WAR
SHADOWS

WAR SHADOWS

A TIER ONE THRILLER

ANDREWS & WILSON

 THOMAS & MERCER

Text copyright © 2017 Brian Andrews and Jeffrey Wilson
All rights reserved.

Published by Thomas & Mercer, Seattle

www.apub.com

Amazon, the Amazon logo, and Thomas & Mercer are trademarks of Amazon.com, Inc., or its affiliates.

ISBN-13: 9781503942035
ISBN-10: 1503942031

Cover design and illustration by Mike Heath | Magnus Creative

Printed in the United States of America

For our parents. Thank you for instilling in us the courage and wisdom to discern the difference between what is right and what is easy and for supporting us when our journeys took us in harm's way.
And for all of you out there, still serving at the pointy end of the spear—you know who you are—safe travels and good hunting.

OGA: Acronym for Other Government Agency, denoting clandestine operations conducted independent of the military chain of command. In most cases, OGA refers to units administered, funded, and controlled by the Central Intelligence Agency, but not all OGA personnel fall under the CIA umbrella. OGA assets conduct counterterrorism operations, intelligence collection, and communication efforts with deep cover assets embedded within enemy organizations. Their existence is categorically denied.

PROLOGUE

Camp Al Qa'im (Formerly FOB Tiger)
310 Kilometers West of the Secret Tier One SEAL Team Compound
Al Qa'im, Iraq
2300 Local Time
2006

The desert is no place for a SEAL, Jack Kemper told himself, but to the desert they sent him again, and again, and again. He'd logged more than eight hundred days in theater over the past four years, and this deployment looked to be the worst yet, kicking off with twenty-eight missions in thirty days. Kemper was raw—raw from the heat, raw from the killing, but most of all, raw from the "moon dust" that covered everything in the far-western corner of Iraq. The Wild West they called it. It was a terrible place, this place. Far from the sea. Far from his family. And far from God.

This was no place for a Navy SEAL.

It was no place for a human being.

He shifted his SOPMOD M4 on his chest and subconsciously tightened his fingers on the grip. *The situation* could *be worse,* he told himself. He could be alone. He could be unarmed. He could be a god-damn spook flying around in some piece-of-shit Russian Ka-27 heli-copter. The CIA was fond of repurposing old Russian helos so as not to attract attention shuttling their war shadows around the red zones. The day Kemper found himself riding around in a Kamov like a spook would be the day he asked Thiel to put a bullet in his brain.

He looked around at the seven other Tier One operators who, like him, were waiting for the go.

"What the hell are you grinning at?" asked Aaron Thiel, Kemper's best friend since SEAL Qualification Training.

"Chafing," Kemper answered, kicking up a cloud of dust with his heel. "Fucking moon dust is rubbing me raw in all the wrong kinda places."

"There's nothing funny about chafing, dude." Thiel shook his head. "I got moon dust in my eyes, in my nose. Hell, I even got moon dust coming out my ass."

"I feel like I swallow a pound of the shit every day." Kemper swiped his tongue along the outside of his front teeth, clearing the grit off what should have been smooth enamel. His mouth was so dry, he couldn't muster the saliva to spit it out. He swallowed instead.

"What the fuck is taking so long? The Head Shed is killing me." Romeo, sitting next to Kemper, was the greenest SEAL on the squad and had earned a reputation for being high maintenance. Despite these shortcomings, the kid had proved himself to be one helluva shooter under pressure. Besides, being the greenest SEAL in a Tier One unit was nothing to cry over—sorta like being the shortest first-round draft pick of the NBA.

"It ain't the Head Shed, bro," Kemper replied. "Captain Jarvis wouldn't tolerate Perry dicking around like this. It's those spooks that came in twenty minutes ago. They're the logjam holding us up."

"Goddamn spooks—why can't they just make up their minds? Let's screw this cat already."

Kemper laughed. He had no idea where the cat expression came from—somewhere in Romeo's twisted mind—but he shared the anxious feeling. During SQT and BUD/S, they had been conditioned for every conceivable form of abuse and punishment, both mental and physical, except for one. The waiting. There was the waiting in the barracks, waiting in the Blackhawk, waiting in the mini-sub, waiting in the water, waiting in the brush, waiting in the dirt, waiting in the dark . . .

Always and every day, the waiting.

Kemper slapped Romeo on the back. "Don't worry, Romeo. Jarvis will get this train back on track."

Romeo didn't bother answering. Instead, he spat a brown squirt of tobacco juice from angry, pursed lips. Kemper shifted his foot to avoid the gob of Skoal splattering over his Oakley boot.

The sound of a door swinging open and then slamming shut made Kemper look up. Senior Chief Perry strode out of the Tactical Operations Center accompanied by some dude wearing civilian cargo pants and a green Timberland shirt. The stranger carried an assault rifle across his chest, wore a drop holster on his left thigh, and had "the look." *Definitely a spook,* Kemper thought, studying the man. The spook's rifle was slung properly, so maybe this jackass knew what he was doing.

The NCO and the spook approached the cluster of wooden picnic tables where Kemper and the rest of the boys had been waiting—fully kitted up and ready to go—for the past forty minutes.

"This is Jones," Perry said to the team, his Alabama twang extra thick tonight.

Kemper glanced across the picnic table at Thiel, who rolled his eyes. Spooks were all either "Jones" or "Smith," it seemed.

"Jones will be joining us on the op," Perry continued. "Tonight's High Value Target is of special interest to our spooky friends, and the consensus is that Jones needs to be there when we hit the *X*."

"Awesome," Kemper snorted under his breath.

"Nothing changes from what we briefed. Two teams of four, only difference is that Jones will be riding fifth wheel—"

"Not it," Romeo interrupted with a grin.

"This plan was vetted by Captain Jarvis, so keep your shit to yourself, Romeo," Perry barked.

Romeo looked at his feet.

"As I was saying, Jones will be riding fifth wheel with me, Kemper, Sanders, and"—the NCO paused, savoring the moment with a smile—"Romeo."

Romeo looked up, flashed his own cocky smile back, and barked, "Hooyah, Senior."

Perry let it slide. Glancing at his watch, he said, "No other changes. We're still on our timeline. Med is set up here, and Qa'im will also be our FARP. The CASEVAC bird is staged here as well, along with the PJs, as briefed. Any questions?"

Behind him, Kemper could hear the slow, rising whine of the engines on the two Blackhawk helicopters from the Army's elite 160th SOAR unit.

"Yeah, I have a question," Kemper said, looking at Jones. "Is there anything *else* we need to know?"

The spook held his stare, and Kemper saw something in the man's eyes. Arrogance? No, nothing so petty. Jones was a man with purpose. He was also a man who had carnal knowledge of the enemy, but Kemper knew that sometimes that knowledge could be a double-edged sword in the field.

"Nothing relevant that wasn't already in your mission brief," the spook said.

Kemper smirked. Yep, he hated these spook motherfuckers. Stingy with their intel and always changing the rules of the game at the last minute. This spook seemed more legit than most, but if Jones had read his Excel spreadsheet wrong, it would be Kemper and his Tier One brothers at the tip of the spear who would pay the ultimate price.

"All right, fellas," said Perry. "Roll Tide."

By the time the boys piled into the back of the Blackhawk, rotor wash had moon dust flying everywhere. Squinting, Kemper clicked his night vision goggles down into place, transforming the desert into an eerie, gray-green moonscape. He scooted to the rearmost edge of the port-side door, hooked in, and let his feet dangle over the skid. As the helo took flight, he watched the Forward Operating Base shrink below. Camp Al Qa'im was unimpressive—a desolate shithole a stone's throw from the border of Syria. Despite the heavy US military presence in Iraq, the border was a porous entry point for weapons and fighters supporting Al Qaeda's growing presence post-Saddam. And despite the Joint Special Operations Command's best efforts, the situation wasn't improving.

Nine months ago, while Kemper was stateside between deployments, a brutal, coordinated Al Qaeda offensive had targeted Camp Al Qa'im. Nine Americans had died and dozens more were wounded defending the base, but ultimately the terrorist attack had been thwarted. The casualties in the jihadist ranks had been higher than those reported by the Western press, but that seemed to be the media's modus operandi these days. Skew and twist. Massage and dismiss. It didn't matter; Kemper's clearance level meant he always learned the whole truth.

When he told Kate that he'd lost two buddies in the firefight, she went ballistic. Even the most dedicated Navy wives had their breaking points. She told him she wanted him out of the Navy, and he understood why. She might as well be a single mom, she cried. Jacob was growing up without a dad. It was time to retire the Trident and become the husband and father he'd taken a vow to be. He'd paid his dues, given his pound of flesh to the War on Terror. It was time to let someone else carry the load. Tier One would survive without him. *For the unit, you're replaceable*, Kate had cried, *but for us you're not.*

Her words that night had battered down his defenses, and he'd promised her he would retire from the unit the next day. But when the next day came, he broke that promise, and now here he was, back in the suck.

The nose of the helicopter dropped, and the green flight line beneath him disappeared as they sped low over the desert floor. Their INFIL point was a short hop, only thirteen minutes away. Tonight's op was a carbon copy of the twenty-eight before it: snatching Al Qaeda leadership and Mujahideen pussies out of their compounds scattered in the barren desert. Their ultimate objective, according to Captain Jarvis, was cutting the head off the snake. But with each passing day, and each hollow victory, Kemper sensed Jarvis's metaphor was fundamentally flawed. Al Qaeda wasn't a snake; it was a hydra. Chop off one head and two more vipers sprouted to take its place. Somewhere in this godforsaken desert, there was a wellspring yielding a seemingly inexhaustible supply of young Muslim men willing to martyr themselves in the name of jihad against the West.

As troublesome as the midlevel jihadists were, the Teams harbored greater disdain for the Mujahideen. The Muj proclaimed themselves leaders, but they never dirtied their hands. Instead, these men used children to fight their war for them. They recruited orphans and kidnapped others to fuel their cub camps, where they brainwashed kids into becoming remorseless gunmen and suicide bombers before reaching age ten. It was the Muj who had incited the growing insurgency against American forces in Iraq, and it was the Muj currently stoking the flames of rebellion inside Syria. In Kemper's opinion, the Mujahideen council was evolving into a terrorism bureaucracy umbrella, making Al Qaeda far more dangerous than before. Which was probably why grabbing high-value Muj targets had become a top priority for the Pentagon. Which in turn explained why the JSOC was running Kemper and his team ragged.

Finding and extracting Mujahideen scattered across the Wild West was both difficult and dangerous—even for operators as elite as Kemper and his Tier One brothers. They'd had several close calls recently, and they found the enemy becoming more tactically competent and evasive as the mission count climbed. On the bright side, after they killed the gunmen and suicide bombers protecting a Muj, the terrorist's boldness always evaporated. Rather than risk personal injury, the pussies always surrendered. That's why the team had to keep going, night after night after night—extract intel, find the connections to other known bad guys, and dismantle the next terror attack before it could materialize . . .

What's wrong with me? Kemper thought, shaking his head. *I'm thinking like a spook.*

He looked up the line at where Jones was sitting, legs dangling out the side of the Blackhawk like a veteran operator. Jones must have felt the weight of Kemper's gaze, because the spook turned to look at him. He had his NVGs pushed up on his helmet, so Kemper could see the man's eyes. In the stark, high-contrast monochrome of night vision, Jones seemed relaxed and confident. Almost bored.

I wonder if Jones was an operator before he became a Jones?

"Kemper," a voice said in his headset, just as he felt the helo flaring above the desert floor—the entire thirteen-minute trip gone in a blink.

Kemper turned and saw Perry miming that he lift the left ear-cup of his headphones.

"Be sure to keep an eye on Romeo tonight," the NCO said, without keying his mike.

Kemper raised an eyebrow, confused. "Say again?"

"I said keep a close eye on Romeo. The kid is more spun up than usual tonight," Perry said, his lower jaw jutting out.

"Roger that, Senior." It wasn't like Perry to play the mother hen. The salty Senior Chief's Trident must be tingling, Kemper thought.

Three minutes later, they were on the ground, two kilometers south of the target compound. The other half of the Tier One strike team was being dropped equidistantly north of the target by a second bird. As their Blackhawk lifted off, the team spread out. Each SEAL took a knee and scanned a sector for threats across their rifle sights. Seconds later, the quiet Blackhawk nosed over, rose, and disappeared into the night, and they were alone. From the corner of his eye, Kemper saw Perry raise a hand, signaling the drop zone was clear. They rose in unison and began the short trek to the target.

Perry led the team to a thinly spaced grove of palm trees, fifty meters from the target house. The trees were a gift, providing rare and valuable cover. Al Qa'im was a border town that had sprung up along the life-giving Euphrates River. Push farther south, and the Wild West became nothing but a wasteland. Even greenery as scant as this had been absent in the shithole they'd hit last night. Romeo had dubbed the place Mos Eisley, after some town in a Star Wars movie. All afternoon, the kid had been annoying everyone in the barracks with his awful impression of Obi Wan Kenobi: "Mos Eisley—you will never find a more wretched hive of scum and villainy. We must be cautious."

What a dork Romeo is.

Kemper smiled at the thought as he surveyed the target—a single-story brown stucco building. The house was large by Iraqi standards, probably seven hundred square feet. Kemper recalled a sketch of the interior he'd seen in the pre-op briefing: a rectangular floor plan with three rooms—a front vestibule, a small kitchen, and a large common room in the back. The compound had seen gunfights in the past; huge chunks of wall had been blasted out of one corner, and the stucco around the windows was pocked with bullet holes. Heavy tarps hung over glassless window frames. Slivers of light escaped from the corners, bright enough to wash out his night vision. Squinting through his goggles, he shifted his gaze to the front of the house, where three vehicles were parked: a white Toyota pickup truck, a small gray sedan with blown-out windows, and a 1990s-vintage Mercedes, no doubt belonging to tonight's HVT—Mahmood Bin Jabbar.

"Left," came Perry's whisper over the wireless headset.

Keeping his body perfectly still, Kemper glanced left. A large man—six feet tall, two hundred pounds—was striding toward them, an

AK-47 slung at the hip. Kemper tensed, a predator waiting for prey to enter the kill zone. He slowed his breathing and played out kill options in his mind. The Iraqi was two meters away now, and Kemper could see the man's attention was focused on lighting the cigarette he carried in his left hand. He shuffled along the tree line, oblivious to the threat lurking in the tall grass.

With his right hand, Kemper silently drew his SOG knife from the scabbard secured to his kit. When the terrorist turned his back, Kemper rose into a crouch. The man took a drag on his cigarette, while retrieving a mobile phone from a pocket with his free hand. Banking on his distraction, Kemper closed the gap in a heartbeat, wrapped his left arm around the terrorist's neck from behind. With his right hand, he drove the black blade into the space between the base of the jihadist's skull and the top of the first vertebra—severing the connection between brain and body. The big man jerked, then collapsed the instant Kemper withdrew the knife. He eased the limp body to the ground and dragged it backward into the cover of the palm trees, where Perry and the others waited.

He looked down at his fallen foe.

The terrorist's face was awash with fear; his brain confused why the call for oxygen now went unheeded. His eyes, controlled by cranial nerves and not dependent on spinal cord connections, darted back and forth in panic. His mouth hung open in a limp, silent scream.

Kemper left the body where it lay and scanned the compound for motion. Seeing none, he whispered into his mike, "Clear."

A click of acknowledgment came in his headset.

Then he heard Perry: "Choctaw Variable, this is Choctaw Actual— On time, on target."

"Choctaw, check—You're a go," came the call from Captain Jarvis on base.

Perry used a double-click of his transmit button to let Jarvis and the other officers back at the TOC know he had heard and acknowledged the instruction. The NCO then signaled with his left hand.

The four SEALs and the spook spread out silently in the brush in preparation for converging on the compound.

"Choctaw Two, One—All set?" Perry radioed to the team on the north side of the compound.

A double-click came back.

"Go," Senior whispered into the mike.

The two teams converged on the target building from opposite directions, four men from the north, five from the south. Each man moved in a tactical crouch, leading with his M4. Kemper scanned for targets over his rifle, following the targeting dot from his PEQ-4 infrared designator. The dot—visible only in night vision—glided over the structure: clearing the walls, door, corners, and roofline. Kemper had danced this dance so many times it was almost as if the little green dot had a mind of its own—searching for threats while Kemper only watched.

Within ten paces of the compound, his olfactory sense kicked in. The smells here were familiar—aromatic cooking spices, cigarette smoke, body odor, and an earthen scent he had never been able to identify but that was prevalent in western Iraq. Just as he could no longer stomach the smell of oysters after a bad bout of food poisoning as a teenager, this cocktail of odors had a primal, overpowering effect on him. This was the smell of danger. The smell of violence.

The smell of death.

Kemper and the other operators fanned out as they drew closer—drifting into tactical positions on both sides of the front door. He crouched low beneath a window obscured by a heavy wool blanket hanging on the inside. He glanced right and watched Special Operator First Class Sanders—Sand Man to his teammates—attach a small explosive charge to the door frame beside the latch. Kemper knew a similar scene was unfolding in mirror image on the other side of the house, the only difference being that the north-side team would use a much larger breacher charge to blow a man-size hole in the stucco wall.

"Roof is clear," a voice said in Kemper's headset. The voice belonged to the overflight drone operator, who was probably stationed thousands of miles away in an air-conditioned room, drinking a cup of hot, fresh coffee. This person—whom Kemper imagined as a clean-shaven twentysomething Air Force nerd without a single scar on his soft, pale body—would go home after his shift. He might grab a burrito at Taco Bell, watch a baseball game, and then fall asleep on the sofa with ESPN *SportsCenter* playing on his TV. No moon dust in his eyes. No risk of bodily harm. No blood on his hands.

What a weird fucking world.

A burst of laughter from inside the house broke the silence, and Kemper tensed.

"My thermal shows three bodies clustered in the front room—seven in the back," said Thiel, who was leading the team on the north side of the compound. This information was helpful, but blooded SEALs knew better than to trust it as gospel.

Perry looked at Sand Man, who was ready and waiting, holding the remote detonator in his hand. Sand Man met his gaze. Perry nodded, then flashed everyone the thumbs-up signal. Kemper pressed his back against the wall. As he turned his head away from the door, he tilted his NVGs up onto his helmet and squeezed his eyelids shut tight. A flash of light, the deep baritone *whump*, and the acrid smell of sulfur left no doubt that Sand Man's charge had just blasted a manhole-size opening in the door.

Inside the house, someone shrieked in pain.

Kemper spun to face the door, brought his rifle up, and followed Romeo through the gap and into the house.

Romeo moved right, clearing right.

Kemper moved left, clearing left.

With the left corner clear, Kemper moved forward, drifting toward the left wall and opening the gap between himself and Romeo. Perry, Sand Man, and Jones entered behind them and pushed forward into the gap. The vestibule was clear, except for a single body writhing on the floor. Kemper glanced down. The poor sonuvabitch must have been reaching for the doorknob at the exact wrong time, because he was screaming and cradling a bloody stump where his right hand had once been. Kemper stepped on the man's uninjured left forearm with his Oakley boot—securing the threat, but leaving his weapon free to sweep. He felt someone move up beside him, and from the corner of his eye he saw Jones crouch down. The spook pressed a knee into the jihadist's chest while covering with his M4.

"I got him," Jones said. "You're clear."

"Thanks," Kemper grunted. He moved forward, toward the arched doorway leading to the larger room at the back of the house. He heard a double tap to his right but kept his focus over his own rifle.

"Clear," Romeo called from his right.

"Clear," he answered and fell in behind Sand Man and Perry, who were now leading into the archway.

"Allahu Akbar!" screamed a voice from the other room.

A single crack from an AK-47 followed but was drowned out immediately by the chorus of pops as Perry and Sand Man fired their SOPMOD M4s in unison.

"Two down, the rest are moving back toward you," Perry said over the wireless to Thiel and the north-team SEALs.

Kemper heard a *whump* as Thiel's breacher charge blew a hole in the back wall of the house. The explosion was followed immediately by the sounds of gunfire and shouting. Kemper advanced through the doorway into the back room. He sensed motion to his left and spun on his heel, but found only a swinging gray blanket hanging over a glass-less window. He moved toward the window. Chunks of cheap cement and stucco sprayed the side of his face as AK-47 rounds peppered the building from somewhere outside.

"Choctaw, this is Ghost—You have three squirters, just exited the west side of the house and moving west toward a tree line." The drone operator's voice was soft and calm in Kemper's ear, in stark contrast to the primal screams and gunfire erupting in the back room.

"Three and Five—pursue the west-side squirters," came the order from Perry, in a voice as calm and cool as the drone operator's.

Kemper felt a hand slap him on the back.

"With me," Romeo said.

Kemper did a one-eighty and followed Romeo back through the vestibule and out the front door, snapping his NVGs back into place as he did.

"On your left," an unfamiliar voice said beside him.

Kemper glanced left and saw Jones advancing with them. The combat crouch position, the rifle carry, the way the spook held himself in the kit—there could be no doubt, Jones was a former operator. The only question left was whether Jones had been a Team guy or an Army SOF man in his previous life, but that information could wait. Right now, all that mattered to Kemper was the fact that Jones was blooded and that he would not be a liability if things got hot.

"At the tree line," Romeo said, angling his trajectory right.

Kemper scanned where Romeo was leading with his rifle barrel and spied two men crouching on the ground in front of the palm trees.

Romeo screamed in Arabic at the two figures, "Facedown on the ground or I'll shoot."

They closed three more meters, and Kemper noted the men were kneeling, not crouching.

The figure kneeling on the right side tilted his head back, raised his arms to heaven, and yelled, "Allahu Ak—"

Romeo's SOPMOD M4 spat fire, and the jihadist's head disappeared in a puff of blood and flying bone fragments.

Kemper was about to shoot the other terrorist, when Jones hollered, "Wait! We need to take Bin Jabbar alive."

"Is that dude Bin Jabbar?"

"Don't know."

"Ghost said there were three squirters," Kemper said, shifting his aim to the stand of palm trees. "Where the fuck is the third guy?"

"I don't see him," Jones said. "You look here, I'll search south."

"Roger that." From the corner of his eye, Kemper saw Romeo advancing on the remaining terrorist.

"Put your face on the ground or I'll shoot you, too," Romeo barked.

Too close, Romeo, Kemper thought, shifting his attention from the trees to his teammate.

Suddenly, the kneeling jihadist propelled himself facedown into the dirt, hands in front, prostrating himself on the ground.

The night went still.

There was a *tink*, and Kemper watched a grenade roll out of the terrorist's hand and wobble to a stop at Romeo's feet.

Romeo looked at the fragmentation grenade and then at Kemper. The young SEAL's expression was sheepish. He flashed Kemper an awkward grin. *Oops—I fucked up.*

There was a flash of mind-numbing white light, a blast of heat, and a punch in the chest. Kemper felt himself flying backward. He hit the ground hard but quickly scrambled into a combat crouch. He scanned the place where Romeo had been, but his friend was gone—evaporated. What was left they would be able to send home in a ziplock bag instead of a coffin.

Jones was yelling—the voice painfully loud in his earpiece—but Kemper ignored the spook. His right calf burned like fire, but he ignored that, too. He donned his NVGs—which had been knocked off by the blast—and with his night vision restored, he scanned the tree line. Through a gap in the palm trees, he saw a distant figure turn and run away. He never saw the man's face, but that didn't matter. He knew exactly who the runner was: Mahmood Bin Jabbar, their mission objective, a Mujahideen coward who'd just ordered his men to martyr themselves so he could slip away into the night.

Kemper took a stride forward in pursuit, but his right leg screamed in protest.

"You need to get a tourniquet on that leg," Jones said, appearing suddenly beside him. "Looks like you caught some shrapnel."

Kemper shrugged off the spook and hobbled toward the tree line.

"You won't catch him with that injury," Jones called. "And neither will I."

Kemper spun, ready to read the OGA bastard the riot act, but the words caught in his throat.

Jones was drenched in blood and pressing a rag against his right eye socket.

Staring at the now one-eyed spook, Kemper keyed his mike. "Choctaw, Three—We're gonna need MEDEVAC . . . ASAP."

PART I

There is a destiny that makes us brothers:
None goes his way alone:
All that we send into the lives of others
Comes back into our own.

—Edwin Markham

CHAPTER 1

Joint Special Operations Task Force Compound
Irbil, Iraq
October 12, 1730 Local Time
Present Day

John Dempsey sat bolt upright in his cot.

He wasn't screaming; he never did that anymore.

His heart was racing, though, and he brought his pulse rate down with slow, measured breaths. When he felt ready, he opened his eyes and let consciousness chase the remnants of the old, familiar nightmare from his mind's eye. Absently, he stroked the jagged, lumpy scar on his right lower leg where shrapnel from the frag grenade that erased Romeo had also torn a chunk out of his calf.

That was Jack Kemper's nightmare, he told himself.

That was Jack Kemper's scar.

I'm John Dempsey now.

Kemper was dead to the world—killed in an explosion in Djibouti during Operation Crusader almost six months ago and buried in Arlington National Cemetery with his Navy SEAL brothers.

All that remained of Jack Kemper were his nightmares.

All that remained of Jack Kemper were his scars.

Dempsey rolled his head in a circle and then arched and twisted his spine—cracking the stiff and aching vertebrae to relieve a night's worth of pent-up tension. Next, he rolled each wrist and ankle, and finished with a crack of his knuckles. Damn his ancient SEAL body. With a grunt of relief, he swung his legs off the side of the cot and checked his watch: *1732*. Just enough time for a piss and a cup of coffee before kitting up and joining SEAL Team Ten for the big op.

Tonight, he was going back to Al Qa'im.

He scratched at his beard and sighed.

Fucking Al Qa'im.

The mission would be very different this time around. The Islamic State of Iraq and Syria owned the Wild West now. The dozen US bases that had provided support and security in theater ten years ago were gone. There would be no Quick Reaction Force providing backup, no fire support from a giant AC-130 Spooky gunship, and no CASEVAC to get them to advanced trauma care minutes away. His boss had arranged for support from the JSOC surgical team, but no Level One surgical hospitals were left in Iraq to help if the mission went south and he got shot to hell. After more than two decades with the Teams, he was no stranger to operating under unpropitious conditions, but tonight's dynamic would be a first for him.

Tonight, he was a fucking Jones.

He had not made it two steps from his cot when his satellite phone rang. "Damn it," he grumbled, turning around. He fetched the phone off the plastic chair he had been using as a nightstand. His bladder would have to wait.

"Dempsey," he said.

"Anything you need?" asked a voice from six thousand miles away.

He couldn't help himself. "Is that a question or a proposition?"

"I don't know, you tell me," replied Shane Smith, heavy on the sarcasm. "You're the one down range."

"In that case, the list is long and obscene."

Smith laughed. "I warned Jarvis that you Tier One SEALs were prima donnas, but he wouldn't listen and hired you anyway. Then, on your very first Ember mission, he let you ride on the VIP 787 and ruined you."

"Never feed a junkyard dog steak unless you plan to feed him steak for the rest of his life," Dempsey fired back. "You guys created me; now you have to live with me."

The words resonated too close to home. He really was a creation of sorts. He shook the odd feeling off.

"Tell you what, I'll pay for a night's stay in the Burj Al Arab and book you a business-class seat on your flight back from Dubai. How's that sound?"

"Ah, I'm just fucking with you, Shane," Dempsey said. "That's not necessary. Right now, I'd settle for a hot shower, some decent chow, and a computer with a faster VPN connection."

"I can't help you with the first two items on your list, but I'll talk with Baldwin about trying to improve your connection speed to the Ember servers."

"Thanks, I appreciate that. Hey, speaking of Baldwin," Dempsey said, getting back to business, "anything new from Ian and his geniuses in Signals? Are we still looking good here?"

"They've been monitoring some chatter, but nothing that's moved the needle. As far as we can tell, the meeting is still on."

"Good," Dempsey said with a nod. "That's good. Do I have the green light?"

The line was silent.

"You still there?" he asked.

"Yeah."

"Look, Shane, I want to nail this bastard. I don't care what it takes, or what strings you have to pull, just get me the green light, okay?"

He heard Smith sigh. Then, the Ember Ops O said, "Have you considered the possibility of leaving him in play?"

"This guy has been in the wind for a decade, he finally resurfaces in Iraq while I'm here, and you want me to leave him in play? Are you crazy?"

"Hear me out, John. Have you asked yourself the question, why has he resurfaced? Why now? Why take the risk? My instincts tell me that this meeting is a precursor to something big. Maybe Al-Mahajer is planning a major offensive. If we could collect intelli—"

"No," Dempsey barked, cutting him off. "That's a dangerous game, and one I don't play. In my experience, leaving psychopaths in play results in dead innocent people. No way, Shane. We grab him, interrogate him, and find out what evil shit he has planned. Then we lock him up and throw away the key."

Smith sighed again. "All right. Jarvis got the green light from the DNI. You're a go."

Dempsey exhaled with relief. "Thank you, Shane."

"Just don't fuck it up. We need this guy alive."

"Understood," he said. "Is CIA ready to help out when I nab the bastard?"

"Yes," Smith said, after a beat.

"You hesitated."

Smith laughed. "Look at you, reading between the lines. Now, if only you can learn how to be a better liar, we might just make a decent spook out of you yet."

"Yeah, yeah," Dempsey said. "Just answer the question."

"My contacts at CIA are all kinds of irritated with me for telling them what to do. Right now, I don't think they'd piss on me if I were on fire."

"That bad?"

"After what happened in New York, what do you expect?"

Dempsey sighed. "I expect them to either put up or shut up. Counterterror ain't a beauty contest; we're all on the same team."

"True, but try to remember who we're talking about. At the end of the day, we still need them. So, try to play nice."

"I'm just looking for a ride, Shane. Nothing more."

"That's exactly the problem. They're not excited to play chauffeur for an asset they're not cleared to know about for an operation they're not running. They're used to being the biggest dog in the yard, and that's the way they want to keep it. But don't worry, Jarvis made some sort of deal behind the scenes, and we're all sorted out now. If you need them, they'll be there."

"Good. Anything else I should know?" Dempsey asked, checking his watch. "I need to get moving."

The SEALs in the Joint Special Operations Task Force would not wait around forever on some damn spook to show up. They'd gladly launch without him if he gave them an excuse to do so.

"Not right now," Smith said. "Stay hot and be sure to check for messages before you launch."

"Will do. I'll call you in a few hours."

"Roger that. And Dempsey?"

"Yeah?"

"Good luck."

Dempsey clicked off the small but powerful satellite phone and slipped it into the cargo pocket of his BDU-style pants. The fact that he was here alone—with no *parental* supervision—showed that Shane Smith, Ember's Head of Operations, and Kelso Jarvis, the Managing Director, were confident with him leading their Special Activities Unit. Dempsey had proved his worth in New York and on several scouting missions during the last several months. His hard work, and Ember's success rate, were causing the fledgling unit's workload to pile up. According to Jarvis, the Director of National Intelligence was already beginning to think of Ember as his own private mini-CIA. The tasking they were receiving lately could easily have been rubber-stamped for CIA, but instead of giving it to Langley, it was being shuttled to Ember.

The reason was simple—speed, stealth, and efficiency.

The CIA had some good folks doing good work, but nimble it was not. They could never have stopped the short-fuse terrorist attack on the United Nations that Ember had foiled six months ago. In fact, Kelso Jarvis's off-the-books unit was created to address the very type of exigencies that the CIA could no longer reliably defuse. Ember was not stymied by bureaucratic oversight and dithering DC politics, nor would it ever be.

Langley was like a battleship—big and powerful, but an outdated relic of another era.

Ember was like a fast boat—small, nimble, and under the radar.

After completing his much-needed trip to the pisser, Dempsey retrieved his duffel bag and unzipped the main compartment. He fished out a drop holster and strapped it onto his right thigh. He checked the magazine in his Sig Sauer 229 and slid it into the holster with a click, then retrieved his Sig 516 assault rifle. He tested the batteries on the EOTECH holosite and the PEQ-4 IR laser designator, twice, then kicked the duffel back under the cot. All of his SCI-level documents—including multiple identities, cash, and mission directives—were in the money belt he wore under his cargo pants. If he didn't make it back for the duffel bag, all he'd leave behind were some clothes.

Dempsey shielded his eyes and squinted as he stepped out of the small hooch that served as guest quarters for the base. Like most operators, he had developed a strong aversion to the blinding desert sun. Down range, SEALs were creatures of the night. Vampires with assault rifles instead of fangs. But he was no longer one of them. He was a guest.

This particular compound was nestled behind the diplomatic mission buildings at the edge of a small airfield. It was, more or less, like every other remote compound he had visited over the past few months as John Dempsey, and over the previous two decades as Jack Kemper. As he wove through a row of white Toyota pickup trucks, an image of Romeo flashed in his head, the kid wearing that dopey-ass grin on his face just before—

"Help you, sir?" a voice said, snapping him back to the present.

The *sir* hadn't been spoken in the manner customary between a soldier and a superior officer. This *sir* was tinged with an almost imperceptible sarcasm . . . *Almost* being the operative distinction. Dempsey knew this because he had used the same exact tone when he'd been working on the other side of the fence in his former life.

In the Spec Ops community, a Jones did not rate a "sir."

Dempsey reached into his breast pocket and pulled out a Department of Defense ID card, which he showed to the camo-clad operator. "John Dempsey," he said casually. "I'm here for the brief."

The operator glanced apathetically at the ID. "Oh yeah," the SEAL said, scratching his beard. "They said you were coming."

"And here I am."

The SEAL swiped his own ID across a card scanner beside the wooden door, and Dempsey heard a click as the magnetic lock disengaged. "Welcome to Camp Little Bighorn, John Dempsey. Try not to get too comfortable."

Dempsey smiled and shook his head. The historical significance of the unofficial name the SEALs had chosen for their Forward Operating Base was not lost on him. Isolated, outnumbered, and tasked with what seemed like an impossible mission, no doubt these SEALs felt like the infamous Seventh Cavalry in 1876. Now that ISIS owned the Wild West, they were embedded in the most hostile of hostile lands.

Once he was inside the perimeter fence separating the Special Warfare compound from the rest of the facility, Dempsey headed straight for the TOC. The building was easy to recognize with its cinder-block walls, spaghetti-mess of data cables, and exterior-mounted air-conditioning units buzzing away. He yanked the door open and stepped inside, like he'd done a hundred times before. To his left was the command center, where a handful of operators sat at workstations, undoubtedly communicating with other assets in preparation for the upcoming mission. To his right was the conference room where the rest of the SEALs were talking and waiting.

"You Dempsey?" a voice said to his right.

Dempsey turned and locked eyes with his welcome party—a tight-jawed operator who was overtly sizing him up. Dempsey did the same, getting a measure of the man. The SEAL was wearing slicks—unmarked BDUs without an insignia or a nametag. Since there were no official military combat operations authorized in Iraq, slicks were the Special Forces equivalent of his own 5.11 Tactical brand clothes.

Dempsey smiled at the SEAL. "Yeah, I'm John Dempsey, but you can call me JD."

To his credit, the operator extended a hand.

Dempsey gladly shook it. He didn't remember shaking Smith's hand the first time they'd met. He'd probably rolled his eyes instead.

"Keith Redman. You can call me Chunk." The operator smiled and tipped his ball cap as if daring Dempsey to ask for the story behind the handle.

Dempsey nodded. No doubt that nickname had a helluva story behind it, but now wasn't the time to ask. In his peripheral vision, he saw another operator approaching from the left. This SEAL was older and wore desert cammies with a Trident on the left breast and gold oak-leaf patches sewn to his collar tabs.

"You must be Mr. Dempsey?"

"Yes, sir," Dempsey said. "Thanks for putting up with me being here. I remember what a pain in the ass it is having a fifth wheel around."

The Lieutenant Commander nodded and looked him in the eyes, no doubt trying to recall if they'd met before. Dempsey had intentionally dropped the hint that he was former Special Ops, hoping it might make things easier. But the decision was not without risk, because revealing potentially compromising information about his past jeopardized his non-official cover. If Smith were here, he would not be happy with him. But Smith wasn't here, which emboldened Dempsey to test the boundaries. There was no rule book for this sort of thing. As far as he was concerned, this was a blind date, and the only way to combat the awkwardness and suspicion was to try to find commonality as quickly as possible. As far as this SEAL team was concerned, anyone who wasn't part of *their* team was just baggage.

"Your being here is not my call," the Lieutenant Commander said with a shrug, confirming where he stood on the matter. "I see you've met Lieutenant Redman. Chunk is the officer in charge of the platoon for this hit."

"Good to know," Dempsey replied, glancing at Chunk. He liked the fact Chunk had not introduced himself as an officer, but he wasn't entirely surprised. He was a SEAL. After that, who cared?

"You got anything to share that will make our job easier tonight?"

"I doubt it, sir," Dempsey said. "But perhaps the three of us could talk for a moment in private before the mission brief?"

The senior officer snorted and shook his head before conceding. "Sure. Why not? We love this cloak-and-dagger spook shit, right, Chunk?"

"Yeah, absolutely," Chunk said, and snapped a can of Skoal in his left hand before taking out a generous pinch and shoving it behind his lower lip. "Things always get interesting when the Smiths show up."

Dempsey gave a tight smile and laughed. "I get it, guys," he said. "I do. I'm gonna tell you everything I can, whether it gets me in trouble or not, so that the team has the best information possible. I'm not CIA, by the way. The folks I work with would not send me here if there wasn't some serious shit about to go down; I can promise you that. I also promise I'll do everything in my power to keep my presence from putting your team at any additional risk. Hell, with any luck, I might prove to be an asset out there."

The two officers eyed him skeptically, but he could tell he'd made an impression. He hoped his easygoing demeanor, straight talk, and humility put him in a different category from the other guys who'd dropped by in civilian clothes over the past few months.

The Lieutenant Commander nodded. "Well, you're kitted up like you wanna go out and play with us—which I fucking hate, by the way—so I guess we should chat. Head Shed says you have a full pass, so we better set some ground rules."

Dempsey nodded. "Of course. Let me tell you what I know first and then you tell me how to best complete my mission without getting in your way."

"I like that," Chunk said, and slipped a plastic water bottle from his cargo pocket and spit some brown tobacco into it. "Step into my office." He gestured toward the back of the room.

Dempsey followed the two officers through the maze of tables and SEALs. Some operators were hunched over laptops, finalizing their individual portions of the op brief, and some were clustered in small groups, bullshitting in whispered voices. A few of the older SEALs looked vaguely familiar, but he didn't recognize anyone he'd logged time with stateside or down range—no one from BUD/S or the time he'd spent with the white-side teams. He felt an invisible weight lift from his shoulders. After he had been blown up in Djibouti, Jarvis had ordered the plastic surgeon sewing him back together to change his face just enough to be unrecognizable to facial-recognition algorithms. Whether the doctor's handiwork would be sufficient to fool a human acquaintance had yet to be put to the test. He still wondered if someone he really knew, a SEAL from his early years with the Teams, would recognize him. He had a few brothers still left out there—men he had fought and bled with, men who knew the parts of him that no plastic surgeon could alter. A true friend would be able to look past his new nose, the cleft chin, and the newest batch of scars and recognize the man underneath . . . right?

Part of him hoped that when the time came, someone who mattered to Jack Kemper would know him.

Chunk held open a door to a small room with an even smaller table and a few folding chairs. It was the down-range version of a conference room. Chunk tossed his ball cap on the table beside his clear plastic spitter and took a seat. The unit commander remained standing, his arms folded across his chest.

"Whadaya got?" Chunk asked.

Dempsey retrieved a small tablet computer in a thick Pelican case from his cargo pant pocket. He pressed his thumb against the biometric reader in the bottom right corner, and the screen lit up. He tapped a folder marked IRB6, and a grainy picture of a man appeared on the screen.

"This fuck stick is Mahmood Bin Jabbar," he said. "He was a mid-level Al Qaeda manager back in the day, before he disappeared for a long while."

"He was Mujahideen," the Lieutenant Commander said, uncrossing his arms and leaning in. Apparently Dempsey had gotten his attention. "I remember this asshole. When I was a JO with Team Four, this guy was on the capture/kill list every fucking day. He was part of a hit where a Tier One guy got killed. Supposedly, they never found the fucker."

Dempsey nodded. The Teams were such a small world—never more than a degree of separation. "Bin Jabbar went off radar after that event."

Dempsey clicked open an even grainier picture taken from a great distance and enhanced. The man was hunched down beside a semicircle of heavily armed men, drawing a picture in the dirt.

"Recognize this guy?"

Chunk squinted at the image. "Bin Jabbar again?"

"Yes, except now he calls himself Rafiq al-Mahajer. Five years ago, we got a hit while he was working as an Al Qaeda mentor with Boko Haram in Cameroon."

He tapped the forward button again.

"This is him with Abubakar Shekau—"

"The fucking leader of Boko Haram?" the senior SEAL interrupted.

"Yeah," Dempsey confirmed.

"Well, shit," Chunk said. "He ain't no midlevel fuck stick now, is he?"

"And he ain't Muj anymore," the SEAL commander pointed out. "He's out there in the suck now."

"Yeah, except he's not Al Qaeda anymore, either," Dempsey said. "After that he disappeared again. Until now."

He clicked to a new picture of al-Mahajer kitted up with an AK-47 and two bandoliers of ammunition. He was standing next to a sign on which Arabic had been spray painted in red over English type. The Arabic translated to *God's Sword*. The English beneath was still readable:

CAMP AL QA'IM.

"That's fuckin' Al Qa'im," Chunk said.

"Yep, five days ago," Dempsey confirmed.

The senior officer pushed back from the table and stroked his chin with one hand. "I see where this is headed, but give me the download anyway."

"This photograph indicates that Rafiq al-Mahajer has risen to a leadership position in the Islamic State's Iraqi front. We believe he will be attending the meeting tonight that you guys are tasked to hit."

"He ain't on my daily list," Chunk said. "He's not one of the three targets we have for the meet, either, unless he's using another alias."

"The spooks kept him off the list on purpose," the Lieutenant Commander suggested. "Right, Mr. Dempsey?"

Dempsey nodded. "But it's not as nefarious as it sounds. My group believes we're the only ones who know al-Mahajer is going to be at this meet. This fucker is slippery and paranoid, so we didn't want to broadcast it to the entire IC and risk getting his antennae up. We're keeping this one close to the vest. Understand, fellas?"

The senior officer snorted again. "And how the hell is that possible? Everything is linked and synced. I take a piss out here and five minutes later I get a text message that the Pentagon, NSA, and FBI are talking about my dick because the CIA snapped a picture of it. It's a joint bullshit world. How do you guys, whoever the hell you are, keep something like this to yourselves?"

"We're outside of those circles," Dempsey said, choosing his words carefully.

"Then where do you get the information?" Chunk blurted out. "The NSA and OGA control everything."

"And who the hell analyzes it?" the commander asked in rapid-fire succession.

A mental picture of Ember's Signals Director, Ian Baldwin, and his two protégés—who Jarvis had dubbed Chip and Dale—popped into Dempsey's mind. He imagined the three men arguing about data sets and intersecting colored lines on a computer screen and somehow deducing where al-Mahajer was going to turn up next. "It's complicated," he said at last. "And anyway, I don't really understand it myself. But I assure you if my guys say al-Mahajer will be there, then there's a ninety-five percent chance he'll be there."

"How bad do you want this fucker?" Chunk asked.

"Really bad," Dempsey said.

"Any special reason beyond the obvious?" the unit commander asked.

"Yes," Dempsey said, and held the SEAL's gaze.

"Got it," Chunk said with a tobacco-stained grin. "Supersecret squirrel shit. I get it. How does this change my operation?"

"For starters, we can expect him to bring a security detail with him—possibly a big one. I imagine for a snatch-and-grab like what was planned for tonight, you were running two teams of six, with offset air . . . right?"

Chunk shrugged.

"Okay, well, I recommend two nine-man teams on site and a reserve squad to secure the perimeter for squirters," said Dempsey, remembering the last time this asshole had squirted and the aftermath that had led to Romeo being vaporized.

Chunk nodded and looked at his boss.

The SEAL commander nodded back and glanced at Dempsey with a look that said, *Go on.*

"You might also want air in orbit and CASEVAC standing by," Dempsey added. "There ain't no cavalry waiting in the bushes in Iraq these days, and Al Qa'im is a long way from Irbil and Baghdad. I don't want any of your guys getting hurt, but in the event someone does, I've arranged for a JSOC surgical team at the diplomatic mission complex here."

The two SEAL officers looked impressed.

"How the hell did you *arrange* that?" Chunk asked.

"My boss made it happen," Dempsey said, and left it at that. The secret surgical team was a Tier One asset that could do damage-control surgery on a short fuse in battlefield conditions. In the austere setting they were operating in now, emergency trauma care could be the difference between life and death if one of the SEALs got hit.

"So are my original targets still gonna be there or is that just a bullshit smokescreen you set up for the mission?" Chunk asked.

"They should be there. My guy is the special guest coming to *inspire* and direct them."

"So we hit the house, we get our guys—or kill them, whatever—and then you take your guy and disappear into the night?"

"Something like that," Dempsey said.

"Fine with me," Chunk said. "You okay with this, boss?"

The unit commander looked at the grainy image on the laptop, and his mind went somewhere else—probably to the Iraq War he had fought before Chunk had even finished BUD/S.

"I'm more than fine with it," he said. "Let's get this asshole." He looked at Dempsey with a little less disdain. "And you'd like to ride along?"

Dempsey nodded.

"And I assume this is not your first rodeo?"

Dempsey laughed. "I've had my eight seconds in the saddle, I promise."

The SEAL commander nodded like he believed him. "Okay. You'll be on Chunk's stick so he can babysit you." Slapping his junior officer on the back, he said, "LT, get with your team leaders and replan this bitch with Mr. Dempsey. I'll go talk to Hal about air."

And with that, the boss was gone.

"Who's Hal?" Dempsey asked.

"The detachment leader for the group from the 160th—that's the Special Operations helicopter detachment we work with." Chunk was up on his feet and looked like a quarterback getting ready to take the field at the playoffs. "Follow me. We've got work to do if we want to keep our push time."

Feeling more than a little nostalgic, Dempsey tried to suppress the grin forming on his face as he slipped the tablet computer back into his pocket. With his rifle in one hand, he slung his vest-style kit—packed with a radio, extra magazines, and other goodies—over his other shoulder and followed Chunk back into the TOC.

All eyes turned to look at them.

A civilian meeting with the leadership meant something had changed.

It wasn't their first rodeo, either.

CHAPTER 2

Two Hundred Feet over the Desert Floor
Russian Mi-17 Helicopter
Western Al Anbar Province, Iraq
October 13, 0145 Local Time

Something warm and wet dripped onto the nape of Dempsey's neck. Scowling, he reached back and used his collar to soak up the offending liquid. He glanced up at a run of hydraulic lines snaking along the ceiling of the helicopter's cargo compartment.

Another drip splattered on his bottom lip.

The SEAL sitting next to him chuckled. "The pilot says if this bird stops leaking oil to let him know immediately." Chunk grinned at Dempsey in the green-gray world of night vision.

"Why's that?" Dempsey asked, wiping the sweet, slimy fluid from his lips.

"Cuz it means this pig's outta oil and we're going to fucking crash."

Dempsey rolled his eyes behind his NVGs. "You sure this piece of shit is flight worthy?"

"It's a coin toss," Chunk said, packing his lower lip with snuff. "She ain't no '60."

"That's for damn sure," Dempsey snorted. He harbored a deep loathing for old Russian helicopters. This bird couldn't hang with a fleet Seahawk, much less the slick, modified MH-60M Blackhawks the 160th usually sported around in. He missed the '60's wide, open cargo doors. He liked hanging his legs out the side during INFIL—rear, port side, every time. He was about to say so to Chunk, when an unexpected wave of nostalgia soured his mood. Snapshot images of his Tier One brothers, murdered in Yemen, swirled in his mind, taunting him with memories of happier times. He took a deep breath and looked out the tiny Plexiglas porthole at the Wild West below.

"What the hell am I doing here?" he mumbled, suddenly feeling out of sorts.

The tightness of his gear, the weight of the assault rifle slung across his chest, the whir of the helicopter rotors as they whisked across the desert at night . . . all these familiar sensations that should be a comfort to him were suddenly having the opposite effect.

It's only déjà vu, he told himself, but it felt different from that. This was *dark* déjà vu—if there was such a thing. He looked around the cargo compartment, expecting to find Romeo, or perhaps Romeo's ghost, but he didn't recognize a single face. This team was loose, confident, and so very young. They were a tight brotherhood, but not his brotherhood.

You should not be here, John Dempsey, Fate whispered in his ear. *But you can't help yourself. You want to dance with me again? Take my hand. Take my hand. Take it . . .*

"Wanna pinch?" Chunk said, waving a tin of wintergreen Skoal in front of Dempsey's face. "Looks like you could use one."

Dempsey ran his tongue along the inside of his lower lip. The offer was tempting. "Nah, I'm good," he said. "But thanks, bro."

He felt a lumbering heaviness as the pilot flared the Russian helo on approach. They were putting out much farther from the target than what would have been necessary for the ultraquiet Stealth Hawks of his past, but tonight's air taxi was taking advantage of an entirely different type of stealth. To anyone on the ground, this Soviet-era bird was indistinguishable from those used by the Iraqi government's dated Air Force. The hope was that this sortie would be seen as another ineffective Iraqi government patrol rather than an American Special Warfare INFIL. As Smith had said to him two days ago, *It's all about keeping a low profile. The folks at home may not know we have American boots on the ground in the battle against ISIS, but the ISIS fighters sure as hell do.*

Chunk gave the signal to make ready, and the SEALs shifted into position. It took two operators to open the bulky, rusted, ridiculously narrow door on the port side of the helicopter. Dempsey watched as they kicked out a single bag of heavy rope. Compared to dual-rope drops, which were standard operating procedure on Blackhawks, this single-rope drop would add precious seconds to their INFIL.

Another reason to hate this goddamn helicopter.

Dempsey patiently waited his turn as the pilot hovered. Finally, he was on the rope, dropping toward the desert floor, followed a heartbeat later by Chunk. Engulfed in dusty rotor wash, he hit the dirt, cleared to the left, and dropped prone. In unison with the other SEALs, Dempsey scanned his designated sector for threats. Chunk let the dust clear and the noise fade before finally raising a hand. Then Custer One—eight SEALs and Dempsey—started their fast march through the desert. Custer Two, the other half of the assault force, was being delivered by a different helo to the north. With perfect synchronicity, they would arrive at the target at the same time.

The team fanned out behind the point man, who periodically glanced at the preprogrammed GPS on his left wrist and made subtle corrections to their course as they hoofed it through the barren Iraqi wasteland. Clusters of trees and grasses began to appear as they closed in on the Euphrates River. Dempsey surveyed the terrain, carefully analyzing each outcropping for cover should they encounter an ISIS patrol before reaching the target. Five minutes later, white lights began to bleed onto the dull, monochrome horizon. *Civilization,* he thought, if there was such a thing left in Iraq. On seeing the lights, the point man altered course to the west. Ten minutes later, they were at the rally point, crouching in a cluster of tall, lush grass along the bank of a small tributary.

From their cover, Dempsey surveyed the target compound. Unlike the hundreds of crumbling stucco shitholes he had hit during missions in Iraq, this compound was swank. Even through his NVGs, the house looked like it could have been plucked from mansion row on Bayshore Boulevard in Tampa and airdropped to the bank of the Euphrates. Looking through the iron gate of the perimeter security wall, he could see several dusty SUVs and one stretch sedan parked on the circular, brick-paver driveway. Beyond the vehicles, a grand, curved stairwell led to a main entrance adorned with ornate glass double doors.

"Eyes," Chunk said.

Dempsey turned his head and watched the operator beside the Lieutenant pull a laptop from his kit pocket and open an umbrella-style antenna. Then, the SEAL checked a separate PDA to locate the particular satellite he meant to link with. After orienting the antenna, he gave Chunk a thumbs-up. "Coming up now. Linking to the Predator."

Chunk leaned onto his side to better see the screen. "Fucking sweet," he said in a low voice. "Gotta love these cloudless Iraqi nights. Much better than in the 'Stan."

Dempsey craned his neck to see over Chunk's shoulder. The feed from the Predator circling twenty thousand feet overhead was perfect. The drone's high-resolution zoom put their POV a couple hundred feet above the compound. Dempsey counted a half-dozen black silhouettes patrolling the walled perimeter.

The SEAL with the laptop tapped an icon, and the image switched to the infrared band. The house transformed from gray to a pale yellow, and the bodies morphed into multihued blobs. Dempsey began counting the orange-red silhouettes inside the house. With multilevel structures, it was difficult to determine which people occupied which floor, but he'd learned some perspective tricks over the years. He counted six men on the upper level and a dozen plus on the ground floor. Most of the figures were moving about, but a cluster of seven men were stationary—undoubtedly seated—in a large room in the left rear corner of the house. An orange figure walked into the room and then, in sequential order, paused next to each stationary figure. *A junior shithead, serving that thick, sweet-ass tea they love to his masters,* Dempsey decided.

Chunk gave Dempsey a nudge. "I count nineteen in the house, and six in the yard. Is that about what you were expecting?"

"Er, actually, I was expecting our guy to travel with a bigger contingent," Dempsey whispered, feeling very much the misinformed spook.

"You said your intel weenie is right ninety-five percent of the time?"

"That's right."

Chunk spit a glob of tobacco juice into the weeds. "Let's hope we're not the five percent, bro."

"Amen," Dempsey said, while secretly praying that Baldwin and the boys back in Virginia hadn't let him down.

Chunk checked his watch and then turned to the operator with the laptop. "Get the air inbound and have them call five mikes."

The SEAL gave him a thumbs-up and began tapping commands into his laptop.

"Custer Actual Two, this is Custer One—Ten mikes as briefed."

Dempsey nodded to himself as he heard the "Roger" from the Head Shed back in Irbil and a double-click from Custer Two over the radio. Chunk had not announced any changes to the plan, which meant the mission would execute as briefed. Both assault teams would breach and hit simultaneously. Once they had secured the compound perimeter, the teams would enter the house and start sweeping. At that point, when the element of surprise was no longer a concern, the little birds would arrive on station to provide aerial fire support. In tandem, a reserve team of eight more SEALs would arrive with two Blackhawks from the 160th. The reserve team, at Dempsey's suggestion, was tasked with rounding up squirters and providing backup fire support if needed. Once the sweep was complete, the two Blackhawks would be standing by to EXFIL most of the SEALs and transport any "crows" off the target for interrogation.

The time dragged, as it always did in the hold, and Dempsey occupied himself by scanning for targets outside the perimeter wall. As his internal clock ticked down toward zero, he redirected his focus inside the courtyard, scanning the stairs leading to the front entrance. Just about the time he felt his muscles tense in anticipation of the go, Chunk's voice crackled over the wireless circuit: "Custer—Positions."

The young SEAL officer raised a hand, and the rest of the team appeared in unison, materializing silently from their hiding places in the grass. Dempsey surveyed the wide gap between the cover of the reeds and the wall surrounding the compound. A surge of adrenaline amped his systems to peak levels in preparation for the silent sprint from safety to the wall. They crossed the gap low and fast. Chunk held them huddled against the wall a moment, listened for any indication they had been spotted. Satisfied his team was still in the dark, he gave a hand signal, fanning them out while a designated SEAL packed a breacher charge into a crack in the mortar.

"Custer Two, One—Set?" Chunk called over the wireless.

"Set," the answer came back from the team leader on the north side of the compound.

Chunk glanced at his watch. "Stalker Two-Five—Position?"

"Three mikes out," the OH-6 helicopter pilot called back. "Sixties two minutes in trail."

Chunk caught Dempsey's eye. Dempsey nodded his agreement; it was time. The Lieutenant flashed him a cocky grin and gave the order to detonate the breacher charge. There was a *whump* from the explosion and the echo of another from the far side of the compound. Dust and the acrid smell of chemical explosive filled Dempsey's nose and mouth—the sweet familiar taste of assault. He popped into a combat crouch and followed Chunk through the hole in the wall; the remaining SEALs fell in behind him.

The SEALs fanned out in both directions from the hole, just in time to avoid the blind fire from the terrorist guards at the locus of the explosion. Dempsey picked his first target, an armed ISIS soldier descending the main stairs from the entry. He squeezed off a round from his Sig Sauer and watched the figure crumple down the steps. He shifted the green targeting dot to a new target—the head of a second terrorist fleeing back into the house. Dempsey's bullet struck the jihadist in the back of the head; a black cloud erupted in the air, painted in high-contrast monochrome.

The staccato pops of SOPMOD M4 fire were now drowning out the deeper bark of the ISIS fighters' AK-47s, signaling to Dempsey that the battle for the perimeter was almost over. He swept his rifle right, across the yard, scanning for targets, but found none left standing. The exterior was won. The battle to claim the house would be much more dangerous.

Chunk signaled for the team to advance on the entry.

Dempsey had not taken more than two strides when the ground around him lit up with tracers as an ISIS fighter fired on them from the roof. At the same time, he heard the whine of the Little Birds screaming in low overhead.

"Custer—this is Stalker Two-Five—strobes on and we'll clear the roof for you."

Dempsey reached up and clicked on the IR strobe on his helmet in unison with the other SEALs. The flashing lights would be visible only in night vision, which he prayed the bad guys didn't have. He looked up and saw an OH-6 gunship banking sharply into position. A second later, there was a loud belch, and a tongue of fire licked out from the side of the little helo. Dempsey ducked his head as chunks of pulverized stucco and roofing material rained down on his helmet and shoulders.

"Roof clear," came the calm, unflappable voice of the Army Special Forces pilot.

Dempsey flinched with anticipation; he had to fight the powerful urge to lead the team in. Beneath the fading whine of the Little Bird bugging out, he detected the growl of approaching Blackhawks. The timing was perfect—'60s inbound meant the reserve force had arrived to secure the perimeter while they mopped up inside. A heartbeat later, Chunk was on the move. Dempsey followed him and two other SEALs up the left side of the curved stone staircase, while three operators advanced up the right side with near-perfect symmetry. The double entry doors were wide open, their decorative frosted window panels now shattered wrecks. Glass crunched underfoot as Dempsey crossed the threshold and stepped into the cavernous foyer. A cathedral ceiling towered overhead, and a spiral staircase to their right arced up to the second story. At movement along the railing, Dempsey sighted and fired. The jihadist crumpled into a heap and rolled halfway down the stairs, his AK-47 clattering the rest of the way down.

"Thought you wanted your guy alive," Chunk said, the corners of his mouth turned up in a sarcastic grin.

"That ain't him," Dempsey grumbled.

The SEALs drifted into a half circle in the foyer, their rifles up and scanning. A beat later, more SEALs, led by Custer Two, entered through the front to join them. By Special Warfare standards, this was an insanely large force to take a lone terrorist compound, but Dempsey was happy to err on the side of overwhelming firepower tonight. He had underestimated the enemy twice before, and both times it had cost him dearly. He would not make that mistake again.

Never again.

Chunk signaled for the new arrivals to ascend the stairs and for his team to hold. Those who remained below covered the balcony and the doorway leading out of the foyer into the main house. Once the ascending operators controlled the landing, Chunk tapped Dempsey's shoulder and gestured that he intended to advance. Dempsey nodded and followed him deeper into the house.

They cleared the doorway only to find themselves in a transverse hallway, forcing Chunk to split the team yet again. Dempsey and three others followed Chunk right, and three other SEALS went left. The next room they entered was a great room littered with upended furniture. ISIS fighters had taken defensive positions behind sofas and chairs—intent on making their last stand. It didn't matter. Chunk and Dempsey were too fast. Too seasoned. Too accurate. In five seconds it was done, four enemy shooters laid out with headshots. For the next half minute, Dempsey heard sporadic bursts of fire echoing about the house, but almost all from American M4s and MP7s.

"Back room, northwest corner," came the call over Dempsey's headset. "Think we got him."

Chunk raised his eyebrows at the news and motioned Dempsey to follow him back in the direction the other three SEALs had gone. They entered the room just as a SEAL was tightening zip ties around the wrists of a kneeling fighter. A second man sat at the head of the table, flanked by two SEALs pointing their rifles at the back of his head. Three other ISIS fighters lay motionless in expanding pools of blood. A family portrait hung crooked on the facing wall.

Once upon a time, this was someone's dining room—before the ISIS usurpers turned it into their private war room.

A burst of gunfire reverberated directly overhead, followed immediately by a calm report over the comms channel. "One, Two—Upstairs is secure. Eight KIA and two crows."

"Copy, Two," Chunk replied into his mike.

Dempsey studied the man still sitting at the expansive dining table. Presumably, this was Rafiq al-Mahajer. The warlord's thick, black beard was wet with Chai, and there was a large brown stain on the front of his gray "man dress," as Romeo used to call them. The sudden memory of Romeo was painful, but he swallowed it down.

No distractions, he chastised himself. *You've been waiting for this moment for years.*

"You made me bring twenty-two operators for *this* piece of shit," Chunk said, sneering at the terrorist. "I hope he's worth it."

Dempsey mentally compared the jihadist's features to the photographs he had studied of Rafiq al-Mahajer, but he already knew: *Nose, too narrow. Eyes, too closely set. Beard, not gray enough, and something else . . . This man is not an Arab . . . Damn it.*

"It's not him," Dempsey said, through clenched teeth.

"What?" Chunk said, incredulous. He pulled a PDA from his kit, tapped it to open a picture of al-Mahajer, and held the screen out beside the man's face. The terrorist stared back at them with dark, angry eyes.

Dempsey saw abject hatred in those eyes, but none of the fear he remembered in the Mujahideen he'd captured before. This man would gladly die for Allah.

"Fuck, you're right. It's not him," Chunk said, and snapped a picture of the warlord with his PDA. He handed the device to the operator beside him—the same SEAL who had set up the laptop with satellite comms outside. "Here, Gyro, find out who this asshole is," he said. Then, turning to Dempsey, "You know this guy? Is he on any of your lists?"

Dempsey shook his head.

While the other SEAL ran a facial recognition search on the terrorist, he let his mind race furiously. Had they hit too early? Could Rafiq have been en route from Qa'im, but running late? Did he know about the attack in advance? Or had Rafiq escaped yet again?

Dempsey pulled on Chunk's sleeve and leaned in close.

"Task the Predator to sweep a two-mile perimeter for squirters, then check the roads between here and Qa'im. Look for a convoy on its way here—or worse, hauling ass back west."

"Check," Chunk said, and looked with disgust at the bearded man at the end of the table. He pulled his comms operator aside to pass the instructions in a whisper.

Dempsey walked over to the terrorist, who was sitting with his back so straight and upright it looked like it hurt. The man stared at him with smoldering hatred. Dempsey clucked his tongue against the back of his teeth. "It's a shame, LT," he said, circling around behind the prisoner. "A shame we didn't have more survivors we could bring back for questioning."

Chunk gave him a quizzical look. "Yeah, I suppose."

"Got any Skoal?" Dempsey asked, looking past the prisoner and smiling.

"Sure," Chunk said, and tossed him the can, his face even more confused.

Dempsey packed a generous pinch of snuff behind his lower lip, then wiped his tobacco-coated fingers on the jihadist's sleeve. The prisoner visibly tensed at the touch. He tossed the can back to Chunk, slid out the chair beside the man, and took a seat. Then he spit a thick gob of brown tobacco juice onto the terrorist's sandaled foot. The man jerked his foot away, disgusted.

"Mar Haba," Dempsey said and leaned forward. *"Shis-mek?"* he asked, inquiring as to the man's name.

The terrorist made a show of turning away and staring at the far wall.

"Taraf tah-chee in-glee-zee?" he continued. *Do you speak English?*

The ISIS fighter glanced at him and then immediately looked away. Dempsey leaned back in the chair. "Yeah, you speak English, you fuck," he said and laughed. *"Wein Rafiq al-Mahajer?"*

The man said nothing.

Dempsey could feel Chunk's eyes on him now.

Time to escalate things a bit.

He leaned forward, trying for eye contact, but the prisoner kept his gaze forward and distant. Then without a word, Dempsey grabbed the man's beard and yanked, smashing his face against the wooden tabletop, and then pushed him back upright in the chair. A small laceration opened on the bridge of the man's nose and blood began to run—down the left cheek until it disappeared in his heavy, dark beard. The jihadist glanced at Dempsey for only an instant, but long enough for Dempsey to see something new in the man's eyes: fear . . . and fear told Dempsey volumes.

This crow knew Rafiq al-Mahajer.

"Lieutenant, give me your knife," Dempsey said softly. He saw the man's eyes flick to the bowie strapped to the front of Chunk's kit.

"For what?" Chunk asked, his tone insinuating he was not cool with where Dempsey's impromptu interrogation was heading.

"I'm gonna cut off this guy's thumbs. Maybe that will help jog his memory about where his boss is." As he said it, he watched the man tuck his thumbs inside balled-up fists. Dempsey resisted the urge to smile. He had no intention of cutting anyone's thumbs off, but this shithead didn't know that. *Knife* any grunt might understand, but *thumbs?* This guy was definitely fluent in English, and that would save time since Dempsey's Arabic was rusty at best.

"Why don't you guys take the other crow downstairs while we chat with our friend here?" Chunk said to the three other SEALs in the room. He gestured at the kneeling ISIS fighter, whose hands were bound behind his back, and then nodded at the doorway.

"Roger that," said the closest SEAL.

Chunk clearly didn't want his team to have any part of what he feared was about to happen—Dempsey respected the Lieutenant for that, but tonight he was OGA. Tonight, he was playing a game with a different rule book. He needed the prisoner to believe torture was in bounds, and he saw no way to achieve that without roping Chunk into the ruse.

"We'll be right down," Chunk called after the junior SEALs shuffling the other terrorist out the door. He pulled Dempsey aside. "This cannot happen here," he said quietly but firmly. "This is my mission and there's no way I'll have my team connected with CIA torture bullshit."

Dempsey met the Lieutenant's gaze. "Then you should go downstairs and join your guys." Without offering a chance for rebuttal, he turned his back on the SEAL and strode toward the seated jihadist. In a single fluid motion, he drew his own knife, arced the blade high over his head, and drove the point down toward the prisoner's hand. "Where is Rafiq al-Mahajer?" he screamed as the knife slammed in the table with a resounding thud.

"*Nein!* Please, no!" the bearded man screamed. After a beat, the jihadist opened his eyes and looked down to survey the damage.

Dempsey watched him slump with relief. The knife was embedded an inch deep in the table and a scant millimeter from the tips of his knuckles.

Dempsey pulled the knife out of the table, but he did not return it to its scabbard. "So, you do speak English," he said, spinning the knife hilt in his palm. "And German."

Chunk shot him a quizzical look.

"This guy's German," Dempsey said, answering the unspoken question. "You gotta check the other database to find him."

The jihadist looked pale. "You are CIA?" he said in a trembling voice.

"You wish," Dempsey said with a laugh. "They got protocols for situations like this. Oversight and ethical guidelines, shit like that designed to protect assholes like you. No, I'm just a contractor. They hire me to take out the trash." He slapped the side of the man's bearded face.

The door opened and the comms operator stuck his head in. For an instant, Dempsey could have sworn he looked disappointed to see the jihadist still sitting upright and lucid.

"Hey, LT?" he said.

Chunk walked over to him and the SEAL whispered something in his ear. Chunk slapped him on the shoulder and he left, conspicuously closing the door behind him. Chunk walked over to Dempsey. "There's nothing going on between here and Qa'im," he whispered. "They're tracking a couple of pickup trucks, but they look like patrols."

"Squirters on foot?"

Chunk shook his head.

Dempsey frowned.

Burned again.

He didn't get it. The intel was solid—Baldwin didn't make mistakes, even with other people's data. If Rafiq al-Mahajer decided not to show, then it meant he'd sent this guy as a proxy. Dempsey shifted his attention to two confiscated laptops and a Blackberry on the table beside the prisoner. If on a scale of one to ten Rafiq rated a seven, then his proxy was a five. Which meant that this mission was not a failure. Proxies had value, and more importantly, so did the electronics they carried. Dempsey probed a pocket for his sat phone. He needed to check with Smith, but he was 99 percent certain Jarvis would want one of their people to take a turn with this guy. That meant escorting the prisoner to Baghdad, where hopefully Smith and Jarvis could make arrangements with the CIA to transport the crow out of Iraq. Suddenly, the thought of flying in the Russian helo turned Dempsey's stomach. Maybe if he was real nice to Chunk, he'd be able to hitch a ride in one of the Blackhawks that had delivered the reserve force.

"What now?" Chunk asked, interrupting Dempsey's mental masturbation about which helo he would be riding in.

"I have a ride waiting to take my new friend somewhere very special," Dempsey said, glancing at the prisoner. The bearded fighter's cheeks were still pale, but his eyes were regaining the fire Dempsey had seen before. Dempsey smiled and spun the knife in his hand one last time before shoving the blade back into its scabbard. "I know what you're thinking, tough guy, but you might as well put that idea to bed right now. Everyone talks eventually," he said. "Everyone."

CHAPTER 3

Mi-17 Helicopter
Eight Hundred Feet over the Desert Floor
Fifty Kilometers Southeast of Haditha, Fifteen Kilometers from Al
Wadi Thar Thar, Iraq
0510 Local Time

The predawn sun kissed the horizon pink across the desert. Dempsey frowned and looked away from the porthole. With sunrise, he would lose his most loyal and reliable ally. For the vampires of Special Warfare, the night was more than a comfort; it was a tactical advantage.

Dempsey slipped off his helmet and snapped it to a carabiner on the side of his kit. The weight of the thing had finally become unbearable, and he didn't need his NVGs anymore with the cabin lighting up. He rolled his neck and got a satisfying double crack. Absently, he ran a fingertip along the serpentine scar that wrapped his left forearm, until Smith's voice played in his head: *You have to do a better job policing your mannerisms. That behavior is something Jack Kemper did. You're John Dempsey now. John Dempsey doesn't do that . . .*

He stopped and hooked his thumbs onto his kit.

Then, he noticed the prisoner staring at him from the other side of the aisle.

Dempsey scowled and swallowed the urge to reach out and smack the terrorist across the face. Instead, he studied the German Islamic convert. Brown eyes that had once brimmed with homicidal rage were now cool and distant. The corners of the captive's mouth were turned down, hung heavy with dread. His flex-tied hands were between his knees, with another flex-tie securing his wrists uncomfortably to the aluminum rail of the helo's bench seat.

Getting caught is a bitch, man, and American justice hits like an iron club. It's only going to get worse for you . . .

Movement toward the back of the loud, rattling helicopter caught Dempsey's attention. He turned to see Chunk rolling with laughter. After a good howl, he leaned back in to continue the discussion with the SEAL across the narrow aisle. Their foreheads nearly touching, they jawed about the things SEALs care about when they're not being stone cold warriors—girls, beer, and sports. And sometimes, maybe which superhero would make the best SEAL . . . Dempsey smiled at the memory of Tito and Spaz, two of the teammates he'd lost in Operation Crusader, laughing and arguing about Spider-Man in the back of a Blackhawk.

He watched Chunk and the other SEAL for a while, envious of their private world—a world only a few feet away, yet out of reach to him. Eventually, Chunk felt Dempsey's gaze and turned his head. Dempsey gave the officer a nod, and the SEAL flashed him a tobacco-stained, toothy grin.

The helo shuddered, sending a drip of warm oil splattering down onto the crown of Dempsey's scalp. He knew better than to look up this time, lest he take a drop in the eye. He shifted his gaze out the porthole beside him. The helo pilot was flying low, following a dirt road that Dempsey was sure he recognized. Yeah, he remembered this particular desert trail. It served as an offshoot, connecting the paved highway to the glistening waters of lake Al Wadi Thar Thar. He craned his neck to get a better view, and two white pickup trucks trailing at their eight o'clock position came into his field of vision. In 2008, two junkers speeding across the desert would not have been cause for immediate alarm, but now the Wild West was hostile territory. Any trucks coming from the direction of Ar Ramadi were surely packed with ISIS fighters. He'd known that crossing this swath of Anbar controlled by the jihadists would be the most dangerous part of the journey.

Why isn't the pilot opening up? Dempsey asked himself. *Give the dude a second . . .*

His stomach was going sour.

Fuck it. I gotta warn him.

Dempsey popped to his feet to make for the cockpit, but in his peripheral vision, he saw the flash of light. "Rocket!" he screamed.

The pilot glanced back for a microsecond, then jinked the helicopter violently to the right. Dempsey's head hit the corner of the passageway leading into the cockpit. He felt his feet slip out from underneath him and his body slam into the deck. Dazed, he pushed himself up onto his hands and knees and shook off the stars. When he looked up, his nose was inches from the smirking face of the prisoner. The German mumbled something and laughed, but Dempsey couldn't tell if it was in German or Arabic. Maybe he was laughing because he knew this old model Mi-17 didn't carry defensive countermeasures and the next rocket fired would certainly finish them off for good.

Dempsey looked aft over his shoulder and saw Chunk and the other SEAL clutching the cargo netting lining the walls of the cabin. Chunk yelled something at him, but Dempsey couldn't make out the words. For a moment the helo was stable, and he thought that the pilot's evasion had worked. But hope evaporated as an explosive shockwave whipsawed the helo in midair. The old Russian bird groaned as steel twisted on itself and it tipped violently left, hurtling Dempsey against the port-side seat rail. His ribcage smacked against something, and he was on his back. The ceiling above him looked stationary, but the sensation of spinning told another story. This bird was going down.

The next thought that ran through his mind was almost comical: *After everything I've survived as a SEAL, I'm going to die as a spook in a piece-of-shit Russian helicopter in fucking Iraq.*

He closed his eyes.

And as the world spun out of control around him, a thought more dreadful than his impending doom occurred to him.

Kate thinks I'm already dead, but I never said good-bye.

I never said good-bye . . .

CHAPTER 4

607 Horseshoe Drive
Queenslake Subdivision, Williamsburg, Virginia
October 12, 2320 Local Time

Kelso Jarvis looked at the phone vibrating facedown on his desk and tried to remember if there had ever been a phone call after 2200 hours bearing good news. He flipped the phone over and saw Smith's name on the screen. He took the call on the third ring.

"Jarvis," he said simply.

"Hey, boss, it's me—on a secure line."

"What's up with our boy in the desert?" He knew the call was about Dempsey, no point in wasting time.

"Dempsey went dark. His helo flight never arrived in Baghdad, and the pilot missed the last programmed check-in forty minutes ago."

"What about the rest of the assault team?"

"Returned to the compound in Irbil on schedule."

Jarvis pursed his lips and drilled a fingertip into his left temple. If Dempsey was discovered—or worse, captured—in ISIS-controlled Iraq, the ensuing firestorm would be one of biblical proportions. From the beginning, the Director of National Intelligence had been reluctant to approve any mission embedding Ember assets with the SEALs in Iraq: *The President has publicly said we will not put "boots on the ground" in Iraq,* Director Philips had growled at Jarvis, *and so as far as the President is concerned, there are no SEALs conducting combat operations in Iraq. The SEALs in Irbil are for the security of the diplomatic mission there. Any media reports to the contrary would discredit the Administration.* But the truth was Jarvis didn't give a shit about President Warner or the media. All that mattered was stomping out terrorism. Everything else was just noise.

Unlike most of the spineless bureaucrats Philips dealt with on a daily basis, Jarvis refused to be cowed. Eventually, he had been able to convince the DNI to green-light the mission by offering unconditional assurance the operation would be completed in absolute secrecy. The promise was wind, of course. Jarvis could not guarantee *absolute* secrecy any more than a meteorologist could guarantee a forecast. However, he was not naïve in this business: the only surefire way to keep his fledgling counterterrorism unit operational was to ensure Ember's activities did not sink his bosses. Smith's report could not have been graver. John Dempsey existed only under non-official cover. If captured by ISIS, his ransom—or public execution, Fate forbid—would be the end of Ember.

"You still there, boss?" Smith asked, snapping Jarvis back to the present.

"Yeah, sorry," Jarvis said. "Did you try him on his secure sat?"

"Yes. Nothing. Baldwin is trying to triangulate a position, but the phone might be powered off or damaged."

"Shane, I think we need to consider the possibility Dempsey's helo crashed."

"That's exactly where my mind was going," Smith said, his voice rife with tension.

Jarvis had watched Smith and Dempsey become close over the past six months—something both inevitable and unfortunate in this line of work. He understood Smith's angst all too well, but angst was a cognitive liability Jarvis couldn't afford to indulge.

"What's your plan, Ops O?" he asked, trying to get Smith on point.

"I want to put the rest of Special Activities on a jet to Iraq and get Dempsey out."

Jarvis paused long enough for Smith to think he struggled with the decision. "No. We have too much exposure on this already. Work with your contacts at the base to task a drone to look for a downed helo, and start planning a rescue mission with the SEAL team. I'll try to get you some satellite time to augment the search. Keep me apprised if Ian finds the phone."

After a noteworthy pause came Smith's, "Yes, sir." The formality flagged his disappointment.

Jarvis slipped into the role of Tier One commander from his past. It was what Smith needed. "He'll be all right, Shane," he said with unbridled confidence. "In case you've forgotten, Dempsey is a very hard man to kill."

"I'm sure you're right," Smith said, his voice reflecting back some of Jarvis's assuredness.

"Hell, what we really need to be worried about is Dempsey taking on ISIS all by himself. He's probably out there kicking ass and stacking jihadist bodies like cordwood. How am I going to explain that to the DNI?"

Smith laughed, then said, "I'll call you with a SITREP in an hour, if not sooner."

"Roger that."

Jarvis tossed the phone onto the desk and added a knuckle to his other temple. He closed his eyes and let his brain do what came naturally. Strategic options and variables began to take shape, organizing themselves into a decision tree with logic gates. Seconds later, he was sketching the details on a piece of paper—his hand flying over the page. As he drew, his mind assigned colors to the different lines, estimating probabilities based on his twenty years of experience planning and running Tier One missions. When he was finished, he had a roadmap to help guide Ember through this quagmire.

Only one of the paths ended with Dempsey coming home safe with his NOC intact. The other outcomes all required various degrees of damage control, and damage control was expensive. Not in a financial sense, but in a parasitic one. Anything that diverted his attention from his penultimate goal was *expensive*. Ember's original charter had been to find those responsible for massacring the Tier One SEALs in Yemen and take any and all action to make sure something like that never happened again. They had made those connections. They had found the mastermind of the attack, VEVAK's Director of Operations, Amir Modiri. They had also identified the US government official who had leaked information to the Iranians prior to the attack. But unlike Dempsey, who still desired vengeance, Jarvis's objectives were more pragmatic: He sought a reckoning. A rebalancing of power in the Middle East. VEVAK, and its expanding network of clandestine operatives, was secretly and quietly wreaking havoc throughout the region. The new "moderate" Iran was a chimera—an illusion designed to hide its growing dogmatic and militant aspirations. If he could unmask Iran's intentions—to leverage the activity of terrorist groups like Al Qaeda and ISIS to aid its rise to global power—then the world would reassess. An Iran that facilitated terror operations was a very, very dangerous development. And so to truly fulfill his charter, he needed to penetrate Modiri's network, learn his allies and operations, and crush them.

He sighed, blowing air through his teeth in a long, measured exhale.

A balloon, deflating.

At times like this, he wished he had a kindred soul he could talk to—an equal to strategize with, parlay ideas, and vet his logic. He glanced at his phone and considered calling Levi Harel. The legendary former Mossad Director was the closest thing to a friend Jarvis had in this mad world. They had not spoken in months, not since Harel had helped him track down one of Modiri's field operatives in Frankfurt. Without the Mossad's help, Ember would have never been able to foil Modiri's brilliant terror plot at the United Nations. In gratitude, Jarvis had promised to reciprocate anytime, no matter the cost, no matter the risk. Harel had yet to call in the favor.

He picked up the secure phone, scrolled through the contact list, and stared at Harel's number. After a long pause, he changed his mind. He knew exactly what he needed to do; no affirmation was required. He went back to his paper and worked on his damage-control plans for each of the possible outcomes of Dempsey missing in Iraq. When the next call came in from Smith, he would be ready to make decisions and give orders without delay.

Then, and only then, would he call the DNI.

CHAPTER 5

Wreckage of the Mi-17 Helicopter
Fifty-Five Kilometers Southeast of Haditha, Eight Kilometers West
of Al Wadi Thar Thar, Iraq
0645 Local Time

Dempsey opened his eyes.

A beam of light streamed in through a porthole window overhead. He was on his back, lying on something hard and uncomfortable. He heard someone groan and then gurgle. A surge of adrenaline burned the cobwebs from his mind, and he immediately understood where he was and what had just happened. He didn't think he'd lost consciousness when they crashed, but maybe.

Maybe.

His hands flew over his chest, abdomen, flanks, and thighs—checking for wetness, deformity, or pain. Feeling none of these things, he wiped the back of his hand across his forehead and saw a smear of blood on his sleeve and hand. He probed and found the wound. It felt small and shallow, a laceration a couple of inches above his left ear. Scalp wounds were bleeders and looked ugly, but so long as his skull was intact, he'd be fine.

He got himself up into a crouch. What remained of the mangled Russian helo was rolled on its side. He was squatting on the starboard wall—now the floor—directly below the port-side slider door.

He stood, and a jolt of pain immediately flared across his lower back and down his left leg. He repositioned his left boot, straightened his hips, and the angry nerve settled down—just an old back injury aggravated by the crash. Given the circumstances, he'd take it. He was fine. Absolutely fucking fine. He'd survived a helicopter crash virtually unscathed. Unfortunately, the same could not be said for his travel companions. The prisoner, still lashed to the starboard bench seat, moaned. The man's left forearm had a new and extra joint. His hand dangled, twisted at an impossible angle where the bones had snapped on impact against the seat rail. Dempsey wondered if the man had a concussion, or internal injuries, or both. Time would tell. He stepped around the prisoner and worked his way aft. In the back of the cargo compartment, he found Chunk kneeling beside the younger SEAL, pulling a dry dressing from his blowout kit.

"You guys alive back here?" Dempsey said, putting a hand on the Lieutenant's shoulder and hunching over for a better view of the injured SEAL.

"I'm fine, but Patch here got himself a new knee," Chunk said, pressing the dressing against the bone protruding through a tear in the SEAL's BDUs.

"Son of a bitch, Chunk," Patch hissed at his platoon leader. "Aggahh . . . the bones ain't going back together, bro."

"Thanks again for inviting us to your party," Chunk grumbled over his shoulder at Dempsey.

"You're welcome. Next time, I'll rent a limo." Turning toward the cockpit, he added, "I'm gonna go check on the pilot, see how he's doing."

"The pilot is kinda fucked," called a strained voice from the front of the helo.

Dempsey worked his way forward, stepping over the dazed terrorist once again. He stuck his head into the horizontal doorway and looked up. The pilot hung suspended, still in his seat, with the control panel collapsed against his lap, trapping his legs. The Army aviator gripped a SOPMOD M4 in his right hand and was straining to see out the shattered windshield.

"You okay?" Dempsey asked.

The pilot looked down at him, face tense with worry. "I don't know," he said. "I don't feel like anything's broken, but I'm hard-pinned. My legs are numb."

"Can you move your toes?"

"Yeah," the pilot said, nodding. "I think so."

"That's good. Any pain?"

"No, not really."

Dempsey put a hand on the man's cheek. His skin was warm and flushed. That was a good sign; had the pilot been cold and clammy, it would have been an indicator of shock. On the flip side, even the most horrific injuries were virtually painless in the heat of battle. He'd seen soldiers with their legs blown off look surprised and confused when they couldn't stand up. There was no way to be absolutely certain whether the pilot was injured until they got him out of that damn chair.

"All right, I need you to listen to me, bro," Dempsey said, all business. "The a-holes who shot us down are coming. I can guaran-fucking-tee that, so we need to be ready."

The pilot nodded.

"How far did we go after we got hit, and in what direction?"

"I turned us northeast toward the lake. The blast didn't take out the rotors, so I kept us flyin' until I lost my hydraulics and flight controls. That's when I brought her in." The pilot let out a slow, shuddering breath. "We flew a bit before we screwed it—ten miles, maybe more. Sorry I blew the landing."

Dempsey shook his head. "Are you kidding me? You did great, man. You saved all our asses. As far as helo crashes go, this ranks as my best ever."

The pilot raised a brow. "How many helo crashes you been in?"

"One." Then, with a shit-eating grin, he said, "Don't go anywhere. I'll be right back."

"Don't worry about me, I'll just be hanging out."

Dempsey climbed back into the cargo compartment and looked at the port-side slider door overhead. If the pilot was right about opening up some distance from the shooters, then he'd bought them some time. If the helo wasn't pouring out smoke like some giant marker beacon, they might be lost on the horizon, well beyond the shooters' line of sight.

Better go find out.

"Chunk, come help me with this door," Dempsey called. The SEAL officer nodded and made his way forward. It took both of them straining to pull back the insanely heavy door. Then Dempsey scrambled out the opening and sprawled prone on the top of the tipped-over helicopter. From the elevated vantage point—nine feet, Dempsey estimated—he began scanning the desert over his rifle sights. Seconds later Chunk joined him, scanning the opposite 180-degree arc.

"How's Patch?" Dempsey asked.

"Compound fracture. Tibia's snapped in half. Fibula seems to be intact."

"Arterial bleeding? Did he need a tourniquet?"

"No. I splinted the leg. He's a tough motherfucker, that one. The whole time I was working on him, the only name he cursed in vain was yours."

"Yeah, yeah," Dempsey mumbled. Far off to the south, a hint of a dust cloud on the horizon caught his eye. "Hey, take a look south, two-zero-zero."

Chunk shifted his body. "That kick-up of dust on the horizon? You think that's the shooters heading our way?"

"It's the right direction."

"Shit. How far you reckon they are?"

Dempsey performed a quick line-of-sight calculation using mental thumb-rules combining the height of the dust cloud and the height of their vantage point. "Twelve miles, max."

"That's not good."

"Anything to the north?"

"No—clear to the north. I can just make out the lake on the horizon."

"Even if we can get the pilot out, we won't make the lake. With Patch on a busted leg and our jacked-up prisoner, we'd be lucky to make two miles," Dempsey said, his anger rising. "Fuck."

"What I wouldn't give for a Little Bird right about now."

"Did you call it in?"

"Can't," Chunk said, grim-faced. "My phone has power but no signal. And the helicopter's comms are toast. How about you?"

Well, shit. Yeah, how about me? Dempsey thought, chastising himself for not checking his sat phone five minutes ago. He rolled onto his side and slid the phone out of his pocket. After a boot-up period, the compact little phone acquired a usable satellite signal. A second later, a small envelope appeared in the bottom of the screen.

Dempsey smiled. "We might be good here," he said to Chunk.

He skipped the message, which of course was from Smith, and pressed the number two on the keypad. There was a single chirp in his ear—the call connected—and then came Smith's worried voice. "Are you okay? Talk to me."

"Been better," Dempsey said, and looked over at Chunk and gave a thumbs-up. "We need an EXFIL, like right fucking now. We got two wounded—a team guy and our ISIS captive—and a pilot who's pinned in the wreckage of the helo."

"What the fuck happened?"

Dempsey shook his head in frustration. "Time for that later." He squinted at the southern horizon, where the dust trail seemed to be growing larger. "We've got at least two trucks, loaded with shitheads, closing on our position. We need the cavalry—a Little Bird or a drone carrying Hellfires."

"I'm messaging Baldwin now to triangulate your signal, and I'm trying to get the JSOC commander online. Stand by and I'll be right back with you."

Smith was gone without a parting word.

Dempsey snapped the phone shut and looked over at Chunk.

"Gonna be tight," Chunk said, his characteristic grin notably absent.

"If the JSOTF has a Quick Reaction Force stood up in Baghdad, we could get a quick launch and still have a chance. Otherwise, Irbil is too fucking far. By the time they get here, it will be over."

"Maybe they have a Predator in the air."

"What are the odds of that?"

"Coin flip at best," Chunk said flatly.

"My thoughts exactly."

"So what's our next move?"

"We have to dig in and plan for the fact the cavalry ain't gonna make it in time. Let's get the pilot free and see if we can't set up the fifty cals. If we can position those heavy machine guns for cover fire, it may buy us some time." Then, looking the SEAL officer in the eyes, he said, "Hooyah, frogman."

"Hooyah!" Chunk barked back.

Dempsey watched him disappear into the crumpled helicopter. It was not lost on him that Chunk had looked to him for both direction and affirmation. In the Teams, a senior NCO like Dempsey, with tons of experience, worked closely with the midgrade officers. Hell, they often led the ops when circumstances demanded. In the heat of the moment, Dempsey had instinctively slid into the NCO role and taken control.

He stared at the phone in his hand and willed it to chirp with good news. "Come on, Shane," he whispered. "I need ya, bro."

"You coming or what?" Chunk called up from below.

"On my way."

He glanced one more time at the dust cloud on the horizon before lowering himself into the hole. Too many SEALs had died in this shithole country on his watch. He had no idea how he was going to get Chunk and the others out of this mess, but one thing was certain . . . he'd either find a way, or die trying.

CHAPTER 6

607 Horseshoe Drive
Williamsburg, Virginia
0055 Local Time

Whether the Fates were conspiring to help him or hurt him, Jarvis could not tell. Dempsey was alive, but beyond that there was little about his situation that inspired hope: shot down in ISIS-controlled Iraq, an injured SEAL, an injured prisoner, two enemy bogies inbound, and no cavalry within a hundred clicks. Without backup, he calculated the odds of Dempsey's survival at 25 percent. Yet somehow, despite the odds, Jarvis couldn't help feeling he'd just dodged a bullet.

Whenever he felt that way, it was invariably time to call the boss.

He picked up his mobile and speed dialed the Director of National Intelligence at his northern Virginia home. The phone picked up on the second ring.

"Yes?" Philips's voice was crisp, clear, and demanding. Maybe it was conditioning from decades of late-night calls over his long and decorated Naval career—commanding F-14 squadrons, then aircraft carriers, then carrier battle groups, and eventually the whole damn fleet. Or maybe the aviator simply didn't sleep.

"I have an update on our operation," Jarvis said, his voice decidedly neutral. "I'm on a secure line."

There was a pause. Perhaps the DNI had been asleep after all, and this was him leaving the bed where his wife still lay sleeping. "Go," Philips said at last.

Jarvis spent the next five minutes updating his boss on everything that had happened. When he finished, Philips simply said, "Well, that's bad."

The gravity of the understatement was not lost on Jarvis. In the world of covert affairs, *bad* ended careers, put untouchables in front of congressional committees, landed demagogues in federal prison, and toppled administrations. Yeah—this was fucking bad.

"Yes, sir," he said, plainly and without excuse.

"I don't suppose you have any good news for me?"

"I do," Jarvis said, willing it to be true. "We have comms with my guy on the ground and a rescue in progress. The plan is to secure the scene, EXFIL our personnel and the prisoner, and be ghosts within the hour."

"What is the visibility here?" Philips asked softly.

Jarvis could tell from his tone that asking this question was a source of personal heartburn. There were men and there were titles. For the Director of National Intelligence, managing the big picture was the top priority. Whether four Americans lived or died was less important than the geopolitical fallout the United States would face from a failed covert operation. That was the business—something Jarvis had made peace with long ago.

"The aircraft is a Russian-built Mi-17—standard Iraqi air asset. Our guys know to sterilize the crash site. Assuming they get out, there'll be no proof our people were ever there."

"If not, the next thing we'll see is a video of your boy on some fuck-ing ISIS website getting his head sawed off with a machete. Are you prepared for that, Kelso?"

"My guy won't let it come to that," Jarvis said.

Philips sighed. "I trust you to clean this up. Get your guy, sterilize the site, and make damn sure the intel we get is worth the ulcer you're giving me. Because if you don't salvage this clusterfuck, the firestorm that follows is going to burn both our asses to embers."

Jarvis smiled tightly at the double entendre. "Will do. We're on it."

The phone went dead. Jarvis admired Philips for not revisiting the disagreement they'd had on the advisability of sending Dempsey into Iraq in the first place. The government was full of blowhard hindsight geniuses, but Philips was not one of them. They both bore responsibility for the decision, and the DNI was making it clear they would manage the consequences together.

Jarvis checked his watch and then pushed the number three on his speed dial.

"Yeah, boss."

"Status?"

"JSOTF has a Blackhawk in the air, inbound. Thirty minutes to the site, maybe less."

"That'll be too late."

"It's gonna be close," Smith replied, taking the more optimistic tack.

"Clean up the mess, either way," he said, and ended the call without waiting for Smith's acknowledgment.

He'd had enough of words that shouldn't have to be said for one night.

CHAPTER 7

Mi-17 Crash Site, Iraq
0725 Local Time

From atop the downed Mi-17, Dempsey watched two white pickup trucks diverge, one circling east and the other circling west. A lump formed in his throat. These assholes were both disciplined and cautious—establishing cross-fire positions while maintaining a safe distance from which to survey the downed helicopter.

They had five minutes until bullets started flying.

Dempsey stuffed his satellite phone back into his pocket. He wouldn't be needing it again until this was over. Smith had called him back with news that a Blackhawk had been dispatched from Baghdad, but the helo wouldn't be on station for another fifteen minutes. That was going to be too fucking late. And there was more bad news. JSOTF didn't have access to a drone within a hundred miles of their position to provide fire support. Dempsey and the others were on their own.

Unless he thought of something soon, this was going to turn into a recovery mission. He well understood the gravity of that scenario—Special Warfare fighters entrenched on the wrong side of a border

Washington said it would not cross. Covert operations were pointless unless they remained covert. It had been this way since President Kennedy had chartered the Teams over fifty years ago, and that governing doctrine would never change. Recovery missions rarely ended well for anyone.

Dempsey looked down through the hatch. Directly below him, Chunk was helping Patch into the cockpit. Behind them, the recently unstuck and miraculously uninjured pilot was carrying the helicopter's only functional .50-caliber machine gun. With the Mi-17 tipped on its side, their firing options were extremely limited: topside or through the shattered cockpit windshield. Since they were being scouted, the latter option was preferable because it was covert until the shooting started. No matter what happened, Dempsey would make sure that his guys fired the first salvo.

As the pilot stepped over the injured ISIS captive, the butt of the .50 cal clipped the prisoner's head. The terrorist moaned and mumbled something defamatory in Arabic. Dempsey studied the jihadist, with his heavy, black beard and bloodstained tunic. He rubbed his own beard—grown to help facilitate embedding with Muslim fighters should he need to while in the Middle East. He smiled as an idea germinated. This plan would never have occurred to the door-kicking SEAL he'd been in his former life, but working with Ember had changed the way his brain worked.

He lowered himself into the helo just as Chunk was crawling back out of the cockpit.

"You think of a miracle yet?" Chunk said, looking up at him.

"Not a miracle, but something that might buy us a few extra minutes until the cavalry gets here," Dempsey said, then outlined his simple plan for the Lieutenant.

Chunk raised an eyebrow. "That's it?"

"Yep. If I can buy you enough time to neutralize one of those pickups, we have a marginal chance at getting out of this mess."

Chunk laughed and shook his head. "You're either one steely-eyed frogman or the craziest sonuvabitch I've ever met."

"I used to be both," Dempsey said, and flashed the boyish smile that had always inspired his teammates back in the glory days. He crawled through the narrow doorway into the cockpit, where the pilot and Patch were trying to position the .50. "You guys good?"

The pilot forced a tight, nervous grin. "We'd be better if we had a fuckin' plan."

"We have a plan," Dempsey said plainly. "Kill all the bad guys and then wait for our ride out of this shithole. Beer is on the EXFIL team when we get back to the embassy mission in Baghdad."

"I thought the rescued, not the rescuers, were supposed to buy the beer?"

"Who said anything about a rescue?" Dempsey said with a snort. "The way I see it, they have the easy job. We're the guys caught in the jihad stampede, thinning the terrorist herd. All they're doing is picking us up after the fight's over."

Patch laughed, despite the raw, raging pain Dempsey knew the man was suffering in his leg. SEALs were remarkable creatures. Patch was the same man in the suck as he was under perfect operating conditions. Through adversity, pain, and loss, a Navy SEAL was a Navy SEAL to the core.

Dempsey helped the pilot kick the smashed windshield out of its housing. There was nothing to mount the heavy machine gun to, so they jammed it into the space between the control panel and the metal frame, now devoid of Plexiglas. Patch was a more experienced gunner than the SOAR pilot, so despite his injury he was the best suited for the job. Taking care with his leg, they moved the SEAL into position on the wreckage of the copilot seat, where he would be able to provide effective fire against any approach from the front of the aircraft.

"You good?" Dempsey asked.

Patch nodded. "Get a few rounds flying, and this damn thing practically floats."

"Hooyah."

"Hooyah."

Now for phase two.

Dempsey moved back into the cabin and slapped the pilot on the back. Then he called up to Chunk, who had taken over as lookout.

"How much time, LT?"

"Minutes."

Dempsey frowned. "You better join the Lieutenant up top, bro," he told the pilot. Then he hollered, "Patch is manning the fifty up front, so I'll lead the other truck aft."

"Check," Chunk said.

"Don't fucking shoot me, Chunk," Dempsey said, only half kidding now.

"Got it."

"But don't look like you're not trying to shoot me," he added.

Chunk glanced down at him with a smirk. "I'll shoot *casual*. How's that?"

Dempsey gave Chunk a thumbs-up, then turned and knelt beside the prisoner. The man's eyes were closed, but he was mumbling something in German. Dempsey unsheathed his knife and cut the terrorist's hands free. The man groaned as his deformed left arm dropped. Dempsey pulled the man's filthy, bloodstained tunic up over his head, and then he shrugged off his kit and his shirt, dropped them on the ground, and pulled the terrorist's "man dress" over his head. He left on his pants, but quickly shed his boots and thick SmartWool socks.

The man stared up at him with glazed, confused eyes.

"Well, how about that," Dempsey said. "Now I look like you."

Then, he smashed an elbow hard into the man's right temple.

He dragged the unconscious man forward to the cockpit by his arms. Once in the cockpit, he flashed Patch and his .50 an evil grin, then shoved the flaccid body out through the other half of the windowless cockpit. On a whim, Dempsey wiped his hand across Patch's blood-soaked BDUs and smeared the SEAL's blood over the right side of his face. Anything that extended the ruse, by even a few seconds, could make the difference between his plan working and being the first guy killed.

"Aft pickup truck is holding and the forward one is swinging around now. Both about seventy meters out," Chunk hollered down.

Dempsey shoved his Sig 516 out the window, then wriggled out through the hole onto the warming desert sand. He quickly scrambled to his feet, slung his rifle across his shoulder, and began dragging the terrorist behind him, moving in an arc along the belly of the helo toward the tail. He rubbed his cheek against a dirty wheel protruding from the upended landing gear as he moved aft, adding more filth to his face. As he reached the end of the fuselage, a white pickup truck crept into view. He pulled back, giving his brain time to process what he'd just seen. Four men—a driver, a fighter in the passenger seat with a rifle, a spotter standing with binoculars, and a gunner manning what appeared to be a DShK machine gun mounted on a tripod in the bed of the truck.

That was bad.

The Russian-made machine gun fired 12.7 x 108 mm rounds at 850 meters per second and was accurate up to 2 kilometers. With a firing rate of 600 rounds per minute, the DShK would tear through the aluminum skin of the downed helicopter and cut everyone inside to ribbons. He hoped like hell that the other truck did not have the same weapon. If it did, they were fucked.

Dempsey closed his eyes, took a deep breath, and practiced the Arabic phrases he would need. Then he opened his eyes, grabbed the still-unconscious terrorist under the armpits, and headed toward the white pickup. The spotter and the gunner immediately trained their sights on him. He braced for the heavy rounds, which at any second could start flying and tear him apart.

"*Le-termee!*" he screamed at the top of his lungs. He made a show of glancing repeatedly back at the helo behind him as he struggled to drag the unconscious prisoner across the sand.

The gunner raised his head up from his circular sight and hollered something at the man with the binoculars. The spotter shrugged and shook his head.

"*Le-termee, le-termee,*" Dempsey yelled again, still moving toward the truck. *Don't shoot, don't shoot!*

"*Awgaf te-ra ar-mee,*" the spotter hollered back. He pointed at the rifle slung under Dempsey's arm. "*Dheb sla-Hak!*" He was telling Dempsey to stop and to drop his weapon.

"*La—La!*" Dempsey said and motioned at the helicopter behind him. "*Amrikan.*"

The man froze. "*Amrikan?*"

Dempsey nodded with both fear and enthusiasm.

The spotter's expression morphed to one of nervous surprise, and he raised his binoculars to take another look at the helo. This reaction confirmed Dempsey's theory. These guys thought they had shot down an Iraqi patrol; encountering American military at the crash site was the last thing they'd expected.

"*Ra-ja-'an,*" Dempsey hollered, his desperate *please* laced with real emotion. Suddenly, he was beginning to second-guess the merits of his plan. "*Ra-ja-'an. Yeg-der aH-Had yi-saa-id-na?*" Can't you help us?

The spotter lowered his binoculars and glared at Dempsey.

Dempsey collapsed to his knees beside his unconscious confederate in the sand and began to sob.

A moment later, he heard the spotter—who was clearly the leader of this crew—begin barking orders. He looked up and watched a man with sunglasses and an AK-47 climb out of the passenger seat of the truck. As the fighter walked toward them, he kept the barrel of his AK-47 trained on Dempsey's chest. Dempsey bowed his head as the man approached, carrying on the charade.

Two sandaled feet stopped six feet away in the sand.

Dempsey calculated he could take the fighter, but when the DShK opened up in response, there'd be nothing left of him but a bloody smear in the sand.

"*Min—wayn in-ta?*" the bearded fighter asked, looking them over.

"Qa'im," Dempsey answered meekly, hoping the man had just asked him where they came from.

The terrorist stared at him blankly.

Sensing uncertainty, Dempsey changed tack. He glanced frantically back at the helo again. *"Amrikan!"* he shouted and pointed. *"Amrikan!"*

"Zein. In-ta ib-'aman," the fighter said and reached a hand out to help pull the limp body of the unconscious jihadist through the sand. Dempsey mumbled on about the Amrikans and began to cry. The bearded fighter huffed and picked up the pace, practically dragging both of them back toward the white pickup. As they approached the truck, Dempsey scanned the other three terrorists. The leader was watching him cautiously, but the driver and the gunner were now focused on the helicopter, looking for the American threat. When they reached the passenger side of the truck, Dempsey stifled a sob and added, *"Shuk-ran,"* thanking the bearded fighter for helping them.

The leader jumped out of the bed of the truck and approached them. *"Ish-Sar?"* he asked, trying to understand what had happened.

"Kha-Tar," Dempsey sobbed. *"Amrikan."* He hoped he sounded like an Arab in shock and not an American speaking Arabic poorly. He bowed his head and placed his right hand over his heart. *"Shuk-ran,"* he said again.

The leader looked unconvinced. After a brief pause, he raised his AK-47 and pointed it at Dempsey's head. *"Dheb Sla-Hak!"* the man commanded.

Okay, Chunk. Feel free to start shooting anytime. Whadaya need, an invitation?

Dempsey cowered, but did not drop his weapon as ordered. Instead, he glanced nervously over his shoulder and said, *"La . . . le-termee!"* Then, throwing both hands in the air, he shouted, *"Amrikans!"*

Two rifle shots rang out, and Dempsey felt the sand kick up against his ankles. He spun around, grabbed his rifle, and fired a three-round burst twenty yards short of the helicopter.

The leader ducked and turned away from Dempsey. *"Termee!"* he shouted to the gunner on the DShK, commanding him to fire at the helicopter.

The bearded fighter standing next to Dempsey raised his AK-47 and began shooting at the helo.

"Ish-ged?" the leader barked, asking how many fighters were in the helicopter.

Dempsey dropped into a tactical crouch and turned, letting his rifle follow. He looked up at the terrorist and smiled. *"Ih-na Amrikan,"* he said. *We are Americans.*

The leader looked puzzled. His eyebrows rose. "Eh?"

Dempsey angled the barrel upward and fired. The 5.56 mm round hit the leader under the chin and exploded out the top of his head. He shifted his aim to the gunner manning the DShK and put a round through the man's left temple. His next round was intended for the bearded fighter, but as he spun to engage the enemy, the fighter grabbed his arm. Dempsey struggled to raise his Sig Sauer rifle against strong fingers digging deep into his right bicep. At the same time, the bearded fighter swung his AK-47 around. Dempsey ducked under the firing arc of the muzzle as it spat flame and metal overhead. With his left hand, he seized a fistful of the fighter's beard and yanked, pulling the man momentarily off balance. In his peripheral vision, he saw the driver jump out of the truck and run back to man the DShK.

Fuck!

Like a pumpkin hit with a sledgehammer, the bearded jihadist's head exploded, engulfing Dempsey's face in blood and brains. Dempsey staggered backward, trying to wipe the globs of the stuff out of his eyes with his fingers. He stumbled over a body as he desperately tried to clear his vision. In that instant, he swore he'd felt the body moving, but that was impossible. He pushed the distracting thought from his mind and swung his rifle in what he guessed was the direction of the pickup and worked the trigger, firing multiple three-shot bursts.

To his immediate left, someone bellowed, "Allahu Akbar!" and Dempsey's heart skipped a beat. He swung his rifle toward the war cry at the same time a SOPMOD M4 echoed to the north. He heard a body fall and the clatter of a rifle hitting the ground. He wiped the blood furiously from his face with the sleeve of the borrowed tunic. With his vision finally clear, he saw his prisoner lying prone in the sand, arms outstretched and bracketing the gory mess that had been his head before Chunk's bullet did its job. He looked left at the pickup and saw the driver hanging limply over the side rail of the bed, a casualty of Dempsey's lucky strafe.

Dempsey turned toward the helo and waved a hand over his head, signaling Chunk, but the exchange was cut short when gunfire erupted on the far side of the helicopter. The other jihadi assault team was engaging with what sounded like AK-47s. He waited for the gut-wrenching rattle of a DShK opening up, but it never came. Instead, he heard the unmistakable tenor of a .50 cal going to work. Two bursts fired by Patch from the cockpit, followed by another two bursts.

"They're repositioning south!" Chunk yelled from his perch on the downed Russian Mi-17. "Out of our field of fire."

Another prolonged burst from the .50 echoed across the desert, and then the machine gun fell silent. Dempsey understood exactly what was happening. The jihadi fighters were flanking. If the second truck was not equipped with a matching DShK, then it probably carried surface-to-air missile launchers—the exact weapon used to shoot them down in the first place. A single rocket would obliterate the helo and everyone inside.

Dempsey would not let that happen.

He leaped over the dead prisoner, sprinted to the white pickup, and climbed into the driver's seat. As with most of the vehicles he'd driven in Iraq, ignition was performed via a toggle switch rather than a key. He pushed a black button with his thumb and the vehicle roared to life. He slammed the transmission into gear, jerked the wheel left, and popped the clutch. The truck leaped forward, a rooster tail of sand spraying behind it.

The plan was simple: hope the bad guys thought he was on their side long enough for him to man the DShK and tear them to pieces. If they identified him first, this would be the last stupid thing he ever did. With the accelerator pressed to the floor, he screamed across the desert, steering a course to intercept the other truck. The instant the second pickup came into view, his stomach lurched. The enemy truck had already repositioned. In the bed, a terrorist was hoisting a missile launcher onto his shoulder, while two other fighters were engaging the helo with AK-47s.

Dempsey slammed on the brakes and rolled out of the driver's seat. With the truck still rolling forward, he vaulted over the side rail into the bed of the truck. He landed hard on his right knee, but ignored the pain and sprang to his feet. Grabbing the twin handles of the machine gun, he jerked back the heavy slide to chamber a round, and then swung the gun around.

A jihadist standing in the bed of the other truck raised a hand to Dempsey, but then froze as realization set in. The fighter did a double take, screamed at his comrade with the missile launcher, and then dove for cover. The man with the rocket launcher tried to swing his weapon toward Dempsey, but it was too late.

Dempsey pressed the trigger with his thumb, and the mighty Russian machine gun spit flame and death at the enemy. The recoil was so violent he thought the little truck might tip over as he walked the stream of heavy rounds across the desert toward his target. His first strafe cut the missile-wielding jihadi in half. Without releasing the trigger, he pulled the laser-line of bullets and tracers to the right, slicing through the cab of the truck and the two jihadists firing their AKs at the helo. Their bodies exploded in unison—large chunks of flesh, bone, and blood erupting in a gory cloud.

Dempsey felt a sharp pain in his left wrist as sparks danced off the DShK's metal housing. *Ricochets.* The fourth jihadi was shooting at him from somewhere. Suddenly, the unwieldy monster in his grip had become a liability. Instinctively, he threw himself backward over the side of the truck, landing on his back in the sand. The impact knocked the breath from his lungs and sent a bolt of mind-numbing pain down his spine and left leg. He disconnected his mind from the pain and reached for his rifle, only to find it missing. His trusty Sig 516 apparently hadn't made the trip with him over the side.

A shadow fell over him.

He looked east to find a scowling, bearded jihadi bringing the barrel of an AK-47 to bear. Reflexively, Dempsey reached for the bowie knife on his kit, but his fingers found only the torn, bloodied fabric of his tunic. He bared his teeth at his enemy, ready for the pain . . .

A shot rang out.

The jihadi's skull opened and spit its contents out onto the ground. A half second later, the body collapsed into a lifeless heap.

Dempsey lay still for a beat, until the pain in his back ebbed enough to stand. When he was ready, he got to his feet and surveyed the bloody carnage around him. Somewhere in the distance, he heard the unmistakable growl of a helicopter. Looking south, he saw a black dot on the horizon, growing larger with each second. He slow-jogged back to the downed Mi-17 helo, but instead of feeling relief, he suddenly found himself awash in irritation.

From the cockpit, the SOAR pilot waved at him. Chunk barked a "Hooyah" and slid down from his perch using the stub of a main rotor blade for support. The SEAL officer hit the sand, whirled, and ran to meet Dempsey.

"Dude, that was fucking insane," Chunk said, gesturing past him at the smoking pickup truck and the mounds of body parts around it. "Holy shit, Dempsey. I've never seen anything like that before. You're like fucking Rambo, man." Chunk swung an arm around Dempsey's shoulders.

"You killed our prisoner!" Dempsey yelled, jerking out of Chunk's grip. "I needed the intel stored in that guy's brain, and you blew it all over the fucking desert. What do you have to say about that, Lieutenant?"

Chunk stopped abruptly and glared at him. "How 'bout *you're welcome*, asshole. Or better yet—next time, I'll just let the bad guys kill your ass."

Dempsey met Chunk's gaze. "What are you talking about?"

"Your prisoner woke up. He was going for an AK. Two more seconds and he woulda smoked your ass."

Dempsey opened his mouth to say something, but the words didn't come. He snapped his jaw shut.

"Oh yeah, and don't forget the other two fuckers I capped for you," Chunk growled and then stormed away.

Dempsey followed Chunk toward the wreck, wondering why he'd ripped into the SEAL officer like that. What the hell had come over him? Team guys didn't act like that. Since when did collecting intelligence start mattering more to him than the lives of the Americans he was trying to protect? Maybe since radical Islam had tossed the rule book for warfare out the window. Thanks to Rafiq al-Mahajer, Romeo was dead. Thanks to men like al-Mahajer, Dempsey's entire Tier One SEAL unit had been wiped off the map. Men like al-Mahajer had to be stopped, no matter the cost. That was his job now. His responsibility.

He shook his head.

Maybe he was becoming a Jones after all.

No way. Never. There had to be a way to do the job without sacrificing his soul. Hadn't he sacrificed enough already? His career, his identity . . . his family.

He jogged to catch up to Chunk.

"We gotta sterilize the helo quick before more bad guys show up. It needs to look like an Iraqi Air Force mission with no signs of Americans," the SEAL officer said without looking at him. "We could use a hand."

"Of course," he said. They walked a half-dozen more paces in silence before Dempsey threw his arm around the SEAL's shoulder. "You know, you're a pretty decent shot—for an officer."

The corner of Chunk's mouth curled up slightly. "And you're a pretty big pain in the ass—for a spook."

"I deserve that," Dempsey said, nodding. Then, after a pause, "You wouldn't happen to have any Skoal left, would ya?"

Chunk smirked and fished a tin of wintergreen snuff from a pocket in his kit. After pinching off a wad for himself, he handed the hockey puck to Dempsey.

"You know," Dempsey mumbled, packing his lower lip with tobacco. "I could've taken that dude with the sunglasses."

"Nah, I don't think so," Chunk said, suppressing a laugh. "He looked stronger than you."

Both men turned to watch the incoming Blackhawk flare on its approach.

"The mission's not a total wash," Chunk shouted to be heard over the roar of the rotors.

Dempsey raised an eyebrow. "How you figure?"

Chunk flashed him a tobacco-stained grin. "Your guy's laptop and Blackberry were packed in a padded hard case. You still got those."

"I'll be damned." Dempsey spat a sour stream of tobacco juice onto the sand. In all the mayhem, he'd forgotten about those. Maybe he had something worth delivering to Jarvis after all.

An encrypted file.

A recovered e-mail.

A phone call placed to Rafiq al-Mahajer's mobile.

Sometimes, that first bread crumb was all it took to find the trail.

CHAPTER 8

Tehran, Iran
October 14, 2030 Local Time

The security guard stopped him five meters from the door. Behrouz Rostami scowled at the hand on his shoulder and contemplated breaking the man's arm. The jujitsu movement was so simple even a child could perform the maneuver.

Only an idiot grabs a man by the shoulder from behind.

"This is private property," the guard said, overconfident. "Turn around and go back where you came from."

Rostami swallowed his aggression and casually shrugged off the hand. He turned slowly to face the young Iranian. While the youth's nondescript street clothing and hapless loitering might fool the neighbors, Rostami had spotted the sentry within seconds of his arrival. "I have an appointment with Director Modiri."

In his peripheral vision, Rostami saw the guard's right hand move subtly toward his waist. Over the years, Rostami had come to realize that killers recognized other killers—the same way one alpha wolf knew another. This puff-chested youth was not an alpha. With the blade sheathed inside his jacket, Rostami could spill the guard's intestines on the pavement before the kid could draw his pistol. He resisted the urge to smirk.

"I was not aware of any appointments," the guard said at last.

"Call it in," Rostami said and began tapping his foot. "Tell the Director that you're keeping Agent Rostami waiting outside."

The guard hesitated.

"Go on, boy. Do as you're told."

The guard's cheeks reddened, but he retrieved a mobile phone from his pocket. After a terse conversation, the guard pocketed his phone. "The Director said for you to wait here."

Rostami sniffed and turned his back on the sentry and the beautiful home he guarded. Rostami had missed the architecture of Iran while in Europe. Not the high-rise condos that grew like weeds in the far-too-Westernized parts of the city, but the homes like this one. The Director's house suggested modern comfort, but it was contained within classic Persian architecture of columns and domes. The call to the Persia of the past was completed with a row of blue tiles along the eaves beneath the roof. Were the homes not so close together here—in the section of Tehran reserved for the political elite of the "new" Iran—it might have been the home of a Shah from a hundred years ago or more.

Modiri made him wait for an eternity, each minute raising his ire. A car arrived, forcing him to step aside as it pulled up to the residence. Mercedes E Class, previous model year, he noted. The driver did not get out or lower his window. Three minutes later, the front door of the house opened. Rostami spun on a heel, but his gaze was usurped by the woman at Amir Modiri's side. She was radiance incarnate. A bonfire of femininity. He watched her, brazenly. She laughed and poked her husband's stomach with a lithe, manicured index finger—theatrical recompense for something said during a conversation begun in the house. Her gait was light and confident. She had an adolescent quality about her, despite being decades removed from her teenage years. He had heard stories of

Maheen Modiri's beauty, but he had never seen the woman's vivacity up close. He felt a stirring inside—primal and hot. He wanted to covet this woman. Possess her. Consume her fire. Drink her vitality and then break her . . . ruin her like all the others.

The driver of the hired car stepped out and opened the rear passenger door. He watched Modiri escort his wife to the Mercedes. She had not so much as glanced in Rostami's direction, but as she kissed her husband's cheek, she met his gaze. *So much mischief in those espresso eyes.* The driver closed the door, and an instant before the black-tinted windows hid her from view, he caught a glimpse of her shedding her hijab. *So brazen, this woman. No wonder Modiri keeps a private security detail. I wonder if she knows he's always watching?*

As the Mercedes backed out into the street, Modiri finally turned to Rostami. VEVAK's Director of Foreign Operations simply said, "Walk with me." Rostami nodded and took a position on the Director's right side. They walked in silence for a block before Modiri finally spoke. "You are not welcome at my private residence. This should have been implicit, given our professional relationship."

"I apologize. I did not mean to—"

"If you ever come to my private residence again," Modiri said impassively, "there will be unpleasant consequences."

"My sincerest apologies," Rostami said, through gritted teeth.

"Why are you here?"

"I have bad news. The safe house in Al Anbar was hit by the Americans."

"Did they get Parviz?"

"He has not reported, so we must assume the worst."

"And al-Mahajer?"

"He sent a proxy."

"Typical." Modiri snorted. They walked in silence for several paces. "But it may be a blessing that al-Mahajer sent a proxy."

A lump formed in Rostami's throat. He'd seen this look in his boss's eyes before. "You're not planning to continue the operation, I hope."

"I see no reason to abort."

"But the Americans have Parviz, and they have al-Mahajer's proxy. It is only a matter of time before they connect the dots."

"And how do you know the Americans have them?"

"Their bodies were not among the dead and they have not checked in. They're gone."

"No matter," Modiri said. "Parviz will not crack. He's one of our very best."

"The same cannot be said for al-Mahajer's proxy."

Modiri shrugged. "Maybe, maybe not, but what I do know is that al-Mahajer would never entrust the complete details of this operation to a proxy. We need to reengage with al-Mahajer and take the next steps."

"Who are you going to send?" Rostami asked, although he already knew the answer.

"You, of course."

Rostami swallowed his anger down like bitter medicine. Collaborating with the Islamic State was like playing with fire. Managing the rise and rhetoric of ISIS had been a challenge for Tehran, but in Modiri's mind it was also a golden opportunity. In typical fashion, President Esfahani and the Supreme Leader preached different messages with different strategic objectives. The Iranian President condemned the atrocities committed by ISIS in the region and extended offers of military aid to Iraq and Syria, with the ultimate goal being to cement Persian influence inside the faltering governments of Iran's two closest neighbors. The Supreme Leader, however, proclaimed that ISIS was the brainchild of the Zionists and America—one designed to sow seeds of discord in the region, turn Muslim against Muslim, and justify making the Middle East into a drone-patrolled police state in a permanent "war on terror." Ultimately, Tehran needed ISIS to fail—and fail spectacularly—thereby paving the way for the rise of Iran and the Persian Caliphate. Amir Modiri's job was to help see this done, while at the same time exploiting ISIS in every way possible to inflict wounds on their true enemies—the Americans and the Zionists.

Rostami suspected that this back-channel mission of offering aid to ISIS was entirely Modiri's idea. Publicly, ISIS proclaimed all Shia Muslims apostates and went so far as to call for their elimination from the Middle East, but behind closed doors the ISIS leadership would conduct business with any entity willing to provide them with weapons or money. Their recent territory and oil losses were making them desperate. Their global reputation made them the perfect scapegoat.

Since his brother's death, Modiri had become obsessed with exacting revenge on the Americans. Rostami doubted that either Iran's Supreme Leader or President Esfahani knew about Modiri's ambitious plan to strike America's heartland using al-Mahajer as a puppet. Modiri was a master of keeping secrets and a god of compartmentalization, but having an agent of VEVAK captured by the Americans during a raid on ISIS leadership would have disastrous consequences for the Director of Foreign Operations. To be caught would not only cost Modiri his career, but quite possibly his head.

"With all due respect, is continuing the mission best for Persia? Like you, I thirst for revenge, but—"

"Don't be an idiot," Modiri said, and struck him like an insolent child on the back of the head, hard enough that Rostami nearly stumbled. "I mourn my brother, but I serve Persia. A successful strike by ISIS in the American heartland will demonstrate America's vulnerability and weakness on the world stage. More important, it will raise their ire at our radical Sunni brothers and provide fresh incentive to escalate their war with ISIS in Syria and Iraq. This accomplishes three goals: First, it safeguards Persian lives and dollars. Second, it distracts the Pentagon from our operations. And third, it drives American foreign policy to acknowledge and support Iran's preeminent role in maintaining a stable Middle East."

"I understand," Rostami said.

"Do you?" Modiri replied, scowling. "I don't think you do. ISIS believes if they burn, pillage, and murder long enough, the world will crumble. Just look at Syria. But I ask you, Behrouz, what use is a caliphate that rules over a land of bones, ashes, and rubble? ISIS is not, and never will be, a functional nation-state. They are incapable of maintaining, let alone ruling, a prosperous caliphate."

"They are fools," Rostami said.

"Yes, short-sighted, barbaric fools, but such men are useful—most especially as martyrs on the front lines of battle. We will use the enemy of our enemy as a pawn in our chess match with the West, just as we did with Al Qaeda. Your job is to convince al-Mahajer to accept our assistance. Use whatever flattery, lies, and promises it takes to do it."

Rostami nodded. He had to admit that his boss was correct. A success in this operation would serve many purposes in their covert war against the West and rise to power in the Middle East. "Understand it's going to be very difficult for me to contact, let alone meet with, al-Mahajer after this last raid," he told Modiri. "He'll go deep underground for months. Even if I do manage to contact him, the Americans will be hunting him."

Modiri swatted the comment away as if it were a buzzing mosquito. "Find Rafiq al-Mahajer. Present him my offer. And don't come back until you do."

"Understood," Rostami said through gritted teeth.

Modiri stopped and turned to face him.

They locked eyes.

"One more thing, Behrouz," Modiri said casually, one killer to another. "If I ever catch you looking at my wife that way again, I'm going to have your eyes plucked out and fed to my dogs."

PART II

When walking through the valley of shadows,
remember, a shadow is cast by a light.
—*H. K. Barclay*

CHAPTER 9

Emek Café
Yenikoy, 34464 Sariyer
Istanbul, Turkey
October 18, 0945 Local Time

Emek Kahve was crowded.

Behrouz Rostami scanned the patrons at the café, looking for an Arab or a Turk who resembled Rafiq al-Mahajer. He had never met the man in person, but he was intimately familiar with his face, having studied every photograph in the VEVAK case file ad nauseam. Finding no matching faces, Rostami walked to the last open table and took the seat facing the entrance.

As he waited, he stroked his freshly shaved chin. For hard-line Muslims, shortening the beard to less than one fist's length was haram; for zealots like al-Mahajer, to go clean-shaven was to be a hermaphrodite. But Rostami was Persian, and with the exception of the clerics and the devoutly pious, most Iranian men did not wear long beards. For the duration of his previous assignment in Frankfurt, he had not worn a beard at all. This decision had been a great boon to his sex life. Allah had blessed him with a strong, square jaw and chiseled, masculine chin. To hide a face as handsome as his under a tangled mass of whiskers was a travesty. Also, the beard aged him a decade, especially now that it was showing hints of gray around the mouth. If Allah had wished him to look like some old, wizened cleric, he would have made him ugly.

Fuck the beard.

Since returning to Persia, Rostami had grudgingly kept a *basiji* beard—three weeks' unkempt growth. In Iran, this particular style was recognized as a military beard, although Rostami had done it for two reasons: first, to facilitate growing a longer beard should his next assignment require one, and second, to distance himself from his German legend—energy-sector venture capitalist Reinhold Ahmadi. It had taken him months to admit it, but the truth was that he had lost himself in his legend. He missed being Ahmadi, with his Italian suits, bottomless expense account, and international élan. But most of all, he missed the women, especially wealthy, naive Western girls. He had loved humiliating them. Hurting them . . .

He had discovered the little waterfront café nestled along the shores of the Bosphorus three years ago, while sleeping with a Turkish girl in Yeniköy, an affluent neighborhood in northern Istanbul. Emek was one of his favorite spots to have breakfast with a lover after a night of passionate sex. The setting was intimate, traditional, and free of tourists. He had specifically selected it for today's meeting with al-Mahajer because the atmosphere would give him a psychological advantage over the Syrian. Al-Mahajer was former Mujahideen—radical, unsophisticated, and more experienced in barbarism than tradecraft. Meeting in a place like this would undoubtedly unnerve the Islamic State commander, even more so because, to Rostami's knowledge, this meeting would be al-Mahajer's first foray outside of jihadi-controlled territory in years.

A Turkish waiter approached the table and asked to take his order. Rostami decided not to wait for al-Mahajer and ordered a coffee and a serving of *menemen* with *pastirma*. Ten minutes later, the waiter delivered his coffee and eggs with chopped beef—steaming hot and served in a traditional double-handled steel dish. Rostami wolfed down the food, never pausing between bites. When he was finished, he raised the little porcelain cup to his lips, tilted back his head, and drained the sweet black coffee in two gulps. When he lowered his eyes, Rafiq al-Mahajer was standing across the table from him, dressed in gray trousers, a gray linen shirt, and a black suit coat.

One point, al-Mahajer, Rostami thought, chastising himself.

"Salam," said al-Mahajer, his voice flat and emotionless.

"Wa Alaikum as-Salam," Rostami replied, and gestured to the seat across from him.

The Syrian pulled out the chair and sat down. His manner was collected and confident; he did not appear nervous at all. Rostami immediately took note that the man's beard was shorter, blacker, and more neatly groomed than in any of the photographs he'd seen. Trimmed to exactly one fist in length and freshly dyed; Rostami could tell because of the deep onyx color and uniform shine.

"You've eaten," al-Mahajer said in Arabic, his tone oozing judgment.

Rostami flashed an easy smile. "Only the first course. Please forgive my impatience."

"You thought I would not come?"

Rostami gave a little shrug. "Given recent circumstances, your absence today would be both understandable and forgivable."

"You are not Syrian," al-Mahajer said, switching from Arabic to passable Farsi.

Rostami's pulse quickened. *Two points, al-Mahajer.*

"No, I'm not," he said, sticking with Arabic. "But I am a true believer."

Al-Mahajer scratched his beard with his right index finger. "What is your message from Tehran?"

"Consider me an emissary of good will," Rostami said, sitting up straighter in his chair. "Here to make an offer of support."

"Your government has publically denounced our efforts."

Rostami smiled. The inevitable chess game, the thrust and parry to massage away the half-truths and find their way to an uneasy trust, had begun. "Words can be written in blood, and words can be spoken in the wind. One is Allah's will, the other is vapor."

"Your government cooperates with America. Your military is working with the Iraqis against us."

"You have slaughtered hundreds of devout Shia Muslims and destroyed Shiite mosques in Syria, and yet we are not your enemy."

The ISIS commander paused for a beat, and then said, "You are *Rafidah*. We do not require your support."

The jihadist's insult was a slap to the face, and Rostami felt blood rush to his cheeks. He'd expected al-Mahajer to be nervous, gullible, possibly even desperate, given the Americans' surprise raid and the meeting here, without his bodyguards. But this man was none of those things. Rafiq al-Mahajer was like a granite pillar—hard, cold, and firmly grounded by the gravity of his own mass.

Time to change strategies.

"But you do need our support, or else you would not be here," Rostami said, clasping his fingers together and resting his hands on the table. "You need our support, because you're losing."

The Syrian stared at him with black-hole eyes—pulling, extracting, consuming. Rostami felt a great void growing inside his chest, as if he were being hollowed out from the inside. *This is the moment,* he told himself. *Falter now, and you'll lose him.* He fought the urge to blink and held the other man's gaze, refusing to look away.

"What can Persia offer the cause that Allah has not already provided?" al-Mahajer said after an excruciatingly long pause.

"A new opportunity. An opportunity which your organization lacks infrastructure abroad to exploit."

"What do you propose, Persian?"

"A way inside. A way beneath the armor of the enemy, so you can strike at his heart."

"Many have tried this. Only one man has succeeded and that man is dead."

"True, but the others who have tried and failed have not had the resources of Persia behind them. We have already demonstrated what we are capable of when pious Muslims put aside petty, sectarian differences between Shia and Sunni and cooperate for a higher purpose."

The Syrian raised an eyebrow. "What cooperation do you speak of?"

"Six months ago, a great blow was dealt to the enemy."

For the first time since sitting down, al-Mahajer grinned. "You speak of Yemen?"

Rostami nodded.

"An impressive operation, yes, but one that came at a great cost."

"Great victories require great sacrifice."

"I do not recall Persia suffering any losses that night."

"Don't be foolish, my friend—Persia risked everything that night. And would again, should you choose to cooperate."

"Why should I trust you?" al-Mahajer asked.

"Because what I'm offering is better than your best alternative, my friend."

Al-Mahajer scowled. "Who are you to pretend you know me? Who are *you* to make such bold claims?"

Rostami savored the moment. It had been a challenge, but he'd finally found a chink in the Syrian's armor. Now, it was time to execute a reversal and appeal to the man's ego.

"We've had our eyes on you for a long time," he said. "Despite all the secrecy and seclusion you've been forced to endure, your reputation as a shrewd tactician and a pious warrior has spread throughout the region. I understand and respect the sacrifices you've made. The path you've chosen has not been an easy one. You've spent the past decade on the move, living in insufferable conditions, always wondering if the next drone strike will be your last. These sacrifices were necessary as you helped transform the Islamic State from a small, isolated faction into the global face of jihad. But now, the time has come for you to leave a mark on history. You know it, I know it, and Allah knows it. You are destined for greatness, and as a fellow true believer, you have my pledge that I will help you achieve that destiny."

Al-Mahajer stared at him for a long moment, taking a measure of his sincerity. Finally, the Syrian said, "Maybe you do know me, Persian . . . maybe we have something to discuss after all."

CHAPTER 10

Hampton Roads Bridge-Tunnel
Interstate 64 Westbound, Norfolk, Virginia
October 18, 1715 Local Time

"Oh, for Christ's sake," Dempsey grumbled. "Just fucking go."

He resisted the urge to pop his horn.

Being shot at in Iraq or sitting in Norfolk traffic . . . hard to say which he resented more.

The car in front of him sped up and then suddenly slammed on the brakes, forcing Dempsey to hit his brakes. He watched in his rearview mirror as the chain reaction rippled through dozens of vehicles behind him. This was exactly the sort of crap that caused traffic jams in the first place. He returned his gaze straight ahead; he could tell from the tilt of the driver's head and the mobile phone propped in his hand that the dude was texting.

If only I had an RPG for that guy.

He turned on SiriusXM radio.

After five minutes of scanning through crap, he turned it off.

He'd moved *maybe* a hundred yards.

He groaned his irritation at the universe, and the universe laughed in his face—the lane next to him started moving while his stayed put.

Had he flown back to the United States on one of Ember's planes, he would have landed at the small Newport News/Williamsburg International Airport and avoided all this bullshit. But since he'd flown commercial on the way out and left his Yukon parked at Norfolk International, he'd offered to fly back commercial and pick up his ride. Apparently, this was his penance for being nice.

His phone chirped, and he tapped the button on the steering wheel to activate the hands-free Bluetooth link. "Dempsey."

"Where are you?"

"Sitting in the idiot parade trying to get to the tunnel."

Smith laughed. "Rush-hour arrival, very nice. Sounds like you should fire your travel agent."

"Okay, you're fired."

"In that case, congratulations on your promotion. You're now the Operations Director at Ember."

Dempsey laughed. "Christ, no. You think I want your job? No fucking way."

"Well, then as your boss, I must be the bearer of bad news."

"No beers at the house?"

"Nope."

"No nap on the sofa after beers at the house?"

"'Fraid not. Jarvis wants you to come in."

Dempsey let out a long sigh. "Sure, why not?" he said.

I've been back in the United States for, oh, less than an hour. What else would I possibly want to do?

"Thanks, brother," Smith said. "See you when you get here."

The line went dead.

He shifted in his seat, trying to find a position where the nerve pain shooting down his left leg was bearable. The helo crash had aggravated his back, and the cramped coach seat on the transatlantic flight hadn't done him any favors. A trip to the chiropractor was probably in order.

As the traffic snaked slowly forward on the bridge, he looked out at the moored ships that made up the balance of the Atlantic Naval fleet—those not deployed at sea. Between him and the hazy outline of aircraft carriers and destroyers, gray Navy helicopters practiced touch-and-go approaches. He watched them flaring, touching down, and then nosing over and screaming past the creeping traffic on the bridge.

Aerial fucking abominations. God, he hated helicopters.

A few minutes later, the tunnel came into view. Halfway through, he knew the pace would magically pick up and traffic would accelerate to highway speed all the way to the exit for Langley Air Force Base. Then, just as inexplicably, traffic would slow back to a crawl until he reached the exit for the Newport News Airport. Ember Corporation—the white-side corporate security company that served as a non-official cover for his black ops unit—had their own hangar at the airport. Beneath that hangar, hidden in a concrete vault, was the operations center for the most covert counterterrorism activity in the world. And right now, the entire team was waiting for him to explain what, if anything, he had to show for two firefights and one helicopter crash that had nearly resulted in the capture of three Americans by the Islamic State.

The proxy's laptop and Blackberry had arrived safely at Ember hours earlier by "another means of transit," that much he knew. Hopefully Ember's crypto weenies had already uncovered something of value. For Dempsey, finding al-Mahajer was not just about settling a blood debt for Romeo's murder a decade earlier. The voice in his head was screaming that something else was coming. Something unexpected. Something nasty. Something no one was prepared for.

It was up to Ember to stop it.

His phone chimed. He glanced at the screen and saw a Facebook notification: Kate Kemper has updated her status. The potency of the urge to pick up his mobile and read the post took him by surprise. He'd not told anyone in Ember—not even Smith—that he was following Kate's Facebook feed. Reading her posts was more than a guilty pleasure; it was more than voyeurism. It was a static line for his soul.

When he'd been with the Teams, he'd despised social media. As far as he was concerned, the only social network a SEAL needed was his teammates. And the only social network a wife of a SEAL needed was that comprised of other SEALs' wives. Not all of the wives shared this opinion, but ultimately, OPSEC ruled the day. The need to protect the secrecy and anonymity of the unit trumped all other considerations, and that had been enough to keep Kate off Facebook.

Everything changed the day he died.

Within forty-eight hours of his death she had created a Facebook memorial page for him. The number of tribute posts and condolences the page received had surprised him. He'd read every single entry, torturing and mollifying his broken heart in the process. Activity on Jack Kemper's memorial page had long since plateaued and tapered off. Now, the only person continuing to post was Kate. Most of the pictures she posted were candid shots celebrating memorable events in the life they'd built together: A picture of them as newlyweds on their honeymoon. Him holding a tightly swaddled, three-hour-old Jacob in the hospital. Him dressed as Blackbeard on Halloween with five-year-old Jake dressed as Captain Hook. Every image made him smile like a kid on Christmas. Every image burned like the Grim Reaper putting his cigarette butts out on his heart. But the existence of the Jack Kemper memorial account had given him something else besides a place to wallow in the past—it had given him a key to the present.

Jack Kemper's memorial page was "friends" with Kate's Facebook page. It had been easy enough to guess the login and password she'd used to create the memorial page, and now he used it to access her personal feed. Unlike the memorial page, on her personal feed she posted about her and Jake's life in real time. In an odd, perverse way, he felt closer to her now than he had when they were newly divorced and living apart. Had it not been for Facebook, he would not have known that she'd sold the house in Tampa and moved to Atlanta to be closer to her parents. Or that she'd enrolled in a painting class at the local community college just to try something new. He liked knowing that she was reading *All the Light We Cannot See.* He'd even picked up a copy with the intention of reading it at the same time. He liked knowing what she was thinking and how she was feeling. And he especially liked hearing about Jake. Most of Kate's posts were about their son. From her last post, Dempsey had learned that Jake, the X-box-playing couch potato, had inexplicably decided to join the swim team.

"Shit," he barked, as he registered his exit drifting by in his peripheral vision.

He swerved across the yellow line to join the exit ramp just before running off the road into the grassy median. He waved politely at the well-heeled woman in an Infiniti sedan who was giving him the finger as he weaved into the line of traffic ahead of her. Five minutes later, he was on the access road for the corporate hangars. He drove to the south side of the airport, across the runway from the commercial terminal, and pulled into a parking spot next to Smith's identical black GMC. He stepped out of his SUV, locked the door with his key fob, and walked to the secure entrance. He punched his five-digit code into a generic twelve-button keypad mounted beside the door, and waited as the entire panel slid upward to reveal a black glass surface. He pressed his left hand against the glass until the system acknowledged with a beep and a green LED flash. A half second later, the magnetic door lock released and he pulled open the reinforced security door.

"Evening, Mr. Dempsey."

A man dressed in gray coveralls had the engine cover pulled off the port-side engine of the smallest of Ember's three corporate jets—a Cessna Citation X. The midsize bizjet, a Falcon 900DX, sat across from the Citation, the access door open and the pull-down steps on the floor. Beside it was nothing but an enormous expanse of vacant hangar floor where the third jet usually sat.

"Hey, Tom," Dempsey answered. "Where's the yacht?" he asked, referring to the 787-9 corporate conversion jet that served as their air-borne TOC.

"Up for its annual," the maintenance man said. "Back tomorrow, I think."

Dempsey nodded and wondered if that was true or if the Boeing had been tasked for a mission he had yet to hear about. Even here, within the group, there were secrets within secrets.

He walked to the rear of the hangar and the oversize, gray, metal tool cabinet. After a quick glance around, he opened the double doors and then reached up onto the top shelf, retrieving what looked like an old-fashioned calculator. He punched a code into the device and hit "Enter," then returned the device to the top shelf and closed the doors. With a soft whoosh, the cabinet disappeared into the floor, exposing the very modern black-walled elevator behind. He stepped over the top of the cabinet, now flush with the floor, and entered the elevator, then pressed his palm onto the glass reader mounted on the wall—identical to the reader that had let him into the hangar from the parking lot. The cabinet rose from the floor in front of him, back into place, and then the elevator began its rapid descent.

A few seconds later and fifty feet deeper, the elevator stopped abruptly. The doors opened, giving him access into a large, well-lit Tactical Operations Center that was the hub of Task Force Ember. He was no longer wowed by the impressive row of flat-screen TVs; the pol-ished, round mahogany table with built-in flip-up workstations; or the bank of computer terminals and servers along the back wall. He glanced, as a matter of routine, up at the two monitors that showed the taxiway leading from the hangar and the parking lot on the opposite side of the building, and saw nothing concerning. A Southwest commercial jet taxied past on its way to the runway, but nothing else was moving.

"Hey, JD," Smith said, as he entered the room through the doors that partitioned off the team locker room and the offices beyond. "Thanks for coming in."

"Hooyah," Dempsey said, with just the right amount of sarcasm to remind Smith he was still annoyed at being called in. "Find anything on the Blackberry or laptop yet?"

"I haven't heard anything from Ian and the boys yet, so I assume the answer is no."

Dempsey nodded. Baldwin's team and the cyber genius Richard Wang—whom Jarvis had poached from US Cyber Command—were good, but they weren't omniscient. "Is Grimes here?" he asked.

Smith dropped into one of the cushy leather seats at the conference table. "Yeah, and so is Mendez."

Salvador Mendez, a former MARSOC Marine with unlimited potential, rounded out Dempsey's small combat team. The plan was to add at least two more members, but Dempsey barely had time to breathe, let alone recruit at the moment. He took the seat beside Smith. The chair was a womb; a wave of drowsiness washed over him. That was how it went for operators—burning stress hormones like human jet fuel until the mission's complete, then when that last drop is used up, the afterburner flames out.

"You good, brother?" Smith asked.

"Yeah," Dempsey said. "Just hitting the wall."

"I remember the feeling. One minute you're going Mach two, ready to take on a tiger, and the next you're barely able to keep your head up."

Dempsey nodded agreement. "And every year older I get, the harder I crash."

"Lemme grab you a cup of coffee. The pot's been warming for hours, so I'm sure it's thick and nasty, just the way you like it."

Dempsey shook his head. "Nah, I'm good."

After a beat, Smith leaned in. "So, how was it?" he asked in a low, conspiratorial whisper.

"How was what?"

"Being out with a SEAL team. Was it weird? Did it get lonely or did you just have wood the whole time?"

Dempsey laughed.

Interesting that Smith had used the word *lonely*, because that was exactly how he'd felt. Paradoxical that he could feel alone in a group of SEALs, but therein lay the irony of human dynamics. Being "one of the guys" was not the same as "the guys plus one." Clearly Smith had experienced the feeling before, or he wouldn't have phrased the question like he had.

"Well?" Smith asked.

"It was good," Dempsey said at last. "The LT from Team Four is someone we should keep an eye on—a real steely-eyed frogman." Normally, he felt more or less ambivalent about junior and midgrade officers in the Teams, but Chunk had been solid.

"Oh, I see how it is," Smith said with a crooked smile. "Can't stand being outnumbered, huh?"

"Not exactly. Think of it more as accommodating a handicap. The way I see it, we need at least two SEALs to offset every Delta on the team."

"At least you didn't lose your sense of humor over there when you were crashing helicopters and trying to get yourself captured," Smith fired back.

The frosted glass door to the right opened and Elizabeth Grimes and Mendez walked in, both wearing desert khaki cargo pants and black 5.11 Tactical sports shirts. Mendez was laughing about something Grimes was saying. They saw Dempsey and stopped.

"Hey, boss," the former Marine said. "Didn't know you were back already."

"Just got in," Dempsey said. He shifted his gaze to Elizabeth. "Lady Grimes," he said with a nod.

Grimes dropped into the chair to his left, swinging her dark red ponytail over her shoulder. She stared at him with those sharp gray-blue eyes that must have melted a lot of hearts in her former life.

"Would you please stop calling me that?" she said with mock anger.

Dempsey grinned. "It's a term of endearment."

"Bullshit it is," she said and punched him in the shoulder hard enough to leave a bruise.

"No, really, it's a sign of respect," Smith chimed in. "He told me as much when we were watching a stripper named Lady at the Mons Venus in Tampa."

"That's right," Dempsey said. "I said she reminds me of Grimes, every inch the lady."

She tried to shoot him an angry look, but started laughing instead. "The day you boys see me dancing naked is the day you've died and gone to heaven."

Everyone busted up, and Mendez gave her a fist bump.

It's good to be back with my team, Dempsey thought, and realized he was suddenly glad he'd been called into the hangar before going home. *They* were his home now—a tribe of NOC-using, gun-shooting, foul-mouth-talking, terrorist-chasing, hot-blooded, American thirtysomethings.

Yeah, I'm home.

The rear door opened and Kelso Jarvis, the head of Task Force Ember, entered, flanked by *the Professor*—tall, lanky Ian Baldwin—with the geek squad in tow.

Jarvis went straight to the center podium and Baldwin sat down in the seat beside him, plugging a laptop into the panel in front of him.

"Welcome back, John," Jarvis said with a nod.

"Sir." Dempsey nodded back. No matter who Dempsey had become, Jarvis would always be Captain Jarvis, former commander of the Tier One SEAL team, and a legend. *Sir* was about as informal as he thought he could get.

"I wanted to get us all reconnected and on the same page," Jarvis said. "Mr. Wang will not be joining us, as he is hard at work on the decryption of the devices that Dempsey retrieved."

"Should have been at work on the prisoner—al-Mahajer's proxy," Dempsey lamented.

Jarvis shook his head. "This was a tough one and you pulled it off with no injury to our cover. No reason to hang your head. From what I understand, your escape was remarkable."

Dempsey shrugged. Like most Tier One SEALs, he had never been much of an "attaboy" kind of guy.

"Now's probably a good time to fill the rest of the team in on what went down out there."

"Roger that, sir," Dempsey said, and stood. "We had intel that Rafiq al-Mahajer would be attending a meeting at an ISIS safe house not far from Al Qa'im in northwestern Iraq. Al-Mahajer is former Mujahideen with deep ties to Al Qaeda, but now he's risen to the position of strategic leader in the Islamic State's Iraqi front. The objective was a capture mission to grab al-Mahajer, but he sent a proxy instead and so the bastard slipped through my fingers once again."

"Once again?" Mendez asked, looking confused. "Did we have him in our sights before?"

Dempsey felt Jarvis's eyes on him.

"This shithead has been in the wind for a long time, since an attempt to capture him nearly a decade ago, a mission during which a good man died." He exhaled and let the ghost of Romeo swirl away.

"So what did we learn, John?" Jarvis asked, getting him back on track.

"The fact that al-Mahajer sent a proxy tells us something. We believe, or I do anyway, that this gathering was far more than just a morale booster for a bunch of crazy jihadists in western Iraq. This was meant to be a face-to-face liaison with someone important."

"Who?" asked Grimes, cutting straight to the chase.

"That's the million-dollar question. Could be a financier, a strategic partner, a petrol broker, or a faction leader planning the next strike. There are plenty of possibilities."

"The *why* is equally important," Smith added. "ISIS doesn't typically play well with others, and not just because of differences in their religious and political ideologies. Unlike Al Qaeda, they use brutality as a recruiting tool. Unlike Al Qaeda, they are not afraid of offending non-radicalized Sunni leadership in the region. Anyone who is not devoted to their pursuit of a pure Islamic State is viewed as a nonbeliever and a threat. They've murdered hundreds and hundreds of Muslims, including women and children. Historically, these differences have kept them at odds with other bad actors, but as we make greater and greater progress in cutting off their revenue streams from oil and drugs, we can't rule out the possibility of alliance building. No one would have thought that all the Al Qaeda faction leaders could have aligned to pull off the Operation Crusader massacre, but it happened."

"Is that what you think the meeting was about? An alliance between Al Qaeda and ISIS?" Mendez asked, his expression chilling.

Dempsey shook his head. "Impossible to know with the limited intelligence we collected during the op."

"But based on the attendees, you don't think so." It was a statement, not a question, from Jarvis. Whenever he asked a question, Dempsey struggled to decide whether the head of Ember was getting an expert opinion or just testing his former LCPO to see how he was evolving. In either case, all Dempsey could do was say what he thought.

"Correct," he said. "I think this was something else. There are lots of ways for ISIS and AQ leadership to hook up without risking a meet in Qa'im. It would have been safer to meet in Raqqa, for example, where ISIS's security is better. This feels different to me. Someone wanted this meeting to take place *outside* of Syria, but who and why I can't even begin to speculate. They piggybacked onto a meeting that was already set up—the one targeted by the SEALs I embedded with."

Jarvis nodded. "Go on."

"Not much more to tell. As you know, we had a little issue with our air transportation en route to Baghdad, and al-Mahajer's proxy was a casualty of that event. Without the proxy to interrogate, we have to hope Baldwin's team can perform a miracle on the confiscated phone and laptop. Maybe we'll find a bread crumb or get a sniff of al-Mahajer's current location. He'll assume he's compromised—expect him to change tactics and locations."

"Thanks, John," Jarvis said from the podium.

Dempsey took his seat.

"Did you consider the possibility of an Iranian connection?" Grimes fixed her cool blues on him. She just couldn't help herself, he thought with a grin.

If I had something like that, don't you think I would have led with it? Uncovering VEVAK's connection to the Yemen attack was Ember's baptismal triumph, after all.

"Good point," Jarvis said patiently. A few months ago, Jarvis had had zero patience for Grimes and her habit of bird-dogging the debriefs, but Ember was gelling into a family. Accepting one another's little idiosyncrasies was part of the team coming together. "We know beyond a doubt that Amir Modiri was the mastermind behind the UN terrorist attack and the Crusader massacre. But what we know and what we can prove are not the same."

Grimes opened her mouth as if to rebut, but then smiled and held her tongue.

"Ian?" Jarvis said, stepping aside for the lanky genius in the rumpled oxford to take the podium.

"Working diligently," Baldwin said with a smile out of place given the context of the brief. "But we must tread carefully, as they've put encryption countermeasures in place. If we trip over one as we pursue decryption, the data will wipe and recovery will be much more tedious—though not impossible for us, of course." He laughed, looked around. Finding no other smiles, he cleared his throat awkwardly.

"So nothing yet to report?" Dempsey said. He was tired. The thought of Baldwin launching into a dissertation about intersecting spaghetti lines of code and how they formed a song whose melody could be as revealing as the lyrics was more than he could take.

"Oh, I didn't say that," Baldwin said, adjusting his glasses on his nose like a graduate-school professor, ready to launch into a discussion that would leave most of the room in the dust. "When you compare these data streams to prior streams—"

"You can go into the details with Dempsey after we're done here, Ian," Jarvis interjected. "In the meantime, just give us your impressions."

"Well," Baldwin said, and put his hands in the pockets of his baggy, wrinkled khakis, "suffice it to say, I believe there is evidence to support John's theory about a liaison. The data patterns suggest that recent communications between the proxy involved two different people with different background languages."

Dempsey was, as usual, amazed that they could determine that from encrypted data.

"What are they saying?" Mendez asked.

"We don't know that, of course—yet."

Dempsey could feel Grimes rolling her eyes beside him.

"But we do know that the pattern of the communication recently changed. We're running an analysis of how the streams compare to all the previous encrypted transmissions we've collected. I'm confident we'll find overlap somewhere."

"So, nothing new or earth-shattering, but sounds like we're moving the ball slowly down the field. Thanks, Ian," Jarvis said with a pat on Ian's back. "That's all, people. Make sure you get a good night's sleep tonight. I want everyone sharp and ready to act on any breakthroughs the guys can uncover."

"We'll be working through the night," Baldwin added excitedly.

"And we'll all be available on an 0300-level alert should something shake loose. In the meantime, rest, people. It's a valuable weapon."

Everyone stood. Dempsey wondered why he had needed to divert to the hangar for this. Then, Jarvis motioned him over. *Shit.*

"Yes, sir?"

Jarvis, who was still standing beside Baldwin, looked him up and down. "How are you, John? Unscathed?"

"Fully operational," Dempsey answered, ignoring the stinger pulsing down his left leg that screamed otherwise. Old back injuries and new helicopter crashes were a really shitty combination.

"We should probably schedule a medical review for you anyway. I need to keep you five by."

"Yes, sir," he grumbled. He didn't have time for that shit. As far as he was concerned, docs were just overpaid paper pushers who lobbied to keep you on the bench when work needed to be done. He wished he knew where Dan Munn had ended up. As a former SEAL himself, Doc Munn was the only physician Dempsey trusted. Of course, an appointment with Munn was impossible under the circumstances. Munn knew him only as Jack Kemper, who had died during Operation Crusader.

He looked up and saw Jarvis waiting patiently for him to finish his mental sojourn.

"John, I want you to work with Ian's team as they decrypt the data on the al-Mahajer proxy devices."

Dempsey laughed and then caught himself when he saw the expression on the Director's face. "Oh, you're serious?"

What the hell is this? Penance for Iraq? If so, being banished to the signals den seems a bit harsh.

"I'm not sure how much I would contribute, Skipper," Dempsey said. "I think I'll probably just be in the way."

"That's exactly the point," Jarvis said.

"To be in the way?"

"To be in the mix. You need to understand all the elements that go into ensuring our operation is maximally effective. You are the Director of Special Activities, and also our most valuable field asset. That helo crash is a perfect example of fate fucking with resources. You never know who or what you're going to lose, and you never know when or where it's going to happen. I need you to be multifunctional. You have come a long way in tradecraft, but what Ian does is an integral part of the modern clandestine world. I'm not ordering you to get a PhD in statistics or computer science, but you do need to understand the ones and zeros."

"Yes, sir," Dempsey said, not sure what else to say. The thought of sitting beside Chip and Dale at a computer terminal for hours was nearly unbearable. Flying in a piece-of-shit Russian helo was worse, but he wasn't sure by how much. He turned to Ian. "Okay, let's go."

Jarvis laughed and put a hand on his shoulder. "I didn't mean now. You're jet-lagged and exhausted. Go home, get some sleep, and be back bright and early. Ian will catch you up then."

"Thank you," Dempsey said, making no effort to hide his relief. He headed toward the door, making eye contact with Smith on the way out.

"Grab dinner before you turn in?" Smith said, a big grin on the Ops O's face.

"Yeah," Dempsey said, a beaten dog.

"A word, Shane?" Jarvis called across the room. "I need about twenty minutes."

Dempsey slapped the former Delta Force operator on the back. "I'll grab Lady Grimes and Mendez," he said. "We'll meet you at the Bonefish Grill in the 'burg when you're done."

"I heard that," Grimes called from the other room.

With a smile on his face, Dempsey shuffled out to gather his teammates. A good meal, a couple of beers, and a good night's sleep were calling . . . and after that, he just might accidently turn off his work phone.

CHAPTER 11

Ember Operations Center
Newport News/Williamsburg International Airport
Newport News, Virginia
1930 Local Time

Jarvis clasped his fingers together behind his head and leaned back in his chair. "You're gloating."

"Am not." Smith shut the office door and took a seat across the desk from Jarvis. "Besides, what do I have to gloat about? I'm not the one who walks on water. That's Dempsey's job."

"What he pulled off in Iraq was a miracle, but last time I checked his initials were JD, not JC. This is exactly the kind of goat rope I want to avoid."

"It's not like he crashed the helo on purpose, boss. We're damn lucky he and the others made it out alive."

"I realize that, but you're missing the point. You and Dempsey made a case for this op, and so I backed you with the DNI. But I can't afford to have Dempsey running wild, kicking doors so he can make good on old vendettas from his days in the Wild West."

"Are you saying that Dempsey did something wrong?"

"No, what I'm saying is managing perceptions is a part of every mission. I don't want the DNI to think that our Special Activities Director is more interested in settling old scores than pursuing the mission objectives."

"You picked up on that, too?"

Jarvis nodded. "Dempsey's got history with al-Mahajer."

"I didn't know."

"You didn't think to ask."

Smith flushed.

"It's all right, Shane, I'm not trying to bust your balls. I signed off on nabbing al-Mahajer because you made a good case and lobbied with conviction. Unfortunately, it went the other way on us and now al-Mahajer knows we're hunting him. God only knows when he'll surface again. If we had made the decision to monitor, we might have been able to gather intel and track his proxy back to wherever he's hiding. The DNI is a patient, pragmatic man, but that patience and pragmatism has its limits. When Philips took the reins as Ember's sponsor, he gave us enough rope to hang ourselves. Let's not tie our own noose. Be sure to convey the message to Dempsey."

"Yes, sir. I understand."

"But?" Jarvis could see in Smith's body language that there was a *but*.

"Permission to speak frankly?"

"Always."

"The only difference between this mission and Dempsey's previous engagements is that this one went south on us. So, if I read between the lines, what the DNI seems to be saying is, we have his support, as long as everything goes right."

"No, Shane, that's not the message. The message is 'stay objective.' Focus on the big picture. For the rest of his life, Dempsey is going to be haunted by the demons of his past. To be effective, he's going to have to learn to compartmentalize. None of us can afford to let our remorse or need for revenge sway our strategic and tactical decisions. Understood?"

"Understood."

"Now for the real reason I called you in here." Jarvis slid a brown file folder across the table. "Meet the newest member of our team."

Smith eyed the folder as if it were radioactive. Finally, he opened it. Jarvis watched his pupils dart back and forth as he scanned the personnel file inside. Smith sighed, closed the folder, and looked up.

"Simon Adamo, career CIA. Please tell me you're fucking with me, sir."

"'Fraid not, Ops O. He was hand selected by the DNI himself."

"Why?"

"In case you haven't noticed, our operations are creating friction with the CIA. Adamo's role is to serve as liaison between us and OGA so everybody plays nice together."

"And how, exactly, does a unit that doesn't even exist need a liaison with anyone, much less the CIA?"

"Due to the very small footprint our charter requires, we're forced to rely on support from the other intelligence communities. Agreed?"

"Of course."

"So we can't always come in and out with a wave of a hand and a warning that 'we were never here.' This is not some Hollywood action movie."

"Mmm-hmm."

"You don't sound convinced."

Smith narrowed his eyes. "An outsider, handpicked by the DNI, thrust into our unit after a screwup—gimme a break. Adamo isn't a liaison; he's a mole. Just like Kittinger forced Grimes onto our team, Philips is doing the exact same thing with this guy." He swallowed and added, "Sir."

"Now *that's* what I recruited you to do—think above your pay grade," Jarvis said, making no attempt to temper his satisfaction. Smith had made the deductive leap without prompting. When he'd poached Smith from Delta, the young officer had been tactically impressive but strategically unsophisticated. Like most SOF operators, Smith had been focused on execution and efficiency, and didn't give a shit about the political gamesmanship going on in the command and control echelon. Now, as the Ops O, Smith needed to worry about motives and power grabs, backstabbing and sandboxing—all the crap operators hated to think about. Someday, Smith would succeed him as Director of Ember, and when that day came, his prodigy needed to be proficient in the tactics of winning inside the Beltway, not just on the battlefield.

"Nice to see you're so happy about turning me into a cynical bastard."

"DC ain't Neverland, Shane. To survive, you gotta grow up."

"So what am I supposed to do? Pretend the new guy's not trying to undermine us at every turn, when I know otherwise?"

"Just because Adamo is not one of us doesn't mean he can't add value. Just look at Grimes. She's fully integrated now and has proved her value time and again."

"That's only because Kittinger's dead."

Jarvis shook his head. "Not true. A month in, she was one of us."

"Except Elizabeth wasn't career CIA; there's a big fucking difference between her background and loyalties and this jackass's."

"Well said," Jarvis agreed. "But Philips, unlike Kittinger, isn't a traitor. I trust him, and so we accept his man Adamo without complaint. You and Dempsey will simply have to figure out how to work with him."

Smith shook his head. "Dempsey's gonna blow a gasket. You do realize that?"

"Dempsey works for you, Shane. Make it work, end of discussion."

"Roger that," Smith said, pushing the folder back across the desk and getting to his feet. "Anything else?"

"Yeah, you have two days to get me a plan to find al-Mahajer. Something doesn't smell right about this whole thing, and I want to know why."

CHAPTER 12

Colored lines danced across the computer screen.

They meant nothing to Dempsey, just as they hadn't for the past four hours. If one stared hard enough, was it possible for data to burn a hole in a man's brain that would lead to his eventual, and merciful, death? Baldwin was standing behind him, one hand on his left shoulder and one on Chip's right shoulder. Or maybe it was Dale's. Dempsey really wasn't sure who was who; they seemed virtually interchangeable, so perhaps it didn't matter. Sitting next to Dempsey and his considerable bulk, the techno whiz kid looked like a middle schooler.

"There, there, do you see it?" Baldwin asked.

Dempsey blinked. No, he did not see "it."

"See how they merge?" Chip-or-Dale asked.

He raised an eyebrow. He actually did see that.

There were seven different lines, each a different color, and they danced around on the screen, each with a very different shape and pattern. As he watched, the green line merged on top of the red line behind it, and for a moment they seemed . . .

"Identical," Dempsey said.

"Nothing is identical," Chip-or-Dale said, and he double-clicked a box at the bottom and began inputting numbers. "But this is a ninety-two percent match."

Dempsey scrunched up his face and stared at the lines. "So this is like a voice match on two different phone calls or something?"

Baldwin sighed. "It's not a voice, John. These are encrypted data streams."

"Right," Dempsey said, frustrated. "But for the hundredth time, I don't know what the fuck 'matching segments of encrypted data streams' means." He leaned back in his chair and pulled at the sides of his face with flat palms. It was like talking baseball with an alien from another planet.

"Okay," Baldwin said and sat down next to him. "Think of these streams as patterns of information. We don't have sentences; we don't even have words, because the data is still encrypted. But the encrypted data yields a pattern nonetheless. Sophisticated encryption systems, like the ones our adversaries use, employ revolving algorithms so even the appearance of the encrypted data from a single source varies over time. Do you understand?"

Dempsey nodded. He didn't really understand, but he thought he had the gist of it: The encryption changed the data—voice, SMS, or e-mail exchanges—into unrecognizable bits of data. On top of that, the encryption itself was ever changing.

"But if you have a library of old data streams, especially data collected from the same adversary using a standardized encryption protocol, you can use a computer to hunt for matching segments of encrypted data to see if they come from a common source."

"That's a leap," Dempsey grumbled.

"Of course," Baldwin said with a chuckle. "I'm giving you the CliffsNotes version."

In other words, Baldwin was explaining chaos theory to a three-year-old.

"But you get the idea?"

"Sure, I guess," Dempsey said. "So you look to match the recently collected patterns to those you have in a database of previously collected transmissions."

"Basically, yes."

"Sounds like you'd need one hell of an archive."

"That database is maintained off-site by a friendly three-letter entity."

"And it sounds like you'd need one hell of a computer to sort through all that data."

"That computer is also maintained off-site by the same friend."

"So what is it that you actually do here?"

Baldwin and Chip-or-Dale shared a conspiratorial grin.

"We create the algorithms, statistical models, and analysis software that does the heavy lifting."

"Ah, the spooky genius math shit."

"Precisely," Baldwin said. "The spooky genius math shit that finds needles in haystacks."

Dempsey rolled his head in a circle, cracking the vertebrae in his neck. Then he twisted his shoulders right and left to crack his back. Baldwin winced as he watched. "So, Professor, now that I understand your flying spaghetti monster on the computer screen, can you please tell me what, if any, actual intelligence you've been able to glean from all this?"

"We confirmed that one of the data streams is indeed from Rafiq al-Mahajer," Baldwin said with a victorious smile.

"So the green line we isolated is al-Mahajer?"

"No," Baldwin said. "The orange line is al-Mahajer. The green line is a new match between that and a source, probably a mobile phone, that communicated with al-Mahajer's proxy's Blackberry."

"Then who the hell is the green line?"

Baldwin shrugged, and Dempsey resisted the urge to turn around, rise from his chair, and strangle the genius. "No idea, but we have a confirmed match in the database."

"A ninety-two percent confidence interval," Chip-or-Dale added.

"Yes," Baldwin echoed, his voice getting excited now. "We have archive data from this source all over the place: Syria, Iraq, Lebanon, Gaza, but also inside Iran."

Dempsey's heart skipped a beat. "Are you telling me this is Amir Modiri?"

"No, no, no," Baldwin said. "It's definitely not Modiri. We have his signature locked down from the Kittinger calls. No, this source is someone else. Very active. Very mobile."

"Wait, I'm confused. Are we talking about al-Mahajer's proxy?"

"No, someone who was in communication with al-Mahajer's proxy."

"Someone present at the meeting in Qa'im?"

"Impossible to tell. I would need all the mobile phones confiscated from all the terrorists in attendance. We only have the proxy's mobile and laptop to work with."

"Shit," Dempsey said, and slammed his hand down on the desk. *I should've grabbed every phone from every crow.*

"Hey, John."

Dempsey turned and saw Smith in the doorway.

"Anything?"

"Yes and no," Dempsey said with a sigh. "We confirmed al-Mahajer was in communication with his proxy, and we found a match with another shithead who has been talking to al-Mahajer's proxy but also has been recorded inside Syria, Lebanon, and Iran."

"Iran?" Smith's brows rose. "Did you check the source against anything we intercepted in Yemen before Crusader?"

"I didn't check that," Baldwin said. "But that's a very good idea."

"I'm on it," Chip-or-Dale said, his fingers flying across the keyboard at his terminal.

"And how is Wang coming on our decryption problem? Any chance we can see the actual messages soon?" Smith asked.

"The decryption is slow going," Baldwin replied.

"Well, go faster." Smith shifted his gaze to Dempsey. "Can you break away?"

Dempsey popped out of his task chair like a rocket. "Thanks for the class, Professor," he called as he bolted for the door. "What's up?" he asked as he followed Smith to his office.

"Not sure. You have a call."

"Here?" Dempsey asked, confused.

"Remember that blind that we set up—the comm line that routes through dozens of nodes in Europe and Asia to prevent traces?"

"Yeah."

"Someone called in on that line and asked for Agent Dempsey."

"Agent Dempsey?"

"Actually he said, 'that jackass agent, John Dempsey.' He said his name was Chunk? I was about to hang up on the clown, but something in his voice sounded legit."

Dempsey smiled. "*Chunk* is Lieutenant Keith Redman from SEAL Team Four. I gave him that number to call me if he found anything he thought I might be interested in from the other crows they pulled off the *X* near Qa'im. Maybe he found something."

"Maybe. Or maybe he just misses you," Smith said, smiling sweetly. He pointed to the phone on his desk. "I transferred the call in here. Line two."

Dempsey reached over and hit the speaker button so they could both hear what the SEAL officer had to say.

"Hey, Chunk," Dempsey said. "You keeping your head down?"

"Nah," the SEAL said with a chuckle. "If I was smart enough for that I don't guess I'd be here."

"Right," Dempsey agreed. "What's up?"

"I'm not usually one to share intel with you OGA types—but we kinda shared some crazy in the suck."

"Just doing my bit to make the earth a safer place for decent people."

"Amen to that," Chunk said. "So listen. Most of the crows we got were usual ISIS shitheads, full of piss and vinegar until the real interrogators come. But this one dude—a guy who we pulled out of that conference room in the house where you grabbed the German proxy—"

"You mean my mission objective who you shot in the head," Dempsey interrupted.

"Right, the guy I shot saving your goat-herding ass. That's the one. Anyway, this other crow turns out to be solid, you know. Iron-sphincter stoic. Wouldn't give up nothing. But the Agency guys got real excited because they got a hit in the facial-recognition database."

Dempsey pursed his lips. "Is he ISIS leadership?"

"No," Chunk said, savoring the moment. "They think the dude is fucking Hezbollah."

Dempsey shot a look at Smith, whose eyes widened. "The CIA guys told you that?"

"No, of course not. Those dickheads wouldn't piss on me if I was on fire, but my combat medic was in the room and heard them talking. They told him to say nothing to no one. But he's a SEAL, you know, so he passed it to me. And now I'm passing it to you."

"Is he still in Irbil?"

"I doubt it, bro. They left in an unmarked civilian jet an hour ago and took him with them."

"No idea where, I'm guessing."

Chunk made a *pffft* sound over the line. "C'mon, Dempsey, they're fucking CIA, what do you think?"

"No problem, we'll find him. I owe you one for this, Chunk, thank you."

"Yeah, well, hooyah and all that. You were locked on when that helo went down. Fucking Rambo, bro. Keep me in mind if you ever need anything down range."

"Will do, Chunk. Stay low."

"Won't be a problem. They're shipping me back to Virginia tomorrow for leave. Something about a helo crash."

Dempsey laughed and ended the call. "Hezbollah?" he said, turning to Smith. "What the fuck? Are all these shitheads cooperating now?"

"We gotta find out where they took that crow," Smith said. "I'll go brief the boss. Hopefully he can convince the DNI to get us in the loop. I'd like to take a turn with this guy."

Dempsey leaned back against the edge of the desk. "Me, too, bro. Me, too."

CHAPTER 13

Covert Hezbollah Training Camp
Cuchumatanes Mountains, Guatemala
October 20, 1730 Local Time

Rostami cursed and smacked the back of his neck.

Something had just bitten him and it hurt. He looked at the red smear in the palm of his hand, littered with unrecognizable insect parts. He wasn't sure which he hated more, the biting flies or the mosquitoes.

"Fuck the jungle," he muttered, wiping his hand on his pant leg as he made his way to the training camp's command tent.

It was ten minutes until sunset, which meant two things: Maghrib and mosquitoes. Last night he'd been eaten alive during the prayer ritual. The buzzing bloodsuckers had gotten him everywhere he'd left exposed skin—neck, ears, face, hands, and ankles. He'd even gotten a mosquito bite on his eyelid, which had swollen up and tormented him all day. Before lunch, he'd doused himself from head to toe in insect repellant. So far, it had kept the mosquitos at bay, but it hadn't stopped the biting flies from trying to take chunks out of him.

At the threshold of the tent, he stopped and listened, hoping to eavesdrop a little before making his presence known. To his surprise, the Hezbollah base commander, Abdel Hijjar, and Rafiq al-Mahajer had bonded immediately, leaving him feeling the odd man out. But now, inside the tent, he heard heated words being exchanged. He smirked, pulled back the flap, and ducked inside.

"I'm sorry, but it is too big of a risk," Hijjar said in Arabic. "The answer is no."

Al-Mahajer turned and fixed Rostami with a caustic, accusatory gaze.

"What is the problem?" Rostami said, glancing back and forth between the two terrorists.

"The problem, Persian, is that despite your promises to the contrary, Hijjar has refused to escort us through the tunnels."

Rostami looked at Hijjar. "Is this true?"

The seasoned Lebanese militant nodded. "An escort into the United States was never part of the agreement."

Rostami balled up his fists as a surge of anger coursed through him. "Iran has given Hezbollah over one hundred million dollars of aid so far this year. Two hundred million last year. And this is how you repay us?"

"Your government has always been a loyal supporter of our cause, and for that we are grateful," Hijjar said, bowing his head ever so slightly, "but our North American operation has been in existence for fifteen years. I will not be the man who breaks time-tested protocols and risks destroying all the groundwork that has been laid."

Rostami dismissed Hijjar's reply with a wave. "Your instructions were to provide us with the training, logistical support, transportation, and arms to complete our mission. Tell me, how does abandoning us in Mexico qualify as fulfilling your obligation?"

"We were very clear about what assistance Hezbollah would provide: local currency; a safe place to conduct operational planning, indoctrination, and rudimentary Spanish-language training for your men; transportation across the border into Mexico; and ground transportation to Mexico City. VEVAK is responsible for chartering a plane from Mexico City to Mexicali. VEVAK is responsible for your passports and US visas. Our relationship with Cartel del Norte is tenuous at best. They do not share our vision; they are business partners. But they *have* agreed to provide you with weapons, tunnel access, and an escort into the United States." Hijjar paused for a beat before adding, "As a concession, I am willing to provide a driver to pick you up at the airport and take you to the safe house."

"Unacceptable," al-Mahajer growled. "I refuse to put my fate, and the fate of this mission, in the hands of apostates. Los Zetas are not true believers. They are not even Muslims. These men are not men of principle. They trade in the drugs of the Great Satan, they worship the God of the Great Satan, and they do not believe in our cause. They are not worthy to stand in our company."

Rostami was about to speak when one of Hijjar's lieutenants—a man with a jagged scar running down the side of his face—abruptly stood and began addressing Hijjar heatedly in Spanish. Taken aback, Rostami watched the two men argue. At one point, the scarred fighter shifted his hand to the butt of a chrome-plated .45-caliber pistol tucked in his waistband. This prompted an immediate conciliatory response from Hijjar, followed by what Rostami could only conclude was a joke, because the scarred man began to laugh and the tension was broken. Two more sentences were spoken, and the scarred fighter walked out of the tent, but not before giving al-Mahajer the evil eye.

"Who was that?" al-Mahajer said, reviving the discussion in Arabic.

Hijjar's jaw tightened. "His name is Arturo Garcia. He is my counterpart in Cartel del Norte. He's picked up quite a bit of Arabic over the years, and he did not appreciate what you had to say. The price to cross the border, it seems, has just gone up."

The look of murder in al-Mahajer's eyes sent an electric charge down Rostami's spine. For a moment, he thought he was about to witness a jungle machete battle between the highest-ranking Hezbollah and ISIS commanders on the North American continent. His eyes darted back and forth between the two warlords ready for blood. It had been months since he'd killed—months since he'd plunged his knife into the back of Effie Vogel's neck after making love to her that fateful afternoon in Frankfurt. The German girl's blood had sprayed hot all over him; the memory was so palpable he could almost taste it. His skin tingled. His pulse pounded, a primal rhythm in his ears.

Do it. Carve each other to pieces, you fools, so I can leave this fucking jungle and go home.

The call to prayer reverberated from a speaker hanging outside the tent—a referee's whistle ending the standoff between two heavyweights about to go twelve rounds.

Al-Mahajer whirled and headed out of the tent. As he passed Rostami, he said, "This is the last time I'll trust a Persian to see Allah's will done."

Rostami sniffed and turned his back on the terrorist without a word.

"Your friend is naïve and rash—a dangerous combination when you're operating in the enemy's backyard," Hijjar said once they were alone.

"He does not understand our foe like you and I do. He is blinded by his beliefs and deaf to any words not his own."

"We serve the same God, but different masters," Hijjar said. "Al-Mahajer's jihad is not the same as mine, and while I applaud his zeal and understand his desire to strike at the heart of those who serve the Zionists, my mission is to remove the Jewish cancer from my homeland. I leave the work of dismantling America to others. My loyalty is to Allah first, my mission second, and my brothers in arms third. Do you understand?"

Rostami nodded.

Hijjar's gaze suddenly flicked to Rostami's right hand. "Which of us did you mean to stab first?"

Rostami glanced down and was surprised to see his six-inch Damascus stiletto clutched in his fingers. With an easy smile, he slipped the knife back into its sheath. "Neither, unless of course you turned on me."

Hijjar laughed, but it was forced. "Allah knows my heart. And yours," he added with a hint of judgment. "In any case, I would like more assurance from you that your friend will not allow his passion to tear down everything Hezbollah has built here . . . built with Persia's generous assistance, of course."

"You need not worry about the Syrian," Rostami said, realizing he was too angry to call the imbecile by his Muslim name. "He needs us far more than we need him."

He cursed silently as the reality of what he must do set in. He had intended for Hezbollah to escort the ISIS team into America, then let VEVAK's sleeper agents handle the logistics on the other side of the border. His plan had always been to book the first available flight from Mexico City to Tehran and watch the carnage on TV from the comfort of his flat in Tehran. Now, thanks to Hijjar's obstinacy, that was no longer possible. There was no question that Modiri would hold him responsible for the outcome of this operation. Amir had not been the same since his elder brother was executed in the tunnels beneath the United Nations six months ago. Since then, Modiri's quest for retribution had been all consuming. What's more, Rostami sensed that Amir held him personally accountable for his brother's death. If this operation failed, he was certain that his boss would task him in operations against the Americans over and over again until the law of averages triumphed and he met his mortal demise.

Rostami smiled at the Hezbollah commander. "I will escort al-Mahajer and his team through the tunnels with the Zetas. And I'll arrange for a team to meet us and transport us to a safe house on the American side."

Hijjar's eyes narrowed. "This is something you can do?"

Rostami understood. If Iran had a network of resources embedded in the United States, why had greater assistance not been rendered to Hijjar's operations already?

"It will be dangerous, but what choice do you leave me?" he said. "VEVAK has just begun an effort to build a network in America," he lied. "It will be risky for my agents, but if that's what is necessary to protect Hezbollah's anonymity, then it is a risk I'm willing to take."

Rostami watched Hijjar carefully, hopeful that he had appeased the man. Hijjar stared hard at him for a moment, but then his bearded face broke into a smile.

"Thank you," Hijjar said. "If Hezbollah fighters were to be captured alongside ISIS operators, it would not only draw new scrutiny to the US border, but it would create incentive for the Americans to shut down our operations in Central America."

"I understand," Rostami said.

"Even without our presence, if you are captured using the cartel's tunnel network, you destroy our single greatest asset for accessing the United States . . . you understand?"

"I understand," Rostami said. "It will not happen, for Allah will blind our enemies and put the wind at our backs."

Hijjar nodded.

In the background, Rostami noted that the muezzin was nearing the final verse of the *adhan*. Time to step outside and serve his body as an all-you-can-eat buffet to the mosquitoes.

"Come," he said, clasping a hand on Hijjar's shoulder. "It's time to pray."

"And after Maghrib," Hijjar said, "we have a serious talk with our Syrian friend. Otherwise, I'm afraid this might end badly . . . for all of us."

CHAPTER 14

Dassault Falcon 900 DX, Tail Number N103M
Over the Eastern Atlantic Ocean
October 21, 2130 Local Time

The Falcon was comfortable, but it was no yacht like the Boeing.

Ember's 787 was trimmed out like a luxury New York apartment, complete with sleeping quarters and a marble-tiled shower, whereas the Falcon had a single cabin with leather seats and a couch. According to the mechanic, the Dreamliner was still out for maintenance, so they were flying the little bird. Dempsey didn't care about the creature comforts, but he sure as hell wished they had more speed. The Falcon had a great range for a jet of its size—more than four thousand nautical miles—but it crept along at only 470 knots. It would take forever to get to Poland . . . at least it seemed like forever. The original flight plan called for a fuel stop in the UK, but favorable winds headed east meant they could do it in one hop. But that still meant seven hours in the air.

"Two hours till we land," Smith said, dropping a hand onto Dempsey's shoulder. "Wanna brief?"

"Not really."

"You're going to have to talk to him eventually," Smith said, shifting his eyes in the direction of their new addition.

Dempsey looked back over his shoulder at the CIA liaison. Simon Adamo looked nothing like an operator. He was dressed in slacks and an open-collar shirt and had his sports coat draped over the seat beside him. The stylish, rectangular-frame eyeglasses he wore had slipped down his nose, and Dempsey watched him push them up with an extended index finger in a strange gesture that resembled him pointing a finger pistol at his forehead. He kept his dark brown hair longer than the operators in Ember, but neater and shorter than Baldwin and the boys. The CIA man had a runner's physique—lean and sinewy—and his face was all angles, as if his skin had been stretched taut over his bones. But he wasn't unattractive. Dempsey had even noticed Grimes sneaking a glance or two in the spook's direction after initial introductions.

At the moment, Adamo was focused intently on his laptop, looking at God knew what—hopefully not the classified bios of the Ember SAD members. Across the aisle, Grimes looked up from her laptop and caught Dempsey's eye. She mouthed the word *relax* and smiled at him.

Dempsey sighed and looked back at Smith. "Fine, let's do it. I don't suppose we can order him to stay on the plane while we do our jobs?"

Smith chuckled. "Afraid not," he said and strolled to the back. Dempsey gestured to Grimes with his head, and she unbuckled and followed Smith aft.

Smith had insisted that Dempsey give the CIA agent a fair chance to prove whether he would or would not be of value to Special Activities. Dempsey had agreed diplomatically, not that he had a choice in the matter. He reminded himself that Grimes was now an integral and indispensable part of his team, and he had deplored her initially. Maybe Adamo would surprise him, too.

Once everyone was assembled around the workstation-size table at the rear of the cabin, Dempsey began. "I have three objectives for this trip. Figure out who this crow is, who he works for, and why he was meeting with Rafiq al-Mahajer's proxy in Qa'im. When we get on-site, first order of business is to get updated by local CIA on any new developments or breakthroughs since our last check-in. Then, we take our turn in the room with him."

"I'd like to be the lead examiner," Grimes said.

Dempsey turned to her. He was about to ask her why, but the fire in her eyes erased all doubts. He reminded himself that she had a personal stake in this, too. Her brother had been one of Dempsey's Tier One brothers and a casualty of the Crusader massacre. Elizabeth was sharp, a closet ubergenius like Jarvis. Over beers one night, Smith had shared a few details from her "real life" CV. Before becoming Elizabeth Grimes at Ember, she was Kelsey Clarke, a rising star at the Office of Science and Technology Policy for the White House. Before that, she'd been a senior analyst at the Brookings Institute, and before that she'd earned a master's from the Kennedy School. So as far as he was concerned, if Grimes wanted first dibs questioning the jihadi, then Grimes got first dibs.

"And what qualifies Ms. Grimes to interrogate a known terrorist?" Adamo inserted before Dempsey had a chance to respond.

Dempsey watched her cheeks flush as she immediately started to defend herself: "My background is—"

"None of his fucking business," Dempsey said to Adamo, cutting her off. "What is important to understand, Simon, is that every member of this team brings a diverse set of skills and experiences to the table. The vetting process for Ember takes place at the highest level. Every single person at this table is more than qualified to conduct investigative interrogation."

"I disagree. Interrogation is a learned skill. Say the wrong thing, overstep a boundary, and you jeopardize all the progress made to date.

From what I can glean of your respective backgrounds, the person best suited to lead the questioning is me, and that's a cold fact."

"Thanks for your opinion, but consider yourself overruled. Grimes will be taking the lead."

Now it was Adamo's turn to flush. Dempsey watched the veins pop out on his neck, but the CIA man held his tongue.

"So, Elizabeth," Dempsey continued. "What's your plan and how can we support you?"

"From an outside perspective, my approach might appear to be unorthodox. It is imperative that you guys keep the CIA off my back during the session. Adamo, you speak their language," she said. "Think you can handle that?"

"It depends on what exactly you have in mind," Adamo replied, pushing his eyeglasses up. "I'd feel much better about this if you outlined your strategy. I hope you're not planning on violating the Administration's moratorium on enhanced interrogation methods."

Grimes glanced at Dempsey.

"It's certainly not our intention, but if this guy was an easy crack, CIA would have already extracted actionable intel, and we wouldn't be on this airplane," Dempsey said. "Unfortunately, we don't have days and weeks to hang out with our new friend, so I'd prefer to keep things fluid."

"That's not how interrogation works," Adamo said, tapping the tip of his index finger hard on the table. "We had to sit on Khalid Sheikh Mohammed for months to get anything real. We eventually got actionable intelligence and used it to abort an attack, but you can't just breeze in, break a guy's thumb, and think you're mining gold when he starts spewing whatever crap he can think of to stop the pain."

"We have twenty-four hours," Dempsey said with his best condescending-asshole smile. "What will be the most helpful is if the OGA guys on the ground get this shithead prepped like we asked."

Smith leaned in. "I spoke with the detail lead on site before we went wheels up. They were already in a deprivation set, and I had them shorten the interval from four hours' rest to two hours' and then keep him in intermittent distress until we arrive. He'll be about as raw as we can get him."

"And less reliable," Adamo chided. "The intel you get will be a mess, if you get anything at all. The protocols used by these interrogators are carefully designed and very thoroughly researched."

"Look, Adamo," Dempsey said, finally getting frustrated, "I appreciate what you're saying, but we're looking for a bread crumb here. We trust your guys will continue methodically, using your protocols, after we leave, but the point is—"

"The point is," Grimes interjected, "we're not building a case here. We're not prosecutors. None of this has to stand up in court. Rafiq al-Mahajer is prepping his next move, that I guarantee. We don't care what the CIA does with this guy when we're done—you can dress him up and take him out to dinner or you can dump his body in the Oder. I don't care—what I do care about is stopping the next suicide bomber from blowing himself up in a park and obliterating a hundred innocent children and their parents in the process. So let's try to get our priorities straight, shall we?"

Adamo and Grimes locked eyes.

"You're just going to have to trust us," Dempsey said. "This isn't our first rodeo and our results so far speak for themselves."

"What results? I'd never even heard of you guys until three days ago."

"That should tell you something right there," Smith said sharply. His patience was wearing thin, too. "Maybe it would be best for you to wait with the plane."

Dempsey sighed. Adamo's presence was already undermining the cohesiveness they'd built these past few months. He couldn't afford to let that happen. "Sounds like we've got a plan. Any questions? No. Good."

Dempsey stood and looked at Grimes. "A word?" He nodded at the pair of captain's chairs at the front of the cabin.

"Sure," she said and made her way forward. "What's on your mind?"

He glanced over his shoulder to make sure Adamo was out of earshot, and then leaned in. "What exactly do you have in mind for this interrogation?"

A vulpine grin spread across her face. "I told you," she said, patting his knee. "It's a surprise."

CHAPTER 15

Kakolewska Apartment Building
46 Ulica Niepodleglosci
Leszno, Poland
October 22, 1430 Local Time

"What would be ideal at this point is if we give him forty-five minutes of sleep and then bring him into the box."

Dempsey looked at the CIA case officer, Brian Black, and then over at Grimes.

"No," she said simply. "Take him out of the stress position and then sit him at a desk with a chair—not in the interrogation room you usually use."

Black looked like he might object but saw Grimes's cold stare and shrugged.

"Okay," he said. "I've got my partner coming to give you the summary of what we've collected so far, but there's not much to tell."

Black left them alone, and Grimes looked at Dempsey.

"I'll get something," she said.

The fire in her eyes convinced him that whatever she was about to do would either break the investigation wide open or send Adamo screaming to the DNI to revoke Ember's charter. Possibly both.

Another man came in with a folder. He sat down, but didn't open it.

"Sam Jacobs," the man said and shook hands with Dempsey, Smith, and Grimes. "I met your guy Adamo already. He's going through the footage we have, but there isn't much to see."

"We'd like a copy of whatever you have," Dempsey said.

"I'm not authorized to release—"

Smith held up a finger and pulled out his sat phone.

"Hey, boss. There is an agent Sam Jacobs here who needs an authorization to release some interrogation video . . . Yeah . . . Leszno . . . okay." He snapped his phone shut and smiled.

"Okay. Well, anyway—" The CIA agent was interrupted by the chirp of his sat phone on his belt. "Jacobs . . . Yes, sir. Hold on, I can give you my code." The agent stepped away and whispered into the phone for a moment. When he returned, he looked at Smith with incredulous eyes. "Okay, well, that was spooky as shit. I guess you guys are like, what, *Mission Impossible?*"

No one answered.

Agent Jacobs shrugged. "So, I'll have the guys burn you an encrypted file and a separate key file to open it." Then he paused and looked back at Smith. "Do you work directly for the fucking DNI or something?"

"You were saying? About the detainee?" Grimes said.

Jacobs shook his head with a *whatever—way above my pay grade* look. "We basically have nothing on this guy. The system tagged him as possible Hezbollah or maybe Iranian."

Grimes looked at Dempsey. "Possible Hezbollah, we knew, but this is the first time I've heard Iranian."

"Possible Iranian," Jacobs reiterated.

Dempsey's thoughts drifted back to the signals lab and the time he'd spent with Baldwin. "The green line," he mumbled.

"What?" Grimes asked, staring at him, perplexed.

"The green line," Dempsey repeated, grinning despite himself. "When I was with Baldwin and the boys, we identified an encrypted data stream from someone who had been communicating with al-Mahajer's proxy's Blackberry. The data matched up with archive data collected on a phone that made calls all over the place: Lebanon, Syria, Turkey, Palestine, Iraq, Gaza, but also inside Iran. Maybe that phone belonged to this guy."

"That would make sense," Jacobs said, nodding slowly. "Facial recognition has him at multiple meetings: Palestine at a meeting with Hezbollah leaders, shortly before the apartment attack in the West Bank last year. We also have him in Turkey, where he was in the company of a known VEVAK agent."

"So was this guy at this meeting in Turkey as an agent of Hezbollah or VEVAK? Pretty important fucking difference," Dempsey said.

"Agreed—and we don't know."

"Don't worry, fellas, I'll sort it out," Grimes said. "That's why we're here—to figure out who this guy is and who he works for."

"What has he given up so far?" Smith asked.

"Nothing. He's a pro," Jacobs said and rubbed his hands across his face. "This dude isn't some disenfranchised Muslim looking to find Paradise. He's tight—well trained at counterinterrogation techniques and experienced under duress. He employs counterinterrogation even at the edges—like in his sleep, literally."

"Languages?"

"At first we thought he was Afghani, because we thought he was speaking Dari when he was in a sleep state, but—"

"But it was Farsi," Grimes said.

"Yeah," the agent said. "The differences in the regional dialects are pronounced, but we're not linguists. I spent a great deal of time with

Afghan special forces, so it sounded like Dari to me, but the linguists back home sorted it out as Persian."

"The two languages are basically the same," Grimes said, looking at Dempsey. "Farsi is generally accepted to be the root language, having spread into Afghanistan and evolving from there."

"When sleep stressed he also spoke fluent Arabic. My partner hears a definite Palestinian dialect there. Flawless. So linguistically speaking, we peg him as either Iranian or Palestinian, but since we have multiple sightings of him with Hezbollah, we like that theory."

"And English," a familiar voice said. Dempsey looked up. Adamo had entered with Black in tow. "With a slight East London accent, by the way, that appears to be acquired."

"All right, I think it's time," Grimes said. "I'm ready to talk to him." The two CIA men stared at her.

"That's not a good idea," said Black.

Dempsey glared at Adamo, who obviously had neglected to grease the skids with his CIA buddies, but Adamo didn't seem to notice . . . or care.

"Female interrogation has not traditionally gone well in these settings with these people," Black continued. "The shit they did in Iraq early in the war with naked women and fake menstrual blood might have caused a big brouhaha, but it never uncovered any real intel."

"Do I look like the kind of woman who plans to lap dance this motherfucker?" Grimes said, her face darkening.

Black took a half step back and opened his mouth for rebuttal, when Dempsey stepped in.

"Look," he said, "Elizabeth is very experienced. Just give her a chance to work her magic, then we'll give him back and he's all yours."

Black folded his arms across his chest. Jacobs looked at his feet, and the corners of Adamo's lips seemed to curl into a smile. Dempsey wanted to smack the lot of them, but he tried the congenial approach. "I realize this is your sandbox. Having someone swoop in and give orders and piss on your turf sucks. And I am sorry for that. But this is happening. Understood? And it's happening right now."

"We have him in a small office with a desk and chair like you asked. He's probably asleep already," Jacobs said, conceding defeat.

"We can watch here," said Black, turning to a bank of monitors. He tapped on a keyboard, and then the six screens all filled with the same image—a bearded man in a gray tunic, his head back and his open mouth toward the ceiling.

"I'll take you in," Jacobs said, and led her out of the room.

Dempsey, Smith, Adamo, and Black all sat down in the faux-leather task chairs and rolled in for a closer view of the monitors.

A beat later, the door behind the prisoner opened and Grimes stepped in. She stood behind the man, her arms folded across her chest, and stared at the top of the terrorist's head as he slept, his head hanging at what looked like a neck-wrenchingly uncomfortable angle. Dempsey watched, fascinated, as Grimes leaned in, her mouth close to the bearded man's ear, and whispered something. After a moment, she put a gentle hand on his arm, still whispering intently.

"What the hell is she doing? I can't hear a fucking thing," Black said, looking over his shoulder at them.

"Relax," Dempsey said.

As Grimes whispered, the sleeping man began to stir. His lips started moving. She smiled and then whispered in his ear again. The man mumbled and then his eyes flickered a moment, but then his head bobbed with sleep.

"Seriously, Dempsey," Adamo said, now clearly agitated. "What is she doing? Where did you find this girl?"

Dempsey ignored him.

Grimes circled the terrorist, paused in front of the desk, and leaned in—her torso obscuring his face from the camera. She had a hand on his chest and her mouth was still by his ear. Then abruptly she stepped back and slapped him across the cheek.

"All right, that's it," Black said, scooting his chair back. "I'm pulling her."

"You will do no such thing," Dempsey said, putting a hand on Black's shoulder.

The detainee was fully awake now, his eyes wild and darting back and forth. He looked at Grimes, and his expression became smug as he wiped a drop of blood from his split lip. Adamo reached out and turned the volume up just as the jihadi yelled something at her.

"He's speaking Arabic," Smith said.

"Palestinian Arabic—a pretty unique dialect," Black said. "He's telling her the CIA is wasting their time sending a woman to do a man's job. He says he has nothing to tell in any case and that it is a violation of international law to hold a man just for his beliefs . . . Now she's talking about his family. How does she know about his family? I don't like where this is heading—"

"You know what, fuck it," Dempsey said, and reached out and muted the sound on the console.

"What the hell are you doing, man?" Black said, whirling around in his chair.

"Letting my operator do her job. You don't like what she has to say, then fine, you can observe the rest in silence. I've had enough of this armchair-quarterback bullshit."

Adamo reached for the volume knob.

"Touch that knob, and I break fingers," Dempsey growled.

Adamo's fingers stopped one inch short of the knob.

On the screen, Grimes was now sitting on the table in front of him, her legs crossed at the ankle. Dempsey couldn't see her face, but it was clear she was talking and that the prisoner, despite his best effort to feign disinterest, was listening. She spoke for several minutes. Then the detainee spoke. Then Grimes. Then he spoke again, this time with an arrogant smirk across his face.

She looked back over her shoulder, up at the camera on the wall, and smiled at them.

Then, she went back to work.

When the prisoner became unresponsive to her circling and questioning, she gently placed her right hand on his left, where it lay loosely secured to the armrest. Then, with the speed of a cobra strike, she dislocated the man's thumb. He opened his mouth and howled in silent pain for an instant, but then quickly collected himself.

"Jesus, she broke his fucking thumb," Black said. "I hope you assholes are planning on taking him with you when you leave. We have oversight up the ass these days."

"Nope," Dempsey replied.

"This is un-fucking-sat, Dempsey," Adamo seethed.

"He'll live," Dempsey said.

The prisoner glared at Grimes. If anything, he was working hard to look amused, now that he was fully awake from the pain from his dislocated thumb. Grimes leaned in again and put her hands on the man's thighs, her face inches from his. Dempsey saw the man's body stiffen under her contact. Then, the prisoner began to talk. When he finally stopped talking, she stepped back and renewed her counterclockwise stalking, reminding Dempsey of a shark circling moments before the kill. To his dismay, he watched as she unsheathed a SOG knife from her boot.

"What the hell is she doing?" Adamo demanded.

Dempsey watched her toy with the blade, drawing it gently down the jihadi's cheek and over his neck, and for an instant he was afraid he'd made a terrible mistake giving her complete autonomy.

"I'm pulling her," Adamo said, jumping to his feet.

"No," Dempsey said. "She won't hurt him."

"She broke his thumb! God knows what she's planning next." Adamo looked at Smith. "Are you seriously just going to stand there and do nothing?"

"Relax, man," Smith said. "It's all an act."

As if she could hear their conversation, Grimes walked around behind the prisoner, looked up at the camera, and winked.

"See, Adamo. Everything's under control," Dempsey said.

They watched the jihadi silently mumble something to her, and to Dempsey it almost looked like the man was pleading. A beat later, Grimes stepped away and sheathed her knife. She walked to the door, but at the threshold, abruptly stopped. She turned, walked back to the prisoner, grabbed his thumb, and with a quick jerk, snapped the dislocated digit back into place. Then, with one final flourish, she whispered something in his ear, smiled, and walked out.

With a sigh of relief, Dempsey looked at Smith, who returned the sentiment with a crooked grin.

"What the fuck was that?" Adamo said, looking for an ally in the group. "Are you kidding me? That was amateur hour. We got nothing, and that's a cold fact."

Dempsey and Smith ignored him. Black said nothing.

Grimes strolled into the room a few seconds later, Jacobs complaining over her shoulder.

"I said I was sorry," Grimes said. "What else do you want?"

"We don't even know who you fucking guys are, and now we have a medical injury to report. It's not like the old days, lady. Careers get ruined over shit like that."

Grimes took a deep breath and plastered on a conciliatory smile. "Look, I really am sorry. You guys are not to blame. You don't design the political culture where a terrorist who kills American soldiers is afforded more rights than the people he murders. You have to live inside the SOPs passed down from on high, but aren't you glad that now you know there are still people out there operating with the authority to get shit done and keep radical psychos like our friend in there from slitting throats and channeling money to terrorists who blow up little girls?"

"The reason the CIA doesn't do this cowboy shit," Jacobs fired back, "is not because of the bureaucracy, it's because it doesn't work. There are tons of data that show coerced intel gleaned under torture and threats is worthless. It is completely unreliable."

"FBI data," countered Smith. "They work in a different world. They're building cases, hunting for details about networks that they want to infiltrate. We know something big is coming and we're just looking for anything to lead us to the next bread crumb before hundreds or thousands of people are murdered. It doesn't have to hold up in court or under scrutiny at The Hague."

"Well, thanks to you, we have a prisoner with a dislocated thumb."

"Oh, Agent Jacobs, relax. I put it back," Grimes said, and blew him a kiss in a perfect Marilyn Monroe imitation.

"Jesus Christ," Jacobs swore and then left the room. Shaking his head, Black followed after him.

"Go talk to them," Dempsey told Adamo.

"And tell them what? They're in the right; they have every reason to be pissed off. No wonder no one is willing to help you guys."

"You work for Dempsey now," Smith said, getting in Adamo's face. "He told you what he needs, now go do your fucking job."

Adamo's face turned red, and he spun on a heel and left the room.

Dempsey turned to Grimes, barely able to contain his curiosity. "So?"

"He's Iranian," she said with a victorious grin.

"How do you know?" Smith asked.

"His fingernails are clean; his hands aren't callused. I could see the line where he used to shave his beard thin, the way Iranian diplomats and government officials do. No one in Hezbollah is allowed to do that. Compared to most, he's manicured," she said. "He defaulted to Farsi there at the end when he was under duress. His respiration rate picked up when I threatened his wife and son in Tehran."

"Wait a minute," Smith said. "How did you know he's married and has a child?"

"I took a chance. Married VEVAK officers in Tehran are no different from married CIA officers in Virginia. They settle their families in nice neighborhoods, put their kids in the best schools. When I was giving him a shave, I made reference to watching his wife picking up his son at Allameh Helli . . . he didn't like that."

"You were fishing?" Dempsey asked.

"Confirming a hunch."

"Okay, so he's Iranian. Now what?" Smith said.

"It's a big win, Shane," Dempsey replied, surprised at Smith's response.

"Don't get me wrong, this is huge. An Iranian agent working with Hezbollah and dialoguing with an ISIS commander is a serious problem, but it tells us nothing about what al-Mahajer is planning. Did you get anything else, anything else at all?"

Grimes looked at the monitor; the prisoner had fallen asleep in his chair. "In the very beginning, he was mumbling in his sleep. He kept repeating the phrase *bawwaba šamāliyy.*"

Dempsey shook his head. "I don't know that expression. Is it Farsi?"

"No, it's Arabic," Smith said. "It means 'the northern gateway,' but it's not a particularly common expression."

"What do you think it means?" Grimes asked, reaching back to fix her ponytail.

"I have no idea. We need someone intimately familiar with the current tactics and code words being used by Hezbollah," Smith said, rubbing his chin, "and I think Jarvis might know just the right guy."

CHAPTER 16

Brussels, Belgium
October 23, 2042 Local Time

Her hand felt small in his. Not fragile, just small. Dempsey hadn't walked hand-in-hand with a woman in a long time. The last time would have been with Kate, but the exact memory was lost to him.

It felt nice, he mused. Only problem was, this was the wrong woman.

Grimes squeezed his hand. "One o'clock. The couple sitting in the far corner."

Les Brassins was impossible to miss, with its fire engine–red facade and oversize plate glass windows. The white privacy curtains were pulled back, and the brightly lit Belgian brasserie was packed with people. Levi Harel and a companion were sitting at a table at the far left side of the restaurant. "Check," he said.

"I wonder what he's like?"

"Who, Harel?"

"Yeah. The man is a legend . . . he's like the Bruce Springsteen of the spook world."

"I have no idea what you're talking about," Dempsey said, looking at her.

She rolled her eyes. "You know, the Boss."

"Yeah, I know the Boss, but what does Springsteen have to do with spies?"

"Seriously? Springsteen is the Boss of rock 'n' roll, as Levi Harel is the Boss of clandestine operations. It's an analogy, JD. What, they didn't teach you about analogies in SEAL school?"

"Oh, they taught us plenty of analogies," he said with a wry smile. "Just not the kind a guy discusses with a nice girl like you."

She laughed. "Nice girl? So that's how you think of me?"

"Actually, you curse like a sailor, you shoot like a SEAL, and you interrogate terrorists like a motherfucker . . . so you're right, nice girl is one helluva stretch." Then, with a smile he added, "To use an analogy, you're like the Madonna of spies."

"Look who's talking, Mick Jagger."

"Jagger? The dude weighs a hundred pounds and struts around like a peacock. We have absolutely nothing in common."

"Not true. You're both geriatric and you both have egos big enough to fill a stadium."

They were both genuinely laughing as they entered Les Brassins—filling the role of happy lovers on holiday in Brussels without looking like they were trying. Dempsey surveyed the restaurant before looking in Harel's direction. Nothing unusual caught his attention in the restaurant. Elizabeth gave his hand a double-squeeze, signaling the all-clear, and they walked over to the Israeli spymaster's table. Harel sat facing them, smoking a cigarette and talking quietly to a woman with her back to them. He was a small man. The gray wool overcoat, which he wore inside, did not manage to conceal his slight build and narrow shoulders. His face was clean-shaven, his expression contemplative, and to

Dempsey, his skin looked weathered beyond his years. He'd seen men with such countenances before, men who shouldered burdens too heavy for a single soul. The spymaster made casual eye contact, put out his cigarette, and stood to greet them.

"Bonsoir," Harel said, extending his hand. "How was your flight?"

"Short and sweet," Dempsey said, shaking the Israeli's hand and uttering the prearranged response confirming that they had not been followed.

"Very good," Harel said and fixed his gaze on Grimes. "You must be Elizabeth."

Grimes smiled. "Yes, nice to meet you."

"This is my daughter, Elinor," Harel said, gesturing to the raven-haired beauty seated across the table from him. Dempsey saw no resemblance . . . except maybe in the eyes.

It's her NOC, you moron, he chastised himself, annoyed that he'd even briefly considered that this woman might actually be Harel's daughter. It was the Mossad man's perfect delivery and adoring fatherly gaze that sucked him into the lie.

Elinor smiled at Grimes and then shifted her gaze to Dempsey. "Bonsoir."

"Bonsoir," they replied in unison, Elizabeth with a decent French accent and him, not so much.

Dempsey stared unapologetically at the Israeli female agent. She was an archetypal beauty—with a perfect Grecian nose, arched eyebrows, high cheekbones, and a deep olive complexion. Elinor had the type of face that belonged on the cover of *Vogue*, the type of face that made men temporarily forget their own name. The last woman who'd had that effect on him was Kate.

"Elizabeth, why don't you take my seat," Harel said. "You and Elinor can catch up while I take a walk with John."

Dempsey watched a flicker of irritation flash across Elizabeth's face, but she smiled and said, "What a wonderful idea."

Dempsey met her gaze, and they reached silent communion on the breach of protocol. If Levi Harel wanted to take a walk, they were going to take a walk. He followed the former Mossad chief out of the brasserie and into the brisk Brussels night. The cobblestone sidewalk was still damp from the rain a few hours earlier. The air felt heavy and tired.

Harel lit a cigarette.

Dempsey ran his tongue along the inside of his lower lip as the craving for wintergreen snuff kicked when the scent of Harel's Noblesse filled his nostrils.

"Show me the scar," Harel said.

"Excuse me?" Dempsey said, confused.

"I don't recognize your face."

"That's because we've never met."

"No, it's because Kelso's plastic surgeon did a very good job, so show me the scar."

Dempsey pulled up his left sleeve. The old knife wound wrapped his forearm like a serpent, pearly white and smooth.

Harel blew a long stream of smoke out the corner of his mouth. "Okay."

Dempsey rolled his sleeve back down and continued to walk beside the legend down narrow Rue Keyenveld, not sure what to say next. The meeting had been arranged by Jarvis—a little detour on the way home from Poland so Dempsey could "pick the brain of an old friend." The clues Grimes had uncovered during her interrogation session with the VEVAK operative were important, but how important they weren't sure. When Dempsey asked Jarvis why he didn't simply ask for Harel's opinion over the phone, his boss had said, "Two reasons: One, because Levi is old school. If you want a favor, you have to ask for it face-to-face, and two, because he said he wants to meet you." Thankfully the former Mossad chief was in nearby Brussels, helping the Belgians with their ISIS problems, rather than in his home base of Tel Aviv.

"They call you Dempsey now?" Harel said, breaking the silence.

"Yeah."

"Homage to the boxer or the general?"

"The boxer."

"Hmm. Suits you."

"You've worked with Captain Jarvis awhile now," Dempsey said, his intonation part question, part statement.

Harel grinned. "Not as long as some, but longer than most. Allies like Kelso are hard to find in this world."

Dempsey nodded.

"I came to the memorial at Virginia Beach."

"He told me."

"I'm sorry about your brothers. We have the highest respect for your old unit."

"Thank you," Dempsey said, choking down an unexpected upwelling of emotion.

"When I was a boy in Tel Aviv, I was small for my age. There was this one boy in my class, Ephraim, who was much bigger. He loved to cause trouble for me. He'd steal my lunch. He'd copy my work, take my pencils. Make fun of me in front of the girls. Ephraim was always goading me for a fight, but I would never take the first swing. Then, one day a new boy, David, arrived in class. Ephraim had grown bored with me, and now he had a new plaything. I watched as he tormented David, I empathized, but I did nothing. I was just glad to get a reprieve. Eventually, Ephraim renewed his old ways, splitting his time harassing both of us. One day, on the walk home from school, David pulled me aside. He told me he had a plan. He'd been following Ephraim; he knew where Ephraim lived. He convinced me that if we aligned together, we could challenge our tormenter. In a fight, one-on-one with Ephraim, individually we would always lose. But together, we could teach him a lesson he'd never forget. So, a week later, on a rainy Thursday afternoon, we ambushed Ephraim. We traded punches—four fists against two— and succeeded in pounding the bully into the mud. In that moment,

David and I were allies. But, fast-forward one year, and David had taken over Ephraim's role as chief bully. He'd drafted three boys into his posse, and their favorite target was me."

"I don't understand," Dempsey said. "Why would he turn on you like that?"

"The why is irrelevant; all that matters is the lesson."

"Which is?"

"That the old adage 'the enemy of my enemy is my friend' is broken logic. Israel knows this. America has never been able to learn the lesson. Your government makes the same mistake over and over—partnering with evil men to defeat other evil men, only to later find itself targeted by the enemy of your enemy."

Dempsey nodded. "You're talking about Iran?"

"Of course. The White House is making a grave mistake thinking that Tehran can be a strategic partner in the War on Terror."

"Ember is not the White House," Dempsey said. "We don't share the Administration's illogic."

Harel took a last, long drag from his cigarette and flicked it into a storm drain. "I know. That's why we're talking."

"Does the name Rafiq al-Mahajer mean anything to you?"

"Number eight on our ISIS most-wanted list. Kelso told me you ran a capture/kill operation on him a few days ago."

"Yeah, but al-Mahajer sent a proxy to the meet, who unfortunately did not survive long enough to provide us with any actionable intelligence. However, one of the other guys we grabbed has proved to be interesting."

"Do you have an ID?"

"We have hits in the facial-rec database, but no positive ID. He's young and he's a pro. Resilient and evasive under interrogation. Fluent in Arabic, Farsi, and English. They tell me he speaks with a unique Palestinian dialect."

Harel tapped a fresh cigarette out of his pack and lit it. "Is that all?"

"No, we have him in Palestine with Hezbollah leadership just before the apartment attack in the West Bank last year. CIA pegged him as midlevel Hezbollah, but Elizabeth is convinced he's actually a VEVAK liaison to Hezbollah."

"I'm happy to run him through our database and see if we can get an ID."

"Thanks," Dempsey said, and handed Harel a USB drive he'd prepped for this very reason.

"What else?" Harel asked, slipping the thumb drive into his pocket.

Dempsey rubbed his chin. "There is one other thing, but it may be nothing."

Harel shot him a look, the kind a father gives his son when the son has just disappointed him. "Let me give you a piece of advice, John. It's the little things in our business that matter. If something gets your antennae up, it's never nothing."

"All right," Dempsey said, nodding. "Does the Arabic expression *bawwaba šamāliyy* mean anything to you?"

"What context?"

"When Elizabeth took a turn interrogating our new friend, *bawwaba šamāliyy* was something she caught him mumbling after a period of sleep deprivation."

Harel stopped walking and stared straight ahead. "I think we have a big problem."

Dempsey's stomach sank. "I'm listening."

"It's no mystery that tunneling has been the cornerstone of Hamas's incursion strategy into Gaza. Israeli Defense Forces destroyed dozens of tunnels in 2014, and we learned a lot in the process. The sophistication of Hamas's underground network and the number of previously undetected tunnels took the National Security Council by surprise and got people asking, 'What about Hezbollah? If Hamas can tunnel into Israel from the south, why not Hezbollah from the north?' So, we started looking at the Lebanese border. We started asking questions and working our network. This has been one of Elinor's projects during the past year. She has been searching for evidence of *bawwaba šamāliyy*. The Northern Gateway. The mother of all tunnels into Israel. If your man is in any way affiliated with Hezbollah and he is mumbling about the Northern Gateway in his sleep, then I want a turn with him."

"I'm certain that can be arranged," Dempsey said. "What else can we do to help?"

"Keep looking for al-Mahajer. Try to figure out why the Islamic State, VEVAK, and Hezbollah are having secret meetings in the desert. My greatest fear is that the day comes when Sunni and Shia put aside their differences and the terrorist factions of the world finally unite to launch an End of Days assault on Israel. Amir Modiri was able to unify the factions of Al Qaeda on the Arabian Peninsula to wipe out the Tier One SEALs. Can you imagine the carnage if he can unite Al Qaeda, Hezbollah, Hamas, and the Islamic State under VEVAK's umbrella? God help us."

"I'll talk with Jarvis. We'll give you all the support we can. It's the least we can do after everything you did for us in Frankfurt. We wouldn't have stopped those bastards in New York if it hadn't been for you and your team."

Harel offered his hand. "That's what allies are for."

"And don't worry," Dempsey said, shaking the spymaster's hand. "I'll find Rafiq al-Mahajer. Failure is not an option."

CHAPTER 17

Covert Hezbollah Training Camp
Cuchumatanes Mountains, Guatemala
October 24, 1840 Local Time

Rostami watched intently as the six dead Muslim men gathered around the table.

He watched them sweat. He watched them fidget. He watched them try to look brave and pious as al-Mahajer used a marker to draw red circles around three American cities where these young, brainwashed radicals would martyr themselves.

"Since our arrival, you have honed your tactical skills—firing hundreds of practice rounds and learning how to handle and proficiently reload pistols and AK-47s. You have been trained how to interact with the enemy and how to avoid drawing attention to yourself. Tonight, we enter the final phase of your preparation. I know that each of you has been patiently waiting for your assignment, and now you are anxious to know the details of how you will make your sacrifice for Allah. I will not make you wait any longer. Three coordinated attacks will be unleashed on America, hitting the Great Satan in the east, the middle, and the west simultaneously. With Allah's guidance, I have personally selected these assignments."

Al-Mahajer squatted, retrieved a suicide vest from inside a box under the table, and set it on top of the map.

"Each of you will be wearing one of these vests. It was designed and built by our Hezbollah brothers here at this camp. The vest is constructed in layers: the inner layer is made of Kevlar, fitted with antiballistic ceramic plates to protect you from enemy gunfire while you complete your mission; the intermediate layer is fitted with a band of high-yield plastic explosive; and the outside layer is loaded with sleeves of twenty-millimeter steel ball bearings. When you wear the vest, you are in Allah's hands; know that He will guide you and comfort you on your mission."

The young jihadists all stared at the instrument of their undoing, pale-faced and speechless.

"You look conflicted, Nabil. Is there a problem?" Al-Mahajer asked, his dark eyes boring into the consternating youth.

"Yes, er, I mean, no," Nabil stammered. "No problem."

Al-Mahajer smiled. "We are all warriors here, sons of Allah, and servants of the Caliphate. Speak your heart, because if you have doubts, it is certain that at least one of your five brothers harbors the same thoughts."

Nabil glanced nervously from al-Mahajer to the young man standing to his right, Faruq. Rostami had seen these two together frequently. Faruq gave an encouraging nod to Nabil.

Nabil swallowed. "I did not realize we would be wearing suicide vests. I thought the plan was to use assault rifles."

"The plan *is* to use assault rifles, but the vest ensures you cannot be arrested and taken into custody. This is a mission of martyrdom."

"Yes, but—"

"How a soldier dies in service of Allah is irrelevant. Your path to Paradise will be paved with the bodies of infidels. The more Americans you kill, the greater your reward will be."

Nabil nodded, but Rostami saw lingering doubt in the young man's eyes.

Al-Mahajer must have seen it, too, because he drew his pistol, pointed the muzzle at Nabil's forehead, and pulled the trigger.

The gunshot roared. Blood splattered. Faruq screamed.

Rostami simply shook his head.

Nabil's body hit the ground with a thud. The five young jihadists—none of whom had witnessed cold-blooded murder before—watched in horror as the body spasmed for a few seconds before going limp.

A heartbeat later, Hijjar and two of his men burst into the command tent, their weapons at the ready. "What in Allah's name is going on?" He surveyed the scene and then fixed his gaze on al-Mahajer. "Why did you kill Nabil?"

"Nabil was not committed to his destiny; he was not prepared to martyr himself for Allah."

"But now you're a man down, and we don't have time to bring in someone new."

Al-Mahajer holstered his pistol and locked eyes with Hijjar. "I am the sixth man," he said coolly. "I will take Nabil's place."

The five stunned young jihadists stared at al-Mahajer with expressions of incredulity, fear, and awe.

After a long, uncomfortable beat, Hijjar addressed al-Mahajer. "We need to talk. Alone."

"Leave us," the ISIS commander barked at his disciples. "And take Nabil's body with you."

Hijjar ordered his two men out as well, leaving the three of them alone.

"What was that?" Hijjar said, gesturing to the bloody mess.

"That was leadership," the Syrian replied. "It was part of the plan from the beginning. I wasn't positive who would be the sacrificial lamb, but Nabil made the decision easy."

Hijjar shook his head and then looked to Rostami.

"I knew nothing of this," Rostami said.

"You intend to martyr yourself in America?" Hijjar asked.

"It's my time," al-Mahajer said. "I'm tired of hiding in the shadows. I'm weary of living like a coward, always moving, always underground. I'm done wondering when an American drone is going to deal death from above before I've had a chance to serve my purpose. This mission will be the culmination of my life's work. It will strike more terror into the hearts of America than 9/11, because this attack will show them that no one is safe—not at work, not at a restaurant, not at a shopping mall, not at a museum. We can hit them anywhere, anytime, and nobody can stop us."

"And what about you, Persian," Hijjar asked, shifting his gaze to Rostami, "do you intend to martyr yourself as well?"

Rostami suppressed the urge to grimace. "Not on this engagement," he said. "I still have much left to do in this lifetime in service to Allah."

Hijjar nodded and turned his attention back to al-Mahajer. "Tactically speaking, your men are ready. I will leave it up to you to decide when they are mentally and emotionally prepared. But I must caution you, don't wait too long, because this is a mobile camp. I rotate the personnel through four different locations. Our next rotation is in three days. You can come with us if you need more time, but you can't stay here."

"Tomorrow they face their final test. Each warrior must wear a vest for twelve hours. The detonators will be deactivated, but they won't know that," al-Mahajer said. "Assuming they pass the test, we will be ready to mobilize into Mexico the following day."

"Very well," Hijjar said, and as he turned to leave, he added, "but next time you are planning on killing someone, please do the courtesy of letting me know."

Hijjar ducked out of the tent and disappeared.

Rostami felt his mood begin to sour. Al-Mahajer was even more dangerous and unpredictable than he'd first recognized. After he'd served his purpose, was the Syrian planning on putting a bullet in his brain when he wasn't looking? How much impiety would al-Mahajer tolerate from a *Rafidhi* before it warranted a death sentence? How many loose ends did he plan to snip? Rostami had no intention of finding out. As soon as they were safely in Mexicali and linked up with the Zetas, he would say good-bye to al-Mahajer and the Islamic State. His orders were to get al-Mahajer and his team into the United States. There was no reason that he had to make the underground crossing into America. He would direct his sleeper agents to rendezvous with the ISIS radical and his team in California and arrange lodging and transportation for the terrorist duos en route to their respective target cities. He would watch the carnage on television from the safety and comfort of his flat in Tehran.

"It's time," Rostami said, feeling better having made his decision.

"Time for what?" al-Mahajer asked.

Pulling his encrypted satellite phone from his pocket, he said, "To prepare for your imminent arrival in the United States."

CHAPTER 18

University of Nebraska Omaha
Omaha, Nebraska
October 25, 1615 Local Time

"Professor Shirazi," a girl's voice called from behind him. "Professor Shirazi, I was hoping I could talk to you for a minute."

Professor Keyvan Shirazi stopped and waited for Amber Conner, one of his top undergraduate pupils, to catch up. "Of course, Amber, I'm heading to my office right now. What's on your mind?"

"I love bioinformatics, you know that, right?" she began.

He smiled at her. "Which is one of the reasons I encouraged you to apply to our graduate program here, at UNO, instead of leaving us for, oh, I don't know, God forbid Kansas University."

Amber laughed, but her body language told him she was nervous.

"What's the matter, Amber?" he said.

"I took the MCAT."

"Nothing wrong with that. How did you do?"

"I did well," she said, screwing up her face in adorable coed consternation. "Really well."

"Superior achievement is nothing to be ashamed of. I would have expected nothing less," he said, reaching for the door to his office. He turned the knob, and ushered her in with a wave of his hand.

"But now I have a problem," she said, taking a seat opposite his desk.

"What's that?"

"My parents," she said. "Now, they want me to go to medical school instead of pursuing a PhD in biomedical informatics."

He eased himself into the plush leather chair behind his desk. "Are they paying?"

"Is that relevant?"

"Money is always relevant, Amber, and anyone that tells you otherwise is being disingenuous."

She thought for moment and then said, "Our deal was that they would pay for college and anything beyond that would be my responsibility."

"Then I think the decision is simple, you—"

His desk phone rang, interrupting him midsentence. He looked at the caller ID displayed, but he did not recognize the number. He did, however, recognize the area code: New York City.

"Excuse me a moment. I should probably take this."

"Do you need me to leave, Professor?"

"No, it's okay. Just a moment." He picked up the receiver and said, "Professor Shirazi."

He heard a series of clicks on the line, and then an unfamiliar male voice said, "Is this Professor Keyvan Shirazi living on 13262 Willow Lane, Omaha, Nebraska 68124?"

"Speaking."

"I'm calling to inform you that your mortgage refinancing package has been approved. Congratulations. You will receive a packet of material in the mail in three to five business days. Please be sure to read the supplied information carefully, and retain it for your records. Thank you for doing business with PTM Bank and Trust."

The line went dead.

The Suren Circle had just been activated.

Despite being seated, he suddenly felt light-headed, as if all the oxygen had been sucked out of the room. He hung up the receiver, his hand trembling as he did.

"Are you okay, Professor?" Amber asked, leaning forward, looking concerned.

He forced a smile. "Everything is fine, but if it's all right with you, can we table this conversation for another time?"

"Of course," she said, grabbing her messenger bag and standing.

"Thank you," he said. "But I would leave you with this advice: Follow your heart. Follow your passion. As you set out on your life's journey, don't beholden yourself to other people's priorities or wishes, because the end result is invariably disappointment for all parties."

"Thank you, Professor Shirazi. I'll remember that," she said with a nod and left.

A wave of mania washed over him. He wanted to scream; he wanted to cry; he wanted to run far away as fast as he could. It didn't make sense. Why, after nearly two decades of silence, was he being called upon now?

What do they want? What must I do?

He quickly gathered his things, locked his office door, and walked as fast as his legs would carry him to his Honda Pilot parked in his reserved faculty spot. Time slipped, and when he came out of his fugue he was pulling into the three-car garage of his suburban home. His wife, Delilah, was standing in the doorway waiting for him, dressed in her hospital scrubs. Like him, she had been called at work. Like him, she had dropped everything and come straight home, executing protocol they had last discussed so very, very long ago.

He turned off the engine, stepped out of the SUV, and met his wife's gaze. She had the strangest look on her face. She almost looked . . .

Excited.

"What are our orders?" she asked as he approached, her cheeks flushed.

"They gave the activation sequence, but nothing else. Instructions will follow."

"I was beginning to think this day would never come," she said, walking with him into their newly remodeled kitchen.

Her enthusiasm only intensified his anxiety. He had expected her to be frightened. He had expected that he would have to comfort her and had imagined that in consoling her he might find his own calm. But this reaction? The look in her eyes gave him gooseflesh, and suddenly, he almost couldn't recognize the woman standing in front of him.

She grabbed him and pressed her pelvis against his; her breathing was growing heavy. It'd been years since she'd . . .

"Take me," she breathed in his ear. "Right here, right now."

But it felt wrong.

It was time to immure his true feelings and play along. He had no choice, because for the first time in his life, he didn't trust his wife.

CHAPTER 19

Ember Hangar
Newport News/Williamsburg International Airport, Newport
News, Virginia
October 25, 1410 Local Time

Dempsey waited patiently while the yellow tow vehicle hooked up to the nose gear of the Falcon. He waited for the click, and then the jolt, as the tug took control. The aircraft doors were still shut, and the cabin air was flowing anemically on auxiliary power, making the passenger compartment stuffy and warm. Normally, he would be agitated, like a caged tiger pacing and pining to escape his cage, but not today. Today, he was Zen. Today, he had decided to give himself a free pass and let somebody else carry the weight of the world on their shoulders.

That somebody was Levi Harel.

It wasn't that Dempsey was happy to learn that Hezbollah, the Islamic State, and VEVAK might be collaborating on a tunnel into Israel to launch terror attacks; it was simply a relief that this particular plot wasn't directed at his homeland. This time, al-Mahajer wasn't targeting his people. If Harel asked for Ember's direct support, he'd hop on the next flight to Tel Aviv without complaint. He'd crawl down whatever shithole they asked him to and trade bullets with the enemy. But helping safeguard Israel wasn't the same burden as being responsible for stopping the next attack on American soil.

Jarvis once told him that Harry Truman kept a placard on his desk in the Oval Office, containing the phrase he had made famous: THE BUCK STOPS HERE. Dempsey knew the idiom, of course, but he'd never known its origin until that moment. A few days later, he'd noticed a simple plaque hanging on the wall behind Jarvis's desk. It read: FOR THOSE WHO CAN'T, FOR THOSE WHO WON'T, AND FOR THOSE WHO CHOOSE TO LOOK THE OTHER WAY . . . Below the text was an engraved image of Ember's logo: a fiery eagle rising like a phoenix from the ashes, clutching a Trident beneath a single star. The message was simple, poignant, powerful. It was the leader's creed: *I will decide, I will act, I will be accountable, even when no one else will.* This was the motto of Ember. It came from Jarvis; he exhaled it. And the longer Dempsey breathed the same air, the more he metabolized his boss's mantle of leadership. Stopping these crazy bastards was his job, his duty, his burden . . . just not today.

Thank God, not today.

Once the Falcon was inside the hangar, Smith finally opened the cabin doors. A precaution against anyone watching via satellite from space, he liked to say. As far as Dempsey was concerned, if the bad guys were watching this location from space then their cover was already blown and therefore Ember was fucked. When he was a Tier One SEAL, their philosophy had been to hide in plain sight. In Dempsey's experience, the more secretive one tried to be, the more attention one drew to oneself. Unfortunately, trying to explain this logic to the Counter Intelligence guys in black organizations was a Sisyphean endeavor, so he'd stopped trying to push that particular boulder uphill long ago. Smith's idiosyncrasy about deplaning inside the hangar was pointless to argue about.

He yawned, stretched, got out of the comfortable leather captain's chair. When he stepped out into the hangar, the first thing he noticed was that the Boeing was back.

Good.

"I'm making a coffee run over to the terminal building," Mendez said, greeting the group of weary disembarked. "Anybody want anything?"

"What have you been up to while we were gone?" Dempsey asked. He liked the former Marine and knew Mendez was eager to get down range, but sometimes the spook business needed a small footprint—or was even done solo—something Dempsey and, he supposed, a team-oriented Marine both needed to get used to.

"Training," Mendez said with a shrug. "We had another day and a half at the Farm, thanks to the boss."

"Time on the range, I hope," Dempsey growled. Then he added with a smile, "You shoot like a Marine."

"I'll take that as the compliment I'm sure it was meant to be," Mendez said with a big—and well-rested—grin. "So, you want coffee or not?"

Dempsey grimaced. He wanted to say no, but some caffeine would help chase the cobwebs away. His body didn't know what the hell time zone it was. He'd flown from Iraq to Virginia to Europe and back to Virginia in a seventy-two-hour window; his internal clock was all out of whack. To top it off, he hadn't been able to sleep a wink on the transatlantic flight home. For some reason, he was worrying about shit he never used to worry about before: Simon Adamo's integration into the team; whether the CIA guys in Poland were going to complain to the DNI; whether he'd made a good impression on Levi Harel; and the raven-haired female Mossad agent, Elinor, whom he found himself strangely drawn to. What the hell was wrong with him?

"No takers? Seriously?" Mendez said, throwing his hands up in mock surprise. "C'mon, JD, you look like you really need it."

"Fine, I'll have the usual," Dempsey said.

"One large, sweet-ass sissy coffee for the SEAL—Check," Mendez said with a grin.

"Make it two," Grimes said.

"Three," said Smith.

"All right then, sissy coffees all round," Mendez said and was out the door. Dempsey felt a hand on his shoulder and stifled a yawn.

"Hanging in there, old man?" Smith said.

"Five by," Dempsey said. "I'm guessing the Skipper wants to debrief?"

"Take thirty minutes," Smith said. "Grab a shower and a change of clothes. No rush."

"Are you politely telling me that I stink?"

"You're a bit ripe, my friend."

"All right." Dempsey laughed. "Too many years in the suck, I can't smell the difference anymore . . . Do me a favor, don't let Chip or Dale steal my coffee when Mendez gets back."

Minutes later he had his forehead pressed against the wall of a shower stall in the bunkroom. He let the hot water run down his back, and he must have fallen asleep standing up, because next thing he knew he was jerking awake from the Romeo dream. He shook off the imagery of his teammate getting blown to pieces—the same dream that had been haunting him for a week—and reached for the soap.

"Jesus," he mumbled. "Nodding off in the shower, now that's a first."

After scrubbing clean, he twisted the handle to cold for a few seconds to jolt his body back to life before stepping out of the shower. He quickly toweled off and made his way to the small bunkroom, kicked the door open, and unzipped his large black go-bag. He fished out a pair of cargo pants, a gray T-shirt, and his camp shoes. While he was putting on his shoes, his phone chimed with a notification. He glanced down at the screen. `Kate Kemper has updated her status.` Curiosity piqued, he swiped to open his Facebook app.

> `Jake swam in his first swim meet yesterday.`
> `He finished third out of sixteen boys in his`
> `very first race! That's him in lane two. The`
> `coach says he's a natural.`

The post included a picture of a swimming pool with eight boys racing freestyle, captured in midchurn. So far, the entry had accumulated fourteen likes. Grinning with pride, he scrolled down through the comments:

> `Way to go Jake! —Aubry B`
> `His dad would be proud! —Diane Stein`
> `He looks like a future SEAL in the making.`
> `—April Rousch`

"What are you doing?" a hard voice said behind him.

Dempsey looked back over his shoulder to find Smith standing in the bunkroom doorway, holding two cups of coffee and staring at Dempsey's phone. "Procrastinating," he said, clicking the screen off.

With a grave face, Smith said, "You can't go there, bro."

He thought about playing the denial game, but what was the point. Smith had busted him; why pretend otherwise? "I know."

"You can never go back. Why torture yourself?"

He blew air through his teeth. "Because . . . because I can't help myself."

Smith sat down on the bunk next to Dempsey. "I never had what you had. When Jarvis found me, I was still married to the Team and wanted to just win the war—not knowing that was impossible without guys like Jarvis. I never married, had no kids. All I walked away from was my Team, and that was hard enough. I can't pretend to know how it feels to walk away from a wife and kid, but before I could embrace this life, I had to say good-bye to the old one. I know it might seem harmless, but Facebook is an umbilical cord keeping you tied to them."

Dempsey nodded. "It's kinda ridiculous. I was the guy who hated Facebook. But now . . ." He smiled. "I just learned that Jake joined a swim team, bro. Jake, the kid who spent ten hours a day in front of the TV playing *World of Warcraft*, is suddenly working his ass off in the pool. He came in third in his first race. I'm so proud of the kid. All our friends posted congratulatory comments."

"You mean Kate's friends," Smith corrected.

"Yeah," he snorted. "Kate's friends."

"I'm not sure if you're catfishing or if you created a ghost account, but this is a nonstarter. Jack Kemper is dead, and John Dempsey doesn't exist. I hate to be that guy, but you gotta check this shit."

"I think you've made your point."

"Good," Smith said, then forced a smile. "Here, take your coffee, grumpy."

Dempsey walked in silence with Smith to the TOC. Grimes, Adamo, and Mendez were already gathered. He dropped into a black chair next to Mendez. "Thanks for this," he said, lifting his cup.

"No problem," Mendez answered and was about to add something when Jarvis came in the door beside the monitors.

Jarvis took a seat, folded his hands on the table, and looked at Dempsey. "Impressions and takeaways?"

Before Dempsey could open his mouth, Adamo spoke up. "I'd be happy to. My impression is that this organization is out of control. And my takeaway is that Ember has taken two steps back from what the CIA has evolved into over the past fourteen years prosecuting terrorists."

Fists balled under the table, Dempsey growled, "You have a lot of nerve coming here—"

Jarvis raised a hand. "It's all right, John. Let's give Simon a chance to speak his mind."

Dempsey fired Jarvis an incredulous stare, but Ember's Director turned his full attention to Adamo.

"The interrogation I witnessed in Poland violated the President's moratorium on torture, as well as the policies that govern agents employed by the United States intelligence community."

"Gimme a fucking break," Dempsey said and rolled his eyes. "She dislocated his thumb. Do you have any idea what VEVAK would have done if the tables had been turned?"

"Hypothetical quid pro quo is irrelevant," Adamo said, pushing his glasses up on his nose. "Nowhere in the Constitution, the legal system, or the charters governing the agencies that comprise the intelligence community is it documented that an agent's behavior shall be modeled after the predicted behavior of the enemy. That's nonsensical. We are Americans. Our operations are governed by principles and principles only; that is what separates us from and elevates us above our enemies."

"Are you fucking kidding me?" Dempsey said and fixed his gaze on Jarvis. "This is the guy the DNI sends us—a lawyer playing dress-up as a spook? It's because of guys like Adamo that Ember was formed. It's because of guys like Adamo that men like Rafiq al-Mahajer are still in the wind plotting terror."

Jarvis held his gaze, and Dempsey waited for him to lash out at Adamo himself. To his surprise, Jarvis directed his comments to Dempsey instead.

"Mr. Adamo is part of the team, John. That was my decision. The DNI sent him, but I accepted him. He is part of the team now, and we will hear his point of view. Ember works because we are all able to share our views and voice our opinions without fear of retribution or ridicule."

Dempsey stared back, in shock. This was the last thing he needed. He was tired, he was frustrated, and he was still reeling from Smith's intervention into what little personal life he had left.

"I thought Ember was formed to get shit done that couldn't get done by Mr. Adamo and his friends. The *only* reason I agreed to join Ember and play Robin Hood with your band of merry men is because you told me that we were immune to this bullshit. Well, I see that didn't last long; back to the same old games."

"What happened is my fault, not Dempsey's," Grimes insisted, her eyes darting back and forth between Jarvis, Dempsey, and Adamo. "The interrogation script was entirely my idea. I didn't brief JD on what I planned to do. I take full accountability." She folded her arms defiantly across her chest. "And it worked, by the way. JD supported my approach, but the interrogation was mine and my responsibility. No one told me to snap that asshole's thumb."

"Accountability flows uphill," Adamo fired back. "You might be to blame, but Dempsey, as the head of Special Activities, is the one who should be held accountable. And that's a cold fact."

"Fuck this," Dempsey said, shoving his chair back from the table and popping to his feet. "I didn't walk away from my wife and kid to be micromanaged by some Dudley Do-Right pogue from Langley. If this is the future of Ember, count me out."

But before anyone could speak, Baldwin burst into the room with Chip and Dale in tow.

"Pardon the interruption," Baldwin huffed, "but I think we might have found him."

"Found who?" Dempsey growled.

A cocky grin spread across Baldwin's face. "Rafiq al-Mahajer, of course."

CHAPTER 20

Dempsey's body was electric—not from his triple-shot coffee, and not from the rage he felt toward Simon fucking Adamo. Baldwin's news that he'd located al-Mahajer had unloaded a week's worth of adrenaline into his system. He was ready to kit up and go, right fucking now, and so it took great effort to will himself back into his seat at the table.

Chip or Dale dimmed the lights, and the other used a tablet computer to populate the wall of monitors in the TOC with images. The leftmost screen filled with an aerial shot—from a drone, Dempsey surmised—looking down at a compound built into the side of a lush green mountain and facing outward into a densely forested jungle valley. White walls surrounded the compound, which he judged to be twenty feet high. A large Spanish-style house with a courtyard sat off to the east and was flanked by two long, rectangular buildings. To the north, he saw what looked like a warehouse, to the west a deforested area that formed what looked like tracks.

"This is a drug cartel compound in the Cuchumatanes Mountains in central Guatemala," Baldwin began. "DEA has monitored activity here for years, but it popped onto NSA's radar when rumors started floating around that Hezbollah had contracted with the Zetas to lease space for training their jihadi fighters. This is only one of several compounds we believe are leased for this purpose—including one much closer to our southern border, in Mexico."

"Wait a minute," Grimes interrupted, "you're telling us that Hezbollah is training terrorists at the narco camps in Central America? How long has this been going on?"

Before Baldwin could answer, Adamo spoke up. "DEA, The Activity, and the CIA have been following this for some time now. Hezbollah fighters usually arrive at the camps in groups of ten or twenty. Upon their arrival, we typically see a surge of cartel soldiers who carry out the training. They do intensive calisthenics, small-arms training, go off into the jungle for land-navigation training, et cetera. We know they train in night vision equipment, tactical assaults, air assault with helicopter support—it's like a weapons boot camp, we think for newbies in Hezbollah's ranks. Typically, we can see the surge. Is that photo the most recent aerial?"

"You beat me to the punch," Baldwin said, and a new picture of the camp appeared next to the first one.

Dempsey compared the photos and immediately noted two differences. The first was that the camp now had four large canvas tents in the area adjacent to the training ground. The second was a quantifiable bump in the number of people milling about. More men occupied the front courtyard, and dozens more were grouped in pockets across the training grounds. In this particular image, it appeared as though the trainees were lined up for an exercise at the rear of the compound—a shooting range, Dempsey surmised.

"That was taken two days ago," Baldwin said.

"What made you decide to look at this particular compound?" Smith asked, joining the mix.

"Because it got flagged this morning for an encrypted sat-phone transmission that is a match in our database."

"Can you narrow it down better than that?"

"Yes," Baldwin said. He had the excited professor look again, and Dempsey could almost see the mathematical algorithms that floated around in the man's head. "We have high confidence this is the same phone that has been communicating with al-Mahajer's proxy as well as the VEVAK operative you have in Poland. And if that's not convincing enough, there's always this . . ."

A new image appeared on the first monitor. The photograph was a close-up—tight, grainy, and blurry—of a man standing with his hands on his hips, staring at something in the firing range area. He had a full beard and was wearing a long shirt. He looked Middle Eastern to Dempsey, but the image was far from conclusive.

"This is Rafiq al-Mahajer," Baldwin said.

Jarvis squinted at the image. "Are you sure, Ian?"

Baldwin looked at his young assistants and they nodded in unison.

"Eighty-seven percent match," said the one on the left.

"It's him," Baldwin said.

"When was this taken?" Dempsey asked.

"Yesterday."

"It all makes perfect sense now," Dempsey said. "That's why al-Mahajer sent a proxy to Iraq, because he's been in Guatemala all along."

"Or," Grimes chimed in, "maybe he was in the Middle East, sent a proxy for security reasons, and fled to Guatemala after the raid. Or, maybe the meeting in Al Qa'im was about something else altogether. Perhaps we need to sort out what the purpose of that meeting was before we jump to conclusions."

Dempsey shook his head. "That would be nice, but it doesn't change where we are. Either way, it explains why our Iranian friend in Poland was in Al Qa'im. VEVAK supports Hezbollah with both money and arms. No matter what the intelligence community has failed to prove these last few years, we've all suspected it for a long time. Al-Mahajer was functioning as the intermediary between the Islamic State and

Hezbollah to facilitate cooperative training. Why train recruits in Syria, amid NATO air strikes and Russia blowing shit up in their backyard, when they could bring them to Central America instead?"

"Not to mention," Grimes added, "that it's a much easier proposition for ISIS to piggyback on Hezbollah's business with the cartels than to try to create a relationship from scratch."

"So are we saying that ISIS is now having their new recruits trained in Guatemala by the Zeta cartel alongside Hezbollah?" Mendez asked.

"It would appear so," Adamo said.

"Holy shit. That ain't good." The former Marine let out a whistle.

"No, it's not," Jarvis said.

"Then what the hell are we waiting for?" Dempsey said, pounding his fist on the table. "We need to go get these guys."

"Agreed," Jarvis said.

"We'll need more shooters," Dempsey said, his mind racing, already working out the details of the hit. "And dedicated drone support."

"Whoa, whoa, whoa. Hold on a minute," Adamo said, waving his hands in the air. "It doesn't work this way. Like I said before, DEA and partner agencies have been watching this camp for years. There are a lot of very talented men and women who have dedicated years of their lives to the strategic prosecution of this particular target—both the camp and the narco-terrorists, not to mention the global crime syndicates that it services. Just because you have a green spaghetti line and a blurry photo of a suspected terrorist does not give you the authority or the right to charge in and destroy years of carefully laid plans."

"First of all," Dempsey said, "Rafiq al-Mahajer is not a *suspected* terrorist. He's a real goddamn terrorist, and I know that because he blew up my fucking teammate right in front of me. And second, if the Islamic State and Hezbollah both have personnel at that camp at this very moment, we have a moral responsibility to act before they disappear into the jungle and we lose them forever."

Adamo started to respond, but Jarvis cut him off. "Enough. I appreciate both your input, but I've made the decision. Dempsey, you have the green light to plan the mission, but Adamo is right, we need to stage and coordinate this with DEA assets in country." He fixed his gaze on the CIA man. "The DNI sent you here for situations precisely such as this, to facilitate cooperation with other agencies so our missions can be effective without stepping on other agencies' toes."

Adamo, red-faced, nodded.

"It's time to earn your paycheck," Jarvis said sternly. "Go, facilitate. I want wheels up in two hours."

Adamo stood, and after a beat so did everyone else.

Dempsey walked around the circular table to Jarvis. "There's a lot of high-speed bad guys in the photo, boss. I could use a few Team guys, maybe a couple of SEAL snipers, to round out our ranks."

"Got someone in mind? Someone who won't piece you together from your old life and blow your NOC?" Jarvis asked.

Dempsey nodded. "You'll have to pull some strings, and we'll need a by-name request through WARCOM."

"Easily done."

"Great. Let me make a call," Dempsey said. "The guy I'm thinking of should be just up the road."

CHAPTER 21

Cuchumatanes Mountains, Guatemala
October 27, 1930 Local Time

Dempsey gripped the oversize monocular in his right hand. It was the model of choice for snipers and operators needing to sight in or to take pictures in difficult terrain. He switched on the optical filter. He wanted one final look at the camp from the hilltop before the darkness forced him to switch to night vision mode and the finer details would be lost. The camp was buzzing with activity, but nothing he saw confirmed that Hezbollah and ISIS fighters were present. There were plenty of guys with beards who could be Middle Eastern, but they could just as easily be Latino. The Predator and satellite overflights had not imaged anyone resembling al-Mahajer since that initial photo. But they'd gleaned other details. Three of the four tents that had been visible thirty-six hours ago were now gone. And current manpower estimates placed forty-three tangos in the camp—deemed exclusively male based on size and gait. Most were heavily armed—at least the ones that Dempsey could see.

The encampment was fortified and designed with defense against incursion in mind. The side of the camp was essentially built into the rocky face of a small mountain, making it completely unapproachable from the north. Two towers flanked the southern walls, one at each corner, and both were equipped with .50-caliber machine guns. The DEA task force they were coordinating with had warned that there would likely be RPGs in the camp. To make matters worse, a known Zeta QRF outpost was located thirty minutes away.

"So?" Lieutenant Keith Redman said.

Dempsey glanced at Chunk, who was lying prone beside him in the tall jungle foliage.

"It's doable," he said, sighting one last time through the scope before the sun retreated behind the western curve of the mountain. He savored the moment—dug in shoulder to shoulder with a kindred operator, scoping the target before an incursion. It felt damn good playing SEAL again, although he could do without the wet chafing that came with jungle ops.

"See any showstoppers?"

"Nah," Dempsey said. "Let's head back."

They crept silently down the hill to where the rest of the strike team was waiting. Dempsey had selected a site for their base camp far from the local dirt road used by the cartels, but close to a small clearing that could serve as the EXFIL site. The Zetas had quadcopter drones that they used to patrol the area around the camp frequently, but irregularly, so it was imperative his team stayed concealed under the dense jungle canopy until after nightfall. In total, he was leading a strike team of eighteen: Ember SAD, Chunk plus four other SEALs, and a DEA augment team of eight. All of the DEA shooters were former military operators, led by a former Army Fifth Special Forces Group Master Sergeant. Dempsey had the talent and the firepower to take the narco camp; the only question that remained was, should he? Without positive confirmation that al-Mahajer and his men were still here, training with Hezbollah at this camp, should he assault now or should he wait?

Back in camp, he regrouped with his Ember team—including Adamo, whom he would have preferred to leave behind in Virginia.

"Get the DEA team leader up here," Dempsey said to Mendez, who nodded and moved off to the south in a combat shuffle.

"What do you think?" Smith asked.

"Easy day to take it," he said.

Adamo made a *pffit* sound—a sound he made frequently and one that was beginning to make Dempsey want to choke the fucking life out of him. "Eighteen assaulting forty-plus heavily armed fighters in a walled encampment with gun towers and surveillance. You call that easy?"

Dempsey gritted his teeth and glared. Adamo had just summed up the odds Dempsey's old unit had faced on practically every Tier One SEAL mission. That was the difference between an operator and an intelligence officer. That was the difference between getting shit done and waiting for shit to happen.

"Sup?" a deep voice said, shaking Dempsey out of his ruminations. He looked up at the DEA strike team leader, a former Green Beret Master Sergeant whom everybody called BT. BT was clad in blue jeans and a black Aerosmith T-shirt under his kit and was barely breaking a sweat despite the sweltering heat and humidity. Now this was a dude who got it.

"So how unusual is it to have forty tangos in this camp?" Dempsey said as the operator kneeled beside him.

BT grimaced and shook his head. "I know where you're going with this, man. You wanna know if numbers alone mean that something hot is going on? Does a population of forty-plus mean that the terrorist shit-heads you're hunting have to be there?" BT sighed. "Problem is there's a huge range. We do overflights constantly. I can tell you from experience that in this camp there's never fewer than twenty or so guys—what we call the organic guys. Think of them as the permanent staff, guys who live here. Anything above twenty is your surge population. I've seen this camp surge to over a hundred, especially when they have new product to ship. They do a lot of combat training here, too—some for the cartel and some contract stuff for whoever. When that's going on, the population can swell up to a hundred and fifty."

"How do the numbers now compare to those you saw a few days ago?"

BT pulled at his shaggy beard. "The camp surged a week or so ago, ten days, I guess. Probably close to eighty. Then the numbers fell, then surged again—twice in the last six days—back to about sixty to seventy."

"What's your gut instinct?" Dempsey pressed. "Do you think the guys we're after are out training in the jungle or have they moved on?"

"I just don't know, man. It could be that your guys have rotated out, which would explain the drop, or your guys could still be there and the drop could be because a couple dozen cartel guys left to do routine shit—check on storehouses, oversee production centers—hell, all kinds of things. Half the population could be your guys and the other half the organics."

"Or," Adamo interrupted, "our guys could be gone, or coming back tomorrow, or maybe they've never been here at all. The point is nobody knows."

"Yes, but uncertainty is not a mandate for inaction," Dempsey countered. "This is an opportunity to gain critical intel. By hitting the camp, we either get al-Mahajer, or we confirm that he's left. Either way, we know more than we do now."

"Why rush? Once we hit this camp, it's over. If they're gone, they're in the wind and they're never coming back," Adamo said. "But if we wait, we retain the advantage. Give it twenty-four hours. If they're out on a training excursion, they will come back. In the meantime, we give Baldwin time to analyze the intelligence and look for something definitive."

"I've been waiting for this motherfucker to show his face for a decade. If you think I'm gonna let him slip away again . . ." Dempsey rubbed his temples. He looked over at BT, who shrugged with a *your call, bro* expression on his face. Then, he looked at Smith.

"It's a gray fucking world," Smith said, "but I say we hit the camp. If we miss al-Mahajer, we can at least pull intel from the camp that gives us an understanding of what's been going down here. Was it training, or was it something else."

"What do you mean by something else?" Mendez asked. "We know it's training, right?"

"Yes, but what kind. Is this indoctrination training or operational training? What if these guys are getting ready for an op? If they're prepping an attack, that's something we need to know ASAP."

Dempsey nodded and looked at Grimes.

"I agree with Simon," she said.

"Seriously?" he said, his mouth hanging open.

"Look, maybe we get another Predator flight and search the area for a mass of tangos in the area around the camp—"

"Wouldn't tell you much," BT said. "There are clusters of shitheads popping up around here all the time."

"Maybe," Grimes said. "But I'm worried if we tip our hand—"

"Yeah, yeah. I heard it from Adamo," Dempsey said, cutting her off. In the Teams, they were expected to police groupthink and share their true thoughts and concerns at all times, which is exactly what Elizabeth was doing. Still, it irked him that she was taking Adamo's side. He looked at Mendez.

"I say light her up," Mendez said, then spat something nasty on the ground.

Three to two, Dempsey thought. *Not that this is decision by committee.* He glanced at Chunk.

The SEAL flashed Dempsey a toothy, tobacco-stained grin. "Never invite a frogman to a fight and send him home empty-handed. You know my answer."

Dempsey nodded, took a deep breath, and said, "We're going."

"That's a mistake," Adamo protested.

Smith put a hand on the CIA man's shoulder. "Decision's made," the Director of Operations said sternly. He turned to the DEA strike team leader. "Pull your guys in and let's brief this thing."

BT nodded and left to gather his team, while Adamo paced away in the other direction, shaking his head.

"You got a good group here, Dempsey," Chunk said and refreshed the wad of snuff in his lower lip. He wore the same infectious boyish grin he'd had back in Iraq.

"Yeah, except for the fucking new guy," he said, gesturing a thumb toward Adamo's back.

Chunk shrugged and spit a brown gob onto the floor of the jungle. "We've all been there."

Dempsey nodded in the direction of the narco camp. "You brought snipers?"

"Yeah, two."

"Can your guys hit the shooters in the towers from the ridgeline where we were earlier?"

The SEAL looked up, apparently doing some math in his head. Then he nodded. "Yeah, if the wind stays like this. But it won't be a quick turn on the second shot from that range, at least four or five seconds."

"That works," Dempsey said. Besides, once the machine gunner in the first tower had his head split open like a watermelon with a sledgehammer, there was a pretty good chance that the second gunner would bolt. Snipers seemed to have that effect on people. "Okay," Dempsey said. "SEAL snipers kick off the show."

Chunk nodded, and then said, "Unless, of course, you want to scream in there alone in the back of a pickup truck like that Rambo shit you pulled at Al Qa'im?"

Dempsey laughed. "I only had one of those in me."

"Good," the SEAL officer said. "Otherwise, I might develop a heart condition."

"Who's going to operate the Raven?" Dempsey asked.

Chunk pointed at one of the two SEALs approaching from the tree line to the south. "Special Operator First Class Hughes," he said. "Hey, Gyro—bring your kit and join us, will you?"

Dempsey turned to Smith. "Get everyone kitted up and teamed like we discussed," he said. "We're gonna do a quick UAV recon and then we'll brief in twenty."

Smith gave him a thumbs-up.

The SEAL called Gyro double-timed it over to them, weighted down by an unusually large rucksack. The three of them then moved back up the hill to the north, through the thick jungle, and then to the ridgeline, where they belly-crawled to the edge, making sure to stay under heavy brush.

A loud, punctuated baritone growl erupted from a nearby tree. A second call answered in deep, throaty barks. Gyro reflexively trained his weapon on the trees. "What the fuck is that?"

"Howler monkeys," Dempsey said, laughing.

Gyro lowered his rifle. "They're fucking loud."

"I think that one likes you, bro," Chunk said. "Maybe after the op, you can get you some monkey lovin'."

"Apparently, you've never met my girl in Norfolk," Gyro said, slipping off his pack. "Believe me, I get plenty of monkey lovin' at home."

Dempsey and Chunk busted up laughing while Gyro rolled onto his back and pulled out a laptop. He set the laptop on his stomach, then pulled out a long green airfoil, followed by a shorter fuselage. He snapped them together and then snapped a small green rectangle into the engine mount.

"What's that?" Dempsey asked.

"New battery—insanely small," Gyro said. "We used to get an hour or so of flight time. This new battery gives us nearly three hours."

"Way better lens on the new camera, too," Chunk added. "Better night vision, better resolution. This ain't like the RQ-11 we had before."

"Quieter, too." After a quick double check of the little drone, Gyro said, "Go?"

Dempsey nodded, and the SEAL brought up a software program on his laptop. He rotated the tiny UAV back and forth, checking the camera. To an outsider, the thing probably looked more like a kid's toy than an advanced tool with a quarter-million-dollar price tag. Gyro handed it to Chunk, who lifted it up over his head and above the brush. Gyro tapped on his laptop and the propeller started to spin. The engine was so quiet, Dempsey could actually hear the sound of the little propeller pulling air. Gyro gave a nod and Chunk tossed the tiny plane down over the ledge. It promptly fell, gained the speed it needed, and then angled sharply up to begin the approach toward the camp just over a mile away. It disappeared almost instantly into the black night, invisible even on the NVGs that Dempsey had tipped down from his helmet to watch the launch. With the drone out of sight, he flipped them back up and crowded in for a view of Gyro's laptop screen instead.

They watched the camp grow as the UAV closed range—the image streaming in real time. Gyro piloted the UAV with the mouse pad while tapping to capture still images, which he dragged into a folder labeled RIGHT FUCKING NOW at the bottom of the screen. The narco camp was well lit, affording them a bird's-eye view with remarkable clarity.

The UAV circled to the west, outside of the camp perimeter, and Dempsey could see that the southeast tower had one man, sitting on a stool and reading a magazine beside the .50-caliber machine gun. The other tower had two men—one sitting on a stool and the other cross-legged on the floor, drinking from a bottle; both were laughing. From the feed, it felt as if the drone were practically inside the gun tower. Dempsey glanced nervously down the hill.

"I'm like eight hundred feet above them and nearly half a mile away," Gyro said. "They can't hear me and they sure as shit can't see me. Don't worry—I'm quieter than a gnat at this range."

The drone circled around the west wall of the camp, where there was little activity. Then it made a pass over the camp from west to east. The dirty canvas tent was unlit, and the training area at the back of the camp stood deserted. As the UAV banked right, the two long buildings came into view. Several dozen men, all with rifles slung over their backs, were hanging out by the side of the barracks. Dempsey could make out the glow of cigarettes and through the windows could even see bottles of liquor on the table. The relaxed mood in the compound was palpable; these guys weren't even contemplating the possibility of trouble.

"Can you show me the rear of the house?"

Instead of banking the UAV, Gyro tapped the function keys on the laptop, and the image switched to a dedicated side-view camera. The rear of the house was open and expansive with an elevated oval balcony that looked out across the camp. A dozen or so men were seated at tables having dinner. These were the senior guys. The dudes smoking and joking down by the barracks were the grunts.

"No heavy weapons other than the towers," Chunk said.

"Yeah, but the DEA guys said to expect RPGs," Dempsey replied.

"Guys on the balcony don't even have rifles, except for that table by the corner."

"Bodyguards, maybe," Dempsey said. "The house probably serves as the Head Shed for these assholes."

"Heavy-drinking group," Chunk said with a smile. "Wait a couple of hours and we could tiptoe in and out."

Dempsey laughed.

"Got what you need?" Gyro asked.

"Yeah," Dempsey said, "but let's give it one more pass."

"Whadaya think about leaving the Raven up?" Chunk asked. "We can park Gyro with my snipers. One less gun but it might be worth it to have eyes—especially if you anticipate they got a cavalry thirty clicks out."

Dempsey raised an eyebrow. Not a bad idea. It would be nice to have the voice of God in their ears for this op. They had more than enough shooters since there were only forty guys, half of which were probably drunk. "Good idea," he said, and then turned to Gyro. "You cool?"

The SEAL shrugged. "I guess," he said. "Hate to miss the fight, though."

"Then you shouldn't have volunteered for the drone class," Chunk said, and slapped his teammate on the shoulder.

"It's cool," Gyro said. "I'll cruise up the road, make one more pass, and then recover for a battery change just ahead of your launch."

"We'll go in thirty minutes," Dempsey said.

"Check," Gyro said, but he was back focused on the video game that was the UAV.

Chunk and Dempsey slid back down the hill toward the base camp. A quick brief and then it was go time.

CHAPTER 22

They circled around him in the rapidly darkening jungle. Dempsey mentally divided the group into two strike teams—one led by him and the other by Chunk, with one SEAL and four DEA strikers on each. For his team he reluctantly took Adamo, but also Mendez, who was a former MARSOC Marine. He couldn't dump Adamo on poor Chunk. He put Smith with the SEAL officer and, with a twinge of guilt, Grimes. He felt obligated to watch after her—she was Spaz's sister after all—but having Adamo forced it this way. Besides, from what he'd seen over the past few months, Grimes could take care of herself.

With all the shooters gathered, he pitched his plan. The two assault teams would move into position, one near the southwest corner and one near the southeast corner. They would stay concealed under jungle cover until the SEAL snipers kicked off the assault by taking out the tower shooters. Then, each team would breach the perimeter wall with breacher charges and move into the compound. The rest was just standard capture/kill mission 101. Once they secured the camp, they'd hold the captured crows in the front courtyard and then toss the house and barracks for intel. The DEA team would defend the compound with the snipers on fire support if an enemy QRF responded. EXFIL would be by air with pickup inside the compound. The primary target was al-Mahajer, but Dempsey planned on taking any ISIS or Hezbollah assholes who survived the assault with them.

"Does it help your operation to haul in cartel guys?" Dempsey asked BT.

"Nah," BT said. "What would help is if this operation looks like it *isn't* a DEA raid. In fact, if the Zetas come away believing that CIA or some black ops team hit them because of their work with Hezbollah, maybe they'll stop this terrorist training bullshit once and for all."

"Amen to that," Dempsey said with a nod. Then to the group he said, "All right, people, final checks and it's go time."

Five minutes later, he was leading his team silently through the NVG-lit jungle. He tried to relax, but that was impossible leading a mixed team with shooters who'd not worked together before. He knew the SEALs—whom he had positioned right-side rear of his V-shaped eight-man squad—were solid. He'd operated with Mendez before, so no worries there. That left the four DEA guys, who BT assured him were solid, and Adamo. He'd positioned the CIA man close on his left in case he needed to be *managed*. Dempsey had expected foot snaps and panting during the jungle trek, but so far, Adamo had been pretty damn quiet.

They weaved methodically through the tangled vines, exposed roots, and heavy foliage, a task that would have been impossible without night vision. The howler monkeys—who had been active at dusk—had settled down, but the jungle had since become a nocturnal circus. The buzz of insects and cacophony of a thousand tree frogs reverberated all around them. The humid, warm air, coupled with perspiration, made Dempsey's clothes cling to his skin. He inhaled the Guatemalan jungle and could almost taste the miasma of decaying foliage, the musk of earth, and a hint of sweetness from tropical flora.

The team mirrored Dempsey's lead, moving in combat crouches and scanning over their rifles through holographic sights as they advanced. The warning BT had given him earlier that day played in his head: *The drug cartels are investing serious cash money in high-tech gear. They've got night vision and drones, so don't count on the darkness alone for providing adequate cover.* Dempsey worked a path through the jungle accordingly, weaving to maximize foliage cover both overhead and in front.

As they approached the target, the bright lights inside the camp told him that the only night vision counterdetection threat they could possibly face was from roaming patrols outside the walls. With so much light inside the perimeter, anyone on greens would go blind—even the shooters in the towers. Twenty feet from the camp, he halted their advance and surveyed the layout. The camp vaguely resembled a medieval castle, with an impressive twenty-foot-tall cinder-block wall and two gunner towers. The cartel had clear-cut and burned a swath of jungle ten feet wide around the outside of the wall. Although not intended to be a moat, the gap had become a nasty bog with standing water where daily rain and runoff pooled at the base of the wall. So far, Dempsey had yet to encounter a roving patrol. Considering the density of the jungle and sloppy nature of the perimeter, now he understood why.

He slowly and silently advanced his team the final few yards into position at the edge of the forest line. Once they were fanned out and set, he keyed his mike and spoke softly into the small boom by the corner of his mouth. "Doobie Two—One—Position?" he said, trying not to chuckle at the call sign Chunk had suggested.

"One—Two is nearly in position. Stand by."

Chunk was cool and collected, just another day at the office.

"Eagles?" he whispered, calling the two SEAL snipers up on the ridgeline.

"Eagle One—tango is lit."

"Eagle Two is no-joy."

Dempsey sighed.

"Wait . . . I have him. Must've had to take a leak. Second tango lit."

"In the tower, Eagle Two?"

"Check."

"Roger," Dempsey said. "Doobie Two, call position and ready."

Two clicks in his headset told him Chunk would let him know when his team was in position.

Dempsey began the familiar kata of checking over his gear, especially his ammo pouches. He felt over his Sig Sauer 556 rifle and looked through the holographic sight to be sure the red hologram target floated out in space. He clicked off his PEQ-4—they would come off NVGs on the assault because of the lights inside the compound, so the infrared laser designator would be useless. Last, he checked that his pistol was secure in the drop holster on his right thigh.

A crackle in his ear and then: "Doobie Two is set."

Dempsey took a deep breath and then scanned the brush line around him. No movement, no bodies. Even Adamo was invisible.

"On the first shot, breachers to the wall for a quick entry."

A double-click.

"Eagles—Go."

Before the single-syllable command was two seconds out of his mouth, Dempsey heard the familiar thud of a long-range, high-powered sniper round. Then he heard the clatter of man and gear hitting the tower deck. The assigned SEAL breacher sprinted to the wall and pressed a brick of C4 into a crevice in the cement. A heartbeat later, he was trailing wire behind him as he dashed back across the brush line.

Dempsey flipped his NVGs up in preparation for what came next.

A baritone *whump* echoed in the night as the Team Two breacher charge detonated on the other side of the camp. A half second later his team's breacher detonated twenty feet away, and he felt the concussive shock wave in his chest. Then he was up and moving through the gaping, smoke-filled hole in the cinder-block wall. Without turning to see, he perceived the flurry of movement behind him as his team followed him into the compound. On the other side, he blinked away the cement dust and smoke, reflexively holding his breath until he exited the cloud of acrid fumes and particulate. He turned left, clearing down the wall, confident that Mendez was clearing right in mirror-image perfection.

With his rear quarter cleared, Dempsey pressed left. Finding no targets, he angled right and advanced toward the heart of the camp. Billowing smoke, backlit by the camp's blazing halogen lights, obstructed his view. Suddenly, a figure emerged from the haze, spraying bullets wildly with a compact submachine gun. Dempsey hit him with a single shot through the temple. The defender's arms went limp, but the legs kept pumping for two strides until the body pitched forward face-first into the dirt.

The staccato pops from his team's M4s and Sig Sauer 556s echoed steady and measured, but soon, erratic bursts of enemy AK-47 fire joined the ruckus.

As Dempsey advanced on the center of the courtyard, he heard BT's voice in his earpiece: "There's a dude climbing up tower one."

He tensed, hoping one of the SEAL snipers made the shot before the .50 cal lit up and ripped his team to shreds. The answer came a second later over his headset.

"Got him," said Eagle One's calm voice, a split second after his sniper round found its mark.

The plan called for one of the DEA strikers on each team to advance to the base of their respective tower and take control. Win control of the .50s, and they won control of the camp.

It wouldn't be long now.

Suddenly he saw a wave of men, machine guns blazing, pouring out of the gap between the mansion and the barracks like hornets from a rattled hive. Within seconds, the defenders were saturating his team with disorganized fully automatic fire. His team returned fire, with deadly and systematic accuracy, and bodies began to fall. Dempsey sighted and fired, sighted and fired, dropping two enemy fighters in as many seconds.

"RPG!" someone shouted.

Dempsey took a knee and made himself small, searching for the rocket. It streaked past him and exploded against the wall behind him wide right. Concrete fragments sprayed everywhere, but the impact point was far enough away that he escaped unscathed.

Time to win control of those .50s.

"Eagle One, tower status?" he asked.

"Both towers are clear," came the report.

"Eight and Sixteen, take the towers," he ordered.

Dempsey sensed movement to his left and turned on his heel, looking over his rifle. A man wearing a silk shirt and sporting a handlebar mustache was waving a long-barreled silver pistol over his head and barking orders in Spanish at two younger men with rifles. Dempsey sighted in, but before he could squeeze the trigger the man's head evaporated in a puff of red as one of the SEAL sniper rounds did its work. Dempsey pressed on, sighting the next asshole in line behind the teetering headless corpse. He took the shot, dropping the first guy as the other tossed his weapon and ran for cover back into the barracks.

"One is going to take the barracks," Dempsey said in his mike. "Still have shooters in the main house."

"Ten shooters down over here," Chunk said in his ear, followed by back-to-back gunshots. "Two will take the main house."

Dempsey scanned the courtyard—another twelve or fifteen KIA on their side, plus three in the towers. They had already cut the opposition force by more than half. The cadence of gunfire was becoming more sporadic. These were cartel shooters they were facing, not jihadi martyrs. No one in this crew was fighting for virgins in the afterlife. Drugs and cash were not the same motivators as faith.

"One, Eight in control of tower one."

"Roger. Light up the assholes on the balcony."

One burst from the .50-caliber machine gun in tower one and the remaining cartel fighters began throwing down their weapons and surrendering. Then Dempsey heard the *pop pop* of a pistol, followed immediately by the sound of an M4 in response. After that, all was quiet. They'd taken the compound without incident or injury on their side. Dempsey scanned for any holdout threats, while his strike team members went to work pressing bad guys' faces into the dirt and flex-tying hands behind backs.

Chunk met him in the middle of the courtyard, where DEA strikers were cuffing the last of the cartel fighters. "Anything?"

"No terrorists in this group," Dempsey said, his head pounding. Had they missed them, or was al-Mahajer out in the jungle with his men somewhere? He motioned the DEA strike team leader over. "Can you figure out who's in charge?"

"We know most of these assholes," BT said. "The guy in charge of the compound is that headless motherfucker in the silk shirt over by the stairs."

"Shit. Then find me someone else to talk to."

"Sure thing. Just so you know, they have a briefing room in the main house."

Dempsey nodded, grinding his teeth with what felt like a lifetime's worth of frustration. "Bring them inside the house. We'll toss the briefing room and other buildings and see what we find."

"Hey, JD." It was Smith in his headset.

"Go," he said into his mike.

"You need to see this shit. I'm in the barracks building—all the way in the back."

Dempsey looked at BT, who gave him a thumbs-up. He turned to Chunk. "Toss the briefing room and the rest of the house. Find me something that explains what the hell is going on here."

"Check," the SEAL said.

Moments later, Dempsey walked through the wooden door at the front of the first long building. The room was bunk-style beds on either side, all unmade with clothes scattered on top. Liquor bottles stood on windowsills and trash littered the floor. The room stank of body odor and cigarette smoke.

"Back here," Smith called.

Dempsey moved quickly through the dump of a room. A narrow door at the back led to the second building, where everything was completely different. Each bed was meticulously made. No liquor bottles, no cigarettes, no trash. Smith stood next to a small writing desk, leafing through a notebook.

"Here," Smith said, handing over the book. "Take a look at this."

Dempsey flipped through the handwritten pages, which were covered in Arabic scrawl. He exhaled slowly through his nose.

"And there's this," Smith said, gesturing at the foot of the bed. "Prayer rug."

Dempsey scanned the room, noting similar prayer rugs rolled up neatly at the foot of each bed. "Think they're coming back?"

Smith shook his head. "I don't think so. No clothes, no bags, no personal items. Nothing but rugs, copies of the Quran, and this notebook."

"So why leave this stuff?"

Smith looked at him and waited, as if he expected him to figure it out.

And then he did. "If they don't intend to survive wherever they're going . . ."

Smith nodded. "We just missed them."

Dempsey's temples began to throb. "How far behind are we?"

"No idea. Maybe hours. Maybe a day."

"Let's go toss the house and interrogate the cartel guys. I don't care how many skulls I have to crack; someone is going to tell me where they fucking went."

Dempsey slipped the notebook into his pocket and then marched out of the barracks straight into the main house. In the foyer, Adamo was standing over two men, both kneeling with their hands behind their backs in flex-cuffs. He was speaking to them calmly in Spanish. Chunk saw him coming and hustled over to caucus.

"I think we got something, bro," the SEAL said. "Follow me."

Chunk took the steps to the second floor of the house two at a time and Dempsey kept pace, eager for good news. Grimes was already in the large modern briefing room, not so different from the Ember TOC under the hangar. She was poring over what looked like a set of schematic prints. She looked up, excited.

"Check this out." She stepped aside as Dempsey bent over the maps and drawings.

"What am I looking at?"

"Tunnels," she said. "These are schematics of the tunnels that the cartel is building and using to move drugs, weapons, and illegals who pay for entry into the United States from Mexico. There are several tunnel designs outlined here."

He suddenly felt nauseated. "Oh God . . ."

"What?" she said, grabbing his hand. "Are you all right? You look a little green, JD."

"Bawwaba šamāliyy," he mumbled. "The Northern Gate is not a tunnel into Israel."

Her eyes widened. "It's a tunnel into the US," she said.

"Al-Mahajer is going to hit us," he said, nodding slowly.

"Oh God," she echoed.

"Where are these tunnels?" Dempsey asked.

"The maps are unmarked," she said. "They could be anywhere. There are dozens of known tunnels—plus God knows how many still yet to be discovered."

"Then how do we know which one they're taking?"

"I don't know. Maybe Baldwin and the boys could have a look at these schematics and—"

"No time," Dempsey said, cutting her off. "These cartel guys have set check-ins—both radio and telephone. They also use social media to convey information with code words. If al-Mahajer is still with the cartel and doesn't know we hit this compound, there's a good chance he will any minute. We need to know which tunnel he's using ASAP."

"How?" she said.

Hot rage took control. Dempsey spun on his heel and headed out the door, pulling his Sig P226 from his drop holster on his thigh.

"What are you going to do?" she asked, chasing after him with Smith in tow.

He ignored her, descended the stairs, and strode quickly over to where BT and Adamo were waiting with two senior cartel leaders.

"What have they told you?" Dempsey said.

Adamo sighed. "Nothing I'm afraid."

Dempsey looked down at the two assholes on their knees. The older man on the right squinted up at Dempsey with a callous smirk plastered across his chubby face. "Ask him when al-Mahajer left," Dempsey said, clutching his pistol at his side.

Adamo said something to the man in Spanish. The man said something back and laughed.

"He says he doesn't remember."

Dempsey raised his Sig and fired a round through the man's knee. The man screamed in pain and surprise and collapsed onto his left side.

"What the fuck are you doing?" Adamo shouted. "Are you insane?"

Dempsey stared into the eyes of the man writhing on the floor. He saw pain, but he also saw terror.

"Ask him if he remembers now," Dempsey said, but Adamo was silent.

Dempsey shifted his gaze to BT. "Ask him."

BT nodded and spoke to the man in Spanish. The man answered, his voice quivering. "He says the Muslims left this morning at nine a.m."

"Ask him which tunnel they're using."

BT spoke again in clipped Spanish. The cartel man began to cry and plead in Spanish. "He says he can't tell us. If he does he's a dead man. Cartel del Norte will torture him and murder his family."

Dempsey looked up at heaven and exhaled. "This is the part of the job I hate," he said, to everyone and no one. Then, he looked down at the bleeding, whimpering drug trafficker, and with a steady hand, pressed the muzzle of his pistol into the center of the man's forehead. "If you won't talk, maybe your friend over there will. Lord, forgive me, but I have no choice—"

"They will cross in Mexicali," the cartel man blurted in fluent English, and began to sob.

"When?"

"Tomorrow."

"What time?"

"I don't know."

Dempsey pressed the muzzle harder into the man's forehead.

"I swear it. The crossing logistics are always decided locally."

Dempsey withdrew the pistol and slipped it back into his holster. Then he turned to Smith. "If you were al-Mahajer and you got word about this raid, what would you do?"

"I would advance the timeline," the Ember Ops O said.

"So would I," Dempsey said with a grave nod. "Call the helicopters for EXFIL. We're leaving, right fucking now."

CHAPTER 23

Cartel del Norte Safehouse
Mexicali, Mexico
October 28, 2130 Local Time

The bedroom door flew open and smashed against the wall, jolting Rostami awake from the first decent sleep he'd had in two weeks.

"Tell your crazy friend to gather his men and equipment," Arturo Garcia said. "We leave in ten minutes."

Rostami glanced at his wristwatch. "What are you talking about? It's not time."

"We have been compromised. There's been an attack on our training camp, and there are indicators that the egress address in Calexico is under surveillance. We're not crossing," the Cartel del Norte man said.

"What kind of indicators? How do you know this?"

"No time for questions," Garcia snapped. "We're not safe here. You have nine minutes, or I leave without you."

A surge of adrenaline vaporized Rostami's drowsiness. He swung his legs out of bed and quickly dressed. Less than a minute later, rucksack on his shoulder, he woke al-Mahajer and told him exactly what Garcia had said.

Al-Mahajer ran his fingers through his hair and let out a weary groan. "I am the one who will decide when and where we go, not the cartel."

Rostami laughed.

A terrible scowl appeared on al-Mahajer's face.

"You think you're in command here? You think the cartel cares about you and your mission? The only thing they care about is money, money that Hezbollah pays to lease their training camps. Best-case scenario, Garcia tolerates us as an inconvenience. Worst-case scenario, he decides we're a liability and he abandons us here, where we can't speak the language, have no support network, and no place to hide. How long do you think it will be before the Mexican authorities find us? How long until we are handed over to the Americans? Don't be a fool, my brother. We have no choice but to do as Garcia says."

"Where is he taking us?" al-Mahajer asked, rolling out of his cot.

"I don't know," Rostami said, "but if I had to guess, Agua Prieta."

Al-Mahajer sniffed. "The backup location?"

Rostami nodded.

The ISIS lieutenant was silent for a moment and then said, "Find out if this is where they are taking us and if they will still support our crossing into America."

"And if the answer is no?"

Al-Mahajer smirked. "Then as a fellow true believer, as the Persian who pledged himself to help me fulfill my destiny, it is your responsibility to negotiate a new plan."

CHAPTER 24

Ember Corporation Boeing 787-9
520 Nautical Miles South of Mexicali, Mexico
October 29, 0125 Local Time

Dempsey stared at the hand-sketched, but remarkably detailed, drawings of the tunnel system. In the schematic, the tunnels formed a complex on the Mexico side of the border, with multiple tunnels originating close together and a third farther away. BT had spent time on the secure line with Baldwin, poring over what they knew about the tunnel systems, where the known tunnels were, and where they suspected new tunnels might now be under construction. Baldwin had used this information—and considerable math and computer time—to confirm that the schematic did indeed suggest the tunnels in Mexicali, with two in Santa Isabel and Mexicali converging and merging together. BT called these feeder tunnels, designed to route product and human cargo to a consolidation site prior to transport across the border. In this case, they converged at a house, and then a single tunnel made a relatively straight shot under the US-Mexico border into California, west of Calexico. Dempsey had no idea how Baldwin and his boys had done it, but they calculated there was a greater than 78 percent chance the tunnels in the schematic ended in a private home at an address on Anza Road.

"What about the other schematic?" Adamo had asked.

"Impossible to pinpoint without more data," had been Baldwin's answer. They'd known to look in Mexicali from Dempsey's violent interrogation. But to find the other site, without any frame of reference, would take time, if it was even possible.

So to Mexicali they were headed.

Dempsey hated not knowing where the other tunnel system was. How did they know that the drug smuggler had told them the truth? It would be far better to cover both tunnels and hit the one with the highest likelihood—but still post assets at the exits to the others.

The current plan was to land at Marine Corps Base El Centro in California and then cross the border in DEA Blackhawks. He would have preferred to land on the Mexico side, but a Boeing 787-9 landing at Mexicali was sure to draw unwanted attention, and now Dempsey found himself wishing, ironically, that they were back in the Falcon for this mission. So far, they had not been able to utilize the wealth of additional gear, including a Humvee, two Suburban SUVs, and several ATVs, that were kept stored in the aft cargo hold, ready to roll into action. On the flip side, it was nice to utilize the 787's TOC with real-time information flow, instead of having data relayed from Ember back in Virginia.

He looked up from the maps and fixed his gaze on Adamo, who sat bent at the waist, his face red, whispering conspiratorially to Smith, who was listening patiently and nodding. It didn't take a genius to figure out what they were talking about. Special Activities was Dempsey's unit, and Adamo would either have to adapt or ship the hell out. He hoped Smith was telling him as much.

He looked back at the schematics. Something was bothering him, but he couldn't quite articulate it. It wasn't the assault plan. The raid was a textbook capture/kill with air support from the two Blackhawks.

Dempsey's team would hit the house in Mexicali and either take al-Mahajer down or flush him into the main tunnel. A DEA task force was already standing by in California, monitoring the exit house in case Ember was too late and the crossing happened before the raid.

But if the crossing had already happened, or if al-Mahajer was in the wind . . . they were screwed.

"Hope they're there," a familiar baritone said.

Dempsey looked up at BT. "Me, too," he said. "I'm just worried they heard about the raid on the camp and pushed the timeline."

"If they go at all." BT dropped into the leather seat beside Dempsey.

"If they're in Mexicali, they'll go," Dempsey said. "They have to because a border crossing like this requires support operations on the other side—which means assets and logistics that were already in motion."

Dempsey looked up again as Adamo took a seat beside the DEA strike leader.

The CIA man shook his head. "I disagree. It's better to slip the timeline than to get caught."

"What you need to understand is that Hezbollah and ISIS use a fractured, independent cell structure," Dempsey said. "They employ old-school techniques like dead drops and face-to-face information exchanges that are immune to cybersurveillance. Individual cells will do everything possible to avoid communications that might leak information to our cyberwarfare community. Once certain elements are in play, there's no easy way to stop the machine."

"So what's your point?"

"My point is that even if they want to advance the timeline or change the location, they might not be able to do so because of the constraints imposed by their communication protocols."

"Granted, but let's not forget who we're dealing with. Al-Mahajer is a tactician. You said it yourself; this guy has successfully avoided capture for a decade. Given recent events, I just don't see al-Mahajer crossing in Mexicali," Adamo said.

Dempsey knitted his brow, confused. "What 'recent events' are you talking about?"

"DEA and the Mexican narcotics task force raided a house in Calexico with a tunnel linked to Mexicali a month ago."

Dempsey looked over at BT. "Is that true?"

"Yes," BT said. "But it was a different system than the one on the drawing. I confirmed that. This is how the game works. We close a hole; they open two more. It's like playing fucking whack-a-mole."

"Whack-a-mole or not," Adamo said, pushing his eyeglasses up on his nose, "these guys aren't morons. If there's heat on Mexicali, then I guarantee they'll look at alternate crossings. They must have a plan B, right?"

BT shrugged. "These guys always have a plan B."

A wave of dread washed over Dempsey. "Shane," Dempsey hollered. "C'mere, bro. We might have a problem."

Smith stood and walked over to them. "What's up?" he asked, his eyes scanning the maps Dempsey had spread out.

"Adamo thinks we're headed to the wrong tunnel." In the corner of his eye, he saw the spook bristle, before he added, "And I'm inclined to agree with him."

"Okay," Smith said. "But the Zeta you shot in the knee said they were headed for Mexicali."

"Maybe they were, maybe they weren't, but according to Adamo they'll think Mexicali is too hot to risk a crossing right now." He looked at BT. "What's DEA's opinion?"

"Look, man, I don't know the MO for the guys you're chasing, but I know the cartel. And if they sense any heat—any heat at all—they'll zigzag. If I had to guess, the cartel will advise your guys to go black, wait it out, and try again when the heat dies down in another two or three weeks."

"Yeah, they could do that, but they risk us unraveling the rest of the plan. Our targets operate differently than the cartels because terrorists and drug dealers have different endgames. The Zetas are playing the long game. Their objective is sustainable, covert drug trafficking. They can afford to wait, because the alternative, getting caught and losing a shipment and a tunnel, is just too damn expensive. For a terrorist, the short game is the endgame. If al-Mahajer is infiltrating the United States to execute a terror operation, then he has a window of opportunity that must be exploited or he fails. Think about Brussels. ISIS moved that attack forward because Salah Abdeslam had been caught. They hit Brussels instead of executing their original objective, which was to hit Paris again."

Dempsey looked up and saw that Grimes and Mendez had joined the group.

"Why did they do that? Why didn't they wait a few months, regroup, reset, and try for Paris again?" Dempsey said, pressing the group to think it through.

No one nibbled.

"Because they'd activated a sleeper agent who, once in play, couldn't be turned off. We've seen this before. We saw it in Germany when we stopped that shit two months ago. We've seen it in the US. They limit communication because it makes their activities impossible to track, but the downside of this approach is limited command and control."

"But it's still better to live to fight another day," BT said.

"Not for these assholes," Dempsey said. "They plan to martyr themselves no matter what. To them it is stabbing the Great Satan in the heart and not missing the opportunity. The most important variable for them is how much collateral damage they cause, not their personal safety."

"Dempsey's right," Smith said. "So if I was al-Mahajer, I'd push the timeline *and* change the crossing site."

"Awesome deduction," Grimes said, "but we have no idea where else to look. We don't know the alternate location."

"I might," Adamo said.

Everyone turned to look at the CIA agent. Adamo stared back only at Dempsey.

"Where?" Dempsey asked.

Adamo grabbed a map and the two schematics. He pushed the one for Mexicali away and pulled the other one closer.

"Do you see the dashed line around this map—a fence of some sort—beside a winding road?"

"And how would you possibly know that?" Grimes asked.

"I spent the last hour online poring through maps of industrial compounds in Mexico, trying to match the layout—the large building north of two long buildings with another square building east. It needed to be on a winding road and surrounded by a fence."

"Aren't Baldwin and his geniuses looking at all of this?" Grimes asked skeptically.

"Yes," Adamo said and clenched his jaw. "But a computer can't fill in gaps from a hand-drawn schematic—assume what is missing and what is maybe less detailed—the way a human can."

"Go on, Simon," Dempsey said.

"So, I narrowed it down to about a half-dozen, but only two are along the border. Of those two, only one has adequate proximity to an airport that would allow them to get to it within the presumed timeline."

Adamo tapped his index finger on the map, just south of the border with Arizona.

"Agua Prieta," Grimes said.

Adamo nodded. "If they cross from Agua Prieta they'll enter the US here, in this little patch of nothing outside Douglas, Arizona."

Smith started tapping on a laptop he had plugged into the pop-up panel in front of him. He clicked his wireless mouse, and the center screen in the bank of large flat-screens on the cabin wall flickered to life. A beat later, the middle screen flickered and Ian Baldwin's face filled the screen.

"Good morning, Shane," he said in clipped tones. "Problems?"

Jesus, does that man ever sleep? Dempsey wondered. *From looking at him, you'd think it's noon.*

"Always," Smith said with a sigh. "Ian, how long would it take to get a drone over Agua Prieta, Mexico? It's located—"

"Just across the border from Douglas, Arizona. I know," Baldwin interjected. "I was just about to call Adamo back. Let him know we ran Agua Prieta through our algorithm. It looks like about a sixty-seven percent chance this is the second location based on the schematic. We may be able to task a drone. I suppose the better question is, how much time do I have?"

"Minutes," Dempsey chimed in.

"That's what I figured."

"You're in a brief with the whole team, by the way," Dempsey said.

"I can see you, John," Baldwin said, with a little smile. "What are we looking for?"

"Activity—vehicles coming and going, armed men moving about, anything that looks suspicious. The target location appears to be an industrial complex west of Agua Prieta. Sorry we can't give you anything more specific, but that's all we know."

"Well," Baldwin said, pulling at his beardless chin, "I can't possibly get any sort of UAV over the site that quickly. But"—he raised a finger and his eyebrows—"I can see what satellite assets may be over the area with our friends at NSA and the boys up in Fort Belvoir. I can also *borrow* time on Homeland's border camera systems. Give me ten minutes."

"Ten minutes," Smith said.

Baldwin leaned in and the screen froze, a close-up of his right nostril the last image before he broke the connection.

"I need to talk to the pilots," Dempsey said.

"Are you sure? We should wait for Ian to let us know what he sees before we divert, don't you think?" Grimes asked.

Adamo leaned in. "She may be right, Dempsey. This is only conjecture."

"Based on the information available to us, is this your best educated guess for an alternate crossing location?" he asked.

Adamo hesitated a split second, then, pushing his glasses up on his nose, said, "Yes."

"Then that's where we're going," Dempsey said, setting his jaw.

"We'll get a data dump on the area and see what we can build on top of that tunnel map," Smith said. Two of the other flat-screens now held Google Maps images of an industrial complex in Agua Prieta situated along a remote stretch of desert outside of Douglas.

Dempsey left the TOC and passed through a short hall with offices on either side. This opened into a sizable galley and then the cockpit. The cockpit door was open, the sport shirt–clad copilot leaning his back against it while blowing on a cup of coffee. The former Air Force tanker pilot looked up and smiled, but shook his head.

"A personal visit? Never a good sign. What's up, Mr. Dempsey?"

"Need to evaluate a change of plans," Dempsey said. He leaned in and nodded at the gray-haired, athletically built pilot sitting at the controls in the left seat. "Hey, Steve. Can we talk?"

"What's up, John?"

Dempsey knew that Jarvis had filched the decorated aviator from the CIA after a full career flying for the Navy and then Delta Airlines. Apparently, the former Hornet pilot wanted back in the game in whatever capacity he could get.

"What would our ETA be if we diverted from El Centro to Douglas, Arizona?"

The pilot began tapping data into the navigation console at the top of the panel between the two pilot seats.

"Where would we land?" the captain asked. "There's nothing on either side of the border with enough runway . . . oh, wait a minute." The pilot saw something and then pulled a chart out of a black case behind his seat. "There is a field with a twelve-thousand-foot runway about fifty-six miles north and west of the border. It's a joint civilian-military field that's run by the city of Sierra Vista and Fort Huachuca—an Army base that adjoins the field."

"Why have I heard of them?" Dempsey asked, searching his memory.

"It's the home for the Army Intelligence Center and NETCOM. Plenty of runway there, and they can probably give us a secure place on the military side of the field if you're willing to read them into your op."

"I can read them in enough to get us in. How much extra time?"

"From here, shit, almost nothing. We're already burning the paint off this pig to get you on the deck as soon as possible. A turn now adds maybe ten minutes, but the longer you wait, the more time you add."

The copilot had already slipped back into his seat and was punching things into his navigation computer.

"Make the correction," Dempsey said. He felt more and more certain with each passing second this was the right call. He was not letting that slippery sonuvabitch al-Mahajer slip away again. "We'll work on clearances and the rest and have it to you right away."

"Roger that."

Dempsey turned around, and as he walked aft he could feel the Boeing banking as the pilot made a correction to the right. In the TOC, Baldwin was back up on the screen nodding, and Mendez and Grimes were crowded around the handwritten maps, which were now reproduced on a monitor with red lines overlaying a size-corrected satellite image. Smith and Adamo sat side by side in front of Smith's computer discussing something, and in the back of the room four of the eight DEA shooters now stood looking around in awe and sipping coffee. Chunk came in with his four SEALs in tow.

"What's all this, bro?" Chunk asked, gesturing to the beehive of activity. "Threw a party and forgot to invite us?"

Dempsey held up a finger. Baldwin leaned back in his chair on the center screen, talking to someone out of view.

"So?" Dempsey asked Smith.

"The last satellite pass is two and a half hours old and not the best angle, but there's definitely vehicle activity in the complex, which based on historical imagery is abnormal for that time of night."

Dempsey felt a twinge of validation at the news. He gave a curt nod to Adamo, who returned the nod. "Any useful camera feeds from the Homeland or Border Patrol?"

"Nothing yet, but they're working on it. The cameras are pretty widely spaced and—no surprise—the facility falls right in between two of them. Probably not much help. Baldwin says he may have new satellite imagery in twenty minutes—which means he will; it's Baldwin after all." Smith crossed his arms and looked at Dempsey. "What do you want to do?"

"Already did it. Talked to the pilots and we're going to Arizona. If we need to divert back to California, we will after Baldwin checks the next sat feed."

"Okay," Smith said. "What about air support?"

"Our best option is Fort Huachuca."

"The Army intel base?" Smith asked.

Dempsey nodded.

"It's the only place with enough runway, but it's perfect. Far enough from the border to not be seen, but only twenty-five mikes from the target in Blackhawks. Simon, you and Elizabeth work on getting us air support for the INFIL—ideally we want '60s—armed '60s—with door gunners for CAS. Shane, please coordinate with the boss back home and try to get us some eyes and ears on the target. Oh, and also see what we can get on the US side for additional support—Border Patrol, local law enforcement . . . anything, I don't care. Any questions?"

No one said anything.

"All right then, let's get to work. We land in under an hour, so be prepped and kitted up by then." He clapped his hands together. "Let's go. Failure is not an option, people."

CHAPTER 25

Rostami paced, the soles of his shoes making a dull scratching sound on the dusty cement floor.

The Americans are coming.

The Americans are coming.

The Americans had carried out the attack on the cartel compound, he was certain of it. The fact that Garcia had shared precious little information with them was confirming evidence. Hijjar had abandoned them in Mexico City just as he had promised, and now Rostami had no way to contact Hezbollah to learn the truth. As a VEVAK operator with years of field experience, Rostami had learned to trust his eyes and his ears. He had learned that the information people refused to share was often just as important as the information they chose to share. Had a rival drug cartel attacked the compound, he would know all the details by now. Garcia's men would be chest pounding and brazenly discussing revenge. But the men were not doing this. Instead, they were silent, solemn, and skittish.

They were afraid.

In recent years, it was common for the American Drug Enforcement Agency to partner with US Special Forces in their "war on drugs." Even in faraway Tehran, there had been rumors that the elite Navy Tier One SEAL team had executed the final raid on the doomed drug lord Pablo Escobar. That the Americans had attacked the Guatemalan compound was not the question—what mattered was whether they were attacking the Zeta stronghold in their war on drugs, or targeting it as a Hezbollah training site. Had the Americans already made the connection between the meeting in Al Qa'im and this operation? Had Amir Modiri been wrong about Parviz? Had the VEVAK operative cracked under interrogation and told the Americans everything? What had the Americans learned from the raid on the Zeta compound? Were they interrogating the senior cartel detainees at this very moment? If so, the only advantage left was time.

Rostami had grudgingly come to respect al-Mahajer for his tenacity and intellect. That the man had survived more than a decade while being on so many capture/kill lists was itself an achievement, but Rostami also knew that al-Mahajer possessed a keen mind for tactics and the psychology of human motivation, surprising for someone who had lived like an animal for so many years. But the closer they marched toward their objective, the more impassioned and committed the Islamic State lieutenant was becoming. En route to Agua Prieta, Rostami had tried to convince al-Mahajer that living to fight another day was an act of prudent courage, all the while knowing he was wasting his breath. When the Syrian announced simply, "We will strike the heart of the devil and we will succeed because it is Allah's will," Rostami had known the debate was over. There was no reasoning with religious zealots, no matter how talented in warfare and covert operations they were.

Rostami had been forced to breach protocol and reach out to his Suren teams, providing them with new instructions for pickup in an entirely new location. It was too many moving parts. He trusted his sleeper agents and had every reason to believe they would be in place, but the rapidly changing plans made him worry more and more. Failure would do more than destroy the jihadist's plan to strike America—it could unmask the Suren operation that had taken decades to implement.

He watched with irritation as al-Mahajer roused his small band of martyrs to find their courage. The man was gifted with an inspirational tongue, but if he truly wanted to serve Allah, he'd best find his way to brevity. Rostami looked at the Rolex Submariner on his wrist. They needed to go—now.

Al-Mahajer finished with a flourish, and his band of brainwashed jihadis all raised their rifles above their heads and began shouting praises to Allah. Rostami glanced at the stoic cartel fighters—Catholics every one—and wondered how many were contemplating gunning down the crazy Muslims who were going to get them killed.

Enough! You fools.

Rostami cleared his throat, loudly. Al-Mahajer looked over, his eyes blazing, then turned back to his men. He walked over and stood in front of the young man called Faruq—friend of the recently sacrificed Nabil. Faruq was kitted up like an operator. He wore one of al-Mahajer's special Hezbollah-constructed bulletproof suicide vests, a Kevlar helmet, and a sidearm, and he clutched an AK-47 in his hands. Rostami watched as al-Mahajer placed a hand on Faruq's shoulder.

"It is time, my brother. The Americans are coming," he said softly. "Are you afraid?"

"No," Faruq said, blood rage in his eyes. "I am afraid of nothing except failing in my service to Allah."

"It is Allah's will that you remain behind, so that we may complete our mission and strike the heart of the Great Satan. You will safeguard our passage. You alone must shoulder this burden."

Faruq nodded. "I will not fail you."

Al-Mahajer embraced Faruq, then beckoned Rostami. "We are ready for you to lead us into the heart of America."

With Faruq staying behind, only five would make the crossing. The rest of the group was dressed in American clothes, each different and carefully curated depending on their cover story and which Suren team was picking them up. Al-Mahajer, having shaved his beard entirely, looked neutered, all the ferocity gone from his face.

Rostami checked his watch again. "It's about fucking time," he said, turning his back on the Muslim. He led them to the tunnel entrance, a hole in the concrete floor next to a row of tool and equipment cages. The hole was normally covered by a thousand-ton hydraulic press that had taken a forklift to move out of the way. Next to the holes stood Garcia, armed and tapping his foot impatiently.

Rostami extended his hand to the cartel man. "Thank you, for everything."

Garcia looked at the hand, but did not shift his own from the grip of his machine gun. "Go now, and do not turn back. When the last of you is below, the hole will be sealed. This is a one-way trip."

Rostami said nothing, slung his machine gun over his shoulder, and eased himself down into the hole until his right foot found the first steel ladder rung. He counted twenty-seven rungs as he descended into the dark tunnel. At the bottom, he switched on his flashlight and wondered how Rafiq al-Mahajer intended to compensate for the loss of Faruq. Would he still try to hit three sites with only five men, or would he try to recruit a replacement? The Suren Circle assets would provide logistical support as well as transportation, but they would not, under any circumstance, participate in the attacks.

When the last of his companions was down, Rostami looked up and watched the eclipse taking place above as the hydraulic press was moved back into position over the hole. All went black, and it was done. No turning back now. Without a word or a glance behind him, he put his right foot in front of his left, and set off into the tunnel at a brisk pace. The tunnel stank of urine, quicklime, and mold, and so he switched from breathing through his nose to his mouth. He wondered how old this tunnel was, and the last time it had been used. How could the Americans, who seemed to possess prescient insight into every foreign clandestine operation in the Middle East, not know about all these cartel tunnels into their country? Unless of course they did know and chose not to shut them down. But why?

"Persian," Rafiq said, jolting Rostami from his thoughts. "I do not know your assets. I will need you to personally and visually confirm their identities before I split my men."

"I wish I could," Rostami said, "but they have been asleep in the US for years, some of them decades. I have never met any of them. We will know them by their vehicle license plates and the challenge-phrase authentication. I assure you that our operation is secure. If the Suren Circle were compromised, we would have known long before today."

"With Nabil's sacrifice and Faruq's assignment, I am one man short for completing the operation."

Here it comes, Rostami thought. *He's going to ask me to martyr myself.*

"You are a man of God," Rafiq continued. "It would bring great honor to your family and your country if you would join our jihad."

Rostami stifled the urge to mock the man with laughter. Al-Mahajer was as unpredictable as he was brilliant. To flat out refuse was to risk a knife in the back when he least expected it. Best not to antagonize the man. "It's a great honor that you would consider me worthy of joining your team. I will contemplate your offer and inform you of my decision after we are safely in America."

As they walked in silence, Rostami calculated their odds of safely crossing the border. He settled on fifty-fifty—a coin flip's chance that he would escape this tunnel alive and disappear into the American night. The irony of al-Mahajer's invitation to join the jihad and martyr himself suddenly hit him. By agreeing to serve as the escort, he had already enlisted in the radical Muslim's jihad, whether he admitted as much or not. Because if the Americans pursued them into this tunnel, he would make his last stand with these five lunatics and have no choice but to martyr himself in the dark.

CHAPTER 26

Military Ramp
Fort Huachuca/Sierra Vista Regional Airport
Sierra Vista, Arizona
October 29, 0255 Local Time

Dempsey ended the call with the DEA support team in California watching the house where the Mexicali tunnel terminated. The report had been exactly what he needed to hear: no activity. When taken together with the latest Agua Prieta satellite imagery showing new vehicles parked at the Cemex complex and armed men walking the fenced perimeter, he had all the information he needed. The next time he saw Rafiq fucking al-Mahajer would be in his gun sight.

The instant the air-stair touched the side of the Boeing, he led his team off the plane. The tarmac was well lit, and he could see the two MH-60 Blackhawks sitting on the skirt in front of a low gray hangar, their blades turning overhead. The whine of their twin General Electric T700-GE-401C engines was as familiar as the feel of his heart beating in his chest. The smell of the jet fuel was an operational aphrodisiac, stirring his emotions in preparation for combat as he jogged across the ramp.

The team assignments were unchanged from Guatemala, with the exception of adding Gyro to his squad. The two SEAL snipers would, once again, provide high-side fire support. Dempsey led his team to the front helicopter, climbed past the starboard-side .50-caliber machine gun, and grabbed a patch of canvas near the front. His teammates piled in behind him, quickly and efficiently. He nodded to the aircrew man on the canvas bench beside him, clad in a flight suit over which he wore a full kit with ammo pouches and an M9 pistol holster on his chest. The man nodded back, and Dempsey tapped his own headset and held up the male adapter that he had pulled from his encrypted radio. The airman nodded, took the cord, and plugged it into the VOX panel beside him.

"Evening, sir," he said.

"You my door gunner?" Dempsey said.

"Door gunner, aircrew, combat medic, and ass kicker, sir."

"PJ?" Dempsey asked with a smile.

"Yes, sir. One of three for your op. Quack over there is our 'buy one get one free' special today, and we've got another guy in bird two."

The other parajumper, Quack, nodded to Dempsey from his seat on the far side of the helicopter.

"Can I talk to the flight crew?" Dempsey said.

The PJ nodded, flipped a switch on his panel, and then gave Dempsey a thumbs-up.

Dempsey moved forward of the big gun, and then, hanging out the door, tapped on the cockpit-door window. The aviator at the controls looked up from his checklist and slid a large rectangular panel backward. He reached out a gloved hand, which Dempsey shook.

"Thanks for the support, Major," Dempsey said, noting the gold oak leaf on the pilot's shoulder.

"Happy to help you spooky motherfuckers," the man said, his voice arriving in Dempsey's headset just out of sync with the movement of his lips, which now stretched into an easy smile. "You got me and Colonel

Boyd in the other seat. They said you wanted experience and we're both AFSOC guys."

"Lucky break," Dempsey said. "Appreciate it again and sorry for the short fuse. You get the details?"

"Yeah," the pilot said and then leaned over when Colonel Boyd pointed to something on the panel. The Major cycled a switch and then gave Boyd a thumbs-up. He turned back to Dempsey. "We'll fly the brief as your guy sent it—helos splitting east and west at the border, crossing at less than a hundred feet and well abeam of your target. We'll converge on the corners at opposite angles. You still want to drop inside the wall?"

"Yes, if possible."

"Okay, can do. But we're not set up for fast roping, so it'll be a touch-and-go delivery. We'll cool the LZ with the fifties first. Only reason to not put into the compound would be if it's too hot. But that won't happen," he said and gestured at the .50 caliber behind his door. Dempsey got the sense that, for this AFSOC pilot, there was never really such a thing as "too hot." He gave the pilot a nod and a tight smile, and then quickly reviewed the tactical channels.

"Copy," the pilot said. "CASEVAC is your call. We got three PJs and then an Army medic in bird two."

"Check," Dempsey said. "Davis-Monthan Air Force Base for flesh wounds and the civilian trauma center in Tucson for mortal injuries."

"Roger that."

Dempsey shook the pilot's gloved hand again and then ducked under the .50 and slid back through the long, open hatch. He hooked in with the safety harness attached from his belt to the canvas bench at the rear and sat with his feet dangling out the door. He looked longingly over at the same seat on the port side of the aircraft—his favorite spot for twenty years with the Teams—and sighed. A moment later, the engines whined, the wind picked up, and the Blackhawk lifted off. A heartbeat later, the helo nosed over and accelerated over the ramp. Once they were at altitude, the pilot banked left and punched the throttle. Dempsey estimated they'd be on the ground in less than thirty minutes.

That thirty minutes vaporized while he went over the assault plan one last time with his team. Normally, briefing on the INFIL would be unheard of—everyone should know his role backward and forward. But on the continuum of short-fuse ops, this fell near the "no fuse" end of the spectrum, so he didn't dare leave anything to chance. After fielding questions, he turned to the sniper sitting on the canvas bench across from him. "You picked your spot?"

"Yeah," he said. "Unfortunately, we can't get super high without a second drop. Don't matter really, cuz there's nothing tall on this target. You guys will be hitting the north building, so we'll take position on the big warehouse to the west. I'll take the northeast corner and Davis will take southeast."

Dempsey nodded. "Let's have the pilots put you on the roof after we off-load inside the fence . . . Cool?"

The sniper gave him a thumbs-up and relayed the new plan to his partner in the other bird. Dempsey relayed the plan to the pilot, who replied with a "No problem. We'll clear the roof with the fifties on the INFIL if needed."

Satisfied everything had been covered, Dempsey leaned back against the bulkhead. The chatter died down as everyone sought the zone. Both birds were completely lights out, screaming across the desert floor at 150 miles an hour. Dempsey felt a powerful wave of déjà vu as he looked out across the terrain—terrain that could have passed for the western Iraqi desert he'd flown over just days ago. In some ways, he felt like he knew that shithole country better than his own . . . just like he'd known his dead teammates better than the wife and son he'd abandoned.

Not now. Not today, he chastised himself. *Only one person matters right now, and that person is Rafiq al-Mahajer.*

He forced his mind out of the gutters of regret and back to the present, mentally reviewing the satellite imagery of the Cemex industrial complex—mapping the assault paths, identifying hides for shooters, noting cover locations for his team in the event of RPGs or grenades. He conducted the complete mission in his head, breaching the north building, tracking down al-Mahajer and his men, and then killing them all before they could make their escape.

The helicopter banked sharply left, and he watched the fence that functioned as the US-Mexico border whiz past them just under his dangling feet, the lights that lit the top every fifty yards little red blurs in the dark.

"Two minutes." The pilot sounded as calm as if he were out for a Sunday drive. "We'll make two low passes first and soften the field with the fifties."

The PJs on either side of the cabin unlocked their machine guns and cycled rounds. Dempsey watched the gunner turn on the IR laser designator and sight it on the ground below to make sure he could see the green dot with his NVGs. Dempsey performed the ritual last check of his gear, weapons, and ammo pouches reflexively, as the other fighters did the same.

He was good to go.

They were all good to go.

"First pass," came the report from the cockpit.

They banked right, and then left, and then dropped down so low Dempsey thought if he stretched a little he could drag a boot in the dirt. Then his guts felt heavy as the helicopter popped up and over the fence surrounding the industrial complex.

An instant later, scattered muzzle flashes punctuated the darkness as shooters on the ground began to engage. He had flipped up his NVGs an instant before the gunners lit the .50s and tongues of white fire licked the night beside him. He watched the tracers tear across the ground and along the fence line. Something exploded to his left, a pickup truck most likely, lit up by the other helicopter. Dempsey grabbed the edge of the door and braced himself a split second before the pilot initiated an evasive maneuver. One of the DEA shooters wasn't so lucky and slipped off the canvas bench, his harness keeping him from falling out of the helo. Adamo helped pull the scrambling operator up and back into his seat.

"Holy shit, this is nuts," someone said on the command channel.

"We're okay," came the relaxed voice of the pilot. "Pass two starting now."

They crossed this time from north to south and the door gunners engaged more effectively. Dempsey watched shooters below flee toward the warehouse, only to be cut down midstride. One poor soul pitched forward and slid all the way to the door, while both of his legs and half of his torso remained five yards behind in the dirt.

The engines whined, and they were pitching up again and banking in the opposite direction.

"This is it, guys. Get ready to drop," the pilot called.

Dempsey unhooked his harness from the bench and leaned out the door of the helicopter, one hand on the rail at the edge of the door and the other gripping his rifle and bringing it up to bear. The helo flared, and before the skids touched down Dempsey was out. He moved right and toward the rear of the Blackhawk, taking a knee and scanning over his holographic sight, watching his green IR target designator dance as he searched for targets. In less than three seconds, the bird was lifting off, the rotorwash beating the hell out of him. The Blackhawk screamed toward the large warehouse to the west, barely pausing long enough for the sniper to leap out. Just to the north, the mirror image was happening as the other Blackhawk dropped the Team Two sniper. Then, the birds were up and gone.

"Spooky One, Thor One and Two are in slow orbit, standing by for support or EXFIL."

"Spooky One, roger," Dempsey answered.

"God is up," came the whispered voice of the sniper duo in his ear.

"Copy, God," he said.

He stood and circled a fist over his head, then led the team at a crouched combat jog across the compound. Mendez fell in beside him, while the group of four DEA assaulters and two SEALs fanned out in an inverted *V* behind.

"Spooky Two is approaching the west warehouse," Chunk said in his ear. The SEAL had moved his team fast to the large warehouse where aerial imagery had shown a contingent of enemy personnel. After clearing the warehouse, Chunk's team would set up a defensive perimeter at the target building.

Sporadic gunfire erupted to the west, followed by shouting in Spanish, confirming Dempsey's concern that the cartel was providing cover fire for their terrorist clients. Chunk's team answered with controlled, measured response fire.

Dempsey vectored his team toward the target building to the east.

"Shooter on the roof," came a call. He heard a shot echo from the roof of the warehouse as one of the snipers engaged the target. "Target down."

A body tumbled off the roof of the target building and hit the ground with a thud.

"Spooky One, this is God. Be careful on your approach. You have a few more tangos on the roof of the target building. Give us a second to clear."

"Roger, that," Dempsey said. "Cap 'em fast."

There were a few more flashes and then the sniper called back. "Target roof is clear. Couple more came up but they changed their minds and went below. Be ready for shooters inside."

Dempsey double-clicked and moved further east. He had expected heavy resistance as they approached the target building, but so far it had been quiet. Too quiet. He heard continuing gunfire from the large warehouse, where Team Two was engaged in a hot gunfight.

"Spooky Two is clearing, but we have a lot of shitheads over here. You guys okay?"

"Check—we're good," Dempsey said. "Do you need us?"

"Negative," came Chunk's cool reply. "We're fully engaged, but expect to secure in two or three mikes."

Dempsey surveyed the target building's west facade. The roll-up doors, elevated concrete apron with ramp, and loading bays confirmed this end functioned as the freight dock for the building. The team scurried up onto the concrete landing and took positions along the wall. Dempsey crouched next to a metal entry door at the end of the row of bay doors. The team split and formed up on either side of the door, two DEA agents taking a knee and facing outward to cover their six during the breach. Mendez crouched opposite the door from him and nodded. Dempsey reached up, grabbed the door handle, and pulled down. The handle dipped, the latch disengaged, and the door drifted open an inch.

Unlocked? What the fuck?

Dempsey put a flat palm over his other fist and popped it away, then flared out his fingers: *Toss a flash-bang.*

Mendez nodded and fished a nonlethal grenade from his kit with his left hand. He pulled the pin and nodded. Dempsey pushed the door open enough for Mendez to toss in the grenade and then shut it. He waited for the muted explosion, and then flung the door open wide. Mendez charged in, crouching low and moving left. Dempsey followed him through the gap, expecting gunfire but getting nothing. He cleared the right corner and continued moving right to make room for the rest of his assault team surging in behind. The main floor appeared deserted, but he noted plenty of hides—behind inventory stacks, inside tool cages, as well as atop two parallel catwalks that serviced an overhead crane. Dempsey cleared the nearby hides then shifted his attention to the catwalks. Just when he thought the steel walkways were clear, movement on his right made him drag the green IR dot quickly to the corner, where he spied a man with a rifle running after someone else fleeing out a second-story window. The man with the rifle looked nervously over his shoulder, but he didn't seem to focus on Dempsey or his team in the darkness below. Clearly, he was still night blind from the flash bang. Dempsey was about to squeeze the trigger when a voice beckoned in Spanish from outside. The man immediately dropped his rifle and dove through the window.

Dempsey's heart sank. These guys were cartel, too.

Shit.

Were they that far behind and the bad guys long gone? Was this the wrong building? Had he misread the intel? Maybe the tunnel entrance was in the west warehouse. He considered calling Chunk and asking him to search for the tunnel in the main warehouse, but he didn't dare make a sound until they'd cleared the building.

Spaced in pairs, they advanced in silent synchronicity—a creeping line converging on a metal partition wall. In the middle of the partition stood a twelve-foot roll-up door and next to it a regular man-size swing door, both closed. Dempsey mentally reviewed the hand-sketched diagram of this facility. On the other side of the partition should be a machine shop. Dempsey had seen similar industrial layouts before, where quadrants of warehouse space were partitioned to separate air-conditioned from un-air-conditioned spaces. He gritted his teeth; there was no telling what was waiting for them on the other side of that wall. To clear the other side would almost be like making another breach. Then, an idea came to him.

He looked up at the catwalks and noticed that they extended past the partition into the other space. He looked at Gyro and BT and pointed at the catwalks and gestured east. They both nodded understanding. He whispered the words "Clear on two clicks" to BT, and the DEA team leader nodded.

Moments later, BT had climbed up onto the south catwalk and Gyro was on the north, creeping silently toward the machine shop. Dempsey gestured for the remaining DEA shooters to watch their flank, while he and the rest of the team trained their rifles on the roll-up and swing doors. He glanced up just in time to watch both operators disappear from sight as they stepped beyond the partition wall. His respiration rate picked up in anticipation of gunfire, while his pulse kept time in his ears.

Ten, eleven, twelve . . .

They had the high ground, which meant they had the advantage.

Thirty-two, thirty-three, thirty-four . . .

Silence.

No gunfire. What the hell's going on?

Then two clicks in his ear.

Dempsey exhaled and keyed his mike. "Roger, we're coming in."

Mendez led through the swing door, sighting over his rifle and moving right. Dempsey followed after him with Adamo right behind. Dempsey cleared the left corner and surged forward, as Adamo stepped up and took the center lane. They cleared the length of the room, scanning around all the equipment, until they reached the far wall. Satisfied, Dempsey waved BT and Gyro down from the catwalks. After regrouping, Dempsey stared out at the deserted machine-shop floor with its hydraulic press, plasma torches, bending machines, lathes, and CNC machines.

"Sorry, boss," BT said with a sigh. "Looks like we missed 'em again."

Dempsey nodded. That same feeling of déjà vu he'd experienced on the helo ride washed over him again, except this time without any of the nostalgia. Something was wrong; he just couldn't put his finger on it. He decided to radio Chunk.

"Two, One, target building is clear."

"Copy, One, west warehouse is clear. Six KIA and a couple of squirters."

"Any dead shitheads, or just cartel guys?"

"Not a single raghead in the mix. Looks like the cartel guys were prepping a shipment though, which explains why they were hanging around. We have a pallet of shit over here that'll make BT smile."

"God, SITREP?" Dempsey said, scowling.

"They're scattering like jackrabbits," the lead sniper answered. "You want us to engage? They're bugging out."

"Negative," Dempsey said.

"One, you want us to come to you, or toss the warehouse and see what else we can find?" Chunk asked.

Dempsey blew air through his teeth, then keyed his mike. "Later. Come help me find this damn tunnel."

"Copy that."

Dempsey looked at Adamo. "What do you think?"

Adamo hesitated a beat. "Just wondering why they split their force. If this is the tunnel entrance, why so much security at the other building?"

"Protecting their product."

Adamo shook his head. "Yeah, I guess."

"You think the tunnel is actually in the other building?" Dempsey asked.

"The diagram showed the tunnel entrance hidden under a hydraulic press in a machine shop. This is a machine shop, and there's a hydraulic press right over there," Mendez said, "but we'll need that fork truck over there if we want to move it." With a grin on his face, he turned and jogged off toward the forklift.

"Dude, do you even know how to drive that fucking thing?" Gyro called and trotted after him.

Dempsey shook his head at the thought of a kitted-up Mendez driving a forklift using night vision. Then, he noticed something that made his heart skip a beat.

"Hey, was that fucking cage door open before?"

He pointed to the right side of the room—the side Mendez had cleared—to a wire-mesh tool-cage door hanging ajar.

No one had time to answer.

Blinding muzzle flares and the roar of machine gun fire sent Dempsey to a knee. Bullets scoured the machine shop and ricocheted off the equipment all around him.

"Shooter in the cage," he yelled, making himself small as he pushed his NVGs up on his helmet and waited for his vision to clear.

"Gyro's hit," a voice yelled.

"Stay down," Mendez boomed.

There were two pops from his right as BT returned fire and advanced on the ambush shooter.

Dempsey's vision grudgingly cleared, and he made out a silhouette standing in a firing stance in front of the tool cage, spraying the room haphazardly with automatic fire. Dempsey sighted in, squeezed his trigger twice, and dropped the shooter. A body appeared in the partition doorway. Dempsey shifted his aim and identified the new arrival as the DEA operator he'd assigned to watch their flank. The DEA man immediately sighted in on the corner and, along with Mendez and a SEAL, closed in on the fallen shooter.

Dempsey had only sighted on the ambush shooter for a fraction of a second, but something about that silhouette was wrong. Years of combat experience didn't lie, and his brain registered the problem. That motherfucker was kitted up.

It's Romeo all over again.

"Stop!" Dempsey screamed. "Mendez, get back."

The explosion knocked Dempsey flat on his back. Hot, wet, fleshy stuff rained down on him. He gasped for air, the wind knocked from his lungs. Despite his brain's frantic call for oxygen, he pulled his rifle up, got to his knees, and cleared the room for other jihadi threats. Still wheezing for his breath, he got painfully to his feet. Someone groaned.

Dempsey looked down and found Adamo sprawled on the ground next to him. The CIA man looked intact, but Dempsey asked, "You hurt?"

"I don't think so," Adamo answered.

Dempsey extended Adamo a hand and pulled him to his feet. Shoulder to shoulder, they walked toward the carnage, Dempsey stepping over a severed leg with half the boot missing as they crossed the shop floor. Mendez, one of Chunk's SEALs, and a DEA operator were gone—nothing left but horrific splatter. The explosion had knocked the hydraulic press over and decimated everything in a ten-meter sphere around the cage.

"Spooky One—SITREP," came Chunk's desperate call in Dempsey's ringing ears.

Dempsey spit coppery blood from his mouth, then keyed his mike. "Suicide bomber," he said. His voice was thick and not his own. "At least three KIA." Behind the forklift, he found Gyro. He rolled the SEAL over and saw wild eyes darting back and forth. "Where are you hit?" Dempsey asked.

Gyro heaved in a spasm of coughing. "In the vest, I think. But then that fucking explosion . . . I'm blind, Dempsey."

Dempsey shined a light on the man's face. It was covered in blood but he saw no major damage. He felt along the man's shoulders and neck and found no wounds. There was a deep hole dead center in the chest of his vest, but he could feel where the 7.62 round spread out on the ceramic plate.

"Round hit your SAPI plate. Didn't go in," he whispered. "You're gonna be okay. The blindness is from the flash. We'll get you out of here."

"My right leg feels funny," Gyro said.

Dempsey felt along Gyro's right thigh, but when he got to the knee everything went mushy. He cocked his head and saw that Gyro's lower leg was turned around further than should be possible. He flicked on his light and saw the operator's BDUs were soaked in blood. He heard footfalls and spun around, raising his rifle. He looked up to find Chunk and the rest of Team Two funneling into the machine shop.

"Gyro needs a tourniquet on his right leg," Dempsey told the Lieutenant, who immediately pulled a blowout kit from a cargo pocket and went to work on his man.

Dempsey keyed his mike. "Thor, One. We need urgent CASEVAC at the target building." His voice was sounding more his own and the coppery taste of blood was going away—unlike the ringing in his ears. He wiped his gloved hand across the side of his face and looked down at the blood and clots he picked up.

"One, Thor. Roger. What else?"

"Maintain overwatch. One bird for urgent CASEVAC and the other standing by for support and EXFIL." He spit a glob of blood onto the ground, saw that Gyro was being taken care of, and then walked over to the gaping hole in the floor underneath where the hydraulic press had been. This was the tunnel entrance he'd lost three men to find. He shined his light down into the hole—no longer worried about stealth or light discipline. A metal ladder, bolted into the concrete, disappeared into the blackness below. In his peripheral vision, he saw Chunk appear beside him and stare down into the hole.

"Drug dealers don't blow themselves up with suicide vests," Dempsey said. "Al-Mahajer is close. I'm going after the fucker. You coming?"

"Hell yeah," Chunk said.

By now, Grimes was on the scene and she went straight to Dempsey. "You need medical?" she asked looking him over, her eyes wide.

"Negative," he said. "We lost Mendez."

All the color drained from her face. "Suicide bomber?"

He nodded. "Where's Smith?"

"Coordinating the helo landing for the CASEVAC."

"Someone else can do that. We're going after al-Mahajer." He keyed his radio. "Smith, to me. Time to hit the tunnel."

Twenty seconds later, Smith was at his side.

"All right," Dempsey said. "Let's go."

Dempsey squatted, and then lowered himself into the hole until his feet found purchase on the ladder rungs. The tunnel was black as midnight, so he pulled his NVGs down and snapped them into position over his eyes. He sighted over his rifle toward the bottom of the tunnel while hanging on to the top rung of the ladder with his left hand.

"Clear," he said and then began his descent.

At the bottom he took a knee, sighting down the tunnel as he waited on Chunk, Grimes, and Smith. The rectangular walls stretched far into the distance before fading into gray-green static. When Smith's boots finally hit the ground, Dempsey popped to his feet. "Stay on me," he said to the group. The time for stealth had passed. If al-Mahajer and his zealots were still below ground, they certainly knew by now that a team was in pursuit. Dempsey wouldn't put it past al-Mahajer to station a second suicide bomber in the tunnel and told his teammates as much.

"Anything moves," Dempsey said, taking off down the tunnel, "kill it."

Moving as quickly as a combat crouch would allow, Dempsey took point. His lower back ached, and stingers flared down his left leg with each footfall. Chunk hugged the left wall, matching his pace, and he could hear the pounding of the other two pairs of boots behind them. After what he judged to be a hundred yards, they came to a sharp turn. Dempsey raised a closed fist and stopped just before it. He listened for a beat, but hearing nothing, he peered around the corner. Seeing nothing, he gestured with his left hand and they resumed the advance.

The tunnel jogged left and right with the occasional dogleg mixed in. At one point, Dempsey felt like they'd doubled back toward Mexico, but it was impossible to know with certainty. His normally dialed-in internal compass was slowly losing calibration with every bend, turn, and switchback. They moved at a quick pace for what he estimated was at least a mile. Had they crossed under the physical border yet? The answer had to be yes, but how much farther until they reached the tunnel exit?

He picked up the pace, his sense of urgency kicking into overdrive. The air was heavy and damp, and sweat was pouring from his brow.

After a bend to the left, the tunnel straightened out. Unlike the buildings at the Cemex facility, the tunnel interior did not afford any place to hide. There were no alcoves, offshoots, or doors. If al-Mahajer had left another suicide jihadi behind, interception was inevitable.

Breathing hard now, Dempsey kept the pace for another four hundred yards, slowing only when he spotted the tunnel's end—a cement wall with protruding metal ladder rungs. Cursing silently to himself, he halted the team a cautious distance from the hole. He let the team form up around him before signaling for them to stay back while he investigated. Expecting a strafe of machine-gun fire or a falling grenade, he eased forward until he was able to angle under the hole and sight up with his rifle. The tunnel exit was covered with what looked to be a piece of plywood.

"Be ready for anything on the breach," Grimes whispered.

"On me," he mouthed, slinging his rifle.

He pulled out his Sig Sauer P229 pistol and headed quietly up the ladder. Four feet from the top, he looked down and saw his team waiting in a line beneath him, Grimes already halfway up. He nodded at her, and then worked himself into a crouched position on the rungs as he took the next two steps, keeping his head below the plywood cover.

He waited, straining to hear anything—movement, the rustling of clothing, breathing—but he heard nothing except for the sound of his pulse pounding in his ears. He took a deep breath and, lodging his back hard against the wood, slowly pressed up with his legs. The board was heavy, heavier than a piece of plywood should be, but he felt it give under his pressure. Grunting, he pressed upward with the power of both legs, lifting the plywood and a layer of fine earth, which poured off the sides and rained down around him. Then, the board tipped and slid off his back. With the weight gone, he sprung the rest of the way out of the hole like a jack-in-the-box, raising his pistol and rolling right. Seeing no immediate threat, he scurried to a crouch and pulled his rifle into combat position while reverse holstering his pistol.

He was in a small wooden building with a dirt floor. As he cleared the room, it became obvious this was a maintenance shed. Tools and yard implements lined the walls, and in the far corner sat a battered, green riding lawn mower along with a red five-gallon gas can.

Dempsey moved to the right toward the wooden door; moonlight streamed in through the slats. Grimes stepped up beside him. A heart-beat later, Chunk moved past him to the far side of the door. He nodded at the SEAL officer and then pressed his gloved left hand against the latch, took a deep breath, and pushed.

The shed door opened into the backyard of a ranch-style house. All the windows in the house were dark, and the only light was from the moon overhead and streetlights in front. The backyard was enclosed on three sides by an eight-foot, wooden privacy fence. He heard laughter and music coming from the next-door neighbors, but this property was dead quiet. He stepped out of the shed and cleared the yard for threats. The scene matched Dempsey's memory of what the confiscated map had depicted. Using private homes to conceal secret tunnels had been an effective strategy for the cartel, and this tunnel was no exception.

He crossed the yard in a combat crouch, his team in tow, keeping away from any windows and the noisy neighbors. With his back pressed against the wall, he slid forward, pressed the latch, and quietly eased open the wooden gate. The street in front of the house was empty and so was the driveway.

Grimes pulled up beside him and whispered, "Now what?"

"We clear the house," he grumbled. "But you know what we're going to find."

"Nothing," she said.

"Yeah. They're long gone."

The operation had been a total failure. Mendez and two others were dead.

And Rafiq al-Mahajer had slipped through his fingers.

Again.

PART III

The woods are lovely, dark and deep.
But I have promises to keep,
And miles to go before I sleep.
And miles to go before I sleep.
—*Robert Frost*

CHAPTER 27

Special Activities Equipment Locker beneath the Ember Hangar
Newport News, Virginia
October 30, 1250 Local Time

Dempsey shrugged the massive duffel off his shoulder, and it hit the ground of his cage with a dull thud. God it felt heavy, much heavier than usual. He stood paralyzed, suddenly too exhausted to even contemplate cleaning his weapons and gear. He took a deep breath. And then another. His vitality was leeched, as if half the blood in his body had been drained out. There was a briefing scheduled in the TOC in thirty minutes, but the thought of rehashing the events of the past twenty-four hours in front of Jarvis was almost more than he could bear.

The flight back from Arizona had been miserable. He'd cleaned himself up, washing the blood of his murdered colleagues off himself, but he'd not slept. He knew sleep was a lost cause, so he hadn't even tried. Instead, he'd sequestered himself at a workstation, searching the databases for clues and conferencing with Baldwin on what new data had been collected or insights gleaned. The answer had been none, nada, zilch. Despite immediately involving local and federal authorities in the search for the terrorists, the Arizona state police and FBI BOLOs hadn't found a thing. Not one suspicious traffic stop, not one drifter picked up along the border roads, not one call from a hotline or a concerned citizen. Even the DEA and FBI guys—pissed off for not being invited to the party until after the fact—had found nothing of value while canvassing the Cemex facility on the Mexico side of the border. No physical evidence had been left behind in the warehouses or the tunnels by al-Mahajer's men. The cartel guys on site were dead or low-level pukes who knew jack shit; everyone important was gone. Al-Mahajer and his band of crazies were in the wind, somewhere inside the homeland, and Ember didn't have a clue about their plan.

And it was his fault.

For the millionth time, he watched Mendez get blown to pieces on the video screen inside his mind. Just like Romeo.

Just like fucking Romeo.

The SEAL inside him knelt and unzipped the black bag. John Dempsey could not bring himself to do anything at the moment, so he let the SEAL do what needed to be done. The SEAL pulled out the Sig Sauer 556 rifle and broke it down—releasing the magazine, clearing the chamber and locking it open, reloading the lone round into the magazine, and then pulling the pin to separate the upper and lower sections of the machine gun. The SEAL laid out all the components on his workbench and methodically cleaned and oiled them. The SEAL put everything back together and stowed the war machine back in the rack among its brothers for the next mission. The SEAL pulled the battery from his radio and dropped it in the charger, cleaned his lights and sights with a lint-free cloth, and finally cleared and cleaned the pistol from his drop holster. And when the ritual was finished, the SEAL returned to the bag for something else to inventory or clean, and finding the bag empty the SEAL left, leaving John Dempsey alone—head down, palms flat on the workbench, eyes rimmed with tears.

"You okay?" Grimes asked.

He didn't answer.

"You haven't moved in a few minutes," she said from the passageway in front of her cage, two down from his. "I've heard SEALs have the ability sleep anywhere, but I didn't know that meant standing up."

After a long, awkward beat, she padded over. She didn't try to touch him. She didn't say anything. She just sat down on the concrete floor, cross-legged in the corner of his cage. When she didn't go away, he turned and glared at her, but she wasn't looking at him. Her gaze was fixed on something in her hands. He watched her rotate a small object over and over, robotically, with her fingers.

"What's that?" he asked, his curiosity eventually getting the better of him.

The left corner of her mouth curled up into a pathetic smile, and she tossed it to him. He caught it midair and opened his palm to find a Lego miniature. The little figurine wore a black mask and cape and had a bat emblem on the chest.

"Batman?" he asked, cocking an eyebrow at her.

"It's my lucky charm."

A poignant memory from his final mission as a Tier One SEAL washed over him. Given all that he and his brothers had been through, it seemed that this one memory was what his subconscious kept coming back to—Spaz and Pablo arguing on a helicopter INFIL about which superhero would make a better SEAL: Batman or Spider-Man? Ironic, that this memory defined who they had been—not superheroes themselves, just ordinary men with extraordinary ambition and the will to do an impossible job for their country. He smiled, a genuine, fraternal smile, and sat down on the floor next to her.

"Your brother had such a hard-on for freaking Batman," he said.

"Yeah, he did." She chuckled. "It started when he was five and he never grew out of it."

"Believe me, I know. We could be in the middle of a firefight, and there was your brother going on and on about Batman." He cleared his throat and then did his best Spaz impersonation. *"Hey, Senior, help me settle an argument. Pablo thinks that Spider-Man would make the best Tier One operator. I told him only Batman is badass enough to make the Teams, much less our unit."* Dempsey started laughing. "God, he really was a Spaz."

Her eyes lit up. "That was pretty good, Dempsey. You sounded just like him." Then, her smile suddenly morphed into a grimace and she started to sob.

"I'm sorry," he said. "I didn't mean to—"

"It's okay," she said, crying and laughing at the same time. "I just miss him, that's all."

He pressed the stupid little Lego Batman into her palm and wrapped his hand around her fist. "Me, too," he said, choking on the words. "Me, too."

"It's not your fault," she said, suddenly turning to look at him. "What happened to Mendez is not your fault. You know that, right?"

He met her gaze. "It absolutely *is* my fault. I led the team into the trap. I didn't see that fucker hiding inside the cage."

She shook her head. "Being ambushed is the implicit risk of every capture/kill op we run. And it wasn't just you who missed the jihadi in the cage, nobody saw him."

"But as the team leader, I'm accountable for the team's safety. When no one else recognizes the trap, I'm the guy who is supposed to. If you don't get that simple operational principle, you have no business being a member of Special Activities, Your Highness."

She exhaled with exasperation. "I don't like when you do that."

"Do what?"

"When you say shit like that. When you call me Your Highness, and Lady Grimes."

"Grimes is your name," he retorted, lamely.

"No, it's not. My name's Kelsey Clarke."

"Not anymore it isn't."

"That's where you and I—and the rest of you NOC-using motherfuckers—disagree. Kelsey Clarke will always be my name. Elizabeth Grimes is just a character. She's a myth; she's a legend. The way I see it, I'm an actor playing a part in Kelso Jarvis's grand film noir. But someday, the director is going to yell 'cut,' and when that day comes, Elizabeth Grimes is no more. When that day comes . . . I finally get to go back to being me."

"Well, la-di-fucking-da for you," he snarled and looked away. "Must be nice."

They sat in silence for a moment before she said, "I'm sorry, John. That was selfish of me."

"Forget it," he said. "If I were you, I'd feel the same way. Hell, I'm no better—stalking Kate and Jacob on Facebook every chance I get."

She scooted closer to him and laid her head on his shoulder. Neither one of them said anything for a long time. "Have you thought about starting over? You know, if you found the right girl, I mean?"

He shook his head. "Don't want to. Kate's the only woman I ever loved. The kind of love we had can't be replaced."

"I understand," she said, hesitantly, "but nobody said you have to replace her. Love doesn't have quotas you know."

"Yeah," was all he said, but he made sure his tone put an end to where he guessed this conversation was headed.

She lifted her head off his shoulder and glanced at her watch. "We gotta scoot. Brief in two," she said and got to her feet.

As she was on her way out of the cage, he grabbed her wrist. "Hey."

"What?"

"If I can't call you Your Highness or Lady Grimes anymore, what the hell am I supposed to call you?"

She smiled at him. "How about Liz, or Lizzie. Or you could call me Beth, maybe Bess . . . do I look like a Bess to you?"

"You're not a Bess, that's for sure," he said, getting to his feet. He studied her face for a beat. "As far as pet names go . . . I'd say you look like a Lizzie to me."

The genuine smile he got back told him he'd made the right choice. "Lizzie, it is," she said, turned, and headed to her cage.

Two minutes later, he was slumped in a chair next to Smith in the TOC. At the end of the table to his left sat Chunk, his eyes wide as he scanned the slick high-tech room that was Ember's nerve center. His fellow SEALs were tucked in at Dempsey's house, with strict orders to contact no one. As far as the world was concerned, the small contingent from SEAL Team Four was forward deployed somewhere in support of OGA. Chunk had spent the last fifteen minutes with Quinton Thomas—Ember's Head of Security—who had told him almost nothing, but instead had explained all the ways he would be fucked if he ever discussed the little bit he did see about their operation. The SEAL still believed that they were a covert team from the CIA, and that was for the best.

As Dempsey watched Chunk, the wonder disappeared and he went back to grinding his teeth. For the first time since they'd met, there wasn't a smile on the LT's face. He must have felt Dempsey's gaze, because he turned and gave a solemn nod.

"You all right?" Smith whispered to Dempsey.

"Yes, Mom," Dempsey snapped, with more venom than he had intended.

Smith narrowed his eyes.

"Sorry," Dempsey said, looking away. "I'm good, boss."

Smith let it slide.

Grimes dropped into the seat beside them. The seat beside her—Mendez's spot—sat painfully empty. Dempsey noticed that Adamo had taken a seat on the far side of the table, away from him and the others. He sat with his arms across his chest, his eyes locked on the empty table in front of him. Something in his expression caught Dempsey's eye—a melancholy he'd not seen before. Maybe Adamo was feeling—

"This won't take long," Jarvis said, entering the room from his office. The screens behind him were dark, not a good sign. He scanned the faces in the room, drummed his fingertips once on the podium, and said, "We all know what happened, no point in rehashing or reconstructing. We lost three good men, and we have a fourth in critical condition. I'm not here to assign blame, and even if I were, we don't have time for that right now. Rafiq al-Mahajer is in the homeland. Right now, as we speak, he is plotting carnage. And I think we're all painfully aware of how effective this terrorist is at dealing out death and destruction."

Dempsey ground his teeth, making his jaw pop, garnering sideways glances from Smith and Grimes.

"I'm going to be straight up with you—we're as blind as we've ever been," Jarvis continued. "For the past three hours, I've been in constant contact with FBI's Joint Counterterrorism Task Force and there's no chatter. It's pin-drop quiet on every media channel. I have NSA doing a signals dump, but that's a long shot . . ."

"They've pulled rabbits out of hats for us before," Smith said, almost hopeful.

"When they knew what they were looking for, but I don't think al-Mahajer is plugged into the regular in-country circles they monitor. He recruited his own fighters outside the US, and he came in black. In my opinion, that was by design. Whatever network ISIS has in place here, he's not touching it. He's compartmentalized and he has OPSEC discipline. Don't get me wrong, I have Ian and the boys looking at NSA data, but the same constraints apply. If he's not talking, they won't find him. We also have our friends in Mossad working on our behalf as well, but so far they have nothing to report."

"Sounds like we're fucked," Dempsey grumbled.

Jarvis nodded solemnly. "Maybe, but failure is not an option. Never give up the fight."

"Never give up the fight," Dempsey conceded. It was the Tier One way.

"We *will* find something, and when we do, I need everyone at this table ready. That means I want you to rest and decompress. I know you all want to honor Mendez and the two other operators we lost, but remember, we are still in mission and sleep is a weapon."

"What about us, sir?" Chunk asked. Dempsey could see the SEAL officer's leg was bouncing up and down with fury.

"I can't tell you what our timeline will be," Jarvis said. "As soon as we get something actionable, we'll mobilize. That could be hours, it could be days. I probably should release you guys back to your command, in case they have tasking for you."

"I'd prefer not, sir," Chunk said. "We're just back from deployment and in training mode at present. Nothing short fuse in our near future. If it's okay by you, we'd like to stay on here TAD and see this thing through."

No surprise there. Chunk had lost one brother, and Gyro was in the hospital. For the young SEAL officer, getting al-Mahajer was personal now.

Jarvis nodded. "We can do that, Lieutenant."

"They can bunk at my place," Dempsey offered. "I have plenty of empty bedrooms." That would help him maintain security on the SEALs as well. They were professionals, and Dempsey trusted them to a point, but Ember couldn't have them in public or in contact with anyone until al-Mahajer was contained.

"Done," Jarvis said. "We're on a one-hour fuse, people, so clean your gear, repack your go-bags, and check your comms so that they're ready to go. When we mobilize, it'll be right fucking five minutes ago."

Everyone nodded.

"Any questions?"

Dempsey was about to ask Jarvis if he would be joining them for Mendez's memorial, but knew the answer, so he held his tongue.

Jarvis fixed his gaze on Adamo, and when the CIA man looked up, the Director of Ember curled his index finger twice, beckoning Adamo to follow him. Without a word, Adamo pushed back his chair from the table, stood, and followed Jarvis out of the TOC. Dempsey watched with equal parts irritation and curiosity as the two men disappeared into Jarvis's office.

I wonder what that's all about.

He felt a tap on his shoulder and turned to find Smith standing beside him, looking down. "Where and when for the toast?"

"My house, say thirty minutes?"

"Roger that," Smith said, and turned to Grimes. "Does that work for you?"

"Yep," Grimes said.

"All right, see you then," Smith said and turned to leave.

"Hey, Smith," Dempsey called after him, getting to his feet. "You gonna be here for a few minutes? Despite my long-standing policy never to let assholes into my house," Dempsey said with a grimace, "if you want to bring Adamo with you, I promise not to make him wait in the car."

Smith flashed him a sardonic smile. "I'm glad to hear that, because I was planning on dragging his ass along no matter what you said. Like it or not, bro, after that op, Adamo is blooded. He is officially one of us."

Dempsey scowled and as he turned to walk away said, "Simon Adamo will *never* be one of us."

CHAPTER 28

Kelso Jarvis's Office
Ember Headquarters

"Have a seat," Jarvis said, gesturing to the chair opposite his desk.

Adamo hesitated. "If this is you firing me, I'll save you the trouble and—"

"Sit down, Adamo," Jarvis interrupted, exasperated. "I'm *not* firing you."

Adamo dropped into the leather chair and folded his arms across his chest. The man looked absolutely haggard—unshaven face, heavy bags under bloodshot eyes, and a gray pallor that was not entirely due to the fluorescent lights. Hell, Adamo looked even worse than Dempsey, and that was saying something. Jarvis stared at the man a long moment before saying, "So, what went wrong out there?"

Adamo screwed up his face. "Your man Dempsey is outta control, that's what went wrong. He rushed into both raids without a fully developed tactical picture and that's a cold fact."

"Ember is a lean organization and our Special Activities Division is a short-fuse entity. Could Dempsey have done more due diligence?

Yes. Would we be any better off if he had? I'd argue no. In fact, we'd probably be worse off because al-Mahajer would have an even bigger head start than he does. Sometimes you have to act on incomplete information."

The CIA man exhaled and met his gaze. "I understand that, but you asked me a straight question and I gave you a straight answer. I'm sure you were hoping the DNI was going to send you some guy who'd come in here and kiss everyone's ass and yes-sir every decision, but that's not me. I'm not here to make John Dempsey's life easy . . . or yours for that matter."

"I know that, which is why I personally requested you for the liaison position."

Adamo sat forward in his chair. "What? That's not how I understood it went down. The DNI assigned me to this post."

Jarvis shook his head. "No. The DNI mandated that Ember have an agency liaison. Then, he gave me pick of the litter."

"And you picked me?" Adamo asked with a laugh. "Why would you do that?"

"I'm not looking to build a task force of clones. I want a team where each member augments and stretches the other members' capabilities. You bring unique skills and field experience to the group. Throughout your career, you've repeatedly demonstrated that you're not willing to sacrifice your integrity for personal advancement. Last and most importantly, I picked you because of your work on the Iranian illegals program."

Adamo shook his head. "That chapter in my life is closed. Permanently."

"I'm sorry to hear you feel that way," Jarvis said, tapping a file on his desk. "Because you work for me now, so consider it officially reopened."

"Trust me, sir, you don't want to go down that rabbit hole. The Suren Circle is a myth. I wasted six years of my life chasing false rumors and ghosts. Take it from a guy who staked his career on it and lost: the Suren Circle doesn't exist."

"I think it does, and I need you to break it wide open." Jarvis leaned forward. "And I need you to do it in the next twenty-four hours."

"Impossible."

"Then hundreds of Americans are going to die on our watch."

Silence hung in the air between them. Jarvis saw the consternation on the other man's face and knew Adamo was in the midst of a mental civil war. He was familiar with the story of Simon Adamo's crusade inside the CIA to prove the existence of an Iranian illegals program—a program run by VEVAK and implemented on a scale and scope rivaling the Russian Rezidentura program. After the unmasking of Anna Chapman, along with nine other SVR illegals in 2010, Adamo's theory gained traction inside the agency. He was given funding, a small team, and marching orders to identify and penetrate the Iranian illegals network in America. But his group was eventually shut down due to lack of proof and progress; the failure rebranded Simon Adamo from one of the company's rising stars into a real-life Fox Mulder, chasing a fringe espionage theory of his own design.

"What does the Suren Circle have to do with stopping al-Mahajer?" Adamo said finally. "I don't care what Grimes and Dempsey think; I'm not convinced that guy in Poland was VEVAK. All we know with certainty is that al-Mahajer is working with Hezbollah."

Jarvis inclined his head. "We have signals intelligence that Tehran has been in the communication mix in the recent past."

Adamo pushed his glasses up on the bridge of his nose. "Encrypted signals data does not a conspiracy make."

Jarvis tamped down his rising irritation. "Before you came here, I presume Director Philips read you in to the events of Operation Crusader and the United Nations terror attack five months ago? Then you know that Amir Modiri, Director of Foreign Operations for VEVAK, has been actively planning, funding, and coordinating acts of false-flag terrorism against the United States and her allies. Al-Mahajer and ISIS could not have pulled off the border crossing without Hezbollah's assistance, but I don't believe for a second that Hezbollah would have agreed to render aid to the Islamic State without incentive from VEVAK."

Adamo nodded slowly. "Let's say you're right and VEVAK is involved, and let's say I was right and the Suren Circle actually exists. Why would Modiri risk exposing such a valuable covert asset to aid a half-dozen ISIS jihadists? Strategically speaking, it doesn't make sense."

"A fair point," Jarvis said, "but you're not putting yourself in Modiri's shoes. Your older brother wasn't shot and killed by Americans. Your religious beliefs don't maintain that the United States and our Judeo-Christian Western society is the root of all evil. And lastly, you are not driven by a burning desire for revenge. To assess the risk-reward proposition, you must first view the decision through our enemy's lens."

"Okay."

"Okay what?"

"Okay, I'll try."

"Excellent. Where do we start?"

"California. I had a CI there who I always believed knew more than he was letting on. Only before, I was constrained," Adamo said, smiling wanly. "As a member of Ember now, I can really put the screws to him . . . that's the modus operandi around here if I'm not mistaken."

"The modus operandi at Ember is this," Jarvis said, pointing to the simple plaque hanging on the wall behind his desk. "We do what others can't, what others won't, and what others are incapable of doing to safeguard innocent American lives. It's counterterrorism, Simon, not rocket science."

"I understand," Adamo said, and stood up from his chair. "Is there anything else, Director Jarvis?"

"Actually, yes there is," Jarvis said, picking up his coffee mug. "And folks around here aren't going to like it." He took a sip, letting the cold, bitter brew linger on his palate before swallowing it down. "For the next twenty-four hours, Adamo, you're in charge."

CHAPTER 29

5209 Brigstock Court
Williamsburg, Virginia
1630 Local Time

"To Mendez, the only fucking Marine I've ever known who smiled more than he scowled," Dempsey said, raising his beer bottle.

"To Mendez," echoed Smith, Grimes, Chunk, and the three loaner SEALs. Adamo had stayed behind at Ember—no surprise there. Dempsey clinked his bottle against the others, much harder than he meant to, sending little puffs of suds up into the air.

As he chugged what was only his second beer, he realized he was already feeling a buzz. *Must be the lack of sleep, lack of food, and dehydration,* he thought, taking inventory of the abuses he'd subjected his body to over the past forty-eight hours. Abuses he'd best soon remedy if he meant to remain functional.

"To Riley and Colt," Grimes said with a heavy voice.

"To Riley and Colt," they answered in unison, and Dempsey realized that he had not known the names of the dead SEAL and the DEA operator until that moment. But Grimes had known their names. Of course she knew their names . . .

"And to Gyro getting out of the hospital and back in the suck with the rest of us," Dempsey added.

"Hooyah," the SEALs said in solemn unison, their minds still fixed on the brother they'd lost.

Dempsey took a long swig of beer and then looked at the bottle in his hand. The red, white, and blue Budweiser label was wet and slimy from sitting in the ice bath–filled cooler. He peeled it off easily with his thumb and index finger. He swirled the beer around inside the now-unadorned glass and watched it fizz. Without the label, the beer could be anything. Slap a different label on the bottle and 99 percent of the people who tasted it would not doubt the brand, which raised the question: Without the label, was it still a Budweiser? He shook his head as the metaphor hit home. Who was Salvador Mendez? The real Mendez—the stuff inside the bottle—not the label Ember had slapped on him. They should be toasting that. They should be memorializing the man, not his fucking NOC. His mind flashed back to the conversation he'd had with Grimes just hours earlier.

Elizabeth Grimes is just a character . . . an actor playing a part in Kelso Jarvis's grand film noir. But someday, the director is going to yell "cut," and when that day comes, Elizabeth Grimes is no more.

What if he'd been the one blown to pieces by the suicide bomber in that warehouse? Would they be toasting John Dempsey and his make-believe life right now? Only Jarvis knew him from before. Smith had made his acquaintance before Yemen, but only Jarvis knew him when the label on the bottle said Jack Kemper. To everyone else in this room he was John Dempsey, and to everyone outside of it, he was already dead. Kate and Jacob would never know John Dempsey. When it was his time to go for real, only his Ember teammates would mourn his loss. He looked down at the slimy paper label stuck to his finger and flicked it into the nearby trash can with disgust.

Then, he chugged the rest of his beer.

"I'm gonna get something to eat," he announced, suddenly remembering he needed to get food in his stomach before the buzz kicked in and took control. "Who needs something?"

"I'm starving. What do you have?" Chunk asked.

"Nothing good," he said, walking to the kitchen. "I haven't been here in weeks." He swung open the pantry door and stared at the barren shelves. "How about I order a bunch of pizzas?" he called out.

"Yes," Chunk called back. "Definitely."

"On me," he heard Smith say.

"Damn right," he mumbled and opened a drawer beside the fridge, fumbling through the half-dozen delivery menus. He pulled out the menu for Zpizza and dialed the number on his cell phone. Before the call connected, he felt his phone disappear from his hand and turned to face Smith raising the swiped phone to his ear, holding up a credit card in his other hand.

"I got this," Smith said.

"Get the spicy Hawaiian," Dempsey grumbled.

Smith shook his head. "Spicy Hawaiian? Dude, now I'm really starting to worry about you," he said, then turned his attention to the call. "I'd like to place an order for delivery . . . uh huh, that's the address . . . yeah, I'll take two large Z-carnivores . . ."

While Smith finished the order, Dempsey walked back to join the others. He was surprised to find Grimes entertaining Chunk and the SEALs with a story about Mendez. As he listened, he quickly realized that he didn't know this particular story. *Musta happened when I was in Iraq,* he thought. When she reached the punch line, Chunk and the boys howled with laughter, and he found himself laughing, too, despite his sour mood. He looked at her, and her tear-rimmed baby blues met his gaze. She looked so vibrant, so strong, and so—

"JD," Smith called from the kitchen.

Dempsey looked over his shoulder and saw Smith holding out his mobile phone with one hand and waving him back to the kitchen with the other. "The boss," Smith said, simply.

"Yes, sir?" Dempsey said, putting the phone to his ear. "Do we have something?"

"Not yet," Jarvis said, but the confidence in his voice conveying that a reversal of fortune was inevitable. "But we're pursuing a new direction. Time to break up the wake and get everyone into the rack. Tell the team—including the SEALs—that I want everyone at the TOC at 0600 ready to go. I need you here sooner—0400 hours."

"I can come in right now."

"No, I need you rested. Take an Ambien if you have to, but get a solid eight down. You need to be ready to go full throttle tomorrow. We'll talk at 0400. Check?"

"Check," he said. Then the line went dead.

Smith was staring at him. "What's up?"

Dempsey shrugged. "Not sure. He says we're going in a new direction, whatever the hell that's supposed to mean. He wants me there at 0400 and the rest of the team reports at 0600 for weapons check, gear loadout, and a brief. Maybe Baldwin is on to something?"

"Maybe," Smith said, without conviction. "We'll feed everybody and then wind down. I'll have Grimes pick up the SEALs on her way in. Cool?" His phone buzzed in his pocket. He pulled it out and checked the screen. "Looks like the Skipper wants to talk to me."

"If it's important, I want to know, Smith. Don't leave me hanging until 0400."

"Trust me, if it's important, you'll be the first to know. But until then, get some sleep, dude."

Dempsey nodded. He felt childish for being irritated that Smith was getting read into Jarvis's plan tonight, while he'd have to wait until morning. Then a disturbing thought occurred to him: Adamo was still at the hangar. Adamo had stayed behind, which meant he had Jarvis's undivided attention. He wondered what that CIA bastard had managed to talk the boss into now. Whatever the "new direction" was, Dempsey had a sinking feeling it was Adamo's doing.

"What's wrong?" Smith said, eyeing him with the same expression the headshrinkers loved to use.

"Rafiq al-Mahajer is what's wrong. I just want to catch this moth-erfucker," he said. "And it's not just about revenge for Romeo and Mendez . . . it's our job, Shane. It's our job to protect and serve the homeland, and right now, we're failing. An attack is coming, and we don't know when, where, or how."

"We'll stop him," Smith said. "Let's just hope he doesn't stay dark."

"Hope is not a strategy," Dempsey said, eyeing his friend.

"I know, but right now, that's all we got."

CHAPTER 30

Dempsey sat beneath the blue umbrella at a picnic table waiting for his mark and wondering if Jarvis had lost his mind. When the Skipper called him in before dawn to "talk," the conversation had been entirely one-sided. Jarvis hadn't called it a demotion, but that's effectively what it was. He'd given Adamo operational authority, and in doing so, Dempsey's worst fear had come true—Ember SAD was now working for the CIA.

Wonderful, here I am back to the beginning . . . full fucking circle.

He took a deep breath and forced himself to stop brooding and look at the book laid open before him—*Cecil's Textbook of Medicine*. If he didn't actually study the material, he knew that an experienced countersurveillance operator would easily spot him "pretending" to read, thus raising suspicion. As he read, he periodically looked up to scan the quad south of the Genetics and Plant Biology Building for graduate student Adar Farhad.

In his peripheral vision, Dempsey saw a tall, lanky male—not Farhad—approaching from the left. The young man was midtwenties, sported green sunglasses and a tie-dye shirt, and had his hair pulled up in a man-bun on top of his head.

"You the TA for Genetics 520?" the kid asked.

"Nah, bro," Dempsey said. "I'm at the med school. Meeting my internal medicine study partner here."

"Oh, I think I'm, like, in the wrong quad," the kid said and shuffled off in his Nike slide sandals with black socks, swinging a large pink backpack over his shoulder.

"That's the future," came Smith's voice in Dempsey's earpiece—as clear as if Smith were sitting beside him. "America's intellectual elite."

Dempsey smiled and shook his head.

"Heads up," came Adamo's voice, all business. "He should be coming out of Koshland Hall any minute."

"I have him," said Smith. "Coming toward you, Grimes."

Dempsey had positioned himself facing west toward the Li Ka Shing Biomedical and Health Sciences building. He looked up from his textbook and made a show of looking exhausted and rubbing his face. He immediately spied Farhad, walking south on the sidewalk between a row of picnic tables and the building.

"Got him," he said softly, arching his back in a stretch.

The face was a match in profile, but the young, muscular Persian confidently striding across the quad did not match the pictures of the drug-addicted kid Adamo had shown them. Evidently, Farhad had cleaned himself up.

Dempsey watched Farhad pull his mobile phone from his jeans pocket. "Phone's out."

"I have him," Grimes said.

Dempsey forced himself not to look south where Grimes was walking on an intercept course from the corner of the Geospatial Innovation Facility and Environmental Sciences building. Instead he looked at his watch, sighed, and started to pack his book and three different-colored highlighters he had been using into his Surf Pro backpack. He stood just as Farhad walked past and pretended to hunt through the pockets of his backpack for his keys. He had the perfect angle to see the planned collision.

Grimes was walking with her head down, mobile phone in hand, sending a fictional text when she slammed into Farhad, nearly knocking him down. She bounced off him and stumbled to the ground.

"Oh my God, I'm so sorry," she said looking up at him from her hands and bare knees.

She quickly scurried over the pavement, picking up Farhad's phone and her own. The handsome Persian extended a hand to her and helped pull her to her feet. Dempsey caught him peeking down Grimes's tank top at her breasts, jostling unrestrained beneath the thin cotton fabric.

"Thanks," she said standing up, both phones gripped together in her left hand.

Back in the van, Richard Wang—Ember's tech genius—was back on the SAD team and was dialed into Grimes's phone, waiting for this exact moment to infiltrate Farhad's mobile.

"Not a problem," Farhad said with a big smile. "I should have been watching where I was going."

"A few more seconds," came Wang's voice over the comms channel, asking her to stall.

"No, it was me. I was walking and texting. Stupid, asshole boyfriend." She looked at Farhad and flashed him a coy smile. "I mean ex-boyfriend," she corrected, looking him up and down and smiling with a blush. She ran the fingers of her free hand through her long auburn hair and laughed. "Sorry. That sounded slutty." She stuck out her right hand, the two phones still pressed together in her left. "I'm Adeline."

"Adar," he said, smiling back at her. "Are you sure you're okay? I think your knee is bleeding."

She looked down at her right knee, the same knee Dempsey had noticed her dragging across the cement moments earlier.

"Oh," she said, looking down at the scuff. "Just a little scrape. I'll be all right."

"Got it," Wang said over the comms circuit.

"I hope I can say the same about your phone." She made a show of inspecting it before handing it back to him. "There's a little scratch on the corner but the screen's not broken or anything."

"It looks fine," he said, giving it a quick perusal. "Is yours okay?"

She flipped her mobile over in her hands. "Yep, fine."

"Well," he said smiling at her, "it was nice running into you, Adeline."

"Yeah, literally," she said with a flirtatious laugh. She started to walk away, then abruptly stopped and turned back. "Hey, listen. I was just on my way to grab a coffee. Do you want to join me? My treat for scratching up your phone." She put her hands behind her back and slipped her phone into the back pocket of her supertight white jeans and rocked her hips back and forth.

Farhad checked the time on his phone and then said, "Sure, why not. I don't have a class until two."

"There's a Starbucks just a few blocks from here," she said.

"I know it well. I live nearby."

"Cool."

Dempsey slung the heavy backpack up onto his shoulder as Grimes and their mark began the stroll south. He followed at a distance, periodically losing visual contact as they passed between buildings and rounded corners. As he walked, he couldn't help but smile at Grimes's performance—babbling on and on like a nervous, flirtatious twenty-something already thinking about the one-night stand ahead.

"Are you a student? I mean, like, oh my God—of course you're a student. I meant what department are you in?" Grimes giggled and Dempsey could picture Smith rolling his eyes.

"I'm a grad student. Finishing my PhD in cognitive neuroscience," Farhad said.

"Good Lord, I don't even know what that is."

"It is the study of the biological mechanisms of cognition. Simply put, how the human brain interprets, processes, and stores data."

"Whoa, sounds complicated," she said. "I'm getting my master's degree in business administration. I'm going to work in pharma—that's where the big bucks are—but I hear it's tough to break into."

He shrugged. "I think you'll do just fine. You don't strike me as a woman who has trouble opening doors for herself."

"Thanks, no one's ever told me that before."

"Have you always been interested in the field of health and medicine? Were you premed in college?"

"Premed—Are you kidding?" she said with a laugh. "I majored in French."

"French, why French?"

"My parents made me go to college, but what I really wanted to do was be a model and live in Paris. I actually landed some swimsuit work, but the agencies all said I didn't have the right body type for runway. It was a stupid dream," she said, looking down at her feet. "I don't know why I'm telling you this."

"No dreams are stupid," Adar said. "And I, for one, think you have a beautiful body type. Those agencies don't know what they're talking about."

"You really think so?" she said, playing coy.

"Of course. Take it from someone who knows. Don't let anyone tell you what you can or can't do with your future . . ."

Dempsey watched and listened as the duo headed down the long steps past the corner of the Biomedical Sciences building, making their way west toward Oxford Street. He had to hand it to her, Grimes was good at this stuff. She'd set the hook and was steadily reeling in the shark. Suddenly, his mind drifted back to something that Jarvis had said to him just before the team had stepped on the plane to fly out here: *To stop al-Mahajer, we need to leverage everyone's skills, insights, and network. And right now, Adamo brings more to the table in those categories than any of us. I'm not saying he has all the answers, but I can promise you that if the two of you don't work together, there's no chance we'll find al-Mahajer in time.* Maybe Jarvis was right. Maybe Simon Adamo wasn't the problem—John Dempsey was. It didn't matter how they stopped al-Mahajer; all that mattered was the end result. The truth was, Dempsey had absolutely no idea how to find the snake, and it terrified him. If Adamo brought that capability to the team, then it was time for Dempsey to check his ego and put his personal feelings about the guy aside.

"Farhad just got a text message," Wang announced, snapping Dempsey back to the moment. "The message reads, 'Wanna meet for beers later?' The number doesn't show up in his contact list."

"Phone's in his pocket," Dempsey whispered.

"Roger that," Wang said.

"Run the number," Adamo said in his ear.

"No shit, Sherlock. This ain't my first rodeo," Wang said.

Dempsey caught himself grinning as he tried to assess every morsel of information from the event and ascribe tactical or strategic relevance, just like the instructors had trained him to do at the Farm:

Farhad received a text but didn't check it. Possible meanings: (1) Grimes has won his full and undivided attention; (2) he's not expecting anyone to contact him with anything important; (3) he's not on a tight leash . . . no domineering boss or girlfriend?

Dempsey continued trailing Grimes and Farhad, while keeping his distance and looking for ticks. As they reached the Starbucks, Farhad was explaining his plan to use the insights gained from his brain research to form a start-up focused on artificial intelligence and deep learning.

". . . in my opinion, artificial intelligence is the final frontier in tech. We're talking about a trillion-dollar market in a decade's time. My father is a venture capitalist, and he's already secured seed funding for my company. I'm putting my team together right now. I could use someone like you—someone friendly and highly motivated with an MBA."

"In that case," Grimes said, "maybe I should be buying you dinner instead of coffee."

"Seated and waiting," Smith said, confirming he was inside the coffeehouse and had taken a table in the back. If there were no open tables when Grimes and Farhad were ready to sit, he'd give up his table just in time for her to take it.

A beat later, Dempsey watched Grimes and Farhad disappear inside. He cleared his six and both sides of the street under the guise of checking traffic. After crossing to the west side of Oxford, he put his phone to his ear to make another fake call.

"Hey, it's me again. Decided to grab a coffee before I head home. Let me know if you want something?"

"Dempsey reporting—All clear outside, coming in. Ready for Adamo on your mark."

"Don't worry, it's not crowded. The wait's only a few minutes," Smith said, pretending to have a conversation of his own.

"Starbucks clear inside. Ready for Adamo three mikes."

Dempsey entered the Starbucks and found a place in line, just as Grimes was paying the tab for two caramel macchiatos. He heard her tell Farhad to wait at the pickup counter while she grabbed a table. In his peripheral vision, Dempsey watched their little game of musical chairs play out with subtle precision as Smith evacuated his table just in time for Grimes to take his seat, a mere thirty seconds before Farhad appeared with their coffees.

Smith cleared his throat.

A moment later the entrance door swung open and Adamo strolled in. Dempsey watched the CIA man scan the crowd, find Grimes, and then casually approach her table in the back. When Adamo stopped beside the table, Grimes looked up and smiled. "Adar, I'd like you to meet my friend, Scott," she said with the enthusiasm of someone who had just run into a long-lost friend.

259

This was the critical phase of the operation. Worst-case scenario, Adar was in play or under surveillance. If so, they could expect company any moment. Best-case scenario, the young Persian made a scene drawing attention to himself and them. Either way, the dude was a flight risk as far as Dempsey was concerned. Managing all of these contingencies was his job now.

"What the hell is going on?" Adar said, his voice taking on a timbre of terror.

"Hello, Adar," Adamo said. "Mind if I join you?"

"No . . . no, absolutely not," Farhad said, shifting in his seat.

"Don't be silly," Grimes said. "Here, take my seat, Scott. I'll leave you two alone to chat about boy stuff."

"Are you fucking kidding me?" Farhad stammered, realizing he'd just fallen victim to a honey trap. "This is bullshit. If both of you don't leave right now, I'm going to call the cops."

"Sit your ass back down in that chair," Adamo said, taking Grimes's seat. "The cops take orders from me, remember? Or have you forgotten what happens when you try to go to the police?"

After an awkward beat, Farhad said, "No, I haven't forgotten."

"Good, then let's talk."

"Back then you told me your name was Brad."

"My name is whatever I say it is," Adamo said and inspected his fingers as if bored.

"Okay, Scott, in that case, there's nothing to talk about. I'm clean now. I'm getting my PhD for God's sake. You have to believe me when I say I'm not involved in that stuff anymore."

"I know, and I'm proud of you for that," Adamo said with what to Dempsey almost sounded like a hint of fatherly pride. Then Adamo's tone turned hard and cold. "Now lower your fucking voice."

Dempsey stepped up to the register; it was his turn to order.

"May I help you, sir?" the pimple-faced girl manning the cash register asked.

"Medium coffee, black," Dempsey said.

"Hot or iced?"

"Hot, and keep the change." He handed her a five and then moved to the pickup area.

"There is nothing I can do for you," Adar was saying—desperation and fear in his voice. "I told you I'm clean. I've moved on."

"Sit still, smile, drink your coffee, you moron. You're drawing attention to us," Adamo said. "Play by the rules and this all goes easy. Make things hard, and I start scheduling meetings with your department chair and the dean. It's not my desire to ruin your life, but I will if I have to, and I won't lose sleep over it."

Grimes left Adamo and Farhad alone, and settled into a lounge chair next to Smith. She made a show of pulling out her phone and surfing the web. Just two strangers, a foot apart and separated by miles of Internet world.

"What do you want?" Farhad asked, defeated.

"I need your help, just one last time."

"Why? I don't know anything. I don't know anyone."

"Let me be the judge of that."

Farhad shook his head. "I'm not going back down that hole."

"I'm sorry to hear that, Adar. Because the last thing I wanted to see was you detained and questioned for your role in aiding and abetting terrorists."

"But, I'm not a terrorist," the young man said, his voice now tight with genuine fear.

"I know," Adamo said softly. "Which would make your imprisonment all the more tragic, but no less inevitable if you don't help me. You still have sins left to atone for, I'm afraid. Do we understand each other?"

"Yes," Farhad said, his voice cracking. "If I agree to help you this one last time, will you promise to leave me alone forever?"

"We both know that's a promise I can't make. I work for the United States of America, not Adar Farhad. But what I can promise you is that if you help me I'll protect you. If you get me the information that I need, I'll make sure that everything in your case file disappears. If something happens to me, the guy who takes my place won't find any skeletons in your closet."

After a long silence, Farhad said, "Okay. What next?"

"I'll meet you at your apartment at six p.m. No guests, no surprises. Between now and then, you go about your day as if nothing has happened. If you call anyone, if you try to run, I'll know and the deal is off. Do we understand each other?"

Farhad nodded. "Six p.m. I'll be there."

Adamo stood and walked swiftly toward the exit. Grimes joined him en route. On her way out the door, she turned and blew Farhad a kiss. An interested bystander, Dempsey turned just in time to see Farhad flip her the middle finger. He wandered to a seat across from Smith, who was tapping furiously on his phone. Dempsey eased himself into the chair and sipped at his coffee. He glanced at Farhad, who was still sitting at the table dazed and lost in thought. A few minutes passed, and he suddenly popped to his feet and stomped past with balled-up fists. He flung open the glass door and stepped outside onto the sidewalk. Dempsey watched him scan the street both directions before turning right to leave—shoulders slumped, head down in defeat.

"Status on Farhad's phone?" Adamo asked over the comms channel.

"Tracking," came Wang's happy reply. "He's moving south on Oxford. So far, he's being a good boy. No calls, no texts."

"You have the mike turned on?"

"Oh please. If he farts, we'll know it," Wang said. "And as soon as he gets back to his apartment and on his Wi-Fi, we own this bitch. I'm all over his keychains."

"Roger."

On cue, Smith departed.

Dempsey lingered behind, leisurely finishing his coffee until he was satisfied no one in the coffeehouse was of concern. Five minutes later, the entire team was gathered in the back of a Mercedes-Benz Sprinter van—a mobile office conversion unit—parked within walking distance of Farhad's apartment. This had been Adamo's show, and Dempsey grudgingly had to acknowledge that the CIA man had run a good op. Although, truth be told, most of the kudos went to Grimes for her performance.

"That dude wanted you bad," Wang said as Grimes shrugged on a sweatshirt, covering up her flimsy tank top and hard nipples in the back of the chilly van. "He was a walking, talking hard-on until Adamo showed up, then . . . *shrinkage.*" Wang made the whistling sound of a deflating balloon and curled his index finger.

"As much as it pains me to admit it, you're not the first person to say I have that effect on people," Adamo said, with a self-deprecating smile.

"Don't sweat it, Simon," Grimes said jumping into the fray. "When your name is Dick Wang, you simply can't help yourself from talking about other men's erections."

Everyone laughed, including Adamo, with Wang howling the loudest of all. It felt damn good to laugh, Dempsey thought. There hadn't been much to warrant levity lately, but they all needed something to break the tension. The clock was ticking, and they all felt it. The hours waiting until their 1800 interrogation with Farhad would be absolute torture for all of them. They needed something to fill the time. Something to keep their focus, so Dempsey looked at Adamo.

"What's on your mind, John?" Adamo said, without missing a beat.

"I was hoping that maybe now was a good time for you to fill us in on everything you know about Adar Farhad and his connection to the Suren Circle," Dempsey said, and for the first time since they'd met, he swore he saw something resembling respect in the other man's eyes.

"I started watching Farhad five years ago when he was a spoiled rich kid with a drug habit. I never believed that he was Suren, but I strongly suspected his parents. They fit the profile I was screening for:

immigrated from Iran between 1990 and 2005, married, financially sound, well educated, with occasional travel to visit family in Tehran."

"So you ran him as a CI?" Grimes asked.

"No, nothing that clean. We worked him for four years, but he was never cooperative. It was very much an antagonistic relationship. Besides the drug habit, he was hotheaded and always rebelling against his parents—parents who he viewed as sellouts and puppets of the West. At that time, Adar was disenfranchised and became enamored with Ahmadinejad."

"Is he a devout Muslim?" Smith asked.

Adamo laughed. "Never. His respect for Ahmadinejad had nothing to do with Islam. He loved the way Ahmadinejad talked shit against the West and got away with it. He loved the audacity and the spectacle of it all. I think in one sense he was modeling his rebellion against his parents after Ahmadinejad's rogue persona on the international stage."

"So what happened?" Dempsey asked.

"He spiraled out of control. Drug use eventually led to drug dealing. At the same time, he began experimenting with radical Islam. Again, not for ideological reasons, but to upset his parents. When he began communicating via social media with domestic extremists, he popped on another task force's radar. Things got a little messy then, because I didn't want to risk spooking the parents. I escalated and that pissed some folks off. Turned out to be all for nothing, however, because the parents staged an intervention and enrolled him in rehab. Six months later, Adar was clean, we had an administration change, and my group was shut down for lack of progress."

"So you never had anything on the parents?" Dempsey asked.

"Nothing actionable," Adamo said, shaking his head. "I was never in a position to force them to break protocol or communicate with other members of the Circle."

"Well," Dempsey said, rubbing his chin, "maybe it's time we change that."

CHAPTER 31

"What's the sour face for?" Grimes asked Dempsey.

"The leftover Chinese stinks," he said, nudging the trash bag of leftovers with his foot. "I don't understand how something that tastes so good can smell so bad. Either it goes, or I do."

"I'd love to see that report to Jarvis," she said with a laugh. "Operation blown on account of counterdetection from stinky Chinese takeout."

"Hey, guys, I'm trying to concentrate over here," Wang said, admonishing them despite the gigantic set of noise-canceling over-ear headphones he was wearing. "Do you mind?"

Adamo, who also was wearing headphones, scowled at them.

Dempsey and Grimes traded impish glances. Clearly, they weren't stakeout material. Dempsey leaned back in his seat and wondered if taking a little nap would rub Adamo the wrong way. Because if so, the SEAL in him could fall asleep on command.

"Put it on speaker. I promise we'll be quiet," Grimes said.

Wang looked at Adamo, who nodded, and then he switched on the cabin speakers. Dempsey heard a rustling as Farhad's phone swished in his pocket as he got out of his car and walked toward his parents' house. So far, he had proved to be compliant, but nothing else. From the time he left Starbucks, to the 1800 follow-up meeting, the kid had done exactly as he'd been told. No phone calls, no text messages, no non-work-related e-mails. The observation and waiting period had been critical to determining his credibility. Everyone, including Adamo, was convinced that Farhad was not being run or monitored by another entity, but only time and vigilance would prove that supposition.

It had taken thirty minutes, but Adamo had expertly and success-fully bullied Farhad into conducting one final task for him. Acting as a human Trojan horse, Adar would go to his parents' house with the mis-sion of instigating a chain of events that would force the two suspected sleeper agents to communicate with their VEVAK handler, with Tehran, or within the Circle itself.

"He's on the front porch," Wang reported.

Dempsey heard a knock, and then a beat later, Adar's mother greeted him at the front door. Mr. Farhad soon arrived and invited the once-prodigal son, now PhD candidate, inside to visit.

"Adar sounds nervous," Dempsey whispered to Grimes.

"Yeah, he does."

"I think they're in the kitchen now," Smith said.

"Audio gain just changed," Wang said. "Phone's out of his pocket. I'm turning on the camera."

Dempsey watched a new video feed populate one of the monitors in the van; it was the streaming video from Adar's front-facing mobile-phone camera. The image was of the kitchen ceiling.

"That's my boy," Adamo said, pleased that Adar had remembered to take the phone out of his pocket. "Now ask for Dad's phone . . ."

On cue, they heard Adar say, *"Hey, Dad, do you have any photos from the anniversary celebration? I'm sorry again to have missed the dinner."*

"*Of course. I have an entire album saved on my phone.*"

"*Can I see them?*"

"*Sure.*"

At that, Adamo made a silent, celebratory fist pump.

Two minutes later, Wang announced, "All right, I own the dad's phone."

"Check audio and video feeds," Adamo said.

"Dude, you gotta knock that shit off," Wang growled. "I know how to do my job."

"Sorry," Adamo said. "Bad habit."

They listened as the Farhads made small talk. When the conversation hit a lull, Adar's father said, "*Adar, you know how much your mother and I love when you visit, but I have to ask—Is something wrong? I can't remember the last time you showed up after dinner unannounced.*"

Dempsey locked eyes with Adamo and mouthed the word *showtime.*

Adamo nodded.

The tension in the van was palpable as they waited for Adar to drop the bomb.

"*Actually, yes,*" the younger Farhad said. "*I hope it's nothing, but something happened I want to talk to you about.*"

"*Does it involve a girl?*" Adar's mother asked.

"*No, nothing like that,*" he said. "*It actually has to do with the two of you.*"

"*With us?*" his father said with a laugh. "*Don't tell me you've run out of money.*"

"*No, Dad. I'm not here for money. I'm here to ask you about the Suren Circle.*"

Adar's father replied first. "*I'm not sure what you're talking about. I've never heard of the Suren Circle.*"

"*Is it a charity you want us to donate to?*" the mother added.

"*Please, Mom and Dad. Please don't make this any harder than it already is. I'm really scared and I need to know what the hell is going on.*"

Adar's voice shook. "Two federal agents approached me today. They told me that you guys were both members of an Iranian spy ring. They said it's some sleeper program and that you have been secretly working for the Iranian government for two decades."

There was a pause, and Dempsey wished like hell he had video other than the ceiling. He wanted to see the elder Farhad's face—see his real reaction.

After a beat, the father said, *"Adar, this is a safe place. You know that your mother and I won't judge you, so it's okay to tell us the truth . . . Have you started using again?"*

"Are you fucking kidding me? I tell you federal agents are investigating you and you ask me if I'm using!" He fired back with enough emotion that Dempsey knew the switch had just flipped in the grad student's head. The kid wasn't compulsory role-playing anymore. The conversation had taken on a gut-wrenching *oh shit, my parents might actually be spies* undertone now.

"Maybe we should call Dr. Magnus," his mother said. *"Schedule a session for all three of us to sit down and talk."*

"No. Absolutely not." When Adar spoke again, the ire in his voice was gone, replaced by the same dispassionate tone his mother had used. "Actually, maybe that's not a bad idea. Maybe we should talk with a neutral third party. I can invite the two special agents to come to the session, too. It would be a delight to watch Dr. Magnus question them about their psychosis and drug-induced delusions as they lay out their case records."

A long, uncomfortable silence hung on the line, while Wang solicited high fives from every member of the Ember team in sequence. "Fuckin' A, way to go, Adar," Wang said while laughing.

"What else did these men say?" Adar's father asked, his voice suddenly grave. "The US media is stoking the flames of Islamaphobia in this country. If we are being unjustly targeted by Homeland Security, I need to know. This could be very serious, Son."

"They told me that you and Mom were recruited by something called VEVAK when you were in your twenties. You were given false identities, money, and the visas needed to emigrate to the US. You became naturalized citizens, but all the while continued working as part of a secret ring of sleeper agents created to infiltrate American business and government and gather trade secrets."

"Adar, we love you, Son, but this sounds crazy and paranoid. After all you put us through, you can see why we would worry. If any of this were true, then why didn't the US government arrest us years ago? Why contact you now after leaving us alone for twenty years? It doesn't make any sense," Farhad senior said.

"I asked the exact same question, and do you want to know what their answer was? Because until now, you were only gathering intelligence. But in the last few days, they said they have reason to believe that your spy ring is planning a terrorist attack."

"That's ridiculous," Adar's father scoffed.

"What's ridiculous? That you and Mom are career spies and you've hidden this fact from me for my entire life, or that you're helping launch a terrorist attack inside the US?"

"Both!" the father shouted.

Someone started crying.

"Who's crying?" Dempsey asked.

"Mrs. Farhad," Grimes answered, narrowing her eyes. "Call it woman's intuition, but I call bullshit. I know it sounds legit, but crying is a great redirect. It's what I'd do if I were her."

"Don't cry, Mom," Adar said. *"Please don't cry, I'm not trying to accuse you of anything."*

"Shit," Dempsey growled. "We're losing him."

"It's okay," Adamo said, looking at Dempsey and Grimes. "Adar did exactly what we needed him to do. He forced their hand. In the next five minutes, one of two things is going to happen. Either they kick him out of the house, or they read him in, but no matter what happens we need to get Baldwin and the boys up and monitoring ASAP because we're about to learn the truth."

CHAPTER 32

Ember Surveillance Van
Parked near the Farhad Residence

Dempsey watched Wang's fingers fly across a workstation keyboard as he messaged with Baldwin back in Virginia. Over Wang's shoulder, Dempsey read the string, only then realizing that the Professor had been tied into the op the entire time. Apparently, from the moment that Wang commandeered Adar's father's mobile phone, Baldwin and the boys back at Ember had been busy requisitioning historical data to start mining.

"Sounds like they're wrapping up in there," Grimes said, talking over the audio feed.

Adamo nodded, but held a finger to his lips.

"Adar, can we please just agree to drop all of this your parents are spies lunacy and focus on what really matters?" Farhad senior said.

"And what is that, Dad?"

"Completing your PhD and building a team for your start-up."

"Sure, that all sounds great, until the federal agents show up at the lab and haul me away for questioning. What the hell am I supposed to do then?"

"You tell them the same thing I'm telling you now, that they must be mistaken with their information, and that if they have any more questions, they need to come talk to me directly."

After a beat, Adar said, "Fine, but when they throw you and Mom in the back of a black van and haul you away for interrogation, don't say I didn't warn you."

"I think you're being a little melodramatic now, Son. Why don't you head back to your apartment? Relax. Have some dinner. Watch a movie. Better yet, why don't you go to bed early and get some sleep? If what you say is true, then I'm sure it's just one big misunderstanding. Give it some time, and I promise everything will be fine."

Dempsey listened to the awkward good-bye that followed as the Farhads ushered their son out the front door. To his surprise, Adar drove away in his car, parked out of sight, then walked back to the van, just as Adamo had told him to do. Dempsey had been surprised by the instruction. It felt wrong letting the kid into their inner circle, but Adamo had been adamant about wanting Adar to listen to the parents' post-op discussion—a discussion the Farhads were just beginning to conduct as Grimes closed the slider door behind the kid. Adar shot daggers at Grimes as he climbed into a seat, but she pretended not to notice, instead focusing her attention on the conversation being retransmitted by the father's hacked phone:

"Do you think he's telling the truth?" Mrs. Farhad said.

"Yes, unfortunately," Adar's father said.

"What do we do?"

"Hush," he said, his voice low and agitated.

When he spoke again, it was in Farsi. Dempsey groaned his irritation at the language change. Now he'd have to rely on Adamo and Grimes to reconstruct the conversation.

The sounds of running water and a kitchen ventilation hood fan being turned on suddenly drowned out their voices.

Adamo looked at Wang. "Is there anything you can do about this?"

"Yeah sure. Hey, Adar, can you run back in there and ask your parents to turn that shit off and talk clearly into the microphone?" Wang said.

Adamo glowered at Wang. "Cut the crap. I'm being serious."

"So am I. There's nothing I can do, man," Wang said. "I have some tech for this situation, but it requires line-of-sight video surveillance. In the meantime, I'm recording everything and streaming it back to the TOC. Hopefully, they'll be able to work some magic and pull dialogue out of all that interference."

Dempsey shifted his attention to Adar.

The kid looked dazed. "I can't believe it," he mumbled. "I . . . I just don't understand."

"Sorry, dude," Wang said with a pitying smile, "but your parents are fucking spies."

"For my whole life, they've been lying to me." Adar looked at Adamo. "While you, someone I despised all these years, were telling me the truth."

Adamo exhaled through his nose. "Do you remember what I said to you the very first time we met?"

Adar nodded, and his gaze went to the middle distance. "You told me that I wouldn't like what you had to say, but the one thing you'd never do was lie to me."

"That's right. And I've kept that promise."

"And what about me? What am I supposed to do now?"

Adamo placed a hand on the kid's shoulder. "You're going to do exactly what your father said. Go home, relax, and work on your PhD. Tomorrow you'll have a new handler, someone to help you manage this situation and answer all your questions, but until then you're on your own. Do you think you can handle that, Adar?"

"My parents are spies. That's not something you can simply pretend away."

"Sure you can," Dempsey said. "My parents were Democrats, but I found a way to manage."

"This isn't a joke."

"I know," Dempsey said, meeting the young man's eyes. "Yes, your parents are spies, but that doesn't make you one. You're an American—a first-generation Persian American with a brilliant mind and a bright future. This is your country, just like it's mine, and his, and hers, and his, and his," he said pointing at each of his teammates in turn. "Our job is to safeguard the lives of all Americans. We're always out there, operating in the shadows. And now you see us. Now you know what we do, and why we do it. As much as you might like to go back to your old life of blissful ignorance, you can't, Adar. You're one of us now—a shadow warrior—and you have a job to do. And if you don't do your job, thousands of people are going to die. So I ask you, can you rise above the fear and uncertainty? Can you cage your personal demons and become a protector of innocent men, women, and children?"

"I think so."

"You *think* so, or you *will*?"

"I will," Adar said, tightening his jaw and nodding slowly. "You can count on me, sir."

Dempsey looked at Adamo. "Time for Adar to head home; we have work to do."

Adamo nodded and escorted the kid back to his car. On his return to the van, Smith asked, "Are we good?"

"Yeah. As soon as we finish here, I'll assign him a handler. Someone we can trust." Then, looking at Dempsey, Adamo added, "Thanks for the pep talk, John. Adar needed to hear that."

"No problem," Dempsey said. "Sometimes all it takes is marching orders and a kick in the ass. Adar knows the stakes; he's a smart kid."

"Hey, guys, heads up," Wang said, his voice amping up a notch. "We've got an outbound call."

"Dad's phone?" Adamo asked.

"Nope," Wang said. "Probably a burner. Baldwin's on it."

"Where's the call to?"

"Hang on . . . looks like the Chicago area code . . . ringing, ringing, three rings, no answer. Call disconnected."

"Can you get us an address?" Adamo said, tension in his voice.

"They're working on it . . . it's a mobile phone. Shit, another outgoing. Fifty bucks says he's working down the hierarchy. This one is an Omaha area code . . . the call picked up."

"Put it on speaker, for Christ's sake," Adamo barked.

"I can't. This is Baldwin's show," Wang said, messaging back and forth at the terminal. "But he's dictating. I'll read it to you guys:

"Hello, this is Keyvan Shirazi . . ."

"Hello, Keyvan, this is Sharzeh Farhad in California."

"Oh, Sharzeh, so good to hear from you. Tell me, how is the family?"

"Fine, fine, no news to report."

"Good to hear. And work, how is work? Any new or interesting projects?"

"Work is fine. No new projects. The only new and interesting thing I have to report are some new people who just moved into the neighborhood. They're very loud and intrusive. I hope we don't have to relocate to a different neighborhood to find peace and quiet."

"That is unfortunate. Please, keep me informed of what happens."

"Of course . . . So, tell me, Keyvan, how is your family?"

"The family is fine, thanks for asking. Nothing new to report with the children."

"And your work?"

"Work is stressful at the moment. I've taken on some new, temporary responsibilities."

"Is that so? What kind of responsibilities, if you don't mind me asking?"

"Nothing I want to bore you with. I'm simply looking forward to wrapping up the project as soon as possible."

"Is there anything I can do to help?"

"No. This is local business, that's all."

"Okay, it was nice speaking with you, Keyvan. Give Delilah my love, and please don't hesitate to call if you need anything⊠anything at all."

"Yes, of course. Thanks for calling, Sharzeh. Good-bye."

"Holy shit," Grimes said, grinning like a schoolgirl. "We got 'em."

"Are you all right, Simon?" Smith eyed the CIA man. "You look a little green."

"Yeah," Adamo said, shaking his head and smiling. "It's just surreal . . . to be finally vindicated, after all these years. It's hard to explain the feeling."

"Congratulations, Simon. Seriously, bro, nice work," Dempsey said. Then after a beat, he asked, "Now what?"

"Now," Adamo said, pushing his eyeglasses up on his nose, "we head to Omaha and pay Keyvan Shirazi a visit."

CHAPTER 33

Omaha, Nebraska
November 2, 1930 Local Time

Somehow, the Americans had found him.

Keyvan's hands were still shaking, no matter how tight he clutched the steering wheel. In broad daylight, in the middle of a campus parking lot, they'd grabbed him, forced him into a black SUV at gunpoint, and given him a shakedown, all without anyone noticing.

A car horn sounded behind him.

With a start, he looked in his rearview mirror and saw a middle-aged man in a Buick throwing his hands up in the universal gesture for *What the hell are you waiting for?* Behind the Buick, he noted the roofline of the black SUV. The American agents were following him, keeping pressure on to make sure he followed through.

The choice they'd given him was simple: cooperate or lose everything in his life that mattered. Just one look into their leader's eyes—the brute with the spiral scar on his muscular forearm—was enough to convince Keyvan this was no idle threat. The people who'd taken him weren't local law enforcement, nor were they FBI. They hadn't even bothered to identify themselves as federal agents or flashed him ID. They were black ops. They were the type of people who made problems disappear. They were ghost warriors fighting America's *real* War on Terror. If he failed, they would make him pay, and pay dearly. And so in exchange for immunity, he'd told them everything, including how the Suren Circle had been activated; how he and Delilah had driven to Douglas, Arizona, to pick up and assist two jihadists who had crossed the border; and that two other Suren sleeper-agent couples were fulfilling similar tasking in different locations. In exchange for a promise of a new identity and a new life with Delilah, he'd agreed to become their double agent and discover the target locations for the other two attacks. Now, it was time to make good on his end of the bargain.

He lifted his foot off the brake pedal and transferred it to the accelerator. His BMW sped forward and through the intersection just as the traffic light overhead changed to yellow. He drove the speed limit all the way home. Somewhere along the way, the black SUV disappeared, but it didn't matter. They were still watching. They were still listening.

He pressed a button on the remote control garage-door opener clipped to the passenger sun visor and waited for the door to roll open. After parking, he pushed the same button on the remote and watched the door lower in his rearview mirror until the last bit of fading daylight disappeared. He loitered in the dark, paralyzed with fear and dread and uncertainty.

What if they suspect me? What if they catch me in a lie? What if they figure out that my phone is being used as a body wire? What if they hurt Delilah? What if they turn her against me? What if . . . what if . . . what if . . .

The door to the house opened and made him jump. He turned to see Delilah's silhouette in the doorway. Her hands moved to her hips, signaling both her impatience and irritation.

Just act normal, he told himself. He opened the driver-side door and stepped out.

"What are you doing out here in the dark, Keyvan?" she asked.

"Nothing," he said and shut the car door behind him.

"I heard the garage door a while ago, you had to be doing something all this time."

"I was just thinking," he said, approaching her.

She narrowed her eyes, scrutinizing him for insincerity, but said nothing else. He leaned in to give her a peck on the lips and she gave him her cheek, something she'd never done before. He was about to ask her what was the matter, but he knew the dreadful answer to this question.

"Come," she said, as if talking to a child. "They're waiting for us in the basement."

He followed her through the mudroom, through the kitchen, and to the stairs leading down to the basement. Their basement was finished, with a full bathroom and a guest bedroom. The rest of the space served as a lounge and game room, complete with poker and Ping-Pong tables—both big-box-store whim purchases, and both never used. Never used, that was, until now. Their two *guests* had transformed the card table into a command center, covering every square inch of surface area with maps and photographs. The Ping-Pong table, on the other hand, was now serving as a weapons staging platform. He scanned the instruments of death and destruction neatly displayed, including two Kevlar vests wired with bombs, two small machine guns whose make he did not recognize, two Glock 9 mm pistols, and several nasty-looking blades of varying lengths. Also, on the table sat a small handheld video recorder.

Since his last trip to the basement, there was one new addition—a black sheet with the white logo of the Islamic State was now tacked to the basement wall. A stool was staged in front of the terrorist banner. This was where they would shoot their web videos, reading self-serving passages of the Quran and taking credit for the devastation they were about to unleash.

"You've been gone a long time," the Syrian said, not looking up from where he sat, typing on a notebook computer.

"I had work to do," Keyvan replied. "I've fallen behind since your arrival."

"Is that so?" the Syrian replied, his voice rife with superiority.

"It is important that I maintain my regular routines and appearances," he said, shoving his hands into his pockets. "You wouldn't want me to do anything to draw unwanted attention to myself or the house would you?"

At this the Syrian looked up and fixed his cold, black eyes on him.

"What?" Keyvan said, nervously.

The Syrian set his notebook computer on the end table beside the sofa and stood up. He walked over to Keyvan and stepped into his personal space.

"You seem nervous. More nervous than usual."

Keyvan looked at Delilah, but her gaze was fixed on the Syrian.

"Why are you so nervous today, Keyvan?" the Syrian said, tilting his head.

"I don't know what you're talking about," Keyvan said, willing himself not to take a step back.

Just then a toilet flushed, and a beat later the Iranian VEVAK operative appeared from the bathroom.

"Professor Shirazi returns," he said, with false bravado. "How many papers did you grade? How many American superstars will have to go home brokenhearted with a B today?"

As much as Keyvan despised the VEVAK operative, he was grateful for the interruption. He chuckled and said, "I gave seven Cs, nine Bs, and five As, if you must know."

"I don't give a shit," the man said. "Get me a drink of water."

"Okay," Keyvan said, turning toward the wet bar on the far basement wall.

"With ice," the Iranian said, glancing at the Syrian with a fox's grin. "In America, it is perfectly acceptable to treat a man like a woman. See, look at how obedient Keyvan has become. He's so indoctrinated in his legend that there is no Persian pride left in him at all."

Keyvan felt his cheeks heat while he prepared a glass of ice water.

"Do you still have your manhood, Keyvan? Or has it shriveled away along with your pride?"

Keyvan felt a surge of anger, and he wanted to throw the ice water in the VEVAK man's face, but he knew that would be a terrible mistake. The Iranian was twenty years his junior and a tactically trained VEVAK operative. The man was a killer; of this much Keyvan was certain, whereas he had no practical experience in such things. He silently cursed his trembling hand as he passed the water to his tormentor. The Iranian took the glass without thanks, and walked over to take a seat on the sofa.

"Prove him wrong, Keyvan," the Syrian said, filling the awkward silence. "I am one man short for the operation. Join me as one of Allah's chosen warriors and cement your legacy as a hero of Persia."

Keyvan glanced at the suicide vests on the Ping-Pong table and felt his stomach tie in knots.

"That was never part of the arrangement," the man from VEVAK said from the sofa.

"Then the arrangement must change."

"Keyvan is not your asset. The Suren are tasked with providing support. They do not take orders from you, and neither do I."

"I think you misunderstand. This is not my will, but the will of Allah. Without a second warrior, the mission will fail," the Syrian said, his voice even and calm. "Who are you to question God's plan?"

The Iranian wagged a finger at the Syrian. "Now you listen to me—"

"I'll do it," Keyvan interrupted, shocking them all.

"What?" the Iranian snarled.

"I said I'll do it," Keyvan repeated. He glanced at the Syrian and saw that the terrorist wore an expression he'd not seen since his arrival . . . *a smile. Keyvan took a deep breath and brazenly* walked over to the card table covered with maps and photographs. This was the closest he'd been permitted to get to the table, which validated the logic behind his decision to volunteer. The *only* exigency that the Syrian cared about was drafting another suicide bomber. Offering to satisfy that need was the only way to learn the details of the operation. "He's right," Keyvan said, looking down at the map of downtown Omaha. He found the Old Market district and quickly scanned the street labels. "I am very familiar with the Old Market. To achieve maximum results, it will take two gunmen. Together, we can herd the infidels toward the intersection of Howard and Eleventh Streets and detonate the bombs on opposite sides of the crowd."

"Yes, yes," the Syrian said, walking over to stand beside him. "This was exactly my plan."

The VEVAK man looked at Delilah. "What is your opinion of this?"

She glanced at each of them in turn, her eyes settling last on Keyvan. "I am surprised at my husband's decision, but if this is God's will, then who am I to judge?"

"Then it's settled," the Iranian said, quickly. He walked to the Ping-Pong table and picked up one of the suicide vests. "This will be your vest. Come here, Keyvan, I want you to put it on for me."

Keyvan swallowed. "Right now?"

The Syrian's enthusiasm darkened. "Is there a problem?"

"No, no, of course not, I just don't see why," Keyvan stuttered, "why I must try on the vest now."

The Syrian narrowed his eyes. "I think you misunderstand me. I'm not asking you to try on the vest. This is not a wardrobe fitting. It is time to begin your training, and your first assignment is to wear the vest for twenty-four hours."

"Twenty-four hours?" Keyvan exclaimed, feeling all the blood drain from his face.

"But of course. A martyr must embrace his destiny, and to do that you must embrace the vest. It must become a part of you, and you a part of it. Do not be afraid, Keyvan. Allah is watching."

Keyvan's feet suddenly felt like blocks of lead. Even if he wanted to, gravity prevented him from taking a step. He looked back down at the card table. "Maybe after we discuss the operation, I'll be ready to wear it."

There was no way in hell he was going to walk around with bombs strapped to his torso. Not for twenty-four hours. Not for twenty-four seconds. His heart was racing now, beating so fast it felt like he was going into Afib. He clutched the edge of the card table to steady himself. Frantically, he scanned the photographs, maps, and documents on the table for clues about the other target locations. Everything on the table seemed to pertain to Omaha, but there had to be something. Some hint or clue identifying the other two cities. He was almost positive there were two other cities being targeted, because three sedans had arrived that night in Douglas, Arizona, and three sedans had departed in three different directions. A large map of downtown Omaha covered the middle of the table, but he spied a sliver of another map peeking out beneath one side. He folded the Omaha map on itself, revealing a map of the continental United States taped to the table below. Three red dots immediately caught his attention: Atlanta, Omaha, and Seattle.

"I just think we should discuss the details of the operation as a group. The tactics we use in the Old Market could also be applied to the targets in Atlanta and Seattle." He noticed that the dot in Washington State was actually located in a suburb of Seattle, not downtown proper. He leaned left to try to read the small black font of the township beneath the dot.

"Keyvan, what are you doing?" Delilah said, her tone both scolding and fearful at the same time.

He stopped and looked up at her.

He saw horror in her eyes.

His heart fluttered.

In his peripheral vision, he realized that the Syrian was standing beside him. He turned his head to find the muzzle of a gun leveled at his forehead.

"What is the meaning of this?" he shouted, trying to sound indignant but his voice cracking instead with fear. "Don't point that at me."

There was a blur of movement, and the center of his face exploded in pain as the bridge of his nose shattered from the blow of the pistol butt. His eyes lit up with a fireworks display of white light and he pitched forward. His knee screamed in pain as it hit the ground. He felt warm blood rushing through the fingers that cupped his ruined nose.

"My God. Why did you do that?"

It was Delilah's voice—frightened and tight.

"Why is Keyvan asking these questions? Who have you been talking to?" the Syrian demanded.

"No one. I've spoken to no one," he tried to yell, but his voice was wet cotton. "I'm a servant of Allah. I've done everything he's asked of me."

The Syrian scowled and kicked him. Pain erupted in his side and he felt a rib snap. He heard a scream, and realized it was his own, reverberating off the basement walls.

"What have you told the Americans?" the terrorist asked. His voice was calm now, almost soft. Perhaps it was over, Keyvan thought. He tried to push himself up from the floor, but his left side and chest shrieked in protest. Without warning, another kick landed between his legs, and he thought he would die before he could suck in another breath.

"What have you told them about the operation? Have you revealed the targets? Tell me and the pain will stop."

"Stop it, you're killing him," Delilah cried.

Keyvan heard more emotion in that cry from her than he had in years, and he knew then that she still loved him. That realization gave him the strength he needed. They could get out of this. They could start over. "I am a servant of Allah. I will martyr myself, to see the Mahdi return in all his glory," Keyvan managed to choke out. The voice, sputtering and begging, was alien to him. The words and promises were coming from somewhere deep and primal, but his plea was only met with another blow.

He collapsed to the floor again, but immediately felt a hand on his collar, jerking him roughly back up to his knees. The pain was clouding his mind, weakening his resolve. The voice inside his head was wishing for a quick end—in a burst of glorious, explosive light—as opposed to this slow death by bludgeoning. He readied himself for the next blow, but it did not come.

"What did you tell them about the Old Market? What did you tell them about Seattle and—"

"Shut up, you idiot. You're making it worse."

"Unhand me."

Keyvan was no longer sure who was speaking and to whom. He willed his eyes open to see what was happening, only to find the gaping black eye of a pistol so close his eyes couldn't focus on it.

Then there was a flash.

And terrible pain.

And then nothing.

CHAPTER 34

Ember SUV
Two Blocks from the Shirazi House
Omaha, Nebraska
2015 Local Time

Atlanta.

Keyvan had clearly said "Atlanta," and now Dempsey could think of nothing but Kate and Jake as the word echoed over and over in his head. His throat tightened, and he felt anxiety the likes of which he hadn't felt since the day he pinned on his Trident. The losses he experienced because he wore the Trident were part of the life he had chosen. But this . . . this was just too much. Kate and Jake were never supposed to be in danger—that was his part of their equation.

A gunshot snapped him from his emotional fugue.

"Oh shit. I think they just executed him," Wang gasped, all the usual flippancy and sarcasm gone from his voice.

"Quiet," Dempsey barked.

The arguing in the Shirazi basement continued:

"Are you mad? We needed to know what he told them."

"*Shut your mouth, you fool. We're not in Raqqa or Ar Rutbah. What were you thinking?*"

"*You're the one who executed him, Persian.*"

"*Because you forced my hand. If the Americans actually did tag him, then they've been listening from the beginning. In which case, you were sharing more information with your foolish questions than he knew.*"

There was a rustling and then a wet thud.

"*He's not wearing a body wire. No electronics.*"

"*Then you killed him for nothing. You killed my Keyvan, you monster. He was doing what we were trained to do,*" the wife sobbed.

"*You saw how nervous he was. The only explanation for his behavior is betrayal.*"

"*He's always nervous, you asshole,*" she screamed. "*That is how he is. But he's always been loyal to me and to Persia, and you murdered him for it.*"

Dempsey heard the sound of a slap.

"*Never speak to me that way, woman. And if Keyvan was loyal to you ahead of his country, then perhaps I should be asking what it is that you're not telling us.*"

"*I've been sequestered here with you since Arizona,*" she cried. "*How could I possibly be working with the Americans?*"

"*Hey, what are you doing?*"

"*Checking his phone.*"

A sudden loud scraping sound caused Wang to dial down the volume on his laptop, which was presently streaming over the Yukon's speakers via Bluetooth.

"*The phone appears to be off.*"

"*Let me see it . . .*"

"*Where is the woman? Where did she go?*"

"*I don't know, probably to the bathroom to be sick.*"

"*No, she's upstairs. She's running. Go after her!*"

Dempsey gritted his teeth. The voice belonged to al-Mahajer; he was certain of it.

"She's my problem, do you understand? You don't touch her."

"Just bring her back. Quickly, you fool!"

Dempsey unbuckled his seatbelt. "She's making a run for it."

Smith whipped around from the driver seat. "Go get her, but John . . ."

"Yeah?"

"If you're seen, we're blown. Better to sacrifice her than the mission."

"Don't worry, I got this," Dempsey said, before slipping out the rear passenger door and heading off into the night to save Delilah Shirazi.

CHAPTER 35

Rostami reached the top of the stairs and saw that the door leading from the kitchen into the backyard was hanging open. He cursed al-Mahajer under his breath. The man might be a genius when it came to brutalizing the locals in western Iraq, whipping up the disenfranchised into a religious fury, and hacking his opposition to pieces, but clearly he knew nothing about clandestine operations in a civilized country. This was not Al Qa'im—this was the middle of America. What a fool.

He sprinted out the kitchen door onto a brick patio, where he paused and scanned both directions for movement. Seeing none, he listened for the sound of a car engine coming to life, but instead he heard the rustle of leaves and the crack of branches straight ahead. Rostami pulled his pistol from his waistband and ran across the backyard toward the wooded expanse that separated the Shirazis' neighborhood from the east campus. He entered the woods, crouched low, and moved quietly in the dark. Every few meters he paused, listening. He heard a rustle to his right and veered toward the sound, all the while cursing in his head. In a span of two days, al-Mahajer had destroyed two invaluable VEVAK assets who had been operating for two decades undetected in America. Keyvan was a nervous woman of a man—he'd been that way since Arizona—but was he brave enough to betray them? Rostami thought not. Now Keyvan was dead, which dictated the same fate for Delilah. He simply could not let her live. Even if she was loyal, fear and anger would render her useless, and he could hardly leave her behind, knowing all that she knew.

He heard the sound of feet on leaves, slightly to his left now. He slowed and moved cautiously and quietly. Delilah had gotten her panic under control. She was hiding now. He took a knee, closed his eyes, and listened carefully—all predator. Thoughts of Delilah's bleached-blonde hair; ample breasts; and thin, fit body flooded his mind. If he had to kill her, he might as well have fun in the process. He would pin her down by her throat on the floor of the woods. He would tear her clothes from her body and fuck her as he dragged his blade across her throat. He would finish as he watched the life drain from her face and then her eyes. Always it left the eyes last.

He heard a soft, shuddering sigh.

He opened his eyes and inched forward . . . very slowly . . . very carefully. He spied a large-diameter tree several meters deeper into the woods. She was hiding behind that tree; he was certain of it. His eyes, now fully acclimated to the dark, could make out one gray running shoe sticking out past the trunk. A smile spread across his face.

He looked over his shoulder toward the lights of the backyard, now perhaps eighty meters behind him. No movement. No sound. No pursuit. The Syrian had not followed him. He looked again at the shoe, which had not moved. If she screamed, he would be forced to kill her immediately. He needed to be quick; he needed to be silent. He reached the tree—raised a hand and rested it on the wide trunk, bending in a crouch. He could hear her breathing now, long and slow.

He readied himself and took a small step, repositioning around the trunk. As he did, her denim-clad left leg and half her ass came into view, the skintight jeans leaving little to the imagination. From her position, he knew she was looking away from him, peering around the far side of the tree. He slipped the pistol back into his waistband holster; took a deep, silent breath; and lunged at her.

At the sound of his attack she tried to spin, but tripped over a root and fell backward instead. She landed hard, her arms flailing. She grunted, but to her great credit—and his relief—she did not scream. He clamped his right hand onto her throat and squeezed. She gagged and her eyes went wide. He stretched his body long on top of hers, pinning her arms against her chest and pressing her into the ground with all his mass. She squirmed beneath him, terror-stricken and panicked.

"Be still," he whispered. "It's going to be all right."

For a moment her eyes filled with a spark of hope. Perhaps he was here to save her from the fanatical al-Mahajer? Perhaps he would protect her? He knew she'd noticed his glances. She must now be building a fantasy in which he helped her escape—somehow got her to safety and away from the crazy Syrian. Rostami smiled a dark smile and slid a hand to unbuckle his pants. Her eyes widened with realization and a renewed terror. At the sight of her fear and helplessness, he had to exert all his self-control not to take her quickly.

Not yet. Not like this. Not until I'm bleeding her life into the dirt.

Unencumbered now, he drew his stiletto from its scabbard. Gazing into her eyes, he pressed the point a centimeter below the corner of her right eye. She whimpered, and he shushed her like a baby. Still pinning her with his full weight, he released her throat. She gasped and gurgled, while he fumbled to pull down her pants—finally snapping the button off and splaying open the short zipper by force. Grinning with anticipation, he tugged, but the fucking pants would not drop past her ass. The tight, hip-hugging jeans the Western whores loved to wear—a look that drove him sex crazy—was now working against him.

He shifted his weight to the right to get more leverage.

Her knee snapped up between his legs with impossible force. He grunted and somehow stifled the urge to yell. Long nails clawed his face—just missing his left eye. He released his grip on her jeans and went for her neck, but she had her chin tucked now. From the corner of his eye, he saw her right hand dart downward. Next thing he knew, she was clutching his scrotum. She squeezed, crushing his testicles and digging her fingernails into his flesh. Unable to control himself, he howled in pain, the knife slipping from his grip as he buckled at the waist and rolled off her. She released her vise grip, and he was aware of her squirming away, but the pain and nausea were incapacitating. As her footfalls disappeared into the night, all he could do was lie there and moan.

CHAPTER 36

Dempsey moved like a SEAL through the brush—deliberate, fast, and quiet. He was in his element now. He felt electric and invincible, which was a problem, because tonight he wasn't kitted up like a SEAL. No rifle. No Kevlar vest. No radio. No NVGs.

Given the choice of all those things, right now, he'd take the NVGs.

His organic night eyes had gone to shit the last few years, along with everything else, it seemed. His back, his alcohol tolerance, his mental concentration—

He heard a wail, but not a woman's wail.

This was the sound of a man in agony.

A beat later, he heard uncontrolled breathing and footsteps moving toward him fast. He dropped into a low crouch, and glided in behind a low bush. He was itching to pull his Sig Sauer from the holster he was wearing, but he couldn't risk a gunshot. Not here. Not now. Even if it turned out to be the devil himself, Rafiq al-Mahajer, Dempsey needed to show restraint. To locate and stop the other terror cells, Ember needed al-Mahajer alive. But if their paths crossed here in the woods, would he have the self-control? Probably not. A wave of dread washed over him at the realization. Was his thirst for vengeance that powerful?

Suddenly, he was regretting his decision to leave the Yukon.

The running figure came into view, and he saw that it was a woman. *What the hell is she doing?* he thought, as he watched her run while trying to hold her pants up simultaneously.

When she closed within ten feet he could make out the expression of abject terror on her face. With no time to second-guess the decision, Dempsey exploded out of the brush and wrapped her up. He clasped his left hand tightly over her mouth and used his right arm to protect her torso from injury as he brought her to the ground and rolled with her into a dense patch of brush. He dragged her along with him, as he crabbed back behind the bush.

Pressing his lips to her ear, he whispered, "I'm here to help you, Delilah. Be silent or we're both dead. Nod if you understand?"

She nodded inside his grip.

"I'm going to let go. Don't bite me."

She nodded again.

He eased his hand off her face, and she immediately whipped her head around to look at him. They locked eyes, and he saw both surprise and uncertainty in her gaze. He kept perfectly still and felt her body shuddering against his, the adrenaline still coursing through her veins.

A twig cracked nearby, and she jerked in his arms.

He held a finger to his lips.

She nodded.

Dempsey looked over his shoulder and caught a glimpse of a figure through a little gap in the foliage—adult male, walking with an awkward gait, possibly due to injury. Dempsey couldn't make out the face in the dark. He glanced back down at Delilah and saw that her blouse was torn and her jeans were ripped open at the hips. His mind quickly filled in the blanks—that motherfucker.

He repositioned his hand to the hilt of his SOG knife clipped to his belt. Delilah saw this and immediately tensed, her respiration rate ticking up. She craned her neck around to look at him, and he shook his head: *Don't worry, not for you.*

The footsteps stopped.

He felt her go stiff in his arms.

Dempsey looked over his other shoulder. Through the leaves, he could just make out their stalker. The man dangled a blade in his left hand while dabbing at his left cheek and nose with the index and middle fingers of his other hand. He held up his fingers for inspection in the pale moonlight. Dempsey heard him sigh heavily and gaze up at the sky, as if saying a prayer to the heavens. Then, the figure looked in their direction. Dempsey tightened his grip on the knife and visualized how the hand-to-hand sequence would unfold.

He waited for the footsteps.

Waited.

Waited . . .

The figure looked away. Shoulders slumped, scanning the woods one last time, before heading back the way he'd come.

Dempsey let out a long, slow breath but continued to hold Delilah. After several minutes passed, he whispered, "Listen to me carefully. I know who you are. I know you're Suren. I know there are terrorists in your house right now planning to launch simultaneous attacks at the Old Market as well as in Atlanta and Seattle."

Her eyes widened.

"Then you also know what happened to Keyvan?" she whispered.

Dempsey nodded. "I'm sorry about your husband."

She began to sob. "They murdered him in cold blood."

"I know."

"Everything got out of control."

"It always does with these people."

"You work for the US government?"

He nodded.

"What are you going to do to me?"

"That, Delilah, is entirely up to you. We can do things the hard way, or the easy way. Either way you're coming with me and you're going to tell me and my colleagues everything you know."

He sensed a wave of fatalism wash over her, and tears began to flow down her cheeks. "I made a terrible mistake, trusting these men."

"Yes, you did," he said, and then let silence do the work for him.

After a minute, she wiped her tears with the backs of her hands. Then, to his relief, she swallowed hard and said, "Okay, I choose the easy way."

CHAPTER 37

The bitch was gone.

And it was al-Mahajer's fault.

Rostami slammed the kitchen door. He wanted to scream. No, he wanted to take his blade and plunge it into the Syrian's fucking neck. He paced the kitchen, walking donuts around the Shirazis' granite-topped cooking island. He paused and looked at himself in the reflection of the stainless-steel espresso machine on the bar. There were two shallow gouges on his cheek and a third along his eye socket that oozed blood down along his nose. The burning between his legs made him almost desperate to check himself out below, but he couldn't risk the Syrian coming up and finding him with his bloody manhood in his hand.

He pulled his gaze away from the distorted reflection, grabbed a paper towel, and began dabbing away the blood on his face. *Killing al-Mahajer is a legitimate option,* he told himself. Without al-Mahajer, the operation would proceed as planned in Atlanta and Redmond. Those cells were on autopilot now. Carnage in two out of three target locations was still a victory. He could fabricate a grand fait accompli about discovering that the Shirazis were double agents and serve up this entire debacle in rich detail to Amir Modiri once he was safely back in Tehran. He was so tired of cleaning up other people's messes. This circus should never have been his responsibility in the first place. This was supposed to be Parviz's operation, but no, Parviz had to go and get himself captured by the Americans in Iraq. Gritting his teeth, Rostami made a silent vow to slit the other agent's throat if the fool somehow managed to make it back to Iran alive.

"Is she dead?" al-Mahajer asked.

Rostami whirled to find the terrorist standing behind him, just inside the doorway to the basement stairs. "Yes," he said, glaring at the Syrian.

"What happened to your face?" al-Mahajer said with a scowl.

"I wanted it to look like a rape. She fought back."

"What did you do with the body?"

"I shoved it down a sewer culvert," he lied. "We need to sanitize this house and go."

"The elite Suren Circle you promised me is a farce. I would have been better off executing this mission alone," al-Mahajer growled as he turned his back on Rostami and headed back downstairs. "I hope my men aren't facing similar issues with their Suren hosts in Seattle and Atlanta."

Rostami followed al-Mahajer while shaking his head. "Keyvan was a coward, but he was no double agent. And Delilah was serving faithfully and obediently until you decided to bludgeon Keyvan in front of her."

"Did you not see what I saw? Keyvan was gathering information to betray us. Delilah was playing the same charade—only she was a much better actor than her husband. If you weren't so stricken by her womanly charms, you would have seen the plain truth as I did."

Rostami decided to ignore the jab and hurried over to where Keyvan's body still lay oozing on the carpet and began rifling through the pockets. "Where is Keyvan's phone?"

"I smashed it," the Syrian said. "We're out of time. A SWAT team will be here within thirty minutes. I packed everything while you were gone. We must leave immediately."

Rostami agreed. He had no intention of ending up in a CIA black site cell next to Parviz, his testicles hooked up to a car battery. He looked at al-Mahajer. "If they were compromised, what is your contingency plan? Do you intend to postpone the operation and reassess?"

Al-Mahajer hoisted a large duffel bag onto his shoulder and laughed. "Postpone and reassess? Oh, Persian, you really are naïve. I'm not postponing anything. On the contrary, I'm going to accelerate the timetable."

"How soon?" Rostami asked and quickly finished packing his own duffel.

"We strike tomorrow . . . at noon."

There was a mania in al-Mahajer's eyes. Rostami's stomach lurched at the implications. "How can this be accomplished without notifying the other two teams?"

"I will contact the other two teams and advance the timeline."

"Would it not be safer to maintain EMCON and strike at the scheduled time?"

Al-Mahajer grinned. "We've prepared and trained for this exact scenario. The equipment is prepared, the target locations set. The time between when I pass the order and they execute is too short for the Americans to react, insh'Alla. Besides, for this operation, the other cells require an authentication from me before they act."

Rostami held his tongue and kept packing his bag. He'd learned there was no point in debating anything with the man, for al-Mahajer was a man whose opinion was immune to influence.

"But I still need your help, Persian."

"My help?" Rostami said, finding the grip of his pistol inside his duffel bag. He looked up and gave the insane Syrian a placating smile.

"Yes, you must fill the void left by your dead Suren companions," al-Mahajer said. "You are responsible for getting me to downtown Omaha and recording my glory. You must promise me to upload the video to the Internet, so that it may spread around the world. Once you have done this one last thing for me, then you are free to return to your life of decadence and impiety in Iran."

Rostami hesitated. Was al-Mahajer telling the truth, or was this some new trick to draw him into a position of involuntary martyrdom by entangling him in the events at the target location? He wouldn't be surprised if al-Mahajer had rigged a video camera with C4. Rostami slid his index finger off the trigger guard and onto the trigger. The safest course of action was to simply kill the Syrian now. "You want me to film you?" he asked.

"Yes. You will be witness to my sacrifice. You will record it and spread it around the world so that it may inspire others to have the courage to strike the Great Satan as well. My name will be remembered forever, and I will be given a seat at the great table with the prophet in Paradise," al-Mahajer said, looking up as if the prophet himself were floating overhead.

Rostami scowled as the implications of al-Mahajer's command and control plan sunk in. He let go of his pistol, leaving it concealed inside his duffel bag. Unless al-Mahajer personally made the call, the other cells would not activate. If the other cells did not activate, then the mission would be a failure. Until al-Mahajer made that call, Rostami would have to bide his time and continue to play the game.

He stood and took al-Mahajer by the shoulders. "Your reward will indeed be great, my brother," he said. "I know we've had our differences, but I swear you can count on me to spread the glory of your sacrifice around the world."

CHAPTER 38

Dempsey shoved the trembling Delilah Shirazi into the back of the SUV.

"Hey, I didn't know we were allowed to bring dates to this party," Wang said, looking up from his laptop.

The joke fell flat.

"Flex-cuff her," Dempsey said to Grimes, brushing the dirt and leaves from his 5.11 Tactical cargo pants.

"Anybody see you?" Smith asked.

"No," Dempsey said, climbing into the Yukon and shutting the door behind him. "But we had a close call. I'll fill you in on that later. What's going on inside the house? What are they saying?"

"They smashed the phone," Wang said with a grimace. "We lost our ears five minutes ago. I've been trying to find another way in ever since. No joy so far."

"Shit," Dempsey mumbled.

"But before we lost the signal, it sounded like they were packing up to leave," Adamo said from the front. The man's jaw was set and confident. "Which means it's time to kit up and go do that Navy SEAL shit you love."

Dempsey raised an eyebrow. He was slowly gaining a grudging respect for the man—just as he imagined Jarvis predicted—but right now, Adamo had him at a loss. "What are you talking about?"

Adamo looked at him with surprise. "We have to hit the house," he said, as if perhaps Dempsey had lost touch with reality. "They're going to get away."

"We can't hit them now," Dempsey said. "We don't know the other two targets."

"Atlanta and Seattle."

"Where in Atlanta and Seattle? Those are two big fucking cities. There are millions of people there." He swallowed and squeezed his eyes shut. He had hurt Kate and Jake so much already—the thought that they might be anywhere near what was coming was unbearable. "We need to know the exact target locations. We need details on the other players. We don't know any of that." His voice was rising to a fevered pitch, and he felt the eyes of his team on him.

"But she does," Adamo said, looking at Delilah.

All eyes shifted to their new guest.

"The intelligence on the operations in the other cities is compartmentalized. They kept it from us. My husband tried to—" She stopped midsentence, epiphany slapping her across the face. "Oh my God, Keyvan was working for you?"

Dempsey nodded. "We picked him up leaving the university this afternoon. We made him a deal, immunity and protection for both of you in exchange for gathering intelligence about the attacks."

"Then you are the ones responsible for his death. You killed my husband!" she shrieked, her face contorting with anger.

"No, ma'am," Smith said, grave and stern. "The terrorists you invited into your home did that. I think you're confusing influence with action."

"We don't have time for bickering right now," Adamo said with mounting agitation. "Our window of opportunity is rapidly closing. Either we hit the house now, or we're gonna lose these assholes *again*."

Dempsey nodded; Adamo was right. If they were going to hit the house, they needed to kit up now. He needed an answer, right fucking now. He turned to the Persian woman. "Cut the crap, Delilah. What are the other two target locations?"

She clenched her jaw and looked out the window in defiance.

"Hey, I'm talking to you," he said, gripping her under the chin and turning her face to look at him. "You agreed to cooperate, so cooperate."

"That was before I realized you were responsible for Keyvan's death."

Dempsey eyed her torn blouse and ripped-open jeans. "Sounds like you're confused, so let me clarify. We're not the ones who tried to rape and kill you in the woods. We're not the ones who put a gun to your husband's forehead and executed him while you watched. We're the good guys, lady. We protect people, even people like you. We're out here gathering intelligence to safeguard innocent lives, but the clock is ticking. Which means you need to pick a side. But pick quickly, because if you don't, you're gonna lose the only friend you have in the whole world right now . . . You have five seconds."

She glared at him, fire in her eyes.

He got it; he really did. She needed someone to blame, and the easiest scapegoat is always the closest one. But he didn't have the time for Delilah Shirazi to work through the five stages of grief and come to terms with her widowhood.

"Time's up," he said.

She exhaled. "I don't know the targets."

"Bullshit," Wang said from the backseat.

"If I knew them, I would tell you," she answered, keeping her gazed fixed on Dempsey. "I suppose I owe you at least that for saving my life."

"Then what can you tell us?" he said.

"I can tell you that there are two terrorists in my basement as we speak."

"Who are they?" Adamo asked, and Dempsey watched the woman carefully.

"One is a VEVAK agent and the other is a senior lieutenant in the Islamic State."

"Those are not identities," Adamo said, pushing up his glasses on his nose. "I could have told you as much—or we wouldn't even be here with you."

The woman fidgeted and swallowed, her desperation growing.

"They were careful never to use their real names. I would tell you if I knew them. What I can share is that we picked them up outside Douglas, Arizona, two days ago, after they entered the US from Mexico using an underground tunnel. And they were not alone. They traveled with four other jihadists, all ISIS youth. At the pickup, they split into three pairs, with orders to strike the assigned targets simultaneously. The two men who came with us are the commanders for the operation. And finally, I can tell you that the attacks are scheduled for the day after tomorrow at 1200 Eastern Daylight Time."

Dempsey looked down at his balled fists. "If these guys are the commanders, it means al-Mahajer is here." He turned to Wang. "Hand me my gear bag from the back. I'm going in."

"Hold on, John," Smith said. "You said it yourself, if we hit the house we jeopardize our ability to discover the other target locations. We have to let this play out. It's going to come down to the wire."

Dempsey shook his head. He needed to know the *exact* locations right fucking now. He needed to know Jake and Kate were safe; he just couldn't tell Smith that.

"I know what I said, but that was before we knew with absolute certainty that al-Mahajer was in her basement right now. I'm going to go in there and get him. This ain't Iraq and it ain't Poland, bro. That motherfucker is going to hit the homeland in less than forty-eight hours. Just let me do my job. I'll get the other target locations out of him. I promise you that." He looked at Grimes. "You coming, Lizzie, or am I flying solo?"

The corners of her mouth curled into a devious grin. "And let you have all the fun? Hell yes, I'm coming."

Wang heaved Dempsey's gear bag over the bench seat. Dempsey grabbed it and set it on his lap. He cracked his knuckles, the anticipation and adrenaline ramping up, and then he unzipped the main compartment to begin the combat preparation ritual he'd done thousands of times.

"Are the other teams being supported by Suren assets in Seattle and Atlanta?" Adamo asked Delilah, the words tumbling out of his mouth so quickly they practically blended together.

"Yes," she said.

Dempsey shrugged on his Kevlar vest.

"Do you know the addresses where the other teams are staying?" Adamo continued.

"No."

"What are the identities of your Suren counterparts in Seattle and Atlanta?"

Dempsey clipped his radio to his kit and plugged in his headset. He was only half listening to the conversation now.

"I don't know."

"Bullshit!" Adamo snapped. "Give me the identities of the Suren hosts in Seattle and Atlanta!"

Dempsey looked past Delilah at Grimes and spoke as if Delilah's interrogation wasn't happening. "I say we cut the power to the house, and go in on night vision. Whadaya think?"

"Agreed," she said, fishing her helmet out of her bag.

"The Suren Circle is an enigma, even to its own members," Delilah insisted. "Communication between members is prohibited, except in the case of emergency or compromise. In such cases, we utilize a hierarchical chain of command based on seniority. Keyvan and I are second in that chain."

Adamo nodded. "The senior couple is located in Chicago?"

"Yes, how did you know this?"

"It doesn't matter. All that matters is finding the identities of the Atlanta and Seattle cells. Would the senior couple in Chicago know this information?"

"Possibly, but they would never share it down the chain without explicit instructions to do so."

"Instructions from who?"

"From Tehran."

Dempsey double-checked the extra magazines on his vest and looked at Grimes. "Ready?"

"Check," she said.

"Let's go," he said. "Wang, come up on channel—"

"Stop," Smith barked, his voice like a gunshot. "We have to leave these guys in play."

"I only agreed to that before I knew who was in there."

"Don't you mean before you knew one of the targets was Atlanta?" Smith said more softly.

"Yes, goddamn it!" Dempsey shouted.

He felt the curious stares of Grimes, Adamo, and Wang on him but refused to look at any of them. "I won't let him hurt my family. I can't let him . . ."

Smith reached back and put a hand on his shoulder. "I understand. Believe me. But going in there guns blazing is not going to get us what we need. This is Qa'im all over again. You go in now, and we lose any chance of identifying the other teams. These guys are sophisticated and determined. They intend to martyr themselves, so wiping out command and control here doesn't stop Atlanta and Seattle. In two days, those other teams will execute, regardless of what happens here tonight. Our best hope is that al-Mahajer recognizes he's being surveilled, feels the pressure, and contacts the other cells to advance the timetable."

"I'm sorry, but I'm with Dempsey on this one," Adamo said, stepping in. "This could very well be our one and only shot to take out al-Mahajer before he kills hundreds of people in Omaha. There's no guarantee we'll learn the other target locations by waiting. Squander this opportunity, and we risk lives here."

"True, but if we don't leave him in play, we are guaranteeing that hundreds of innocents will die in Seattle and Atlanta. If al-Mahajer communicates with the other cells in the next twelve hours, we'll be able to take out all three cells," Smith said.

"And if he doesn't, then what?" Adamo said, shaking his head at Smith. "Leaving him in play is insane."

Smith blew air through his teeth. "I know, but that's the world we live in now."

"So you're making the call?" Adamo said.

"No. This is a capture/kill operation, which means Dempsey's in charge, but before the decision gets made, we each have an obligation to speak our minds and make a case for what we think is right," Smith said. "That's the Ember way."

Dempsey suddenly felt the yoke of responsibility settle back on his shoulders. Technically, Smith could overrule his decision, but Dempsey knew that wouldn't happen. He clenched his jaw. Like Adamo said, if they hit the house now they would stop one team for sure. But what if Smith was right? What if by intervening now, his action guaranteed that the two other attacks were executed? He was lying to himself and his teammates to guarantee he could take al-Mahajer alive and get the bastard to talk.

Don't let family cloud the decision, a voice said inside his head. *The odds of them being at the target location at the time of the attack are probably a million to one.*

But even if his family wasn't there, someone's family would be. Someone's son. Someone's daughter. Someone's mother, wife, father, husband . . .

"Fuuuuuuuuuck!" Dempsey bellowed, shaking his clenched fists in the air.

The inside of the Yukon fell so quiet he could hear the thump of his pulse in his ears. All eyes were fixed on him, waiting for the decision that would determine the fate of hundreds, possibly thousands of American lives.

Dempsey closed his eyes and imagined what Jarvis would say if he were present: *The difference between operating for Ember and operating as a Tier One SEAL is delayed gratification. We're playing the long game, John. And to win the long game sometimes requires making decisions that in the heat of the moment seem counterintuitive. Making those decisions requires courage. Without courage, leadership can't exist. Without leadership, the bad guys win every time.*

He took a deep breath and opened his eyes and looked at Wang. "So Keyvan's phone is deep-sixed?"

"Yeah, boss."

"Okay, so how else can we track these guys?"

"At a minimum, one of them needs to power on a phone—and by that I mean a phone that they are taking with them," Wang said. "So far, that hasn't happened."

"What about hacking into Keyvan's BMW? Can you use the Lojack or built-in GPS to track it?"

"Yeah," Wang answered. "I hacked it already, when we were following the professor here from the university."

"Perfect."

"But that won't do us any good if they EXFIL on foot or take another vehicle."

"True, so we observe their exit. If they take the BMW, we're golden. If not, we tail them old school," Dempsey said.

"So we're not hitting the house?" Adamo asked with incredulity.

Dempsey shook his head. "Believe me, dude, I want to. I want to so bad I can taste acid in my mouth. But we can't. These guys are too good. Despite what I said, even if we manage to take al-Mahajer, I can't guarantee he'll talk. He's planning to martyr himself in two days; he'd rather die than crack. And after what we saw in Poland, I think any intel we extracted from the VEVAK operative would be questionable at best.

I promise, we'll take these fuckers out before they can execute here in Omaha. But we have to give them a chance to communicate with the other teams; it's our only hope of saving Seattle and Atlanta."

Adamo nodded, accepting the decision without further debate.

"The priority now is getting tactical teams en route to the other targets." Dempsey's personal need to go to Atlanta was almost overwhelming, but he fought it back. He needed to stay in Omaha. Al-Mahajer had beaten him twice; he wouldn't let it happen a third time. "I'll remain here as team leader with Wang. To round out our team, I want an HRT unit here ASAP. Wang, let Jarvis know I want a name request for Hansen and his guys from our New York City UN op six months ago."

"Typing the request now," Wang said.

"Adamo and Grimes, you're team Atlanta. Chunk and his SEALs are on standby at Ember; I want them to be your augment."

"Agreed," Adamo said to his surprise. "It's the right play."

"We won't let you down," Grimes added, and in her gaze was an unspoken promise to safeguard more than just the city.

"Which leaves Seattle," Smith said. "And me."

"You good with that?" Dempsey asked. "We can augment you with West Coast SEALs or some of your old Delta buddies."

"A couple of names come to mind," Smith said with a nostalgic grin. "Don't worry, I'll take care of my own augment. You just focus on Omaha and Atlanta. I'll brief Jarvis en route, and get the TOC stood up back home to start lining up eyes and ears for us. God knows we're going to need it."

"Roger that," Dempsey said. "All right, everyone, that's the battle order. The mission is simple: locate and eliminate."

Everyone nodded in agreement.

"Well, what the hell are you waiting for?" he growled. "Get the hell out of my Yukon and get your asses to the airport. We have work to do and the clock is ticking."

CHAPTER 39

Embassy Suites Downtown/Old Market Lobby
540 South Twelfth Street, Omaha, Nebraska
November 4, 0615 Local Time

Special Agent Scott Hansen walked into the lobby looking exactly like Dempsey remembered—big, confident, and his face creased with a permanent scowl. The kind of scowl like a man trapped in an elevator with a flatulent stranger. Even in civilian clothes—cargo pants, a black sport shirt, and a cheap gray sports coat bulging around the pistol on his hip—Hansen oozed "operator." Hansen was a team leader in the FBI's Hostage Rescue Team. Like Hansen, the vast majority of the nearly one hundred operators who made up this Quick Reaction Force were former military Special Operations. Dempsey pegged Hansen as Army SOF, the same unit Smith hailed from, but he'd yet to confirm this.

Dempsey extended his hand in greeting, and Hansen shook it with a grip like a hydraulic press.

"Was there something I did in New York that made you think I was okay with being OGA's on-call bitch? Because I don't remember giving you that impression," Hansen said. Impossibly, the scowl on his face deepened, but Dempsey knew this ruse. Hansen's dark-green eyes sparkled with the look of a man glad to be turned loose outside the wire after a dry spell.

"Sorry," Dempsey said, releasing Hansen's thick, calloused hand. "We're in a real shit storm here, and I really needed someone I could trust."

"By that you mean someone who's already seen your super spooky ass in action and kept his mouth shut after," Hansen said. "That's the real reason I pinged on a 'by-name request.'"

Dempsey laughed. "Yeah, well, there is that. Let's go upstairs and brief. You have a team setting up?"

"Roger," Hansen said. "I have the same tac leader you met at the UN—former frogman like you, plus a six-man team, all senior. Just like you requested. Two are combat medics—retired Eighteen Deltas. They're set up at the airport, waiting for instructions."

"Very good," Dempsey said, leading him to the elevator. "We need to present a really low profile on this one. Our target will spook easily, and if that happens, we're screwed."

Hansen pursed his lips. "You know we're not really set up for that kind of thing. Our operations at HRT are, by design, obscenely overt in signature."

"I understand," Dempsey said. HRT was deployed for tactical strikes when the FBI's Critical Incident Response Group needed big guns and special operators. Power projection was a tactical component of most HRT operations. "Our situation here requires operators of your caliber, but we'll need more of a stealth presence. Adapt and overcome, right?" he added, mimicking the Special Forces mantra.

"Right," Hansen said, both his voice and expression dubious.

They rode the elevator to the sixth floor. As they were stepping off, Dempsey asked, "You got the brief from our guys?"

"We got the grainy pictures of the two guys you ID'd as your bad guys, but the report was vague on specifics. Can you share more details about the operation?"

"Unfortunately, not much," Dempsey confessed as they walked down the hall to the king suite they were using as an op center. "We know the principals, but we're unclear on the other players. We know the general target and the time, but no specifics on the attack itself or precise location."

"Awesome," Hansen said through a sigh as Dempsey swiped them into the room.

Inside Wang sat hunched over one of six laptops he had lined up on the table in front of him.

"Special Agent Hansen, this is Dick Wang, our tech genius and field SIGINT guy," Dempsey said. "Wang, this is Special Agent Hansen."

Wang glanced up, gave a campy wave, then hunched back over his laptop.

"Where are we?" Dempsey asked.

"Same," Wang said and combed his thick black hair out of his face with his fingers. "They're still holed up in the hotel near Twenty-Fourth Street. No one has left."

"Based on mobile GPS, the Lojack, what?"

"Nah," Wang said. "Their phones are still off. The BMW is sitting in a lot a few blocks away. Right now, we're stuck with a single channel—eyes in the sky."

"Satellite?"

Wang shook his head. "That's my backup. Degraded resolution, because Ian is using the same satellite for us in Seattle. So, he gave me overlapping drones—super high-res shit—streaming real time from their command center in Colorado. Nobody's left the hotel all morning. When they do, I'll be able to tell how much change is in their pockets."

"I don't like it," Dempsey said. "What happens if you have to take a piss?"

Without taking his eyes off the screen, he pointed to a one-liter Aquasana bottle on the desk, filled halfway up with yellow liquid, and said, "Dude, I got this."

Dempsey shook his head and looked at Hansen.

"What task force did you guys say you were with?" Hansen said, his scowl back and uglier than ever.

Dempsey gave a tight-lipped grin. "Okay, moving on . . ."

Hansen squinted at the screens of some of the other laptops Wang had set up farther down the table. "You said two other cities. Omaha isn't the only target?"

"Correct," Dempsey said. "Our intel suggests simultaneous attacks in Atlanta and Seattle."

"Jesus," Hansen said, letting out a whistle. "This is some serious shit. Islamic State?"

Dempsey nodded. "With outside help."

"And you guys aren't CIA?" Hansen mumbled.

"No, but aren't you glad we're here?" Wang said over his shoulder, his boyish grin finally free.

"I'll answer that question after it's all over," Hansen said.

A knot formed in Dempsey's stomach as a new and terrible idea occurred to him. "Wang, is it possible that al-Mahajer already called the other cells in Seattle and Atlanta and we missed it?"

"Sure, anything's possible," Wang said, his eyes still locked on his laptop. "But highly unlikely."

"That doesn't make me feel better," Dempsey said. "If he made the call and we missed it, then Atlanta and Seattle are screwed."

"Yes, I know, which is why we're using every SIGINT technology in our arsenal to monitor for that call."

Dempsey sighed, not sure what else to say, but also not satisfied with the situation.

"Look, Dempsey," Wang said, turning to look at him. "I know what room they're in. I know what car they're driving. As of two hours ago, I own the room next to them and I have equipment inside."

"When did you pull that off?"

"When you were sleeping," he said with a grin, then turned back to his laptop. "Don't worry about it, dude. You do your ninja shit out there, and I'll do mine in here. I'm not going to miss that call."

To his surprise, Wang's confidence actually took the edge off his nerves. "So when the call happens, then what?" Dempsey asked. "Can you hack and track the phones on the receiving end?"

"Yeah."

"So if fuck stick calls his boys in Atlanta, then you can hack and track the phone in Atlanta?" Dempsey asked. Kate and Jacob popped into his mind for the hundredth time in the last few hours.

"I can track 'em," Wang said. "But that doesn't mean they'll carry the phone around with them. Odds are, they're all using burners and they all ditch after final instructions are given and received. But once we get the phone's location—which takes only seconds—we put eyes on them, just like we're doing with al-Mahajer. Even if they ditch their phones, we can still track them, but instead of using GPS we're following the rabbit."

"Following the rabbit?" Hansen asked.

Dempsey looked at the FBI man. "Following a target with just line of sight. No signals. With drones and satellites. Less than ideal, obviously, but doable."

"More than doable," Wang corrected. "The new drones can probably read a VIN number for me off a windshield if needed. Don't worry, guys, we'll find the bastards."

"How do you know?" Hansen asked.

Wang shrugged. "Have to. The alternative is inconceivable."

Hansen scowled at Wang for a long moment, then turned to Dempsey. "So, what do you need from us?"

Dempsey walked him over to a paper map of downtown Omaha, spread out on a table. In the middle, the cobblestone-paved streets of the Old Market, laid out between Tenth and Thirteenth Streets and the five blocks north to south between Farnham and Jackson Streets, were highlighted. The quaint entertainment district was one of Omaha's most popular attractions, for both tourists and local residents alike. As the go-to dining destination for downtown Omaha, the Old Market was a perfect lunchtime target on a sunny fall afternoon like today.

"As I said before," Dempsey began, "we don't know if al-Mahajer has selected a specific target inside the Old Market, or if he's just planning to wander around, machine gun blazing. Hell, he could kill dozens by making a single pass down Howard Street during lunch hour."

Hansen leaned in for a better view. "Could be worse," he grumbled.

"If we split up into two-man teams, we can cover the majority of the market. We can either start at the corners and converge, or assign teams different key intersections. If I was al-Mahajer, I would launch the attack at the intersection of Twelfth and Howard, but he's a wily, deceptive bastard. The point is we need to be really kinetic here and adjust in real time once we see how it unfolds."

"Can we intercept prior to arrival?"

"We can certainly try, but I think they'll come in on foot. I'll take the northwest corner, so I have a better chance of making a visual ID."

"Okay," Hansen said. "How many shooters are we talking about?"

"We think two."

"Once we pick them up, then what? Kill on sight?"

Dempsey shook his head.

"We have every reason to think they will have explosive vests and no idea how they will detonate." He wished they had been able to examine the vests or knew more about them. He realized that they had learned almost nothing from the woman, Delilah. "They might have dead-man's switches, like the assholes in Brussels who had gloved-hand switches that detonate on release. In that case, manual detonation is also a concern, if they spot our patrols."

"Jesus. So why not just take them now? Wang said he knows their room number. My guys can get there in a few minutes. That has to be lower risk of collateral. They may not even be kitted up and armed yet."

Dempsey shook his head. "We're still waiting for the outbound call. If we take al-Mahajer now, we don't get any intel on the other targets and those attacks will happen on schedule and we won't be able to stop them."

"Okay, so we surround the hotel covertly, wait for the call, and then kill them."

"It all depends on what's communicated during the call. If al-Mahajer is using 'Go, No-Go' protocol, the other teams will be waiting for a last-minute signal to proceed. In that case, we have to wait for the green-light call, or the other teams will alter their plans."

"So you're willing to risk letting this attack happen? Christ, Dempsey. That is some scary cowboy shit, man."

"If we can get the teams from all three targets ID'd on the first call, we'll hit them all right away. If not, we have to wait."

Two minutes later, they were consumed by angles, lines of fire, escape routes, mass casualty plans, and where to place their snipers. Dempsey locked thoughts of Kate and Jacob in a black mental box and dug into the details of stopping al-Mahajer as they waited for the outbound call that he feared might never come.

CHAPTER 40

Econo Lodge, West Dodge
Omaha, Nebraska
0710 Local Time

Rostami looked up from where his forehead was pressed against the cheaply carpeted hotel room floor and watched al-Mahajer pray his last prayer to Allah. Al-Mahajer had woken him at 4:30 a.m. to share a pot of tea. Then, they prayed the sunna of Fajr, beginning precisely when 5:15 a.m. had passed. Afterward, Rafiq had kneeled and stared at the wall, not speaking, for an hour. It was not permissible to offer voluntary prayer between the Fajr and sunrise—more specifically until the sun had risen a spear's length above the horizon. Twelve minutes' apogee was the accepted time period since compact pistols had long ago replaced spears as the instruments of jihad, but al-Mahajer had waited a full fifteen, no doubt extra cautious today of all days.

Rostami watched a tear fall from al-Mahajer's tightly closed eyes and drip onto the floor beside his mobile phone, where a compass app pointed to 42.33 degrees, the line of bearing to the holy shrine of Ka'bah 7,262 miles away in Mecca. If the ISIS commander had not been so stubborn with his decision to wait until the last possible moment to activate the Atlanta and Seattle teams, then Rostami would not be in this situation. If the call had been made, he could have already put a bullet through the man's head. But al-Mahajer had not made the call, and Rostami's anxiety was following an exponential curve. Last night's events would not go unnoticed. Delilah Shirazi was out there, and that meant the Americans were coming for him. He could feel it in his bones. They were close and getting closer. Every minute that lunatic waited to make the call was a minute closer to capture.

He will martyr us both if he keeps this up. Only I no longer believe in a paradise awaiting me in the afterlife.

Al-Mahajer's eyes sprung open suddenly, and he sat bolt upright on his knees.

Rostami squeezed his eyes shut and began to move his lips in final, feigned prayer. He did manage one short prayer, just in case: *Allah, please allow me to survive this madness.* After a minute, he opened his eyes and took a long, slow breath as if completing a deep and solemn prayer. Then, he looked over at al-Mahajer with a tight smile.

"Today is a great day for true believers, my brother," Rostami said. "Your reward for your sacrifice will be great."

"I'm weary of your false flattery." Al-Mahajer turned to look at him with cold, black eyes.

"What are you talking about?"

Al-Mahajer laughed sardonically. "Do you think me blind? Do you think I don't know your heart, Persian? You might have charmed me at the Emek Café, but I've come to know the real you these past days. You, Behrouz Rostami, are not a true believer. Like all *Rafidah*, you are an opportunist who cares only for yourself and sating your most carnal desires. Allah knows this, too, and has no place for your kind in Paradise."

"You have misjudged me," Rostami said, while instinctively inching his right hand toward the pistol tucked in his waistband.

"You want to kill me?" al-Mahajer said, narrowing his eyes. "You've been contemplating it since Guatemala, but you can't do it now for the same reason you couldn't do it then. Your masters in Tehran will put a bullet in your brain if the operation fails. Our destinies are entwined."

"So it would seem," Rostami said, through gritted teeth. "Is it time to make the call, *brother*?"

Al-Mahajer scooped up his phone and got to his feet in a single fluid motion.

"It is," he said and powered up his phone.

Rostami watched him select and dial the first of only two numbers in the contact list. Then, al-Mahajer surprised him by turning on the phone's speaker. The phone rang once and picked up.

"God is great," al-Mahajer said in Arabic.

"May God be with you," came the reply, strong and confident—much more so than Rostami had imagined.

"I am moving up the timeline."

"When?"

"Today we shall be together in Paradise, my brother."

The pause that followed spoke volumes.

"Today?" the voice said at last.

"Yes," al-Mahajer replied.

"God is indeed great. We will be ready."

"Only the day changes," the ISIS commander instructed. "The time and the target remain the same."

Confidence had found its way back into the voice on the line: "Praise God."

Al-Mahajer looked into Rostami's eyes and smiled a devious smile as he spoke his next words. "I will make another call at precisely one minute before the appointed time. Should that call not come, then something has happened to me and you will change to the secondary target at the alternate time. Do you understand?"

"I understand. We will be ready and will await your call to strike."

Al-Mahajer severed the call without a parting word, his black-hole eyes still fixed on Rostami. "It appears, Persian, that we will be together until the glorious end."

"Praise and glory to God," Rostami said robotically.

As al-Mahajer dialed the second team, Rostami's mind was racing. He had not expected the call would be made only in the final seconds of the attack. Al-Mahajer had thought of everything . . . Now he needed to devise an escape plan from the Old Market, because the opportunity to send al-Mahajer to Paradise early was forever lost to him.

CHAPTER 41

"Got him," Wang shouted, his fingers flying over his keyboard. "Now I just have to lock the coordinates and move the drones. We need a solid visual fix for backup, in case they power the phone off."

Dempsey walked over and squeezed Wang's shoulders—the universal ops center *attaboy*.

"I'll do it," came Baldwin's voice, calm and professorial from the second laptop screen. "You stand by to lock the second phone."

"Okay," Wang said. "They're in downtown Atlanta . . . tracking just off the intersection of Carnegie Way and Cone Street . . . looks like they're in a parking garage. You gotta be fucking kidding me. Damn it."

"Calm down, Richard," Baldwin said slowly and softly, a teacher to a student. "I have a fix, and I'm recording the call. Please prep for the next call. I'm sure the Director would prefer to hear the live audio as opposed to your commentary."

Wang mumbled something under his breath, then glanced over his shoulder at Dempsey.

"We can track them out of the garage, right?" Dempsey said.

"If they keep the phone powered on. If not, they could drive away in any of a dozen cars and without eyes on the ground, we wouldn't know which one," Wang said as he typed and clicked.

"Shit." Dempsey saw a new number flash on one of the laptops. "Is that the second call?" he said, pointing to the center screen.

Wang slapped his hand away. "Hands off, dude. That's, like, a touch screen. You're gonna jack up my shit."

Dempsey pulled his hand back and Wang tapped the screen, this time bringing the audio up on the speakers.

The speakers greeted each other in Arabic. Dempsey felt his fists and throat tighten hearing al-Mahajer's voice.

"What are they saying?" he asked.

"Moving up the timeline. They're going today, but at the same time as previously planned. God is great. They're going to Paradise to bang virgins. Blah, blah, blah. Now something about a second call one minute before and instructions to change targets if the call isn't received."

The words hit Dempsey like a punch in the gut. "Fuck." He turned to look at Hansen.

"How'd you know, Dempsey?" Hansen said. "How'd you know they'd pull that shit?"

"Because this is not my first rodeo," Dempsey said. "We've seen this tactic before."

He watched Wang's hands fly across several different laptops. The second screen to the left was zooming in spurts, magnifying a particular section of Seattle. Wang ignored the map and satellite feeds, his fingers typing code furiously on the computer beside it.

"Almost got it."

"Got what?" Dempsey asked but then bit his tongue, trying to be quiet.

"Oh yeah!" Wang shouted and raised his hands over his head. "I own you bitches." He looked up at Dempsey with the smile of an eighth grader bringing home an A+ on his science project. "Now I'll just run the GPS in the background." He was back to tapping again, this time on the center keyboard. "Got 'em," he said, and a blue dot now appeared on the satellite image.

The camera zoomed in on a neighborhood situated like a little peninsula surrounded by the Broadmoor Golf Club. It was located just south of Route 520 and less than five miles northeast of downtown. The image zoomed again, and soon he was looking at the top of a big white house with a circular brick driveway cutting through well-manicured hedges. In Seattle, it had to be a $3 million home—maybe more. The dot flashed in the northwest corner of the house.

"Can you tell me what floor they're on?" Dempsey asked.

Wang looked up, eyebrows raised. "Sure," he said. "Do you need that?" He started typing again.

"No, I was kidding. I just—"

"The device is 15.6 feet from ground level—so second floor."

"Christ, Wang. Where'd Jarvis find you again?"

"This ain't 'find my iPhone,' man," Wang said, gloating now. "I'm using some seriously high-speed shit, dude."

"I'm in," Baldwin said from the other laptop. "The encryption is generic on this phone. I'll dump the data for the team to sort through. Also, I have a drone on the way."

"For the Seattle location?" Wang asked, clarifying.

"Yes, Seattle."

"What about Atlanta?"

"I should have it . . . wait a moment," Baldwin said, his voice terse, but still measured like a college professor lecturing.

"Shit," Wang said.

"What's wrong?" Dempsey asked. All the screens looked the same to him.

"The Atlanta phone powered off." Wang was typing again, this time on the last laptop in the row. "But if the battery is still in, then I can interrogate the GPS in 911 mode. Much less precise, but still useful . . . Shit! It's gone. They must have taken the battery out."

"It's not your fault, Richard," Baldwin said.

"Tell me you at least got a data dump from the Atlanta phone before it powered off?" Wang asked.

"Incomplete," Baldwin said. "The Atlanta phone had better encryption. Why don't you periodically try to power it back on, just in case they put the battery back in. If you succeed, let me know immediately so I can export the remaining data from it."

"No promises," Wang said, "but I'll try."

"You focus on that, and I will sift the data from the Seattle phone for coordinates or anything pointing to the specific target location."

Dempsey stared at the zoomed-in image of the house in Seattle. *This is good,* he told himself. Very, very good, but . . . it wasn't enough. He looked at his watch: almost 0800. The attacks were scheduled for 1:00 p.m. in Atlanta, noon in Omaha, and 10:00 a.m. in Seattle. That gave the tech weenies four hours to figure out the target locations. He watched Wang work for several minutes, until he decided that him hovering wouldn't help the process go any faster.

He walked over to the map of the Old Market and began running tactical scenarios in his head, laying them on the map with his mind. It wasn't long before thoughts of al-Mahajer intruded, derailing his concentration. He'd been beaten twice by the bastard, and both times because he'd made the same mistake—he thought he'd gained the upper hand, let down his guard for an instant, and then paid dearly for it. There was nuance to how al-Mahajer utilized his suicide bombers . . . but Dempsey couldn't articulate what it was. Like a forgotten question, impossible to answer without first being recalled. To beat al-Mahajer this time, he would have to solve this strategic puzzle *before* the terrorist's vest went boom.

CHAPTER 42

Ember TOC
Newport News, Virginia

Jarvis paced the TOC, tapping the side of his stainless-steel coffee tumbler with his thumb. For the hundredth time, he glanced at the center display and the static blue dot superimposed over the target address in the upscale Broadmoor neighborhood north of Seattle. The dot had not moved on the map for hours, and now he was beginning to worry. He resisted the urge to sigh. He resisted the urge to clench his jaw. He resisted the urge to curse his adversary, and the limits of technology, and everything else in the universe that seemed to be conspiring against them. Events were not unfolding like he had anticipated. Soon, he would start second-guessing himself, and that was a road he did not want to go down. He looked up at the row of digital clocks above the screens, each giving the time in a variety of US and international time zones: 1215 EDT / 1115 CDT / 1015 MDT / 0915 PDT. They were forty-five minutes from showtime with no fix on the terrorists in Atlanta and no intelligence on the target locations in either Atlanta or Seattle.

"Where are we with Atlanta?" he asked Baldwin, who was sitting at a computer terminal in a row of terminals along the wall.

"No change," Baldwin said. "I can put the drone imagery up, but it's just circling downtown."

"You still have Wang trying to interrogate the phone?"

"Yes, but with no success. We believe they removed the battery. In which case, our next and only window of opportunity to get a fix will be when al-Mahajer makes the 'Go, No-Go' call just before the attack."

Jarvis nodded gravely. "Any other ideas how we can—"

"We've got movement," Baldwin interrupted.

Jarvis looked up at the monitor left of center as the aerial imagery from an MQ-9 Reaper drone slowly rotated and began to zoom in. He watched as a silver sedan pulled out of the garage and backed down the driveway. A beat later, a red triangle appeared in the middle of the high-resolution image, indicating that the target had been acquired. Then, the zoom accelerated dramatically until the crystal-clear image of an Infinity Q70 sedan filled most of the screen. The targeting system on the MQ-9 Reaper drone matched the movements of the vehicle perfectly. On screen, the sedan appeared motionless, the only indication of movement being the asphalt slipping by underneath as the drone tracked the target with miraculous precision.

"Thermals?" Jarvis said.

"Standby . . . one signature," Baldwin said. "Just the driver."

Jarvis slammed his coffee tumbler down on the conference table, causing Baldwin to jump. "Damn it!"

"What do you want me to do?"

"We need to track the Infiniti *and* keep eyes on the house. They are supposed to be two-man teams."

"You think the Infiniti could be a decoy?" Baldwin asked.

"Yes. What are my coverage options?"

"Satellite for the next twelve minutes; after that we're going to have problems. There's weather moving in."

"You're fucking kidding me."

"I wish I were. It's raining in Everett and creeping south."

"Bravo One, did you hear that?" Jarvis said on the open channel.

"Copy," came Smith's voice back over the TOC speakers. "Want me to send a vehicle to the house? Bravo Two could be there in ten mikes, but be advised it could impact our response once the target location is identified."

"I could circle the drone?" Baldwin said.

"No, keep the drone on the Infiniti," Jarvis said, then louder, "Bravo One, send a vehicle to Broadmoor Drive."

"Copy," said Smith.

"Where the hell is he going?" Jarvis said, pointing to the blue dot, which was now moving on the map in sync with the Infiniti's real-time position as tracked by the Reaper.

"He's heading north on Foster Island Road," Baldwin said.

"Yes, I can see that, Ian. But why is he getting onto 520 East?"

"I don't know."

"What in Christ's name is going on?"

A phone chirped beside Baldwin, and he picked it up. "Yes? Okay, then walk over and tell us."

Jarvis looked at Baldwin.

"Chip and Dale have a theory where he's going," Baldwin said and then focused back on his screen.

"Zoom out on the Reaper. Half-mile radius," Jarvis said, and immediately the Infiniti began to shrink on the screen. He watched as the sedan took 520 East across Lake Washington, away from Seattle, toward Bellevue.

A second later, the TOC doors burst open and Chip rushed in, nervous excitement on his face. "I think I know where he's going. Central Park East Apartments, located south of 520 and just east of Highland Crossroads."

"Where is that?" Jarvis said.

"Right here," Baldwin said, as a digital pin materialized in the center display, approximately halfway between Bellevue and Redmond.

"How did you get this address?" Jarvis asked, turning to face the analyst.

"The browser history we pulled from the hacked phone showed several Google queries. One of the queries was for this apartment complex. We also see they used the map function several times, zooming in and scrolling around; they generated two different route maps to the apartment complex from the residence on Broadmoor Drive."

Jarvis allowed himself a slight smile. "Nice work. We'll know in the next few minutes, but I think you just ID'd the pickup location for the shooters."

"But we still don't know the target," Baldwin said.

Jarvis walked to the conference table and picked up a stack of printed probability distributions—each for a different target location and each calculated using Ember's Monte Carlo simulation software. He had run thirty-seven simulations to generate a list of probable target locations—twenty for Atlanta and seventeen for Seattle—based on a specific list of factors, including accessibility, visibility, crowd size, crowd density, native security presence, financial value, name recognition, social significance, and distance to closest law enforcement first responders. The highest-probability target for Seattle had been the Space Needle. The iconic structure satisfied multiple criteria, and it had been Jarvis's instinctive first choice before running any stats. But the time of the attack, 10:00 a.m., severely impacted crowd size. The Waterfront also scored high marks across all criteria, but took a similar hit on crowd size and density at the target time. Now, with the driver heading east away from downtown, the probability distributions were changing rapidly in real time.

He didn't have time to rerun the simulations, but as a synesthete, he possessed certain gifts when it came to numbers and figures. As he flipped through the pages, he perceived the ink changing colors: red,

red, red, red, red, blue, yellow, red, yellow, blue, red . . . When he was finished, he pulled the blues and set the others aside; as he scanned the new short list, connections formed in his mind. Al-Mahajer was not hitting a single target; he was hitting three. His goal was not to simply maximize civilian carnage but to send a powerful message of fear. That message was: *Americans are not safe anywhere. Whether you live in Boston or Boise, Orlando or Omaha, big city or small town, whether you're going out to shop, to dine, to play, or to work, you're not safe . . .*

Jarvis looked up to find both Baldwin and Chip staring at him. He selected the page with the brightest blue font—color that only he could perceive—and slammed it down on the table. "They're not hitting downtown," he said. "The target is the Microsoft campus in Redmond."

Baldwin's eyes went wide, and then he whipped around in his chair to face his terminal. As his fingers flew across his keyboard, he began rattling off information: "Eighty buildings spread out across a five-hundred-acre campus, serving thirty thousand employees. On-site dining. On-site gym. On-site post office. On-site day care—"

"It's the perfect target," Chip chimed in. "It's a microcosm of Seattle."

"Bravo One, are you copying this?" Jarvis asked into the ether.

"Copy," Smith said. "Be advised, we're downtown and Bravo Two is arriving on station at Broadmoor."

"We know your locations, Bravo."

"Then you understand that our tangos have a big head start. Prosecution could be difficult."

"Copy that, Bravo One." Jarvis turned to Baldwin, who read his mind and nodded. "We're working on a backup solution just in case."

"Do you want me to reposition now, or hold until you confirm the pickup?" Smith asked.

Jarvis considered the question for a beat. "Reposition to intercept. Hold Bravo Two in position as a backup in case I'm wrong and we need quick reaction downtown."

"Roger that," Smith said. "Bravo One ready for coordinates."

While Baldwin transmitted real-time routing guidance to Smith's vehicle, Jarvis returned his attention to the monitor with the drone footage. But instead of seeing the Infiniti, all he saw was gray haze.

"Goddamn it," he barked. "We're going to miss the pickup. Baldwin, get me lower. Now."

"Be advised, sir, radar shows the cloud base for this system at eight hundred feet. At that altitude, everyone, including our shooters, will see the Reaper."

"Damned if I do, damned if I don't," he murmured, running his fingers through his hair.

"What's that, sir?" Baldwin said, looking up at him expectantly.

"Nothing." He took a deep breath and then gave the order. "Coordinate with the pilot and take her down. Whatever it takes, Mr. Baldwin. Do you understand? We cannot miss this pickup."

"Understood." Baldwin picked up a handset and called the drone pilot seventeen hundred miles away.

The conversation lasted only twenty seconds.

"We can stay at cloud base and pop in and out," Baldwin said after hanging up the phone. "Hopefully catch the pickup but minimize exposure of the drone."

"Not hopefully," Jarvis growled. "We need visual confirmation of the pickup."

Baldwin pursed his lips.

Jarvis shot him a look. "You disagree?"

"Well, no—not entirely," Baldwin said. "Visual would be nice, but this is an all-weather drone. The new tracking system allows it to maintain the target designation it already achieved on the Infiniti."

"Your point, Ian? I'm sorry but we have a time issue here."

The middle screen was still filled with only dense gray clouds.

"My point is that, regardless of the clouds, we'll continue tracking the Infiniti. We'll see it stop and confirm the location that Chip

329

identified from the map display. Thermal imaging will cut the clouds and confirm the number of people in the vehicle."

Jarvis considered this, but he wanted to *see* the shooters enter the vehicle. Three decades' experience of hunting shitheads was worthless if his eyes were stuck in the clouds. Yet, Baldwin had a point. If the two or three signatures were added and the vehicle resumed track toward Redmond . . .

"All right. Circle in the cloud base. When the vehicle stops, I want a short drop out of the clouds to try and get a visual. If the thermals confirm a pickup, we follow the Infiniti with the drone and continue Bravo One to the intercept and leave Bravo Two at Broadmoor as backup for downtown."

Baldwin nodded and spoke again into his handset, coordinating with the drone pilot.

And they waited. It was minutes but felt like hours.

Jarvis checked the feeds from Dempsey in Omaha and Adamo and Grimes in Atlanta, but no new information was available to him to distract his racing mind. He tapped his metal thermos. He paced and watched the blue dot on the map display and the clouds on the center screen.

"They took the exit for Highland Crossroads—they're a minute or so from Chip's projected pickup point."

"Stand by to dive the Reaper."

Seconds dragged, and dragged, and dragged . . .

"Okay, they've stopped," Baldwin said. "On your mark."

Jarvis closed his eyes and pictured men moving swiftly from the apartment to the car on the street. He watched them in his mind and counted off their steps . . . "Now," he said, opening his eyes.

"Roger."

Jarvis watched the white-gray mist dissolve and become green foliage bisected by the black asphalt of Route 520. The image refreshed and he was looking at the Infiniti, dead center in the large screen. The right front passenger door was swinging closed, and he glimpsed a ponytail, trailed by a thin forearm. Definitely female. A larger body, sporting a mop of black hair, jumped into the rear seat. The door closed, and he got a short glimpse of a black boot as it disappeared. On the far side, another male was stepping into the car. He was hurrying, and Jarvis noted the unnatural bulge between the shoulder blades under the jacket he wore.

A beat later, the image turned gray and then white as the Reaper pulled back into the cloud base.

"It's them."

Baldwin looked at Jarvis with a frown and then down at his screen.

"We have four thermals in the vehicle. The target is pulling away from the curb," Baldwin said. "I didn't see weapons."

"It's them," Jarvis said again. "The Suren couple in the front and two ISIS jihadis in the back."

He looked at the map and saw the blue dot move in step with the Infiniti as it pulled away from the curb and then made a U-turn. He watched the blue dot head north and take the ramp onto Route 520. He noted the green dot, Bravo One, was also on Route 520, but only now crossing Lake Washington.

"You need to haul ass, Bravo One," Jarvis said. "Pickup confirmed. The shooters are en route to Microsoft."

CHAPTER 43

Old Market
Omaha, Nebraska
1120 Local / 1220 Atlanta / 0920 Seattle

Dempsey needed to get his head in the game. The more time he spent worrying and wondering about Kate and Jacob, the less effective he'd be. This was exactly the reason Jarvis had Baldwin segregating comms and information flow for all three target operations out of the TOC. It was unrealistic to think he could prosecute his own target while coordinating Bravo and Charlie teams.

And I can't prosecute al-Mahajer while I'm worrying about Kate and Jacob.

Hansen sat beside him in the passenger's seat. The other six HRT agents—uneasy with their street clothes and gym bags holding their rifles and gear—were assembled at the rear of the SUV.

Dempsey pulled his mobile phone out of his small backpack on the floor beside Hansen's foot, entered his pass code, and then tapped the Facebook icon.

"Checking something?" Hansen asked.

Dempsey thought of three lies simultaneously, but went with the truth.

"Yeah," he said, as the app opened, "I have a wife and teenage boy in Atlanta. I'm just checking to see where they are. Not sending anything."

"Didn't ask," Hansen said. "I sure as shit would let my family know if there was an attack coming to my hometown."

Dempsey nodded. Direct communication was impossible for him. He was dead after all, and unlike in Stephen King novels, the dead did not speak to their spouses and children, via Facebook or any other form of social media. The air caught in his throat as he read Kate's last status update from less than an hour ago.

```
Teacher in-service day. Taking Jake downtown
for lunch and an afternoon of shark watching.
Great kid. Great day.
```

She'd posted a selfie of the two of them standing in front of a town house. His son looked insanely tall—no longer the little boy Dempsey still pictured in his mind's eye. Jake was looking sideways at his mom, smiling awkwardly but with adoration.

Fuck.

"Everything okay?"

Dempsey turned to Hansen, who wore a look of concern that he imagined pertained to Dempsey's role in the mission more than anything else.

"Yeah," he said. "Everything is five by." He turned on the radio in the inside pouch of his black jacket and spoke into the air, the comms picked up by the micro-Bluetooth in his ear. "Mother, any data on the Charlie Team target?"

There was a long, uncomfortable pause.

"Negative, Alpha One. Charlie Team is in hot standby, ready to go. Stay focused."

"Copy," Dempsey said with pursed lips. Did Jarvis know something, but wasn't telling him? Doubtful. Atlanta was hundreds of miles away and he was here. His thoughts went to Grimes and Adamo, and he said a little prayer that they'd keep his family safe. Then he reminded himself that there were wives, and children, and husbands at the Old Market he needed to worry about. He owed those families his undivided attention.

Dempsey let the SEAL inside him take control, and he slipped into his familiar tactical routine. He checked his gear—pistol in the waistband of his pants, the extra magazines on his left belt, and wireless earbud. He exited the truck and met Hansen at the rear of the vehicle, where the other four agents milled about, hands in pockets, looking awkward.

Dempsey gave them a tight grin.

"You guys look like Marines on liberty. Untuck your shirts. Relax your shoulders. Try to look casual. When you're in your sector, you can't just stand there. Mingle, browse. Buy something in a shop. Order a coffee at the Starbucks. Pretend to text or pretend to be on the phone. If the bad guys see FBI-looking dudes standing on the corner scanning the crowd, we're blown. Got it?"

"Yes, sir," one of the agents—almost certainly a former MARSOC guy, like Mendez had been—said, and Dempsey winced.

"All right, get moving."

"Don't worry, they'll be fine," Hansen said after the two teams assigned to the southern end of the market wandered off. "But good call putting those teams south." He laughed.

The remaining two agents stood beside them, arms folded, waiting for orders.

"You guys set?" Dempsey asked.

They both nodded.

"So, you're with me," he said to the shorter one. "We walk together and we talk, we laugh, we bullshit around. We look like guys just heading to lunch, got it? You see something suspicious or anybody who looks like our tangos, you let out a big laugh, and lean and tell me like it's a raunchy secret. Can you do that?"

The guy nodded. He was older and looked more confident than his colleagues.

"You're the SEAL from New York City, right?"

"Right," the guy said without a smile. "You can call me Basher. I was the tactical team leader. And you're the *should I take the red pill or the blue pill* SEAL from the Matrix nobody talks about?"

"Yeah, I'm that guy. I took the red pill."

The SEAL laughed. "Morpheus showed you the real world, huh?"

Dempsey thought about the strange universe of counterterrorism Jarvis had pulled him into. The metaphor fit. He grinned wryly. "Something like that."

"Well, you were solid at the UN," Basher said. "I'll trust your spooky ass on this one."

"Cool," Dempsey said. Then looking at the other pair, "You guys good?"

Hansen nodded.

"We'll work that northeast sector and stay in touch. I'm keeping the VOX off for bullshit chatter unless we see something, all right?"

Dempsey nodded.

"Yeah, same here."

Dempsey clipped a small black disk to the button closure of his shirt. The camera was no larger than a button cell battery, but it would stream high-resolution real-time video back to Jarvis in the TOC at Ember. He and Basher hiked in slowly, two friends with some time to kill. Dempsey had spent more hours than he cared to remember recently doing just this drill—scanning the crowd for a target while looking like he wasn't. They were still a bit early, so he wanted to get the lay of the land and then move back to the north where he expected al-Mahajer and his partner to enter the market on foot. If the phones were still off, the high-altitude drones should, he hoped, track their INFIL.

Wang spoke in his earpiece as if he had read his mind. "Phones are still off. No movement from the hotel, but it's getting kind of busy over that way."

"Don't miss them," Dempsey said harshly, but then turned to his SEAL teammate and laughed. The man chuckled back and shook his head. Basher was a better actor than Dempsey had expected.

"I won't," Wang said. "I'm running the camera and the pilot has control of the bird. I can see everyone leaving the hotel."

"Are you in position?" Dempsey asked.

"Check. I'm on the top floor of the parking deck in the truck. I'm good, Daddy-O."

"Is he always like this?" Basher asked.

"No," Dempsey said. "Sometimes he's annoying and immature."

The agent laughed for real now.

They stopped at Scooter's coffee a block into the Old Market, at the corner of Howard and Twelfth Street.

"Heads up, JD, I got them," Wang said.

Dempsey felt his pulse quicken and forced himself to slow down as he paid for two coffees. "Thanks a bunch," he said and handed the barista a ten-dollar bill. "Keep the change and have a great day."

"Thank you."

"Yeah, it's definitely them," Wang's voice said in his ear. "Moving on foot. Two tangos. They left together but have stretched out. I think it's al-Mahajer in the lead and now the other spanky is a half block back. Heading east. Coming your way."

Dempsey and Basher loitered in the coffee shop and waited for Wang's next update. He forced himself to make small talk and sip his coffee casually. They had time. Al-Mahajer had several blocks to cover.

"They're turning east on Harney now, the lead guy anyway. Second guy in trail nearly a block back now. The lead guy is wearing a jacket and carrying a bag. The second guy is wearing short sleeves and has no carry. Weird. He can't be wearing a vest; no way he's packing anything bigger than a subcompact. He's texting on his phone now."

Dempsey nodded at Basher and stepped outside Scooter's. He set them on an intercept course, striding casually through the Old Market. "Maybe he's not the guy," he said to Wang. "Sure you didn't see a third?"

"Negative."

That was weird, Dempsey thought. Delilah Shirazi had been clear about al-Mahajer prepping two suicide vests in her basement. Was the other bomber coming in from another route? Was the guy walking with al-Mahajer a decoy? Shit. He had planned to move the two south teams to the mid-Market once they had a visual, but now . . .

"Alpha Three and Four, stay south," he said softly, then elbowed his partner and laughed. The SEAL glowered at him instead of laughing, which played to anyone watching. "Two, we're gonna stage at the bus stop on Harney and Thirteenth on the southeast corner. You guys slip behind us to midblock on Howard between Twelfth and Thirteenth." He thought a moment. "Actually, Two, split your team—one guy to Howard, the other patrol that northeast corner. The guy trailing al-Mahajer is probably the VEVAK operative, which means there could be a third player we don't see."

Dempsey hated splitting his team, but he had no choice. They only had so many guys, and there was a lot of market to cover.

"There've been no other comms from these dudes, if that helps," Wang chimed in. "If they met up with another shithead here in Omaha, I missed the call. They've been dark since the calls to the other target cities."

"Check," Dempsey said, and then a thought occurred to him. What if al-Mahajer had prestaged explosives around the market? That was exactly the type of devious shit the bastard would think of. "Guys, make sure you're looking for abandoned bags, packages, et cetera. They may have prestaged IEDs."

"You want us to canvass the shops?" one of the patrolling operators asked.

"Negative. That would keep you out of the game too long," Hansen said on comms.

They made it to the bus stop and took a seat on the bench. Dempsey pretended to show something to his "buddy" Basher on his phone, laughed, and started sipping his coffee. He set his bag on the bench beside him and pulled the zipper back halfway. Inside he could see the Sig 556 compact rifle with the stock collapsed to its shortest length. The SEAL in him wanted to take it out, recheck the round in the magazine, and sling it across his chest.

"Tango almost to you," said Wang in his ear. "Across Harney and coming to the corner at Thirteenth."

Dempsey looked at the corner and spotted al-Mahajer, and his blood went cold. He hadn't expected to feel such a visceral reaction. Images of Romeo in Iraq and Mendez in Mexico flooded his mind, and he willed the ghastly, grisly memories back into the black lockbox in his head.

"Contact," he whispered and forced himself to look away.

"Crossing the street south, but staying on the west side of Thirteenth."

"I have him. Where is the other asshole?"

"He is in tow, but—wait—he's turning south now on Fourteenth."

"Two—pick up tango two on Howard or if he turns east toward you. Three and Four, stay alert."

He turned to his teammate and laughed and slapped the man on the back, earning a scowl and a fake laugh. He watched in his peripheral vision as al-Mahajer passed on the far side of the Thirteenth street.

Once he passed Dempsey activated his VOX.

"Here we go, Alpha," he said. "Mother, Alpha has the target." He tapped the camera disk on his shirt. "Streaming to you now and moving south."

"Roger, receiving you, Lima Charlie."

Hearing Jarvis's calm voice brought Dempsey into the zone. He tapped the former SEAL on the shoulder, and they stood, gym bags in hand, and began walking. They were twenty-five yards behind the ISIS terrorist he had been hunting for a quarter of his life.

As he walked, al-Mahajer pulled out his mobile and raised it to his ear.

"Mother, this is Alpha One. Al-Mahajer is making a call. I repeat, tango is making a call."

"Copy, Alpha One," came Jarvis's voice. "Interrogating now."

Dempsey watched al-Mahajer lower the phone, look at the screen, and then raise it to his ear again. "Mother, Alpha One, tango is making a second call. He's activating the other cells."

"Copy, Alpha. We're on it."

He knew he shouldn't ask the question, but couldn't help himself. "Did you get the Atlanta location?"

After a long beat, the answer came back: "Affirmative, Alpha One. Charlie Team is moving into position. Just keep your eye on the ball. Mother out."

Dempsey swallowed hard and tried to cage his emotions.

They'll be fine, he told himself.

And as he watched the ISIS terrorist drop his mobile phone into a trash can, the little voice inside his head reminded him that nothing with his old nemesis was what it appeared to be. Al-Mahajer had one last trick up his sleeve, and Dempsey still had no idea what it was.

CHAPTER 44

Ember TOC

"We've got the Infinity just a few minutes from the Fifty-First Street exit," Baldwin said. "Three tangos inside plus the driver."

Jarvis shifted his focus from Dempsey and Omaha to watching the green dot, Bravo One, in pursuit of the blue dot, the Infinity Q70 sedan. Both vehicles were driving north on Route 520 toward Redmond. Smith's SUV had closed the gap, but was still a mile behind. A missile strike from the drone had become the primary solution. Unfortunately, Route 520 was not cooperating with this plan. This was not some backcountry rural highway; it was the major commuter artery between Redmond and Seattle. A remote stretch suitable for a missile strike without the risk of collateral damage simply did not exist. Traffic wasn't rush-hour bumper to bumper, but it was heavy enough that an aerial attack at highway speed would result in significant civilian injury—orange numbers scrolled in his head. His best bet, he decided, was to hit them on the exit ramp of 51st Street as they looped east on the exit toward 148th Street and the entrance to the vast Microsoft Redmond campus. If that did not pan out, he would strike the target as they entered the complex on Microsoft Way. Everything depended on collateral damage.

"Bravo One, keep trying to close the gap. We're going to need you if collaterals prevent a strike."

"I'm doing ninety," came Smith's voice. "Three miles to the exit."

Jarvis shifted his gaze from the map to the Reaper feed—imagery inside a gray cloud with streaks of rainwater forming and sliding to the bottom corners of the lens. The red triangle in the middle marked the Infiniti—if the clouds weren't in the way. He looked back at the map and the blue dot and the green dot.

Too far.

He made his decision.

"Bravo One. Be advised we're going with the aerial solution. We still need you to confirm the kill afterward and assist in the case of collaterals."

There was a pause as the words sunk in for his Operations Officer. Finally, Smith said, "You have control of the kill? Can you confirm?"

"Yes, Bravo One. Aerial attack on the tango."

He expected a protest from Smith, but got one from Chip instead.

"We're going to launch a drone strike on American soil? Really?" the analyst said, his face going pale. "Is that even legal?"

Jarvis looked at him and nodded. An attack on American soil by an armed military drone was actually not unprecedented, but he doubted anyone involved with supporting this mission or even their extended chain knew that.

He turned to Baldwin. "Get me Colorado on the red phone, please. I'll talk to the boss; you brief the pilot."

"Yes, sir. Ringing him now . . . you're speaking to Colonel Benjamin Price," Baldwin said softly and handed the wireless phone to Jarvis. Usually wireless was best avoided, but the whole of the Ember underground complex was shielded from any outside electronic interrogation.

"Good morning, Colonel," Jarvis said.

"If that were true, why am I getting a call on this line from an untraceable number?"

"Sir, my name is Brian Smith. I head a secret Joint Counterterrorism Task Force answering to SecDef and the DNI. DNI is sending you an authority code for this mission. My men are briefing your pilot, who will, in about ninety seconds, need you to release his restrictions."

"This is the shit in Seattle, I assume."

"Yes, sir. We are going to authorize a missile strike on the target in less than two mikes."

"Well, fuck me," came the tense voice. "I have your authorization code from DNI coming in now. My pilot is ready, and we are secure in our SCIF. Transmit the targeting data."

"He has it already," Jarvis said. "The target is locked."

"Roger that," said the salty Colonel a thousand miles away. "Can you give us a laser designation on the target? A blind shot from cloud cover is one thing in the middle of nowhere Iraq. But this is down-fucking-town Redmond."

Jarvis thought a moment. Bravo Team had a Northrop Grumman GLTD II laser target designator. It was not as bulky as the AN/PED-1; it also didn't have the warm-up time that the larger device needed, but the precision was similar, and certainly good enough to confirm the target already locked by the Reaper. He looked up at the map and saw that Bravo One was five hundred meters and closing. "We have a ground asset. I'll make the call and try to light the target so you can confirm that you're tracking the actual target. Then, we wait for a shot that will mitigate any collateral damage."

"Mitigate or minimize?"

Jarvis paused. He understood. No one was going to come asking questions of a task force that didn't even exist.

"This mission is critical to saving American lives, Colonel. We will have your back, I assure you."

"I've heard that before."

"Not from me," Jarvis said. He weighed the situation. The Colonel would follow his orders either way. Still . . . "Sir, my name is Captain Kelso Jarvis. You come and find me if anyone comes fucking with you after this."

There was a tight chuckle. "You're all good on our end, Captain Jarvis," the Colonel said. "We know what we signed up for at this command."

The line went dead.

Jarvis looked at the screen again. The Infiniti was just a few moments from taking the exit.

"Bravo One, did you hear the last?"

"Yes, sir. We have the handheld and have a visual on the target. Still closing the gap, but we'll be good to light the target in another hundred meters. Shit . . ." There was a pause. Jarvis waited. "There's a car ahead of the tango and a minivan behind it on the ramp."

"We can't see them, Bravo One. The drone is in the clouds. Light the target and call the shot."

In his mind, Jarvis could see the three cars tightly packed on his moving map and behind, Bravo Team's SUV. Jarvis let the two columns of numbers stream through his mind—one representing the collateral damage risk and fallout and the other the targeting opportunities still left.

"Reaper, do you have the target locked?" Jarvis said to the open room. The link to the SCIF where Colonel Price and his operator controlled the drone was now on speaker.

The green triangle switched to red.

"Target is locked." The pilot sounded tense—maybe even a little scared. "Waiting to confirm with the laser designator."

"Hold fire for my order," Jarvis said.

"Roger."

The blue dot was stopped near the bottom of the ramp. The green dot was at the top of the ramp, decelerating but closing.

"Bravo, be advised the tango will be turning right," Jarvis said.

"Check," Smith said. "Looks like the car ahead of the tango is turning left."

Jarvis watched the screen and saw the blue dot creep forward to the intersection and the green dot come to a stop within a car's length.

"Fuck. The minivan has its right turn signal on," Smith reported. "There are kids in the minivan, boss. I can see them watching a cartoon on the video player through the back window."

"We have from now until they reach the entrance to the campus to take the shot," Jarvis reassured him.

"They're probably going there, too, sir. Microsoft has a day care program. Can you hold? We can engage from here. We're ready to go."

The numbers scrolled through his mind's eye. "More risk of collateral that way, Bravo One," he said. "Any other vehicles approaching from the north?"

"Negative, sir," Smith said. "But the minivan—"

"I need a visual, pilot. Right now," Jarvis barked. "Drop below the cloud base."

"Mother, Bravo One. Tango is turning. Hold your fire until my mark," Smith said, his voice rife with tension.

On the drone feed, the gray haze disappeared, and Jarvis saw the Infiniti sedan turning right. A second later, the minivan began its right turn, but before it could finish, Bravo One's SUV clipped the van's right rear panel, spinning the van ninety degrees and perpendicular to the road. The van stopped, still at the corner of the exit. Smith's SUV then accelerated around the van, veered into the southbound lane, and then immediately swerved back into the northbound lane, narrowly avoiding a head-on collision with a passing Honda. Smith's maneuver was genius and executed perfectly—stopping the minivan while protecting the family inside. Jarvis watched as Bravo One accelerated after the Infiniti.

"Lighting up the target," Smith said, breathless from the tension and the accident he had just caused. His passenger rose head and shoulders out the SUV's sunroof, lighting up the Infiniti with his hand-held laser designator. "Target is lit!"

"Now, Reaper," Jarvis barked. "Engage."

There was no reply, but the triangle on the screen that represented the targeting system of the Reaper flashed. Fire streaked across the lower right side of the screen. A heartbeat later, the blue dot representing the Infiniti flickered and disappeared as the missile hit. The drone feed went gray as the pilot played peek-a-boo again, disappearing the drone back up into the clouds.

"Direct hit," came Smith's voice. "Target is . . . um . . . gone. Nothing left but a smoking hole and a couple of wheels. Nice shooting, Mother. No collateral damage from the strike to us or the minivan."

Jarvis turned to Baldwin. "Get on the horn with the locals—police and FBI—and find someone to help manage this." Then louder he added, "Bravo One, get the hell out of there."

"Copy," came Smith's reply.

With Seattle safe, and no time to waste, he turned his attention to Dempsey's feed. On the screen, he realized he was looking at Rafiq al-Mahajer walking through the Old Market in downtown Omaha, a suicide vest beneath his jacket and only moments from blowing himself up.

CHAPTER 45

Old Town Market
Omaha, Nebraska

Dempsey grabbed his partner's arm and laughed loudly, shoving his mobile phone at the man with his left hand.

"Look at this, dude. I mean how drunk do you have to be to post this on Facebook?"

His right hand was reaching in his bag now, his fingers tickling the cool metal of the Sig 556 and the warmer composite plastic of the grip farther back.

Basher stopped walking and leaned over the screen for a look.

"Oh shit, bro!" Basher laughed, playing the part. "Dude, I know that girl. We used to date."

Al-Mahajer's eyes floated over them—then past them—not registering them as a threat. Then the terrorist crossed west to east directly in front of them, heading back toward Twelfth Street on Howard Street.

"We are one half block in trail," came Hansen's voice.

"Hold," Dempsey said softly, then louder to Basher, "Are you serious, dude? No way."

They let al-Mahajer disappear around the corner, and then they continued walking, crossing to the south side of Howard Street and stopping just past the corner, out of view. Dempsey pressed against the wall and counted to three. Then he stuck his face around the corner and pulled it back again, recalling what his eyes had seen. Al-Mahajer was crossing at the corner to head south on Twelfth Street.

"Wang, where is our secondary tango?" Dempsey whispered.

"One block south of you heading east—toward Twelfth Street."

"Anything south, Three and Four?"

"Negative."

Dempsey waited to see if Jarvis—call sign Mother—would chime in. He didn't.

"Three and Four, move toward Twelfth and then slowly north. Head on a swivel. Whatever is happening is happening soon. Two, move a block south and get behind the secondary. We have the primary."

Double-clicks from all three teams confirmed his orders.

Dempsey led and Basher followed swiftly down the south side of Howard and Twelfth Streets. He peered around the corner and then pulled back. Al-Mahajer was walking toward a makeshift stage on the east side of the cobblestone street where the first band was already warming up. Dempsey had seen signs plastered all over town for the music festival playing today through Sunday. The city had blocked off two blocks of Howard Street to vehicle traffic. A small crowd had already gathered around the stage, and the surrounding cafés and restaurants with outdoor seating were packed with patrons.

Dempsey knew exactly what al-Mahajer intended to do.

He pulled the zipper on the gym bag over his shoulder the rest of the way back and reached in and gripped his assault rifle, leaving it in the bag. Cries from bystanders would alert al-Mahajer, so he had to time the reveal perfectly. He sensed his partner fanning left, so he drifted right. Then, his stomach sank as the terrorist reached into his bag.

Fuck.

Al-Mahajer was definitely wearing a suicide vest beneath that barn jacket—one undoubtedly packed with ball bearings or washers that would fly shrapnel in all directions when he detonated, dealing death in a wide sphere. Dempsey performed a quick collateral assessment: the band, the crowd, and people dining at the two outdoor cafés behind the stage would be obliterated. With enough shrapnel and a powerful-enough charge, people across the street and even down the block would die as well. So, he couldn't risk *intentionally* detonating this asshole under any circumstance, but knowing that didn't solve the problem of how to prevent an unintentional detonation. If al-Mahajer was finger-ing a detonator inside that bag, a head shot now would save everyone. But if the terrorist was gripping a dead man's switch, a head shot would kill dozens of innocents.

"I've lost tango two," said Wang's voice.

He had no time for that now. Hansen would have to unfuck that.

"Tango two went in the side entrance of a café. Pursuing," came Hansen's voice.

Al-Mahajer mounted the steps to the stage, his hand still in the bag. The lead singer of the bluegrass band stopped strumming his gui-tar and smiled awkwardly at their uninvited guest. Dempsey pulled his rifle from the bag and sighted, putting a floating holographic dot on the back of al-Mahajer's head. *No coin flips today*, he told himself. He needed to see the terrorist's hand: thumb on the button, it's a dead man's switch; thumb off the button, a detonator. Before he could take the shot, he needed to confirm the trigger mechanism.

Suddenly, an idea came to him.

"Allahu Akbar, Rafiq al-Mahajer," he shouted, keeping the floating red reticle on the man's head and his eye on the hand in the bag.

Al-Mahajer turned, looking furious rather than frightened. As he did, his hand came out of the bag—holding neither a dead man's switch nor a detonator. Instead, Dempsey identified the object as a compact 9 mm fully automatic assault pistol.

The logic clicked in Dempsey's mind: the bastard was going to mow down as many people as possible with his machine gun before blowing up those who tried to escape.

"*A'salam*, motherfucker," Dempsey said and squeezed his trigger.

"Everyone down on the ground!" he heard Basher scream. "FBI—everyone get down!"

Dempsey watched with satisfaction as his 556 round went through al-Mahajer's left eye and then exploded out the top of his head, taking with it bone, blood, brains, and a chunk of hairy scalp. The man's arms flew outward, his left hand empty, the right squeezing the trigger of his assault pistol. A few rounds coughed from the gun into the crowd and then up and over Dempsey's head.

Dempsey hit the deck and pressed himself to the ground.

People were screaming and scurrying now, some leaping over the fallen and others tripping on them. Instead of heeding Basher's order to get down, the crowd's reaction was to panic and run. Dempsey waited for the white light and the searing flash, but it never came. No body parts raining down on him. No blood in his eyes. He waited a slow three count. Then he looked left at Basher, who was also on the deck, looking at him, his head shielded beneath his arms. The man's eyes were wide, but he managed a smile.

"Still glad you took the red pill?" Basher asked.

Dempsey tried to think of something clever but came up empty. He smirked instead and then pulled himself up to his knees. Then, he raised his rifle and scanned the fleeing crowd around him.

"Two, One, status on the secondary?"

"Lost him in the café," came Hansen's curt reply.

"Wang?"

"Nothing from above. I have the crowds to deal with. Easy to blend in. Especially if he changed his shirt or put on a hat."

"Keep looking, everyone. Find that sonuvabitch. Three and Four, move north on all four blocks. We need to find tango two."

About half of the civilian bystanders had fled, but the rest were mostly clustered into a herd about thirty yards away from Dempsey and Basher. Others were standing in ones and twos taking pictures with their smartphones. Dempsey moved cautiously toward the stage, where al-Mahajer's lifeless body lay leaking blood and other fluids.

Time to call Jarvis.

"Mother, this is Alpha One. Al-Mahajer is down."

"Alpha One, Mother. Is he wearing a suicide vest?"

"Check."

"But no dead man's switch?"

"He didn't go boom," Dempsey said, staring at his fallen adversary. Then, with a queasy this-ain't-over feeling in his stomach, he added, "But I need EOD here ASAP to disarm . . . just in case."

CHAPTER 46

Zio's Pizzeria
1109 Howard Street in the Old Market
Omaha, Nebraska

Rostami lost his tail by cutting through the Hyatt Place Hotel at Jackson and Twelfth Streets. He snagged a sports coat from a bellman's cart and then slipped on sunglasses as he exited the lobby down the hall from the first-floor rooms. At the end of the hall, he exited to the alley that ran between the hotel and the building housing Zio's Pizza and a seafood restaurant. He entered Zio's via the side door marked EXIT ONLY and smiled at the couple at the table beside the door, nodding and saying, "Bonjour." The couple, if they remembered anything about him at all, would remember the happy French Algerian who came in the wrong door. He moved to the main entrance, which faced Twelfth Street.

"Can I help you?" said the young woman at the hostess stand.

"Un moment, s'il vous plaît," he said. He picked up a menu from beside her and perused it as if deciding. He turned his back to her, and looked out the window, just in time to see al-Mahajer sprint up the stairs onto the music stage.

Rostami smiled and backed away from the large window beside the glass door. When he saw the Syrian move his left hand into his coat, he would move back farther and hit the deck, though he might have to do so sooner if the ISIS zealot pointed the machine pistol in his direction.

The crowd started screaming, pushing at one another, but then a voice—a loud, booming voice—screamed something in Arabic from the corner to his left. He couldn't see far enough around to identify the source.

Rostami moved backward, beyond the hostess stand where the young woman stood. He watched her walk toward the window, mouth open, oblivious to the fact she would soon be riddled with bullets and shrapnel. Rostami dropped to the floor, anticipating the onslaught. Then, a single gunshot rang out, not the burp of the machine pistol he expected to hear. He rose up enough to see al-Mahajer pitch over backward, his pistol firing haphazardly into the air. Several bullets struck the plate glass; the window exploded inward. The blast would come next. Rostami closed his eyes and pressed himself against the floor.

Seconds passed.

Nothing.

He opened his eyes.

Something was wrong.

He got to a knee and looked out the shattered window. Huddled on the floor beside him, the hostess was sobbing, but she was very much alive and intact. She cradled her left arm, trying to stem the bleeding from a laceration that looked to be from flying glass rather than a bullet.

And then Rostami saw him.

The devil himself, moving forward in a combat crouch, looking over a Sig Sauer 556 assault rifle. It was the same rifle. It was the same stance. It was the same fucking man from the tunnels beneath the UN—it had to be. This was the man who'd stalked him in Frankfurt, pursued him to Vienna, and thwarted him in New York. Because of this man, Masoud Modiri was dead, a loss Amir Modiri would never forgive him for.

The devil was waving his left arm and moving through the crowd.

Rostami reached for the pistol under his untucked shirt, rage in heart, intent on putting a bullet in the back of this devil's head. But then he spied another man behind him, also in a combat crouch that marked him as Special Operations. But how could they have responded so quickly? How had the Americans found them unless . . .

Delilah.

If only he'd gutted the Suren bitch when he'd had the chance.

He left the pistol in his waistband. Allah only knew how many American counterterrorism operators were moving in disguise through the crowd. If he took the shot, they'd pursue him and he'd have no chance of escape.

"Oh my God!" said a restaurant patron, a young man in his twenties who stood beside him and began to film the chaos in the street with his mobile phone. The American devil was only yards from him now. Rostami raised his own phone and began to record. Motion to his right made him turn and he saw several more men, rifles at high ready, weaving through the rising tide of screaming people. Two-thirds of the people ran in all directions, but the other third, like him, stood gawking with cell phones raised above their heads.

Time to leave.

As he joined the panicked throng running north, he focused his phone camera on the American counterterror specialist with the Sig 556. The operator was talking—via a wireless radio system, he assumed—to his command and control. As Rostami passed, he filmed the operator's face in profile, passing within three meters of him.

I have your face now, you cowboy motherfucker.

Then he looked away and slipped his phone back into his pocket. He scooped up a trampled blue baseball cap off the cobblestone street; it was embroidered in white with the letters KC. He pulled the ball cap down on his head and disappeared into the panicked crowd. As he fled the Old Market, he said a little prayer for the dead Syrian to explode and rid the world of the American devil once and for all.

CHAPTER 47

Georgia Aquarium Lobby
1304 Local / 1204 Omaha

Jacob Kemper smiled.

The past six months had been the hardest of his life, but today he was happy.

For the first time since his mom had dragged him to Atlanta, he saw the move for what it really was—a gift. By leaving Tampa behind, his mom had given him both the physical opportunity and the spiritual permission he needed to start over. He had a new house, a new school, a couple of new friends, and most importantly of all, a new perspective. He now realized that his dad's death had not been the beginning of his downward spiral, but rather the hard landing at the bottom. He loved his dad, and he missed him, but during his parents' two-year separation, Jake and his mom had been trapped in a Tier One purgatory—his dad unwilling to commit to them, but also unwilling to let them go. Now, they were free to live again.

"What do you wanna see first, bud?" his mom asked.

He smiled at her. She had started calling him bud about a week after they arrived in Atlanta. At first, it had pissed him off, because that had been Dad's nickname for him. But once he realized that she was doing it subconsciously and not of her own volition, he actually kind of liked it.

"How about the Ocean Voyager thing," he said. "I wanna see the scuba divers with the sharks."

"Fine, but don't get any bright ideas. Diving with sharks is completely off the table for you," she said as she presented their admission passes to the ticket checker at the main entrance doors. "Never gonna happen, so don't get your hopes up."

Jake shook his head and rolled his eyes—the requisite response of a sixteen-year-old—but he laughed inside. It had practically taken an act of Congress to get her to agree to the scuba lessons. He didn't dare tell her that the thought of diving next to a shark made him queasy. He liked that she saw him as someone fearless enough to actually dive with sharks.

Someone like Dad.

"We'll see," he said, mimicking her favorite line and throwing in a cocky half smile for good measure.

"Oh, we'll see all right," she fired back, laughing as they walked into the main entrance vestibule.

To their immediate left, a bright orange information kiosk beckoned.

"How about I ask for directions?" she teased. "I know how you love it when I do that."

"Don't you dare," he said, tugging her by the hand away from the kiosk and toward the Wall of Fish—the tunnel aquarium leading to the massive Atrium. From there, visitors could access all the exhibits, the gift shop, and a cluster of restaurants and snack shops.

They strolled through the tunnel, watching the permit and jacks zoom by, swimming in their endless underwater loop. As they exited into the Atrium, someone shoulder-checked Jake, hurriedly trying to squeeze by on his left.

"Hey, watch it, dude," he said to the asshole's back.

"Jake, come here," his mom said. There was something in her voice that made him uneasy and he turned. She grabbed his wrist and pulled him toward her, her eyes on the dark-haired, dark-skinned man. A second man strode after the first and bore such a resemblance they easily could pass for brothers. Both appeared to be midtwenties and wore canvas barn jackets despite the warm fall day. The jackets, the hurried movements, and the way their heads swiveled nervously around in all directions—sizing up the crowd—made Jake's inner voice scream with alarm.

Dad used to say—especially right after returning from a deployment, when his gaze still had that dark, faraway thing going on—to watch for certain traits in a crowd. These two guys were hitting all the marks. Suddenly, Jake found himself counting off the exits, scanning the Atrium for shelter, and trying to identify persons who could be of help. It was as if his dad were standing beside him, quizzing him on "the checklist." Jake twisted his wrist free from his mom's hand and stepped in front of her.

"I think we should leave," she said, a trembling urgency in her voice, and he wondered if Dad had also quizzed her on how to spot trouble during their date nights in Tampa.

"Hold on, Mom," he said. "Something is wrong."

He pulled the SEAL Team Ten hat—one of so many gifts from his father—off his head and handed it to her.

"Jake, what are you doing?"

Commotion erupted ahead. A concessions employee with a food tray dropped at his feet was shouting, but Jake couldn't make out what the guy was saying. All around him, people began shuffling. A chair at one of the restaurants tipped over. A baby started crying.

The crowd was beginning to sense that something was wrong.

Ahead, the two men briefly caucused and then diverged—one rushing ahead toward Ocean Voyager, and the other turning back toward the tunnel, his eyes on the throng of people behind Jake streaming into the Atrium through the Wall of Fish. Jake locked eyes with the man, and gooseflesh stood up on his neck. For the first time in his life, he saw murder in another man's eyes, and at that moment, he knew these guys were terrorists.

He grabbed his mom's hand and pulled her to the right, hoping to give a wide berth to the terrorist. "Stay behind me," he commanded, and to his surprise, she listened. A bird's-eye view of the aquarium popped into his mind, and he wondered how he could possibly know the layout of the place. But then he remembered having glanced at the back of the trifold tourist brochure while they were waiting in the ticket line. Somehow he remembered that the gift shop was to his immediate right and there was an emergency exit just beyond the Tropical Diver exhibit at his two o'clock. A woman running with a toddler in her arms smashed painfully into him. The woman screamed, the baby wailed, and he lost his grip on his mom's hand.

Across the Atrium, he saw two fully kitted-up warriors enter from the Cold Water Quest exhibit, moving in a combat crouch. He blinked and wondered if he was hallucinating—imagining what he wanted to see—because these guys were definitely SEALs. With the exception of actual Team guys like his dad, no one knew SEALs better than Jake. He watched the two operators fan out quietly through the crowd, so quietly that the terrorist they were converging on didn't hear them coming. In mere seconds, the two SEALs had the first jihadist spread-eagle on the floor at the entrance to Ocean Voyager. The taller SEAL had the terrorist stretched out in front of him, his hands gripping the wrists while the other pointed an assault rifle at the back of the man's head.

To his left he heard someone shout, "Everyone clear the Atrium!"

Two more operators materialized out of the tunnel as pandemonium erupted in the Atrium. Someone screamed, and then it seemed like everyone screamed. The noise reverberated and echoed in the cavernous hall with a disconcerting effect. People—mostly women with small children—hunched over and darted in all directions. Jake looked back at the operators and registered that they were dressed different from the SEALS, with nonissue cargo pants and black T-shirts under their black combat vests. Then, he realized that one of them was a woman, sighting over an MP5.

The second terrorist saw them and veered left, putting him on a collision course with Jake's mom. Jake watched—everything happening in slow motion—as the man opened his olive-green barn jacket, revealing a small machine gun in his grip. As the barrel rose, Jake surged forward, anger trumping all fear. A simple thought took shape in his head: this guy was about to shoot women and children. Men like this guy were the reason he didn't have a dad.

He crossed the distance between them in a second, but it felt like minutes. The man was looking away, mouth open and screaming. Jake saw fire lick out of the machine gun and heard more screams. He twisted his body, driving his left hand out and up, just as his dad had taught him in their backyard Krav Maga lessons. He nailed the terrorist's wrist, forcing the thundering machine gun barrel toward the ceiling. Jake rotated his hand, repositioning it to grip the man's wrist. At the same time, he pivoted on the ball of his left foot, stepped through the space between them with his right, and drove his right fist up into the terrorist's jaw. The terrorist stumbled backward and almost fell, but at the last second regained his balance and wrenched his arm free from Jake's grip. Jake stumbled forward and tried to tackle him by the waist as he fell, but the shooter stayed upright.

Jake felt a sharp, crushing pain as the terrorist drove the rifle butt down against the crown of his head. He hit the ground and immediately rolled onto his back, his arms up defensively. He blinked hard to clear the white spots from his eyes and felt hot blood running through his hair and onto his neck. As his vision cleared, he saw the man sighting in on his face over the machine gun.

"Allahu Akbar!" the man screamed, eyes wide with pure and absolute hatred.

Jake wanted to close his eyes—so he wouldn't see the muzzle flash—but another part of his brain refused. "Fuck you!"

There was a loud pop and Jake's body jerked.

But instead of a stream of bullets ripping Jake's face apart, the terrorist arched his back, his rifle arcing away and spitting at the tile floor. The terrorist's body twitched violently, still upright, as another pop followed the first. Then another. Blood spilled out of the man's mouth and over his chin. A big red bubble formed and then burst from between his lips. Finally, he pitched forward and fell, his face smacking the floor with a wet thud, the rifle clattering away.

Jake felt strong hands clutch his arms, and he realized he was being dragged backward into the tunnel. He looked down and saw the black gloves and turned to see who had him, half expecting and half hoping to see his dad. But he didn't recognize the man. He locked eyes with the woman with auburn hair running beside them.

"You're not SEALs," he heard himself say from far away.

Then the world was filled with light.

And heat.

And he disappeared into a soft but comfortable darkness.

CHAPTER 48

All hell had just broken loose, and Jarvis was in the middle of the firestorm.

The center monitor was streaming drone imagery from Seattle where Bravo Team was circling the smoking hole that had once been a luxury sedan full of terrorists. The Seattle map was gone from the left screen, replaced with split-screen live streams from Dempsey's and Special Agent Hansen's body cams in Omaha. Jarvis watched their cameras pan as they walked through the now-deserted Old Market.

Rapid movement on the right monitor usurped his attention. It was streaming Grimes's body camera feed as she entered the Georgia aquarium. This was it.

"Everyone clear the lobby!" Grimes shouted.

Chaos ensued—screaming, running, and shooting.

"Shooter at your three o'clock," Jarvis said, but she was already converging.

He watched in awe as a random teenager in the crowd rushed into view and assaulted the terrorist while he was firing into the crowd. There was something familiar about the way the kid moved. The kid delivered a punishing blow and almost succeeded in disarming the shooter, but then the terrorist regained the upper hand. Jarvis watched in horror as the terrorist knocked the teenager out and brought his weapon to bear for the kill.

"Take the shot," Jarvis barked, and prayed his instincts were right.

Grimes's muzzle barked, and the jihadi buckled. As she advanced on the fallen terrorist and the kid, he finally got a good view of the shooter.

"He's wearing a bomb vest," Jarvis said. "Egress, egress, egress!"

A beat later Grimes was running alongside Adamo, who was dragging the kid to safety.

Suddenly, the monitor flashed white, flickered, and went to static.

Jarvis's heart skipped a beat.

He'd stood OTC in enough TOCs to know what had just happened—the terrorist's suicide vest had exploded.

"Charlie Team, report," he said. "Charlie Team . . . report?"

"Stand by," came Adamo's coughing reply.

"Switch to Adamo's feed," Jarvis ordered Baldwin.

The right monitor flickered and a new feed appeared.

"Charlie Two, report."

Grimes's voice was strong and clear, but tense. "You were right," she said. "Suicide vest. Must have been on a kill switch, but I didn't see anything in his left hand. He blew after we killed him . . . less than thirty seconds. Probably nothing left of him, but if you hold on, I can walk over and take a look."

"Your camera is Tango Uniform," Jarvis said. "We're on Adamo's feed."

"Copy," she said.

"Charlie Three, status report," Jarvis said.

"Mother, this is Charlie Three," came Chunk's voice, loud and clear. "We're five by and have the other shithead in cuffs and isolated."

"Was the other shooter wired to blow?" Jarvis asked.

"Hell yeah, that's why we got him isolated," said the SEAL.

"And he didn't have a handheld detonator?"

"No, sir," came the reply.

"So what's the trigger?"

"I do not know, sir," Chunk said. "But I am not walking over there to ask the motherfucker. You wanna know how that shit works, then call EOD."

"EOD is en route," Baldwin announced.

"You made the right call, Charlie Three," Jarvis said. "Keep him isolated. EOD has been called and is en route to your location."

Meanwhile, Adamo had walked back through the Wall of Fish into the Atrium. "That tunnel saved our asses," Adamo said as he made a slow arc, showing Jarvis the aftermath. A few dozen bodies lay strewn among the rubble that had once been the food court seating area. Most of the fallen were moving, but several were not. He saw lots of small bodies—children. There was a little boy's empty tennis shoe—Spider-Man lighting up red and blue—at the edge of the debris.

"Charlie Team, injury report," Jarvis said.

"Charlie Three and Four, no injuries," Chunk called in.

"Charlie One and Two are okay," Adamo answered. "Just scratches. And the teenage boy is okay."

"Sir, you need to warn Dempsey," Grimes said, her voice tense. "There is definitely some variety of kill switch in play. This guy blew up *after* he was dead. Kill shots at the other targets need to be planned accordingly."

"Check," Jarvis said, not telling her that it was already too late for that.

He looked at the monitor with Omaha feeds. On the right side of the split screen, he saw that Dempsey was approaching the body of

Rafiq al-Mahajer where it lay supine on the ground. Dempsey's body cam was focused over his Sig 556 rifle directly on al-Mahajer. The top and right side of his forehead had been blown off.

"Alpha One, hold," Jarvis barked.

Dempsey stopped immediately. "Copy. Is there a problem? A problem in Atlanta?"

Jarvis hesitated a moment. Dempsey would ask that question only if he'd been checking in on Kate. They both knew that Kate and Jacob were somewhere in downtown Atlanta, but neither of them knew their fate. That question would be answered soon enough, but right now Jarvis needed his operator focused.

"Atlanta is contained," Jarvis said, "but we had a tango go boom after a kill shot. These guys must be using a novel type of detonator. Not a conventional handheld dead man's switch, but something new. Is al-Mahajer wearing gloves?"

Dempsey inched forward, then stopped. "Negative."

"Evacuate the area and get to a safe distance."

Dempsey's body cam video stream panned left and right, showing Jarvis the scene in the Old Market.

"We have a fair number of wounded here, sir," Dempsey said. "The target is down, but we have people down around the stage and others sheltering in place at the restaurant. If he blows, then we're gonna have collaterals." Dempsey paused, but Jarvis knew what he would say. "I'm gonna move in and see if I can disarm the vest. Wang, you there?"

"Wait," said Wang, his voice uncharacteristically grave. "I'm headed to you."

"Stay put, Wang. I got this," Dempsey said. His video stream showed the HRT operators converging on the area. "I need everyone out of here, right now," Dempsey ordered. "I'm going to try to disarm this sonuvabitch."

CHAPTER 49

Old Town Market
Omaha, Nebraska

Dempsey kept his rifle up and pointed at the body of al-Mahajer, despite the truth staring him in the face.

"Boss, this guy is fucking dead," Dempsey said into his mike. The information seemed redundant since Jarvis could see for himself that more than half of al-Mahajer's forehead was missing. He could also see the wet stain that always formed around a corpse when all of the body's sphincters gave up at once, even if he couldn't smell the stench of death like Dempsey could.

"Check his wrist," Jarvis said evenly. "EOD in Atlanta just reported they caught their crow trying to tear off a wristband while his hands were flex-cuffed together behind his back."

"Roger that," Dempsey said, slinging his rifle as he knelt beside the corpse of the terrorist who had eluded him for more than a decade. He had no time to relish the moment. He pulled his 5.11 Tactical TAC glove off his left hand with his teeth and pressed two fingers into the groove beside the trachea on the terrorist's blood- and brain-spattered neck.

Holy shit.

"Sir, you won't believe this, but I have a pulse on my tango," he said, hearing the surprise in his own voice. "How is that possible?"

"Highly improbable, but medically feasible," came Baldwin's voice in his ear. "You see how your bullet took out his frontal and temporal lobes, and—yes, it looks like his occipital lobe is partially missing as well, you see?"

"I don't know what the hell any of that means, Professor." Dempsey pulled gently on the left arm of the near-corpse, which had ended up behind the terrorist and beneath him. Using a booted foot, he raised al-Mahajer's torso up, fully expecting to be blown to bits in the process.

"Do you see how the target was de-cerebrated?"

"No," Dempsey said. He looked down at al-Mahajer's left wrist and spied a narrow black watch with a black LED strip—only it wasn't a watch. It was one of those fitness trackers with a built-in heart-rate monitor everyone was wearing these days. He shifted his gaze back at al-Mahajer's gory mess of a head. "Just give me the eighth-grade explanation, Baldwin."

"Your bullet destroyed the target's front brain, but the brainstem is still preserved. The brainstem controls all of the automatic, involuntary actions—like breathing and heart rate. Al-Mahajer is technically brain dead, but he is not, well, dead-dead."

Dempsey studied the fitness band on the terrorist's wrist. The narrow LED display had numbers on it, and beside it was a picture of a heart, which was flashing on and off, presumably in time to al-Mahajer's still-beating heart. The digital readout was flashing "55."

Suddenly, it hit him. This was his final test. Al-Mahajer's final deception. The same devious stratagem yet again.

He draws you in, gets you to let down your guard, and BOOM!
You lose.

"How long, Baldwin?" Dempsey asked.

"Until what?"

"Until he's dead-dead."

There was a pause. "Maybe seconds, maybe minutes. I'm not a physician, John. I would imagine it depends on blood loss?"

"I think the suicide vest is linked to a heart-rate monitor," Dempsey said. "I think it must be programmed to detonate if the heart rate goes to zero, or maybe below a certain rate? If his heart stops before we can clear the wounded, we're fucked."

"How bad is the bleeding, John?"

"He's missing half his head, what do you think?" Dempsey said. The dark puddle of blood around the dying terrorist's head was still growing even now.

"Then stop the bleeding!" Baldwin said, with more urgency and emotion than he'd ever heard from the man.

Dempsey pulled his blowout kit from his left cargo pocket and tore it open with his teeth. He grabbed the dressing from the plastic bag and balled it up and then pressed it deep into the pulsating mass of gore at the top of the terrorist's head. The dressing soaked instantly.

"I need a medic here," he said.

"Coming up," came the call from one of Hansen's men.

"And I need Wang."

"Right here, JD," came a voice in his headset but also beside him. He looked up and met Wang's gaze.

"I told you to stay back," he said. "I could have relayed details over comms."

"This will be quicker," Wang said and knelt beside him, pulling his right knee back to avoid the expanding pool. "We don't have much time."

The medics were coming, and in the meantime Dempsey held pressure on the brain cavity. The terrorist's one remaining eye stared off to the left, the pupil filling the entire iris. Dempsey figured this was what *brain dead* meant.

"Can I look at the vest?" Wang said.

Dempsey glanced at him. "Do you really want to mess with the explosive vest?"

Wang bit the inside of his cheek, but nodded. "There are no wires to the vest from the activity monitor, so if you're right, it has to be communicating wirelessly to something on the vest. These devices usually have an app you can put on a tablet or a smartphone."

"Go ahead and look, if it will help you," Dempsey said. Then, he looked at Hansen, who was standing at the foot of the stairs leading up to the stage. "Get everyone back," he said. "And then you and your guys get back, too. Have the medics slide their gear up to me and then haul ass out of here."

Hansen nodded and turned to the loitering civilians, cell phones raised and recording. "We need everyone back. Right now. Everyone back."

Wang pulled al-Mahajer's barn jacket open and revealed what looked like a standard-issue black tactical combat vest. Except it had long vertical rows that bulged out, no doubt filled with shrapnel, four gray bricks of explosives—two to a side—and in the middle was a maze of wires, a control unit with LED lights and an alphanumeric display with a German word he assumed said "armed." The control unit was connected with a USB cable to a smartphone held to the vest with duct tape. On the screen was the same flashing "55" for the heart rate.

"Talk to me, Wang," Dempsey said. He watched the heart rate drop to "52" on the screen. He looked at the fitness tracker on the dead man's wrist, which matched the number.

"The fitness tracker is transmitting wirelessly to the cell phone app here. If this was my rig, I'd have it programmed with a lower threshold so when the heart rate falls below the target number—maybe zero—it will send a signal to the detonator system here." He pointed with a pinky.

"And when that happens?"

"Boom," Wang said with an accompanying hand gesture for effect.

"Great," Dempsey said. "How do we disarm it?"

"I don't know. I could try to hack into the detonator via the mobile phone, but that'll be complicated and would probably take too long."

"Awesome," Dempsey said. The heart rate now said "50."

"But," Wang said, an "aha" finger in the air and his eyebrows up, "I could try to hack the activity monitor instead—maybe trick it into thinking the heart rate is still above the alarm parameter."

"Yes, very good," Baldwin's voice said in Dempsey's left ear. "If it's wireless, that should be easy. If you can't access the fitness monitor directly, hack the phone because we know they're paired."

"Yeah, good," Wang said. He dropped down and sat cross-legged, opened his notebook computer on his lap, and started mumbling to himself.

"John," Baldwin said in his ear.

"Yes, Ian," Dempsey said patiently. He was trying to keep his thoughts away from Kate and Jacob, whose faces kept popping into his mind.

"I'm worried that if al-Mahajer's blood pressure drops, the sensors on the monitor won't be able to sense the pulse and might detonate even if the heart rate remains above the target."

"That's just great, Ian. What the hell can I do about that?"

"You need to give him fluids and try to raise his pressure. Maybe a little Trendelenburg?"

He saw a medic with a large backpack moving toward them in a sprint. It was one of Hansen's men, but he carried an Omaha EMS bag as well as the backpack.

"Trendel-lah-who?" Dempsey said.

"Trendelenburg position—Elevate his legs above his heart," Baldwin said patiently.

Wang was staring at his laptop and pulling at his chin. Dempsey slapped his arm with a bloody hand. Wang looked up.

"Stick my gear bag under his feet," Dempsey said, gesturing with his head while keeping pressure on the top of al-Mahajer's head.

Wang dragged Dempsey's gym bag into position, then lifted al-Mahajer's legs and dropped them onto the bag. Then, he scrambled back to his laptop and started typing.

"Toss me the kit," Dempsey said to the HRT agent with a medical bag, which Dempsey now saw held a cardiac monitor and a defibrillator.

"You're the SEAL in charge, right?" the man said, ignoring him and mounting the stairs.

"Yes, but listen, bro. You do not want to be up here."

"Boss told me the situation," the guy said, kneeling beside him and opening up the large bag. "Sounds like it's a big deal to keep this guy's heart going a few minutes. I was a Green Beret 18-Delta medic long enough to know two things. I can keep a heartbeat going in a rock for a few minutes when I want to, and ain't no squid gonna be able to do what I can do. So, way I figure, you need me."

Dempsey surveyed the scene. The square was still in chaos around the stage. Some people were milling about in a daze, dozens of others were lying on the ground where they had been trampled, and still others were pushing past the police, cell phones in the air, trying to post snippets of the most exciting day of their lives on their Instagram feeds.

We've got to disarm this bomb, or all these people are going to die.

"Okay, what do I do?" Dempsey said, looking back at the medic.

"Set up the IV while I get the monitor hooked up."

Dempsey nodded and quickly tore open an IV setup and spiked the IV bag, just as he had done countless times in their "live tissues" training sessions with the Tier One SEAL medics and a half-dozen times in the field for injured brothers.

"Wang? How's it coming?" he called, while he finished the IV.

"Another couple of minutes."

The heart rate dropped to "42" and the light on the detonator panel turned yellow. Dempsey's throat tightened.

"What just happened?"

Wang looked up at the detonator display and then back at his computer where his fingers were flying on the keyboard.

"Looks like the threshold for arming the bomb is forty-five beats per minute," he said.

"And what's the threshold when it blows up?"

"Uh, I don't know," Wang said, flustered. "Just try to keep him above forty-five, okay!"

The medic beside Dempsey suddenly jammed two fingers into the man's remaining eye socket and the pulse rate shot up to "44," and then to "48." The yellow light flickered and went off, and the green light came back on.

"What technique is that?" Dempsey asked.

The medic shrugged. "One that would make my heart rate go up," he said. Then he stabbed a large needle into al-Mahajer's arm at the crook of his elbow. Dark blood came back, and the medic slid the plastic catheter off the needle, pulled the needle out of the hub, and then hooked the IV tubing to it. He adjusted the wheel on the plastic clip that controlled the flow and then squeezed the bag with both hands, forcing fluid into the vein.

"I'm in!" Wang said. "Had to hack the phone like Baldwin said. It's using an app paired to the activity monitor."

"So now what?" Dempsey said. He was very eager to get everyone, including himself, as far away as possible from the human bomb. "Can you just turn it off?"

"Not sure. I need to think about that . . . I don't want to fuck this up."

"Great idea," the medic said and then added, "Shit, guys. We've got a problem."

Dempsey looked at the panel, which was yellow again, and then at the fitness tracker display on al-Mahajer's wrist. The heart rate blinked "38."

"Fuck," Dempsey said. "What should I do?"

"Start CPR," the medic said.

"Seriously?"

"It measures heart beat at the wrist, right? It can't tell the difference between the heart and your compressions. Dude, fucking start CPR!"

The flashing number now said "28." The yellow number flickered, and beside it a red light flickered as well.

Dempsey put the heel of his hand on the dead man's breastbone, covered it with his other hand, and with locked elbows began pressing rhythmically up and down. The flickering of red stopped and the yellow held steady.

"Faster," the medic ordered, now squeezing the IV bag with all of his might. He dropped the bag on the ground and sat on it, then pulled a black case out of his duffel. He unzipped it and pulled out a long-needled syringe. "I'm gonna give some epi," he said, talking more to himself than Dempsey.

The green light flickered, but then the yellow came back on. Dempsey couldn't help but laugh at the irony. *I'm giving CPR to the man who I want dead the most in the whole world.*

Dempsey's torso was churning like a piston, pumping at least a hundred times a minute, but the number on the fitness monitor still said "42."

"Wang," Dempsey said in a low, urgent voice. "Hurry!"

Wang began to chew on his right index finger. Then his eyes lit up. "I have an idea." His fingers danced on his keyboard again. "Demo mode!"

"Yes, yes," Baldwin said calmly in his left ear. "Brilliant. But hurry."

The light turned green and then suddenly the number shot to "135."

"What just happened?" Dempsey said, stopping the compressions.

"Epinephrine, dude," the medic said. "But now his heart is gonna push the blood out that gaping hole in his head real fast. When BP falls this time, that'll be it."

"Wang?" Dempsey said. "Tell me you got this."

Wang ignored him, laser focused and working.

Dempsey watched the puddle of blood grow beneath them and felt it soaking into the knees of his pants where he knelt.

The heart rate on the monitor fell to "80" and then "60."

Poised over the half-dead terrorist, his hand still on the breastbone and set to restart CPR, Dempsey turned to the medic. "Now?"

"Go."

The medic hesitated and then, seeing he'd done all he could, slapped Dempsey on the back. "Good luck, brother. Hooyah."

"Hooyah, bro, now get outta here."

And the man was gone.

Dempsey started CPR, but the number kept falling.

The heart-rate monitor fell to "50" and then "42."

The detonator light turned yellow.

"Just you and me, Wang," he said softly. "It's now or never."

He stared at the display on the monitor, pressing down on the breastbone now as hard as he could. He felt the sternum split under his weight, cracking in half.

The heart rate fell to "20" then to "0."

Dempsey stopped his rocking compressions, closed his eyes, and waited for the pain. But the white heat didn't come. He opened his eyes and looked at the wristband. The little heart icon was gone and the pulse rate said "0." He turned to Wang, who was smiling, a tear running down his left cheek.

"I did it," Wang sobbed.

Dempsey looked at the detonator panel with its glowing green light. The app on the phone showed a heart rate of eighty-two, the little heart flashing in time to the simulated pulse.

"You sure did, bro," he said. He wrapped Wang up in a bear hug. Then he pushed him back. "Go," he ordered, "and tell Hansen to send in EOD."

Wang set his laptop down and sprinted from the wooden stage on shaky legs, dodging and jumping over people lying on the street as he cleared to a safe distance.

Dempsey stood.

Then, looking down at the one remaining eye of the dead, nearly headless ISIS commander, he said, "Fuck you, Rafiq al-Mahajer . . . I win."

CHAPTER 50

Ember TOC
Newport News, Virginia
November 5, 2030 Local Time

Dempsey folded his hands in his lap and looked up at Jarvis as Ember's Director spoke to the team.

"Success in our world is hard to measure," Jarvis said to the room. "We lost three teammates and six civilians stopping al-Mahajer—a terrible loss—but the death toll would have been four to five hundred, and the wounded toll three times that, had we failed. Tonight, we remember the wounded and the dead but celebrate the lives we saved." He stepped from the podium, signaling he was done. "Now secure your gear and get the hell out of here. I'll see everyone back here tomorrow at 1600 hours for a final debrief."

Everyone stood.

Handshakes were exchanged. Smith found his way to Chunk and his SEALs and led them to his office for the requisite paperwork drill before they were released back to their unit. Dempsey traded nods with Adamo, acknowledging the new and awkward kinship they had forged over the past forty-eight hours. Had it not been for the spook's insights and instincts, they would never have found al-Mahajer in time. As he shifted his gaze to Grimes, he felt a hand on his shoulder.

"A word?" Jarvis said.

Grimes flashed him a knowing smile and looked away.

"Sure thing, Skipper," Dempsey said and followed Jarvis to his office. He crossed the threshold and opted to stand instead of taking a seat opposite the Director's desk. "Everything okay, sir?"

"Fine, I just need a minute to talk."

A lump formed in Dempsey's throat. He knew what this was about. "Sir, I know the Facebook thing was way out of bounds, but I can assure you—"

Jarvis raised a hand to stop him. "I have no doubt the Facebook *thing* has run its course. That's not why I called you in." He clicked the mouse on his laptop and then spun the screen around to face Dempsey. "This is footage from the Georgia Aquarium and it's something you need to see."

"Sir?" Dempsey asked, confused.

Jarvis offered him a crooked half smile and walked out, leaving Dempsey standing alone with the computer.

Dempsey exhaled, rolled his neck, and was rewarded with a triple pop of his vertebrae. He sat down in front of the computer and clicked the wireless mouse to play the recording. He immediately noticed that Jarvis had the sound turned off and the frame rate set to one-quarter speed. In the upper left corner of the screen in white letters was the name GRIMES, and beside it was a clock with eight digits, displaying military time in hours, minutes, seconds, and hundredths of seconds. This video was from Grimes's body cam.

A dark cloud seemed to envelop the room as he reminded himself the operation had not been a complete success. There had been eleven people wounded at the aquarium—including two kids—and one man had died. He leaned in, resting his chin on his right hand, his elbow on the mahogany desk as he watched a terrorist with an assault rifle in his right hand turn in an arc, fire spitting slowly out of the barrel. A hand entered the frame from the right. Then the forearm.

Dempsey clicked and froze the image.

The forearm was slim, muscular, and familiar.

Dempsey squinted at the watch on the wrist. That was *his* watch—an old watch from the Teams that he had given his son, Jake, on the boy's twelfth birthday. Could it really be . . . Jake?

The oversize Casio Pathfinder no longer looked like a daddy's watch on a boy's wrist. It fit this arm. Just above it was a paracord bracelet—the one that they had weaved together, Dempsey patiently showing Jake how to keep the strands tight so the bracelet would be taut.

Oh my God, that's my son.

He wiped a tear from his cheek and clicked "Play." Jake's left palm and wrist drove the shooter's hand and machine gun upward. Then, Jake's other hand came into view, striking the terrorist squarely in the jaw. Then his son's face entered the screen, and Dempsey paused the video again.

He studied Jake's face. He expected to see fear and doubt. Jake had always been timid and cautious. So risk averse, in fact, that it had been the family joke that Jake had gotten all Kate DNA and no Frogman DNA. But that had never mattered to Dempsey. He'd always loved his son, and over time he had learned to admire Jake for having the self-awareness to recognize and acknowledge his fears and limitations. The difference between father and son was that Jake had never been afraid to be afraid. In that way, this video was proof that Jake had accomplished something Dempsey never had.

Jake had faced his greatest fear and won.

The face on the screen was a warrior's face.

When did that happen?

Dempsey surprised himself by breaking into a sob, his throat becoming tight and painful. He missed his son so much. He loved him so much. And now, it seemed, he didn't know him anymore. Then he watched with helpless dread as the terrorist's rifle butt smashed into the top of his boy's head, and his son crumpled to the ground. The terrorist swung the barrel, bringing the muzzle in line with Jake's head, and Dempsey felt like all the oxygen had been sucked out of the room.

Then, a muzzle flare lit up the screen, as Grimes made her headshot, dropping the jihadi where he stood. The video clip ended ten seconds later. Dempsey watched the video until completion. Then he laid his head on his scarred left forearm and let the tears come; they ran in rivulets over the pearly white serpentine scar and pooled on the table. He couldn't remember crying like this—not ever. And when a hand squeezed his shoulder, he didn't startle. He didn't spin around, grab the wrist, and rip the intruder a new one. This was his home now; no one here wanted to hurt him. No one here judged him for his demons.

He looked up at Smith.

"I counted six stitches," Smith said.

"What's that?" Dempsey said.

"On the news, I counted six stitches on Jake's forehead when he was being interviewed. The news is eating this up. He's all over Fox News. Brian Kilmeade is hailing him as a hero: 'The son of a slain Navy SEAL tackled a terrorist suicide bomber at the Georgia Aquarium. The son of a SEAL risked his life to save others.'"

"You saw him on TV?"

"Oh yeah," Smith said, with a grin so wide you'd have thought Jake was his own son. "He's shy and soft-spoken, that Jake of yours, but he has the eyes of a warrior. The soul of a warrior . . . just like his dad."

"I miss him so much," Dempsey said, gritting his teeth and trying to corral his emotions.

"I know, bro," Smith said and sat down beside him. "You've gotta be so proud, dude. Did you know Jake would become such a steely-eyed badass?"

Dempsey grinned and then started to laugh. "Never."

"He saved lives today," Smith said. "Those moves, those instincts, you taught him well."

"No," Dempsey said, shaking his head. "That's all Jake."

They sat in silence for a moment, two brothers, with nothing else to say.

Dempsey wiped the last tear from his chin. "But after seeing that, I hope his mom makes him become an accountant or a pediatrician or some shit like that. The world doesn't need another John Dempsey."

"Amen," Smith said with a laugh. Then he stood and clamped a hand on Dempsey's shoulder. "You gotta let them go, brother."

"I know," Dempsey said, his voice cracking.

"It's not for you, JD. It's for them."

Dempsey nodded.

"I know," he said. After a beat, he pushed his chair back from Jarvis's desk and stood. "Time to go have a beer and toast the dead fucking remains of Rafiq al-Mahajer."

"Now you're talking," Smith said, wrapping an arm around his shoulders. "Baldwin and the boys are gonna join us. Hell, even Jarvis said he might stop by. Grimes already has Chunk and the Team guys headed to your house."

"Why my house?" Dempsey said as they walked out of the TOC, the automatic lights going dark behind them.

"In case something gets broken," Smith said. "If you haven't noticed, when this crew gets together, something always does."

EPILOGUE

Behrouz Rostami shifted in his chair. His right leg had gone numb from sitting for so long. It was coming up on two hours that Modiri had made him wait past their scheduled appointment time. This was intentional, Rostami knew. Modiri loved to play his games. Penance and punishment. Submission and servitude. Games didn't bother Rostami; he played them with people, too. The only thing that upset him in a boss was incompetence, and Amir Modiri was anything but incompetent. Unfortunately, the same could not be said for others in the upper echelon of VEVAK.

His escape from America had been surprisingly easy. He simply rented a car and drove north on I-29 all the way to Winnipeg, entering Manitoba using a VEVAK-obtained Canadian passport. For operations in America, he always posed as Canadian, since Canadian citizens did not require a visa and typically suffered few questions from US border officials. Going the other way was even easier.

Modiri's secretary's phone buzzed.

She answered it, acknowledged her boss's terse instruction, and motioned Rostami in. Modiri had chosen a homely, middle-aged thing for his admin, no doubt so as not to upset Maheen. The Director's wife was not permitted access to this floor, but that was irrelevant. Maheen was a queen bee, and the queen's spies were everywhere, buzzing, buzzing, watching, and buzzing.

Rostami was surprised to find all the shades drawn in Modiri's office and the lights off. When he closed the door behind him, the office fell as dark as night. Modiri was sitting behind his desk, perfectly still with his eyes closed. Despite the pins and needles still pulsing down his right leg, Rostami took a seat opposite the desk. He did not speak, just stared at his boss and watched him breathe and wait. After a very long time, Modiri bowed his head and began massaging the skin under the curve of his eye socket.

Rostami resisted the urge to speak. It was obvious; Modiri had a migraine, and it was best not to antagonize the man in any way.

Modiri exhaled loudly but spoke softly. "The Suren Circle is compromised thanks to you."

"I do not accept responsibility for the Circle's undoing. They were soft, stupid, and weak. Corrupted by their time in the West. Useless to you," he replied, the harsh words incongruous with the careful, hushed tone he used to convey them.

"Not useless. The Circle has returned one hundred times our initial investment in intellectual property, equity holdings, and cash. They proved to be far better financiers and thieves than spies. That is not lost to us."

"With all due respect, it was your idea to utilize them for this operation, not mine."

Modiri opened his eyes. "You speak brazenly for a man who just failed his mission."

"I did everything that was asked of me and more. If you are looking to assign blame, blame someone else."

Modiri smiled and then winced for doing so. "You know, Behrouz, you're right."

Rostami was taken aback by his boss's words, and fought to keep his expression neutral.

"You'd think after all these years I would have learned my lesson," Modiri said.

"And what lesson is that, sir?"

Modiri took another deep, cleansing breath and said, "The same lesson I forget over and over and over again." He reached into his top-right desk drawer, the drawer where Rostami knew he kept a Beretta 9 mm pistol. "If you want something done right, you have to do it yourself."

I'm about to get a bullet in the head, Rostami realized.

He watched Modiri's right hand come into view, but instead of clutching a pistol, the Director's fingers held a file folder. Rostami exhaled relief and tried to bring his heart rate back under control as Modiri opened the folder and leafed through a short stack of photos. He selected one photo and slid it across the table.

"Do you know this man?" Modiri asked, rubbing his eye socket again.

Rostami brought the photograph close to his face and squinted to study the image in the near-total darkness. It was a photo he had taken of the American Special Forces operator who had foiled al-Mahajer's attack in the Old Market. In the image, the operator was sighting over his rifle, his naked left forearm visible with a disfiguring scar that cut across the cords of muscle like a coiled snake. "I know this man," he seethed. "Just not by name."

Modiri slid another picture across the desk and then a third.

Rostami picked them up. They were pictures of the same man from different angles and in different locations. One background was wooded; the other looked like a city street.

"Where were these taken?"

"The first one is from security camera footage recorded in the grounds around a lake house outside Geneva."

"The house where we met with your brother? The house where one of our security men disappeared?"

Modiri nodded. "And the other photograph was taken by one of our New York agents documenting the American counterterrorism response at the UN six months ago."

"Do we know who he is?" Rostami asked, staring at the picture.

"No. He doesn't appear in any database."

Rostami smirked and returned the photos to Modiri's desk. "So, you want me to find him and kill him?"

"You'll never find him," Modiri said, closing his eyes and leaning back in his chair. "Or the organization he works for. To kill this man, we need to make him come to us . . . and I think I have the perfect plan to do it."

ACKNOWLEDGMENTS

We would like to acknowledge and give special thanks to the team at Thomas & Mercer. We are indebted to our editors: JoVon Sotak for taking a chance on John Dempsey, and Jessica Tribble, who works tirelessly behind the scenes to make sure the series reaches its maximum potential. From developmental edits, to line and copy, to cover art, to marketing and promotion—all the pieces of the puzzle are managed and executed with excellence and care. Our team is the best in the business, and we want the world to know it.

Thanks to Sarah Burningham, whose incredible and tireless PR work introduced the Tier One Series and John Dempsey to hundreds of thousands of readers.

Thank you Rick Fox and Chris Schneider for all you've done to support us and help put our work in front of our brothers and sisters serving in the military. Your commitment to the United States Armed Forces is unparalleled.

We owe a special thank-you to our agent, Gina, the best damn literary agent in the world. You created us, and you bring life and enthusiasm to every book we write.

And last but certainly not least, we'd like to thank our wives, who work tirelessly and selflessly to support our writing careers. Without family, it all means nothing. We love you.

GLOSSARY

- AQ—Al Qaeda
- AFSOC—Air Force Special Operations Command
- BDU—Battle Dress Uniform
- BUD/S—Basic Underwater Demolition School
- BZ—Bravo Zulu (military accolade)
- CASEVAC—Casualty Evacuation
- CENTCOM—Central Command
- CIA—Central Intelligence Agency
- CO—Commanding Officer
- CONUS—Continental United States
- CSO—Chief Staff Officer
- DEA—Drug Enforcement Agency
- DNI—Director of National Intelligence
- Eighteen Delta—Special Forces medical technician and first responder
- Ember—American black-ops OGA unit led by Kelso Jarvis
- EMCON—Emissions Control (Radio Silence)
- EOD—Explosive Ordinance Disposal
- EXFIL—Exfiltrate
- FARP—Forward Area Refueling/Rearming Point
- FOB—Forward Operating Base

- HRT—Hostage Rescue Team (FBI)
- HUMINT—Human Intelligence
- IC—Intelligence Community
- INFIL—Infiltrate
- IS—Islamic State
- ISIS—Islamic State of Iraq and al-Sham
- JCS—Joint Chiefs of Staff
- JO—Junior Officer
- JSOC—Joint Special Operations Command
- JSOTF—Joint Special Operations Task Force
- KIA—Killed in Action
- LCPO—Lead Chief Petty Officer
- MARSOC—Marine Corps Special Operations Command
- MEDEVAC—Medical Evacuation
- MOIS—Iranian Ministry of Intelligence, aka VAJA / VEVAK
- Mossad—Israeli Institute for Intelligence and Special Operations
- NCO—Noncommissioned Officer
- NETCOM—Network Enterprise Technology Command (Army)
- NOC—Non-official Cover
- NSA—National Security Administration
- NVGs—Night Vision Goggles
- OGA—Other Government Agency
- OPSEC—Operational Security
- OSTP—Office of Science and Technology Policy
- OTC—Officer in Tactical Command
- PDA—Personal Digital Assistant
- PJ—Parajumper/Air Force Rescue
- QRF—Quick Reaction Force
- RPG—Rocket Propelled Grenade
- SAD—Special Activities Division

- SAPI—Small Arms Protective Insert
- SCIF—Sensitive Compartmented Information Facility
- SEAL—Sea, Air, and Land Teams, Naval Special Warfare
- SECDEF—Secretary of Defense
- SIGINT—Signals Intelligence
- SITREP—Situation Report
- SOAR—Special Operations Aviation Regiment
- SOCOM—Special Operations Command
- SOG—Special Operations Group
- SOPMOD—Special Operations Modification
- SQT—Seal Qualification Training
- TAD—Temporary Additional Duty
- TOC—Tactical Operations Center
- UAV—Unmanned Aerial Vehicle
- UN—United Nations
- UNO—University of Nebraska Omaha
- USN—US Navy
- VEVAK—Iranian Ministry of Intelligence, analog of the CIA
- Zeta—Colloquial name for the Mexican drug cartel aka Cartel del Norte

ABOUT THE AUTHORS

Brian Andrews is a US Navy veteran who served as an officer on a 688-class fast-attack submarine in the Pacific. He is a Park Leadership Fellow and holds a master's degree in business from Cornell University. He is the author of the Think Tank series of thrillers (*The Infiltration Game*, *The Calypso Directive*). Born and raised in the Midwest, Andrews lives in Tornado Alley with his wife and three daughters.

Jeffrey Wilson has worked as an actor, firefighter, paramedic, jet pilot, and diving instructor, as well as a vascular and trauma surgeon. He served in the US Navy for fourteen years and made multiple deployments as a combat surgeon. He is the author of three award-winning supernatural thrillers: *The Traiteur's Ring*, *The Donors*, and *Fade to Black*. He and his wife, Wendy, live in Southwest Florida with their four children.

Andrews and Wilson also coauthor the Nick Foley Thriller series (*Beijing Red*, *Hong Kong Black*) under the pen name Alex Ryan.